THE HARLECH BEACH KILLINGS

A DI Ruth Hunter Crime Thriller #2

SIMON MCCLEAVE

STAMFORD
PUBLISHING

The Harlech Beach Killings
by Simon McCleave

A DI Ruth Hunter Crime Thriller
Book 2

❀ Created with Vellum

THE DI RUTH HUNTER SERIES

#1 *The Snowdonia Killings*

#2. *The Harlech Beach Killings*

#3. *The Dee Valley Killings*

#4. *The Devil's Cliff Killings*

#5. *The Berwyn River Killings*

#6. *The White Forest Killings*

#7. *The Solace Farm Killings*

#8. *The Menai Bridge Killings*

#9. *The Conway Bridge Killings*

#10. *The River Seine Killings*

#11. *The Lake Vyrnwy Killings*

#12 *The Chirk Castle Killings*

#13 *The Portmeirion Killings*

THE DC RUTH HUNTER MURDER CASE SERIES

#1. *Diary of a War Crime*

#2. *The Razor Gang Murder*

#3. *An Imitation of Darkness*

#4. *This is London, SE15*

THE ANGLESEY SERIES - DI LAURA HART
(Harper Collins / AVON Publishing)

#1. *The Dark Tide*

#2. *In Too Deep*

#3. *Blood on the Shore*

Your FREE book is waiting for you now

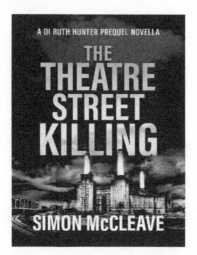

Get your FREE copy of the prequel to
the DI Ruth Hunter Series NOW
http://www.simonmccleave.com/vip-email-club
and join my VIP Email Club

For Nicola, Izzy, George and Tilly

Underservedly, you will atone for the
sins of your father.
Horace

The apple will not fall far from the tree
Welsh Proverb (dated 1803)

When the sins of the father do
visit us, we do not have to play host. We
can banish them with forgiveness.
August Wilson

Prologue

November 2010

THE VILLAGE OF BEDDGELERT LAY TO THE WESTERN SIDE OF Snowdonia and fifteen miles from the coast of Wales. Mount Snowdon dominated the skyline to the north and some of the most popular routes up its mountainside originated in the village. For centuries, locals and travellers alike stood in awe of the great mountain as it loomed up before them over 3,500 feet above sea level. The name *Snowdon* came from the Old English for Snow Hill but the Welsh preferred to call it *Yr Wyddfa*, meaning burial place.

The mountain's grey, snow-filled crevices and dark tracks held the blood of many a battle and failed invasion. Without words, those who came upon the sight knew in their very souls that Snowdon was a sacred place; somewhere that, if they gave it time, could still their minds and expand their imaginations.

A mile to the south of the village, the mighty River

Glaslyn had forced itself through a narrow passage and cut a steep-sided valley, draining a large lake that had covered Beddgelert after the Ice Age. The surrounding wooded area was one of Wales' most famous beauty spots; the Welsh Highland Railway ran through the Aberglaslyn Pass and its spectacular scenery drew tourists from all over the world.

At the top end of the village of Beddgelert, there was a row of five small, narrow mid-nineteenth-century copper-miners' cottages built from grey stone.

As the afternoon faded, large flakes of snow began to appear in the colourless sky and pepper the rooftops, fields and trees like a strange sprinkling from outer space.

The evening darkness came and the air around the miners' cottages was now heavy with wind-blown snow and the redolent smell of burning wood and coal.

The end cottage had a white, wooden oblong sign: *Gower's Cottage.* The building was built from dark stone and local slate. Inside was cramped with low ceilings and beams. An old wood burner, around which cheap furniture and a large television had been arranged, warmed the living room. From somewhere, 'Angels' by Robbie Williams was playing loudly on a radio.

In the kitchen, two sisters sat at a wooden table eating their tea and giggling. One girl had clips in her blonde hair and wore a pink tracksuit top which had *Los Angeles – LA* 7 written in swirly silver writing on it.

Her sister wore glasses and was still in her school shirt and bottle-green tie. She watched their mother singing to the radio. The girl knew she was faking it to make them feel better. She joined her mum and sister in the song until all three of them were singing and laughing at the tops of their voices. *'And through it all ...'*

. . .

HOWEVER, THE GIRL SAW HER MOTHER GLANCE AT THE time on the kitchen clock. Their day was about to get significantly worse. It always did at this time of day, like clockwork.

Hearing the noise of the front door closing, a boot on the floor and the distinctive sniff, the girl glanced at her sister and mother. The atmosphere in the room had changed. The singing stopped and now there was fear and tension.

A few seconds later, a short man with a shaved head wearing oil-stained overalls came in noisily. He shook the snow and leaves from his jacket, with little thought of the mess, and put a red toolbox down on the sideboard with a forceful crash. Her dad ruined everything. The tension in the kitchen was unbearable. She hated the very sight of him, the very smell of him.

'They say the snow's not going to stick.' Her mum's smile was uncertain; she was trying to gauge his mood. Sometimes she wished her mother would just stick a carving knife in his back. Their lives would be so much better without him.

The girl watched as he turned the radio off with a snap. The music was annoying him. *Everything annoys him*, she thought to herself.

'Heard this joke at work.' Her dad's words were slurred. 'A wife told her husband she was fed up with him being a flamingo. So, he thought it was time he put his foot down, once and for all. Funny that, you know what I mean?'

Her dad grinned, slumped down and began to untie his boots and then glared at her. 'Give me a hand will you, daft bitch?' The girl could see he had been drinking, and when he was drunk, he was volatile and violent.

Her mum immediately knelt on the floor like a well-

3

trained servant, quickly unlaced the snowy boots and carefully took them off. The girl got angry at her mum. *Why does she let him treat her like that? No man would ever talk to me like that.*

Pushing back her wonky glasses on her nose, the girl sighed audibly and gave him a look of disdain from under a fringe of untidy hair. She wasn't scared of him. He was a bully.

Within a flash, he pounced, pulling her hair tight and looking directly into the girl's eyes.

'Are you going to be trouble again?' he thundered into her face. She could smell the pungent stink of beer and whisky on his breath. She met his eyes defiantly and gave him the hint of a smirk just to piss him off. 'Got something to say, you little slag?'

'No …' she said with a shrug. But one day the answer would be different. One day she would have her say before slitting her dad's throat and watching him choke and bleed out like a wriggling pig.

'No, what?' her dad asked, now pulling at her hair and putting his grease-smeared hand around her jawbone. She could feel the grit and engine oil on her skin. He seemed angrier than usual and it was unsettling.

'No… Dad,' she muttered reluctantly and turned her face towards him.

'Look at this face. This beautiful face.' He shook his head in wonder and smiled.

'Dewi …' her mum whispered.

He put his thumb onto her sister's lips and gazed as he pushed his thumb inside and against her tongue, 'This mouth, eh? Make some man very happy with this, you will. Some lucky man …'

4

'For God's sake, Dewi,' her mum pleaded with him.

He turned and with the back of his left hand, he struck her hard across the jaw. *Crack!* She staggered, but he wasn't finished. He swung his right fist, and as it connected with the side of her skull, it virtually lifted her off the ground.

'Just shut up! For once!' he roared.

Her sister froze in her seat and let out a muffled whimper.

The girl's mother collapsed to the floor like a doll. She groaned as she tried to curl into a ball, appearing to slip in and out of consciousness.

Sick with anger and fear, the girl rose in her seat but was shoved back violently. The wood of the chair banged painfully into the base of her spine.

'Sit down, or I'll leather you too!' her dad bellowed in her face.

Looking left, she saw a silent tear roll down her sister's face and fall onto her food. Then she saw that her sister had wet herself. The cerise tracksuit bottoms were darkening across her thighs. Reaching out, she touched her sister's hand. *It's going to be all right. I will look after you.*

Possessed by rage, her dad shook his head sadly, went over to his wife and sighed, 'You had this coming, you stupid bitch!'

He raised his foot and stamped on her mother's throat. *Snap.*

A bone cracked like when they snapped dry sticks to put in the burner.

It didn't feel real. It was like they were all in a nightmare. How could this be happening?

'That's me putting my foot down once and for all,' he said to no one in particular.

In that instant, the girl realised that her mum was dead.

And now her mind was trying to process what would happen next.

Her heart was thumping hard, and she felt sick to the pit of her stomach. Was he going to kill them all? Like the stories she had read in the paper. The man who had killed his two sons and then jumped off a cliff on the North Wales coast.

Taking a knife from his pocket, her dad looked at the girl and beckoned with his finger.

'Your turn. You can come upstairs with me today for being a bad girl,' her dad said and then turned to her sister. 'And you can stay here and clear up.'

At first, the girl's stomach flopped and rolled like she had gone over an enormous humped-back bridge. Her hands were cold and trembled. She had no choice but to go. Like she had done before.

And she wanted to spare her sister. She was weak and fragile.

Going to the stairs, she looked down at her socked feet and her white shins. He was just behind her and his hand touched her back between her shoulder blades to guide her upstairs with a shove.

'Go on ...' he grunted.

And then quietly, she disappeared into herself. Reduced her very being, in that moment of terrible, protective self-preservation, to nothing. A disassociation from all thought and of all feeling. It was too much to bear again and again. She was no longer consciously present. Her mind, her consciousness, was far away in a safer place.

The girl that went upstairs with him was no longer her.

14 FEBRUARY 2018

. . .

DETECTIVE SERGEANT NICK EVANS, AND DETECTIVE Constable John 'Mac' McDonald, were out on a shout for a suspected fight and assault in Porthmadog. It was six o'clock and raining heavily. *Happy Bloody Valentines' night*, Nick thought to himself. Stuck in a car with a chubby Scottish bloke who ate prawn cocktail crisps like his life depended on it. And the chemically fishy smell that permeated the air in the car. He buzzed down the window to get some fresh air. If he got wet, he didn't care.

'Bloody hell, can't you eat ready-salted?' Nick asked.

'Why?' Mac sniffed his fingers. 'These smell like my wife's knickers. And that reminds me of my Valentines' treat when I get home.'

Nick pulled a face. Mac was a good bloke but his crude sense of humour often offended female officers in the CID office at Llancastell nick.

'TMI mate,' Nick said shaking his head and smiling in mock disgust.

'Eh? TM-what?' Mac asked.

Mac really was a clueless dinosaur, but he was bloody funny. This was the man who during a conversation about films claimed that he thought Sean Penn was the capital of Thailand.

'Too much information, you bell-end,' Nick laughed.

Mac mimed masturbation with his hand at Nick. 'What's your Valentines' plan, lover boy? Microwaved lonely-man lasagne for one and a cheeky wank?'

NICK GAVE MAC THE FINGER AND THEN TURNED ON THE radio. 'Hey, I'm having sex with someone I love,' Nick quipped.

In his early thirties, Nick was lithe and handsome with a dark beard. His skin and eyes were unusually clear as he was heading towards ten months of sobriety, which was a record for him. Prior to this unbroken period of recovery, Nick liked to tell others that he had been doing 'the old Alcoholics Anonymous hokey cokey'. '*In, out, in, out, shake it all about.*'

THAT MEANT SOBERING UP, GOING TO MEETINGS, TALKING the talk, before relapsing. Then he would disappear for months only to return to meetings with his tail between his legs and admitting that his period of 'more research' – an AA euphemism for a relapse – had once again proved that he had no control over alcohol and never would. Back to step one, like an AA game of snakes and ladders.

Turning the dial on the radio, Nick tried to find some suitably cheerful music to lift his mood.

There was no judgement from those in AA. It was a shitty disease and the only disease that convinced the victim that you didn't have it. A cunning, deadly fox of a mental illness that would be, as someone once personified it, 'waiting patiently as it slowly tricked you into drinking again and then trying to kill you before you came back to your senses'.

An hour ago, Nick and Mac had been given local intel that a young man, named Mark Ferguson, had been involved in a fight. That meant Nick and Mac needed to investigate. Ferguson was 'a significant person of interest' to them in an ongoing drugs operation they were running with Merseyside Police.

In the autumn of 2017, North Wales CID had set up surveillance on a housing association flat in the socially deprived Heol Y Parc area of Porthmadog. There was intel that it was being used by a 'cuckooing' drugs gang, the Croxteth Park Boyz, from Liverpool. The gang had targeted Timothy Evans, a vulnerable adult with learning difficulties, and taken over the flat as a base from which to sell and keep drugs and store guns and cash.

The head of the Croxteth Park Boyz was the notorious Curtis Blake, a psychotic gangster who ran a sizeable chunk of Liverpool's drug trade. He had contacts in the Netherlands where he owned drug factories. He had used violence and intimidation to seize the supply of class-A drugs within Scotland's major cities, in particular Glasgow, where he had cousins who helped him out.

Nick hated everything about Blake. His creepy grin during arrests and questioning. His perma-tan and expensive veneers. His cars, Mediterranean villa and yacht. His fondness for starving his massive American Bully dogs – originally bred from American pit bulls and Staffordshire terriers – and then locking his enemies and rivals in a room with them, laughing at the screams as they were torn to pieces. Nick thought he was a disgusting excuse for a human being.

Nick also had a more personal reason for hating Curtis Blake. An ex-girlfriend of his from school, Laura Foley, had got hooked on drugs while at Liverpool University. She quickly became a heroin user. On a beautiful August evening in 2003, Laura had overdosed and died in the house she shared in Toxteth with three other smackheads. Nick couldn't bear to think of her like that. Even though Nick was only a uniform PC on the beat at that time, he did some digging around the investigation into Laura's death. It was clear that Curtis Blake had supplied the heroin that had killed her. So if he was honest, Nick was obsessed by getting Blake sent to jail or seeing him die horribly.

At the beginning of February 2018, a rival Merseyside gang, the Bootle Crew, sent a nineteen-year-old runner called Mark Ferguson to lay the ground for a county lines drug operation. However, Dylan Woods, from the rival Croxteth Park Boyz, spotted and recognised Ferguson from Liverpool. They knew exactly why he was there. They hatched a plan to protect their turf by attacking Ferguson. It would send a message back to Liverpool that Porthmadog was Croxteth Park Boyz territory.

What Nick and the other members of Llancastell CID didn't know was *when* they would attack Ferguson. To make matters worse, Ferguson had a knack of knowing when he was under police surveillance and then giving them the slip.

For a moment, Nick looked up at the wall of rain falling from the sky. There was a laziness to rain, he thought to himself. How raindrops obeyed gravity and just fell with no resistance. Now that the noise of the engine and heater had stopped, the rhythmic drumming and splatter of the drops was thick and steady. He gave up trying to find suitable music and turned the radio off.

A patrol car, yellow and blue markings, stopped beside them and a uniformed constable got out. The rain was easing a little as Nick got out of the passenger side of their unmarked car. He slammed the door behind him.

'No sign of anyone, sir,' the PC said.

'Okay, thank you, Constable. Can you liaise with the retail park security team and see if we can get any CCTV?' Nick asked.

'No problem, sir,' the PC said getting back into the car.

Nick shrugged the rain from his coat. He thought that for the first time in a while he was content. He was enjoying his job, and he was enjoying sobriety. He felt the rain trickle from his scalp, down his forehead and fall from his nose. The air smelt of fresh rain and cooked donuts from a nearby fast-food place. He might get some on the way home.

It was a wasted journey but Nick's mood meant that it didn't matter. He was missing his favourite AA meeting of the week but there would be another tomorrow. Ferguson was probably in a local pub, playing pool and selling drugs to the local teens to keep him in kebabs and beer.

Nick looked at his watch. If the traffic was okay, he might just make it back in time to the weekly meeting at the church hall.

Turning back to the car, he heard a distant noise that sounded like the low groan of an animal. It might have been Mac belching in the car. Glancing over at the large steel industrial recycling bins, in the far right-hand corner of the car park, he saw something move. There were plastic bags, the highlights of which were caught by the floodlights of the car park, that seemed to move and fall away.

Nick assumed it was the wind and rain and turned to go. It was a shitty night and North Wales did cold, torrential rain like nowhere else.

Then the same noise again.

It wasn't coming from the car. It was coming from over by the recycling area.

Squinting through the drizzle, Nick could see that there seemed to be a figure lying on the ground. There was another figure crouched over as if they were wrestling each other.

Then there was another moan. This time more urgent and then a stifled yell of a word that sounded like, 'Help!'

Mac had now got out of the car as well.

Breaking into a run, and with water splashing from the concrete onto his socks, Nick yelled, 'Oi, police! Stay where you are!'

The crouched, hooded figure spotted him coming, stood up quickly, ran to a mesh wire fence, vaulted over it and then was away. *He's agile and quick,* Nick thought. *And now I've got to bloody chase him!*

'Stop! Police!' Nick hollered knowing it would have no effect.

Glancing down at the injured figure on the ground, Nick could see he was in a bad way but knew that Mac was close behind.

'Stay with him. I'm going after the runner, Mac!' Nick yelled back at him.

The escaping figure turned to look back for a moment. Black hoodie, black mask covering his mouth and nose, black gloves, North Face jacket. Gang uniform. Nick could tell just from a glance at his eyes and his stature that he was late teens. Maybe even younger.

Nick grappled over the fence and then followed full pelt over the rubble and uneven ground that led away from the car park. Beyond that was the main road.

The teenager was putting some distance between them. Nick cursed his lack of fitness. He lost his footing for a moment. A sharp stabbing pain in his ankle. He'd have to run it off. Ten years of being a half-decent rugby player in North Wales had taught him how to run off pain.

They sprinted down a steep bank, past trees and towards the main road. Nick was now into his stride and gaining on him. Twenty yards now. Any closer and Nick thought he could rugby tackle him. He hadn't been a winger for Llancastell Rugby FC for nothing.

Ten yards.

Suddenly the teenager side stepped off the pavement

and into the middle of the road that dissected the retail park. It threw Nick off his stride for a moment.

The blue and yellow sign of Lidl on the right and the olive green of The Outdoor Superstore to the left.

The lactic acid was burning Nick's lungs. Sucking in air, he put in one last spurt. He was seconds away from launching himself and taking the little wanker down onto the wet concrete. *Come here, you fucker!*

From somewhere, a car engine started and then revved deeply. Up ahead, the red taillights of a black Mercedes 4x4 glared and bled into the darkness of the night and rain.

The back door of the car opened in readiness for the teenager's getaway.

Sod that! He's going nowhere.

The teenager reached the Merc and, without breaking stride, jumped in.

As the car started to move, Nick caught him up and grabbed hold of his jacket through the open door. The teenager kicked him hard in the arm and chest but Nick wasn't letting go.

If I hold on tight, I'll pull the little bastared out of the car.

But he was wrong. The car accelerated away violently, and Nick lost his grip on the jacket and then the door handle, which he tried to grab.

'For God's sake!' Nick shouted as he gasped for air and winced.

Just as the back door slammed, a head came out of the passenger-door window and looked back at him. Baseball cap, face mask. The blue eyes glinted at him in dark amusement.

It was Curtis Blake.

He knew those eyes anywhere. Bastard.

'See yous later, copper!' he said in his thick Scouse accent, the tyres screeched and the 4x4 sped away.

One day he would get in a dark alley with Blake and dish out some natural justice for the hundreds of lives he had ruined.

But Nick didn't have time to think about that. His major concern was the injured man he had left with Mac.

Despite feeling physically sick and out of breath, Nick turned and sprinted back the way he had come.

As he pounded towards the car park, he could see Mac crouched over the man lying curled up on the concrete beside the mesh fence.

Nick got closer. The victim's jeans were dark from blood and rain, and he was shaking. One of his black Adidas trainers lay a few feet away, lost in his desperation to run and escape.

'This is not good, Sarge,' Mac said.

'Have you called it in?'

'Yeah. Paramedics are on their way. Ten minutes though.' Mac sounded concerned, and that was rare.

'Ten minutes? Let me have a look.' Nick crouched and put his hand on the man's shoulder who was injured and in pain. The man rolled over.

'Try to keep still. I'm a police officer,' Nick assured him.

Nick instantly recognised the whitening face as that of Mark Ferguson. He still had the remnants of teenage acne and a patchy growth of hair on his chin and top lip. The kind of 'bum fluff' that Nick would sardonically joke could be removed with a hairdryer.

Ferguson was soaked in blood and it looked like his throat was slashed. He looked up at him and Nick stared back into the frightened eyes of a dying nineteen-year-old. At this moment, Ferguson looked younger, like he could

14

still be at school. His hands shook and he put them to his neck.

'Where's the bloody ambulance?' Nick shouted and looked up at Mac.

Nick took off his coat, rolled it quickly and pushed it against Ferguson's neck to see if he could stem the bleed. It wasn't any good, there was blood everywhere.

Ferguson gurgled, 'Help me …' as blood bubbled from his mouth.

'Try not to talk,' Nick told him.

Ferguson wasn't going to make it. Nick was helpless and even though Ferguson was a toerag, he was also a teenager, somebody's son, and he was bleeding to death in front of him.

Nick pushed his coat tighter and warm blood seeped through the material, through his fingers and trickled down the back of Nick's hands and his forearms.

'Come on, mate,' Nick said urging Ferguson to fight against what he knew was inevitable.

Ferguson's breathing was becoming shallow and then the tension went from his body. His eyes darkened as the irises dilated.

The young man was dead.

A moment of quiet as Nick looked at his frozen expression and then he threw his blood-soaked coat away angrily.

'For God's sake!' Nick bellowed to no one except maybe God.

Nick looked up at Mac, shook his head and sat in the blood and rain.

That night he knew he wouldn't be able to sleep. This was Curtis Blake's work. Another life destroyed.

After a debriefing with DCI Drake at CID, Nick eventually got home at midnight. Despite a long, hot shower, he still had the smell of the bins, the blood, rain and death on him. And drink was the only solution to the pain, trauma and anxiety. *Who the hell wouldn't drink?* He had held a young man and watched him bleed to death in his arms. How the hell was he supposed to cope with that?

Nick sent a text to his AA sponsor:

Bill, I watched someone die in my arms today and I've picked up. I'll call you when I come out the other side. Sorry. Nick.

Bill called Nick almost immediately and sent texts for the next seven days. But it would be too late.

Chapter One

S*ummer 2018*

The tidy school classroom was thick with heat as fifteen-year-olds slumped in grey plastic chairs. Some of the girls fanned themselves and groaned at the temperature. The boys just kicked each other under the tables.

It was July, and the UK was in the middle of a heatwave and the temperature was nudging thirty degrees daily. The black roller blinds were half pulled down and all the windows were open, but the air was baking. Walls were decorated with colourful examples of students' work but it looked a little frayed and tattered as it was close to the end of the academic year. Everyone was winding down for the summer break and attention spans were non-existent.

Detective Inspector Ruth Hunter had been talking to the teenagers about new laws on 'sexting' and the legal implications of getting caught. She had shown them an information video called 'Don't cross the line ... into Cyber Crime!'. The title's rhyme made Ruth squirm. It was just the sort of thing that made teenagers think that adults were 'sad' and out of touch, but someone in the North Wales' Police Communications Department, who was definitely paid more than her, thought it was witty and clever.

Ruth was about to turn fifty, attractive with chestnut-coloured hair that just rested on her shoulders. She wore a dark-blue blouse with a delicate pattern and smart black trousers. Her lined lips, baggy eyes and crow's feet were a testament to the stress of 'the job', smoking and drinking a little too much.

Ruth could feel the sweat on her top lip and the back of her neck. God, the heat was stifling. Her main purpose was to talk to the students about careers in the police force. To one side, Police School Liaison Officer Euan Jones sat in shirtsleeves, his face red and sweaty.

'There really are very few barriers to beginning your career in the police force,' she explained as she indicated the next slide of her hastily assembled PowerPoint. As always, Superintendent Jones had given her next to no warning that she was giving this talk.

Ruth's audience were restless, bored and the low-level noise of laughter and conversation was growing. A pen went flying across the room and landed noisily on the floor.

The young female teacher glanced apologetically at Ruth and then at the students, 'Year Ten, I know it's hot in here. But please remember our manners, especially as we have several guests in school today,' she barked in an angry but weary tone.

A new slide from the PowerPoint presentation was

being projected on a screen, not that anyone was vaguely interested.

Am I eligible?

Applicants from all backgrounds and ethnic groups are encouraged to apply.

Basic guidelines for applicants:

There are no minimum or maximum height requirements

There is no formal educational requirement, but you will have to pass written tests.

RUTH WONDERED WHAT THE HELL SHE WAS DOING THERE. How long was Superintendent Jones going to 'phase' her return back into proper CID work?

Ruth had been signed off work in May, which was then extended to June and July. The Dinas Padog murders had taken their toll on her very being and had been the proverbial straw that broke the camel's back.

In April 2017, two teachers from the same school in the sleepy Snowdonia town of Dinas Padog had been murdered within a week of each other. Ruth, who had just arrived on a transfer from the London Met Police, was appointed the senior investigating officer. She had run what everyone had considered a thorough investigation. However, when the murderer's identity was eventually discovered, it had sent shock waves through the community and Llancastell CID. The murderer had not been on anyone's radar. Ruth knew that as the SIO, she would be held ultimately responsible. Therefore, the investigation had technically been a failure. There had been various scathing press articles accusing the North Wales Police, and Ruth in particular, of gross negligence.

The Independent Office for Police Conduct had found in favour of Ruth and her team but the stress and length of that investigation weighed heavily on her. She started having panic attacks, and problems breathing, sleeping and even functioning. Her GP and the North Wales Police HR Department had signed her off with work-related anxiety and stress. No one was surprised. The North Wales Police Federation had already reported in 2017 that eighty per cent of its members were suffering from some form of anxiety or depression and that morale was at an all-time low.

Superintendent Jones had ticked all the right boxes and on the surface was supportive of Ruth being signed off. However, Jones was a political animal, self-absorbed with his own agenda. Ruth suspected that when she returned to work, Jones would marginalise her to show the top brass that Ruth was accountable for the mistakes in Dinas Padog and thus distance himself from it.

It was usual for a CID officer of her rank to be phased back to work by sticking to desk work such as statements, strategising or chasing leads. Jones seemed to have other ideas. She suspected that Jones was making her life intolerable hoping she would transfer out or take early retirement. She assumed he didn't want an officer in CID with ongoing mental health issues. Her phased return to full work was at best dull, and at worst demeaning, and essentially it was covert bullying but there was nothing she could do about it.

Being sidelined was beginning to grate on her because being a detective was all she ever wanted. She loved the challenge of trying to work out what had happened, why, and putting the pieces of the puzzle together, getting to court and securing a conviction and stopping people doing terrible things. She felt she had made a difference throughout her career.

Ruth had experienced the bullying culture in the police force before and watched when junior officers were too scared to confront or report their bosses over misconduct. When she first joined London's Met, it was one big bully-boys' club that gave a consistent message that criticism or not toeing the line was very career-limiting.

Ruth had had her fill of 'silverback' leaders who were charismatic, with enormous egos, and drove performance through fear and intimidation. It was well-known that in the past, police chiefs had been guilty of predatory, sexual conduct towards junior colleagues. There was a terrible culture of entitlement and being untouchable at chief-officer level. In 2015, a report by HM Inspectorate of Constabulary found that over half of officers in the Met wouldn't whistle-blow on colleagues' corruption or misconduct because of fears of repercussions. In the same year, seventy-five Met officers were accused of corruption. Eleven were convicted while the others were allowed to retire or continue to work.

Ruth looked at the yawns and rolling eyes and so tried a different tack to see if she could elicit any response from the class. Christ, she couldn't blame them – she was boring herself.

'Okay. Forget the PowerPoint. I was once sixteen, it's boring, I know. But I also knew from the time I was about ten that I wanted to be a police officer. What about you? What do you want?' Ruth asked. There were a few heavy seconds of awkwardness. 'When you're eighteen or when you're twenty, where would you like to be?'

'I'll be blazing up a fat one,' a shaven-headed boy said with a grin, miming smoking a spliff. The class howled with laughter at his bravado.

'Pregnant and with a council flat,' a girl mumbled to her friend but loud enough for Ruth to hear.

'YouTuber millionaire.'

'Gonna shag a footballer …'

'Professional gamer, like.'

Ruth gave a wry smile of amusement. She had heard all this before back in London – their lack of ambition wasn't a surprise. In deprived areas like Llancastell, ambition wasn't cool. And mugging off a teacher or a police officer was a badge of honour.

'Owen wants to be a primary-school teacher,' another boy shouted.

Ruth nodded and smiled. 'Well that's great.'

'Yeah, that's cos Owen's a paedo, miss.' The class laughed again.

Ruth rolled her eyes. It struck her, at that very moment, how different her life was to when she was in the Met. She had joined the North Wales Police Force eighteen months earlier. As the well-worn cliché went, she had had enough of 'the mean streets' of South East London and some of the archaic attitudes within the Met. Knife crime was going through the roof and she'd seen too much murder and mayhem. There were family connections in North Wales and Conwy had been the location of many an idyllic family holiday.

The North Wales Police Force seemed to offer a different style of policing. Or so she presumed until she had been flung headlong into a double murder case as soon as she arrived.

A FEW MINUTES LATER, THE PRESENTATION WAS OVER. Ruth received a half-hearted round of applause and some mumbled *thank-yous*. The teacher thanked her too, made her excuses as she was on duty, and raced away.

Ruth felt disheartened as she went over to retrieve her memory stick from the computer and projector. All she had really achieved was to confirm these teenagers' preconceived ideas that the police were out of touch. Maybe that was the point? She was out of touch. Even her own daughter was grown up and in her twenties. And Ruth was born in the sixties for God's sake, even if it was only by a few months.

When Ruth had joined the force in the early nineties, there were no mobile phones, no internet, her football team Chelsea were the fifth best team in London and Donald Trump was only known for his New York tower and making a cameo appearance in *Home Alone*.

However, as Ruth gathered her things, she saw a girl hanging back near the door. The girl had long, dyed black hair, a nose ring and pale skin.

Ruth smiled at her. 'Hi. I didn't catch your name?'

Lucy swayed awkwardly, 'Lucy, miss.' There was a moment of pause while she plucked up some courage. 'Did you really know from the time you were ten that you wanted to be in the police?'

Ruth nodded, and she approached. 'Yes. Yes, I did. I guess I was lucky that I knew what I wanted to do. What about you, Lucy?'

Lucy's voice was quiet as though she was admitting to some heinous crime. 'I really want to go into the police when I'm older, miss.'

'Good for you. And why do you think you want to be a police officer?'

'Suppose I want to do something worthwhile. Try to help people, you know?'

'Yes, I know exactly what you mean.'

'My dad doesn't. He says the police are the enemy. But my auntie's in the police and she's a total lege.'

'Is she? That's great to hear you want to join the police.' Ruth fished out her police card. 'Here you go. If you've got any more questions or want to chat, just give me a call.'

Ruth smiled at Lucy whose face beamed as she read the card.

Chapter Two

The summer sun sank imperceptibly in the sky as the orange glow of day began to drain away, surrendering to the soft pinks and velvets of dusk. The wind was still unusually hot, and it picked up a little across the ragged cliff tops that peered warily over the smooth sands of Harlech Beach, which was now virtually empty. Dry rye grasses, *lolium perenne*, and thrift, *armeria*, bent gently back and forth. The swathes of green fields that undulated away towards the mountains of Snowdonia were beginning to tinge with brown due to the heat and lack of rain.

The sound of sea birds squealed urgently in the distance as they lunged and dived over the iridescent Irish Sea. Dublin was less than a hundred miles across the water, due west, although Pan-Celticism wasn't high on anyone's priorities these days.

In the distance, the white glint and blue lettering of the *Stena Adventurer*, a 43,000-tonne Stena Line passenger ferry, was taking 1,500 people from Holyhead to Dublin. South of that was an enormous 120-tonne Liberian crude oil tanker, the *NS Lion*, heading for the Russian port of Murmansk.

Harlech, twinned with Riec-sur-Bélon in Brittany, France, was a picturesque seaside town on the west coast of Wales. Technically in the county of Gwynedd, it lay within the ancient boundaries of Merionethshire and over half of the inhabitants spoke Welsh. The town's name was said to have derived from *llech*, meaning high, and *hardd*, meaning fine or even beautiful.

By now the flamingo-pink hues of the sky over Tremadog Bay had blended and faded a little more. To the east of Harlech, Snowdonia National Park stretched for over fifty miles before it gave way to Llangollen, Llancastell and the English border. To the north, commanding mountain tops towered on the horizon.

At the southern end of the Harlech cliffs, there was an impressive, modern five-bedroom house – an enormous two thousand square feet of clean angles and symmetrical glass. Everything about this home was high spec; underfloor heating, granite work surfaces, solar panels and a hot tub. It was more Malibu than West Wales and the panoramic views out to Cardigan Bay and the backdrop of Snowdonia were staggering in their sheer beauty.

A middle-aged man, slim with greying blond hair, came out onto the Norwegian hardwood decking and looked out at the fabulous view. He wouldn't want to be anywhere else on the planet. A small springer spaniel trotted obediently at his side. He looked like the amiable television presenter you might find on a nature programme. He wore Ralph Lauren pastels and a gold Rolex watch.

Owen Ankers felt comfortable in his own skin and relatively at peace with the world. Especially today. Today of all days.

For a self-made millionaire, he was proud that his beginnings had been so modest, working as a teenager on his taid, grandfather, Tommy Ankers' sheep farm just outside Blaenau Ffestiniog, twelve miles north-east of Harlech.

Captain Thomas Ankers had bought the farm in 1926 after a decorated career in the army, winning the Military Cross at Ypres. He had paid one thousand pounds for just over a thousand acres and unlike many of his neighbours, Ankers was new to sheep farming. In fact, sheep farming had existed in Snowdonia since the Iron Age.

Owen could still remember the farmhouse where Taid Tommy and Nain Eirlys lived. The mismatch of Deco and arts-and-crafts styles that seemed so ancient in the late seventies. The smell of Pond's soap, home cooking and the wood burner. His curiosity at the wrinkled skin on the back of his nain's hands and her simple gold-band wedding ring.

The work was tough and Owen's father and taid were uncompromising in what they expected from him. Days were long and the weather relentless. There was a great responsibility too. He remembered having to skin a dead lamb and place its coat over an orphan lamb so that a nearby ewe would adopt it.

Thirty years later, the company he formed with his school friend Callum, Ankers & Webb, sold organic vegetable boxes online to over seventy thousand homes a week and made an annual turnover of thirty-seven million pounds.

Owen had the right to look confident in himself; he had just sold a stake of his empire to the private equity firm TP Creed Global Management for forty-eight million pounds.

Owen thought it was ironic that at first, he didn't give

a toss about anything organic. In fact, quite the opposite. It was a bloody middle-class, hippy fad. Then his friend, Callum Webb, showed him how potatoes were mass produced in a vast metal shed. The black image of the skull and crossbones on the nitro-fertilisers and chemicals, with names like Nitrophoska Blue, Big K and Viking 13, made him shudder. From then on, Owen and Callum began to grow and sell organic vegetables, targeting the wealthy of Cheshire and Chester over the border. Restaurants, health-food shops and private homes. They nearly gave up after two years when they were still living hand to mouth. In fact, it took eight more years of hard work to see a healthy profit but as eating organic became increasingly popular, so did Ankers & Webb. As a recent interview in *The Sunday Times* pointed out, 'It all started with some Welsh bloke named Owen and a bag of spuds in 1990.'

Ankers & Webb became a pioneer and a leading advocate of fair-trade at the turn of the millennium. He was invited on panels and spoke to government working parties. Owen was also more than aware of his company's carbon footprint and refused to use airfreight for the ten per cent of their products that came from abroad.

Owen looked back up at the house he had had built nearly a decade ago. It had just been valued at over one million pounds, but Owen wasn't interested in selling, despite his marriage failing in the past twelve months.

A large bird fluttered and landed on the wooden and glass balustrade that separated the deck from the steep beginnings of the clifftop. It was a *brân goesgoch*, or a red-billed chough or crow. It was sometimes seen along the coast and was the rarest member of the crow family. There was a legend that King Arthur, whose mythology was so intertwined with that of Snowdonia Park, transformed into a red-billed chough as he died. The bird was therefore seen as an omen.

The faint white outline of the moon was now visible, but the air wasn't getting any cooler. Owen felt the sweat on his brow and noticed that the sharp shadows of the day had faded a little. He looked around as a figure came out of the house and onto the decking. Owen smiled and beckoned, 'Come on. We'll take Hector for a walk on the beach.'

He motioned to his mobile phone, which he put on the table with a flourish, and said, 'And I'll leave this bloody thing here.'

The Queen Elizabeth II Law Courts, in Derby Square, Liverpool were a modern set of buildings, pinky brown and stone that ribbed like corduroy. They were first opened in the 1980s and contained the city's crown courts, some of the busiest in Europe. The unremarkable architecture was somehow meant to reflect the towers and turrets of Liverpool Castle, which had stood on the site since the thirteenth century.

Having swigged three good mouthfuls of Aldi's finest Tamova vodka, that he had decanted into a Sprite bottle, DS Nick Evans took his place in the busy public gallery of Court One. Sprite bottles were the perfect camouflage for the alcoholic as the green plastic hid the actual colour of any liquid being consumed.

The alcohol calmed the anxiety and resentment that Nick had felt throughout the first few days of this trial. Curtis Blake was on trial for conspiracy to blackmail and pervert the course of justice. Not for cold-blooded murder, for the savage, crippling beatings or dealing drugs to the impoverished areas of the North West. If the trial continued, Blake was likely to serve some prison time and Nick's mate in the Crown Prosecution Service thought a four-year sentence likely. Although the maximum sentence for blackmail was ten years, the Prosecution were struggling to show that Blake had threatened violence, which would make the sentence far lighter.

Nick was looking forward to watching Blake squirm at any sentence that saw him having to serve time. He was an evil destroyer of lives and deserved far worse.

Grinning like he had just remembered a joke, Blake sat in the dock. Many knew him as 'Uncle' and it was reported that Merseyside criminals kissed his hand when meeting him in the backrooms of The Acorn pub where his crime empire was based.

When Merseyside Police tried to enter Blake's nondescript terraced house in Lower House Lane, on the border of Croxteth and Norris Green, they realised it was no ordinary family home.

Officers told Nick that Blake's front door was so well fortified with steel plates that they had to smash a hole in a side wall. Once they were in, rooms were sectioned off by heavy metal gates and the house windows were triple-glazed, mainly because that made them bulletproof.

Upstairs, detectives broke through a soundproof, four-inch-thick steel door and found Blake's torture chamber. This was where rivals would be fed to the starving dogs. There were also two large black metal hooks that had been screwed into the ceiling and wired to the mains. Victims were suspended and beaten between electric shocks.

However, someone had tipped Blake off and they had stripped the place of everything and meticulously cleaned the previous week. Blake himself had fled to Majorca.

There were mutterings that Blake had someone on the take inside the Merseyside Force who was feeding him intel. Another local 'snout' said the bent officer was in the North Wales Police Force.

The next two hours of the trial mainly revolved around the Prosecution explaining the contents of a mobile phone tap to the jury who then were handed typed transcripts.

Nick had taken a growing dislike to the barrister for the defence, Stephen French. He was balding with pointed ears and blue eyes behind glasses and had an unpleasant arrogance to his manner. He moved sleekly around the courtroom. When questioning, he had demonstrated his bodkin-sharp intellect and a meaningful stare that was more for the jury than anyone else.

Once in a while, as the jury were taken through the labyrinthine details of the case, Blake gazed disinterestedly around the courtroom, sometimes searching the public gallery for family members, friends or 'associates'. Nick knew that even though Blake feigned indifference, he was using this trial as part of his education in the way that UK law enforcement worked. That was the catch. Police officers had to divulge how evidence was obtained – taps, surveillance, informants. If Blake was found not guilty, he and his gang had been given a two-week crash course in how the police had gathered evidence against them stretching back years. As veteran prisoners always said, 'Don't serve time, let time serve you.' Blake would spend hours in his cell in HMP Altcourse reading depositions and testimonies.

There was always a huddle of knuckle-headed men near the back row of the public gallery. They seemed to come and go in shifts. They swapped mobile phones and bits of paper at regular intervals. Most wore North Face jackets, although a couple of the older men, such as Fat

Tone, wore sharp suits, ties and tie pins like extras in a Scorsese movie.

And then it happened. What Nick had feared the most. Ahmet Nadir, a member of a small Turkish drug gang, had done a runner to Venezuela and so could not appear as a witness against Blake. The UK had no extradition treaty with Venezuela, so Nadir could stay there as long as he wanted.

Nick knew what was coming and had gone for a 'vodka break'. After some heated discussion, the judge, His Honour Judge Alan Coren QC, looked at the jury. 'The Prosecution's failure to produce Mr Nadir today as part of the case against the defendant means that there is no evidential basis to link the two men to each other, or to the accusations of blackmail. Mr Nadir's written testimony is therefore also inadmissible in this case. It is the ruling of this court that, as a result of this, there is insufficient evidence against the defendant, Mr Blake, and the defendant is now free to go.'

There were whoops and whistles from the public gallery. Nick felt sick. Blake had ordered the murder of Mark Ferguson, the young man who had died in his arms a few months ago. Blake caused misery and mayhem for thousands across the region and yet no one could even mount a decent case against him.

Blake punched the air with a yell and gestured to the gallery. 'No one can touch me!' He turned and pointed at the Prosecution team. 'You lot, you'll never bloody get near me. Ever! Untouchable.'

STANDING TO GET A BREATH OF FRESH AIR OUTSIDE THE court, Nick saw the defence barrister, French. He stank of privilege, public school and Oxbridge.

As Nick approached, French let out a thunderous guffaw as he strode away from the court buildings with his young, eager legal clerks in tow.

Nick intercepted him. 'Mr French?'

French frowned, 'Sorry, I ...'

Nick flashed his badge, 'Detective Sergeant Evans. Llancastell CID.'

'How can I help, Sergeant?' French asked with a touch of impatience in his educated accent.

'How do you do it?' Nick said, starting to seethe at French's whole demeanour.

'Sorry, I ...' French shot a bemused smile at the clerks around him.

'What just happened in there.'

'Do you mean getting justice for my client?'

'How do you sleep at night? I mean, we both know that Curtis Blake is a violent, murdering drug dealer who has caused misery and pain to hundreds of people, many of them innocent.' Nick could feel his pulse quickening. He just needed to make sure that he kept control.

'Sergeant, you know how the British legal system works. Every defendant, no matter who they are, has the right to the best legal defence that his counsel can provide. So, I sleep very well.' French's tone was infuriatingly pompous.

'And the truth?' Nick glared at him directly, wanting to punch him in the face.

'That's for the jury to decide.' French said calmly with a shrug and went to walk on.

'So, you're just doing your job?' Nick asked, moving in front of French to block his way.

'Yes. Not everyone I defend is guilty, Sergeant. Now if you don't mind ...' French huffed as he tried to circumnavigate Nick.

'You've never been into a crack house or a drug den, have you?' Nick wasn't going to let French get away until he had his say.

'No, I haven't,' French snapped.

'The people in there look like survivors of a concentration camp. They are barely alive, addicted. Families are destroyed, children without parents. Utter misery. Curtis Blake makes money from their misery and kills and maims anyone who gets in his way. And you actively help him do that, which makes you no better.' Nick was now shouting – he couldn't help himself.

'I'm sorry but I don't have time for this,' French said and this time he managed to sidestep Nick and walk away.

'Tell your client we're coming for him. And won't stop until we've got him,' Nick shouted as French strode off.

A couple of passers-by looked at Nick and gave him a wide berth. He lashed out and kicked a nearby bin.

Suddenly from out of nowhere a teenager appeared in front of Nick. He was wearing a hoodie, baseball cap and a black North Face balaclava mask. For a moment, Nick jumped back, assuming he would be attacked.

'What the hell are you doing?' Nick yelled, looking to see if the teen was holding a knife.

The teenager shrugged and snorted. 'I ain't shankin' you, fed.'

THE TEENAGER TOOK SOMETHING OUT OF HIS JACKET. IT was a fifty-pound note. He flicked it onto the pavement in front of Nick. 'Mr Blake says you like a drink. So, he wants you to have a drink on him.'

The teenager laughed, turned and jogged away. Nick watched him go. When he got to the road, a black Mercedes 4x4 pulled over to pick him up. It was the car that Nick had seen Blake sitting in on the night of Mark Ferguson's murder in Porthmadog. The car pulled away and disappeared around the corner.

Grabbing his phone, Nick called the only person that really understood him at Llancastell CID. DI Ruth Hunter might have been sidelined in recent months, but he knew he needed to tell someone.

'Boss?' Nick said as Ruth answered the phone.

'What happened, Nick?' Ruth's voice betrayed her fear that Blake would walk.

'It's over. The case was dismissed mid-trial,' Nick explained darkly.

'I'm sorry to hear that,' Ruth said.

'You should have seen his face, boss.'

'Let it go for now. Blake will slip up. Arrogant wankers like him always do eventually,' Ruth said.

'Not before he's caused a load more mayhem and misery. Part of me wants to get a gun and do the world a favour by blowing his brains out,' Nick said. He had imagined it many times.

'That would be your life over too,' Ruth said.

There was a moment of silence on the phone.

'It's good to hear from you, Nick. It's been a while,' Ruth said. He knew she was trying to change the subject.

'Yes, boss. We'll have to meet for a catch-up soon.'

'Yeah, I'd like that. Now go home, try to move on, and don't do anything silly,' Ruth said, sounding maternal. What she meant was, don't go home and drink yourself into oblivion.'

'Yeah, thanks, boss. I just needed to speak to someone,' Nick said.

'Anytime, Nick. I'll see you soon,' Ruth said and hung up.

. . .

35

NICK DROVE HOME IN A DAZE AND DID THE ONLY THING HE knew how to do. He drank to black out.

Ten hours later, Nick squinted as he came to and rolled over on the sofa. He had no idea if it was morning, afternoon or evening. The light outside at this time of year didn't help as it could be 5 a.m. or 5 p.m. The inaudible US sitcom on the television was no clue either.

The rug and wooden floor beside him were strewn with two empty bottles of vodka, cans of cider and a plate of untouched food from the chippy. He was losing weight fast, but he had no appetite. That sinking feeling of being back in the middle of an alcoholic relapse was overwhelming. He was trapped. Again.

Already Nick could feel the sweat dripping down the back of his neck as his body began to crave alcohol. He sat up and noticed that some of his lower-order motor neurone skills weren't functioning yet. His balance was lopsided and his legs were heavy and didn't feel like they belonged to him.

And, of course, the overpowering question – was there any booze and where was it? He shook a couple of cans of cider but they were empty. The panic started. He was in no fit state to drive. Then he hit the jackpot – an unopened four-pack of strong lager that he didn't even remember buying. He cracked open the first can and watched his shaky hand try to hold the can steady. Then he 'pinged' it down in about three gulps. It was warm and tasted foul, but this was medicine, nothing more. Sod the crisp blend of malt and hops. It was 5.3% abv, and that was the only thing that mattered.

A gurgle deep in his stomach, then movement in the chest and the back of his throat as he projectiled the whole can onto the floor. He reached for the lemon and salt that were on a side plate on the coffee table. He sucked the lemon and licked the salt. The combination was meant to help keep the alcohol down in his stomach. He pinged another can, then the salt and lemon and waited. Whoosh – within a second, he had wretched and vomited again.

Nick lay back on the sofa, his eyes watering. Jesus, if this wasn't hell on earth, he didn't want to know what was. Third time lucky. Plenty of lemon and salt. Another warm can followed by more lemon and salt. He sucked in some air and sat back. He closed his eyes and kept his breathing deep and regular as he waited for the alcohol to get into his bloodstream and take away some of the withdrawals.

Until four months ago, Nick had been sober for ten months and four days. Seven weeks off his first AA birthday. And he had done everything right. He was going to meetings, got himself a home group and a sponsor with thirty years sobriety. He was doing his readings and gratitude lists. The craving for alcohol had been removed from him and he didn't know how. It was a bloody miracle, and he was happy to tell people in the AA meetings that he felt blessed.

And now that was all gone. He was trapped in the madness again.

Nick picked up his phone. He knew he needed to reach out to his sponsor, Bill. As he squinted to try to focus on the screen, he noticed that he had a missed call. At first, he thought he must be seeing things. But there it was. Something he had never seen before.

A text from his dad.

ALL RIGHT, LAD. YOU OKAY? HAVEN'T SEEN YOU FOR A WHILE. Give me a ring when you can. I've got something I want to ask you about.

· · ·

THE SKY HAD DARKENED A LITTLE — THE ORANGE WAS DEEP and burnt, and a rich blue now reflected in the glistening silver of the wet sands of Harlech Beach. Owen Ankers was heading at a strolling pace north along the wind-blown shoreline. A figure walked beside him as they tried to chat over the swirl of the wind.

Owen looked right, over at the mighty and time-worn thirteenth-century castle that jutted dramatically from a two-hundred-foot rocky outcrop. The castle's architect, James of St George, constructed a medieval fortress that combined a powerful sense of majesty with a great visual beauty of line and form. When viewed from the high bluff of rock to the south of the town, he knew the view of this foreboding castle, the Irish Sea and the mountains of Snowdonia created a panorama that was spectacular.

Ahead of them, was an undulating sand dune system which made up much of the soft Meirionnydd coast, extending from the Mawddach estuary in the south to Black Rock Sands in the north-west.

A Springer Spaniel hopped and jumped in and out of the dusty dunes a hundred yards from the figures. The shapes of the dunes seemed to mimic the very landscape and mountains of Snowdonia behind them, like a scale model. These undulations closest to the beach were barren and devoid of plant-life except for a few patches of marram grass, a lone lost crab and the dark, incoherent scribble of seaweed.

Whooper swans and a large flock of widgeon, pintail and mallard flew south across from the Glaslyn Estuary. Skylarks and butterflies added to the richness of the back-drop, while fungi, including waxcaps and puffballs, grew in the sandy hillocks.

Owen Ankers strolled calmly along the sand, whistling loudly at moments for Hector the Spaniel to keep up. The sweat was making his scalp itch and his calves were straining a little. His overriding emotion was gratitude. He had an opportunity to put things right. As the saying went, 'There's no softer pillow than a clear conscience.'

For a moment, Owen's mind had been drawn away to business. His company was drawing up plans to invest in underground farms, or 'Urban Farms' as they were being called, where sites such as the old networks of World War II air-raid shelters were being used to grow fruit, veg and herbs. He had already discovered that there was seven thousand square feet of unused space under Clapham Common tube station.

Owen's attention was half drawn back to the figure he was walking with. Their conversation was stilted, awkward but not confrontational. He turned to look at his companion as they walked, squinting at the setting sun as the wind picked up some sand. But something about them, their expression, made him stop in his tracks and he tried to refocus. He still had the images of modernised World War II bunkers full of pea shoots, rocket, red mustard, pink stem radish, garlic chives, fennel and coriander in his head.

Owen gazed up into the sunlight and watched as the small insects flew translucent across its glare.

It was a glorious evening and he wouldn't want to be anywhere else.

Chapter Three

The morning air was burning hot, especially on the sixth floor where the sun glared angrily through the windows of CID Incident Room One. Nick squinted at the light as he kept his head down and kept walking. He hoped that the mints he had just crunched on would hide the smell of booze. The dismissal of the case against Blake and the text from his dad were whirring around his head. What did his dad want to talk to him about? They hadn't spoken properly since Nick had left him unconsciously drunk on the floor of his cottage eighteen months earlier. To say their relationship was dysfunctional didn't really do it justice.

The room was buzzing with chatter and the odd boom of laughter. Coffee, tea and unhealthy food was being consumed as files and paperwork were passed between officers. There were around a dozen Welsh CID officers, mostly male and middle-aged.

As Nick helped himself to coffee, Detective Chief Inspector Ashley Drake stood at the front, bringing officers up to speed on ongoing CID operations. He was six foot, black, slim with a shaved head to disguise a balding hairline. His forehead was lined deeply. He had transferred from the Manchester Police Force just after Christmas when a DCI position had become available in Llancastell. But Nick knew him from the Dinas Padog murders, where the Manchester Force had been brought in.

Drake was originally from York and although there was an accent, it wasn't quite, 'Ee by gum, lad.' However, he was proud of his roots, having been born into poverty above a pet shop in the city centre. After a few pints of warm Timothy Taylor's Landlord bitter, Drake's accent would thicken as he would happily recount how the infamous Roman Ninth Legion Hispania had marched down his road in 80 AD. And that Sir Francis Drake, Guy Fawkes and Robinson Crusoe were all famous sons of the city.

Nick sipped from his black coffee, closed his eyes and shook his head for a moment to focus his attention on the briefing. He was in a vodka-induced haze and it was taking longer than usual to clear.

Drake had started off by airing his concerns about how much of North Wales' CID's manpower and resources were being used to tackle 'county lines' drug gangs. In North Wales, criminal drug gangs from Merseyside, and to a lesser extent Birmingham, were taking over the drug trade by intimidating local low-level dealers or putting their own dealers on the ground. Children and vulnerable adults were being used to transport and store drugs, money and even weapons. Gangs would establish a base in the local location, such as the home of local vulnerable adults by force or coercion, and this was known as 'cuckooing'. It was becoming increasingly common to bang on the door of a suspicious property in North Wales and find a group of young men with Scouse or Brummie accents.

A partnership between the North West Regional Organised Crime Unit, Operation Titan, and North Wales Police had been established to tackle the growing problem but it was labour intensive and sapping the budget.

Drake perched on the edge of a table. 'Right, let's get down to today's business everyone. What have we got? Mac?'

Mac approached. He was heavy-set and what was left of his hair had been shaved. Nick had looked up to Mac when he first joined Llancastell CID. And Mac, who had been a CID detective for over twenty years, took him under his wing. Mac had no interest in going up the ranks and had mocked Nick when he decided to take his sergeants' exams. As far as Mac was concerned, rising up the ranks took you further and further away from proper police work.

Pressing the button on the computer, Mac pointed to an image of a teenage boy, about eighteen years old, dressed in a blue hospital gown and lying with his eyes closed in a hospital bed. His face was visibly bruised around one eye.

'Boss, IC1 teenage male was found unconscious last night on a stretch of ground between Harlech Castle and Harlech Railway station. As of yet, we have no idea who he is. There was nothing to identify him on his person except six-gram wraps of what we think is crack cocaine in his pocket,' Mac explained.

The crack cocaine instantly resonated with Nick – a county lines operation.

'How bad are his injuries?' Drake asked.

'He has a fractured skull. There are also bite marks on his shoulders and upper arms.'

Bite marks? Drake looked at them. 'Given the severity of the injuries, we should treat this as an attempted murder.'

'If he has bags of crack on him, then can we assume he's a low-level dealer working for a county lines gang?' Nick suggested.

'I've had no intel on county lines dealing going out as far as Harlech but we can't rule that out,' Drake said.

'Maybe he was attacked for being on someone else's turf?' Nick suggested. He and Mac had been working on and off with Merseyside Police and the National Crime Agency, NCA.

Detective Constable Luke Merringer, with his balding ginger hair, goatee beard and a bulging waistline, looked up from his notepad. He was softly spoken, meticulous to the point of nerdy and Nick thought he was the perfect antidote to Mac in the CID office. So much so, they bickered like an old married couple.

'Boss, we are waiting for the toxicology reports but the nurses have said that he smelt strongly of alcohol when he was brought in.'

Drake rubbed his nose and then nodded. 'Okay, so where was he drinking? Pub? Outside somewhere? Who was he with? How long had he been lying where he was found?'

On the other side of the office, Detective Constable Sian Hockney answered a phone.

'First thing to do is to identify him,' Nick suggested.

'I'm sending the details over to the Missing Persons Unit. They will send photos of any possible matches so we can do any comparisons. SOCOs will be in Harlech today so we'll get forensics back, if there are any,' Mac explained.

Drake looked over at them and took a moment to think. 'If he's in a county lines drugs gang, he won't be reported as missing. Luke, liaise with Merseyside CID and the NCA. See if there's any intel their end about Harlech.'

Luke scribbled and nodded. 'Boss.'

. . .

HAVING FINISHED HER PHONE CALL, SIAN CAME ACROSS THE office to join the team. 'That was the hospital. They can't find the unconscious male that was brought in from Harlech last night?'

Drake frowned. 'What? How can they lose an unconscious patient?'

'I don't know, boss.'

'I thought there was a uniform officer stationed there?' Drake asked.

'Apparently he was out of the ward for five minutes getting a coffee,' Sian explained in sardonic tone.

'Bloody hell! Sian, go with Mac to the hospital and check their CCTV. We need to know how an unconscious drug dealer vanishes from a hospital.'

BY THE TIME RUTH GOT TO THE TOP OF THE STAIRCASE OF the sixth floor of Llancastell nick, she was a little out of breath. *Stop smoking or at least cut down,* said a voice somewhere in her head. If you added in the thick heat and Ruth's lack of challenging work, she was in a foul mood and didn't have the patience to listen to Jones's bullshit. The previous evening Ruth had even been online to work out when and how she could take early retirement. She had had enough and wanted out.

As she turned the corner, Ruth spotted DC Sian Hockney heading towards her, although she was blissfully lost in thought and hadn't noticed Ruth yet. Ruth's pulse quickened a little and her stomach skipped, as they always did at the sight of Sian. *You're acting like a bloody teenager.* But Ruth thought Sian really was very attractive. It was a shame that Ruth was so rarely in CID these days for them to form a proper friendship – or more.

Sian looked up and smiled. 'Boss. I was going to try and find you today.'

Ruth's neurons sparked. *Was it to say that you've had a crush on me and needed to tell me straight away?*

Sian's green eyes twinkled as she gave her a knowing but humorous look. 'Seems you made quite an impression on my niece, Lucy, at school yesterday.'

'OH, DARK HAIR, NOSE RING?' RUTH NODDED, remembering the girl she had given her card to. *Now that was karma for you*, Ruth thought.

'That's her. Singing your praises, she was…' Sian gave her a meaningful look. 'Thank you, boss. You taking an interest in her yesterday gave Lucy a massive boost. Things aren't great at home. Her dad's a right know-it-all twat.'

'Anytime. Sounds to me like you're her hero. Actually, you're a total "lege".' The fact that Ruth had been given an unexpected boost in Sian's estimation was giving her a real buzz.

'She tells me that you knew from the time you were ten that you wanted to be in the police force?'

'Yeah, it was either that or join Bananarama,' quipped Ruth.

Sian laughed and said, 'You'll have to tell me about it. We should go for a drink after work one night?'

Ruth paused for a moment, and then bit the bullet with a smile. 'You're on. I'd love that. Maybe in the week sometime?'

. . .

SIAN WENT TO GO. 'YEAH … LOOK FORWARD TO IT. AND thanks again, boss. You're the "lege".'

Ruth tried to hide her grin as she headed the other way with an added spring in her gait. Apparently, she was a 'lege'. Sian had been on her gaydar for a while and even though she had no idea if she was gay, straight or bi, a drink with her would be a welcome change to her routine.

She knocked on Jones's door, heard the customary inaudible mutter from the other side and went in. Jones sat at his desk and for a moment didn't look up. Ruth had grown used to all his outward signs of self-importance. He was far too busy to acknowledge her properly. *What a twat.*

'Have a seat, Ruth,' Jones mumbled and gestured while typing something on his laptop. *Let the little games commence, you dinosaur with a small dick.*

'Sir.' Ruth sat down and waited for Jones to grace her with his full attention. She looked at the idiotic wisps of greying hair above his ears that only served to highlight his baldness. She tried to avoid office gossip as much as she could but how many marriages was it now? Five or six? She had lost count. Although she did find herself wondering how Jones had managed to remain childless. A deliberate act or biological malfunction? She hoped it was the latter. She caught sight of the drapes of fat that leaked over his belt and his flanks.

Jones stopped typing, took a breath, pushed his chair away from the table and looked over at her. 'How are you, Ruth?'

He was so full of shit.

'Fine, I'm fine, sir.' She knew that Jones had no interest in how she was.

'Good, good …' Jones said as though he hadn't even registered her answer. He reached for some papers and handed them to her. 'There's a missing person I want you to look at for me.'

RUTH COULDN'T HELP BUT LET OUT A SIGH. WAS HE bloody joking? That was a job for the woodentops, at least in the early stages. 'Is that the best use of my experience, sir? I understand that Operation Titan could do with more CID officers.'

RUTH KNEW ABOUT THE JOINT COUNTY LINES OPERATION with Merseyside and the NCA and it was the kind of case that she wanted to get her teeth into.

'This is not you being sidelined, Ruth, I assure you. The assistant chief constable has asked me personally to give this priority,' Jones explained, but Ruth wasn't listening to his bullshit. There were several ACCs in the North Wales Police Force and she had no idea who he was talking about.

Jones handed over an A4 photo of a middle-aged man, expensive overcoat and navy scarf, sitting by a beach with a Springer Spaniel dog. He was smiling. A natural smile that caught his amusement at the strength of the wind that blew against him.

'Owen Ankers. Forties. Self-made millionaire. Went missing at the weekend. Failed to show up to his brother's fortieth birthday celebrations in Abersoch. No answer from his home or his mobile phone. Then he failed to show up at his company's head office yesterday. All completely out of character,' Jones explained.

'Have uniform been round?' Ruth asked.

'Twice. Nothing. No sign of anyone,' Jones said.

'What's the assistant chief constable's interest?' Ruth

asked, wondering if she would be told to mind her own business.

'ACC Davenport used to be married to Owen Ankers until last year, when they divorced.'

'Beth Davenport?' Ruth knew Assistant Chief Constable Beth Davenport only by reputation. But she had been a trailblazer for UK female police officers and had at one time been president of the British Association of Women in Policing, BAWP. She was a bit of a hero to Ruth, especially with her work on gender equality in the force.

'You know Assistant Chief Constable Davenport?' asked Jones, pompously reminding Ruth of her correct title as she was a superior rank.

'Only by name. I've never met her. I knew that she worked up this way in recent years.'

'She was based at Colwyn Bay but she's been on secondment to Hendon. And she has a desk here on the ninth floor but I hardly see her these days. Anyway, she's worried about Owen's disappearance. And she's a very experienced copper, so that makes me worried.'

For once Ruth agreed with him. Coppers were realistic and pragmatic people. If they got spooked, it was normally for a good reason.

'Of course, sir. What do we know about Ankers?' Ruth asked.

'He's a bit of a hero in Harlech. Local boy made good. Funds the local football club and youth club. Charity work. Commander Tope and Ankers go way back.' Jones gave her a knowing look. 'And they're in the same Masonic lodge.'

'BIG SURPRISE.' RUTH RAISED AN EYEBROW.

She knew all about the historic link between the police force and Freemasonry. There had been a suspicion for over the past century that the Masons had exerted a huge influence over the police and law. During the sixties, there had been allegations of bribery and corruption when it had been discovered that police officers, criminals and judges all belonged to the same Masonic lodges, which allowed for the very real possibility that the law could be completely compromised. She remembered that just before she left the Met, there were fresh allegations that senior police officers in the Freemasons were blocking the progress of women and officers from black and minority ethnic communities and thwarting reforms in policing.

'I'll look into it and get back to you, sir,' Ruth said through a forced smile. She hated all the bullshit that went with secret boys' clubs and their silly handshakes.

'Great. Assistant Chief Constable Davenport is going to meet you at Owen Ankers' property tomorrow morning,' Jones informed her.

Even though she was certain this would be another dead-end job, Ruth was looking forward to meeting ACC Davenport. Any woman who had worked her way from bobby on the beat to assistant chief constable was deserving of her respect.

RUTH HAD BEEN SITTING IN THE HORSE AND JOCKEY PUB for fifteen minutes, sipping slowly at her gin and tonic. She was meeting DS Nick Evans for a catch-up. Ruth and Nick had worked together on the Dinas Padog murders the year before and, after a rocky start, they formed both an excellent working partnership and a growing friendship.

However, since the shocking revelations of those murders and Ruth's absence from work and 'phased return', they had had little to do with each other. Nick had sent her a couple of texts to see how she was. There had been a few grabbed words but nothing more than pleasantries. She had missed both his humour and his supportive ear.

'Sorry I'm late, boss.' Nick came over, looking a little flustered.

'Thought you'd stood me up,' Ruth said with a smile. It was good to see him, even if he looked drained. She suspected he was drinking again.

'Drink with a cockney MILF? I wouldn't miss that for the world,' Nick said with a cheeky grin.

'Christ, you don't change. What do you want to drink?' Ruth asked, rising from the table.

'It's all right, boss, I got this,' Nick said as he headed for the bar.

Ruth suspected he was going to have a sneaky double at the bar. She'd seen him do it before but she wasn't going to judge.

After a minute, Nick returned, plonked a pint on the table and sat down. He sucked an inch off his beer and sat back. 'That's better.'

Ruth indicated his beer. 'I'm not going to ask about your drinking.'

'Don't. It's "an ongoing issue" according to HR,' Nick said, rolling his eyes.

'Any more developments on the Blake case?' Ruth said.

'Total sham. Again. I used to believe in karma, but if there was anyone that disproves its existence, it's Blake,' Nick said.

After their recent phone call, Ruth knew how much Blake got under Nick's skin. From what she could remember, it was a hatred that went back over a decade.

'What about you, boss? You still helping little old ladies across the road?' Nick quipped.

'Don't bloody joke. I was giving a talk in a school yesterday to a bunch of braindead teenagers,' Ruth said.

'Jones is a self-serving dickhead. Always has been. And at the risk of blowing smoke up your backside, you're a brilliant detective. We need you in CID,' Nick said.

'Blow away. I could do with a bit of an ego boost.'

Nick smiled, glugged at his pint and looked at her for a moment.

'What?' Ruth asked. She could see that he was weighing up whether or not to say something.

'Ironic though. I think there was part of you that came up to North Wales for a quieter life. Bit of paperwork, talk at a school, looking for a stolen tractor,' Nick said.

Ruth nodded. Nick was spot on and one of the only officers she had worked with that she felt comfortable talking like this with.

'Yeah. Grass is always greener. I think being a detective in CID is now in my DNA. When I'm not doing it, I miss it. I don't want to do anything else.'

'What does Jones say?'

'He's given me a mispers case to look through,' Ruth said wearily. 'Mispers' was the police abbreviation for a missing-persons case.

'That's bollocks,' Nick said. 'Anything interesting?'

'A businessman up in Harlech. Owen Ankers. Very rich. He seems to have vanished off the face of the earth.'

'Harlech?' Nick asked.

'Yeah, why?'

'We had an attempted murder up there a couple of days ago, that's all. I always thought Harlech was a sleepy little place where tourists went,' Nick explained.

'So, no Mrs Right in your life at the moment?' Ruth asked, changing the subject.

'No chance. Look at the state of me.'

'You scrub up all right. Sometimes.'

'Sometimes? Charming. Anyway, I'm not really your type, what with me having a penis and everything,' Nick said with a chortle. 'What about you?'

Ruth laughed. She hadn't hidden the fact that she was a lesbian from Nick, and even though he made the odd joke, he was discreet.

'I've got my eye on someone. But not really,' Ruth said, thinking of Sian and wondering why she had even flagged it up.

'Anyone I know?' Nick asked.

'No, no … Anyway, here's to us, two sad wankers,' Ruth chuckled as she raised her glass.

'Two sad wankers!' Nick said as she chinked her glass.

Chapter Four

The following morning, Nick was on a shout to the tiny village of Maentwrog, which lay in the Vale of Ffestiniog just below Blaenau Ffestiniog and within the Snowdonia National Park. A body had been found in the River Dwyryd, which ran alongside the village. Nick had already made his mind up – accident or misadventure. That was the usual outcome of this type of discovery. Inexperienced tourist in a canoe or drunk local staggering home in the dark of night. Maybe suicide.

Maentwrog meant 'Twrog's stone'. According to legend, a giant known as Twrog threw an enormous boulder – *maen* meaning stone in Welsh – from the top of a hill down into the village, destroying a pagan altar the villagers had built. Where the stone landed, a Christian church was then founded, now called St Twrog's Church. Legend tells that if anyone rubs this boulder, they are destined to return to the village. There are many that also believe that this return will be for sinister reasons.

As Nick pulled into the picturesque village, 'Howlin' For You' by the Black Keys was playing. The Astra's air

53

conditioning rattled on full blast but he could feel the heat of the day coming through the flash of sunlight on the windscreen. His face and neck were sweaty but that was as much the alcohol withdrawal as the heat. He pulled at the collar on his shirt for a moment's relief. The orange, digital read-out told him it was thirty degrees outside. He continued along the A496, past the tiny shoulder-to-shoulder stone cottages and then crossing over the River Dwyryd on the bridge that had stood strong since its construction in 1780.

Nick parked his car alongside one of the two marked *Heddlu/Police* response cars with their yellow and blue markings. Pushing his sunglasses down the bridge of his nose, he blinked in the sunlight. It took a few seconds for his eyes to readjust. He reached into the glove compartment watching two uniformed officers who were around a hundred yards away and redirecting traffic away from the bridge. He took a litre-bottle of vodka, slid down in the driver's seat so he was out of their sight, swigged a couple of mouthfuls and then put it back. He let out a sigh. That was the power of alcohol. His brain and body relaxed just with the knowledge that it was soon going to be in his bloodstream.

Nick slid his sunglasses back up, got out, assessed his balance and looked out over the river that glistened silver in the sunlight. The banks on both sides were open, dotted with the occasional magnificent umbrella-shaped field maple, and beyond them swathes of fields with sheep grazing languidly.

Scene of crime officers, SOCOs, were already on site and had sealed off the area with white police tape and a blue sign that read: *HEDDLU Arafwch – POLICE Slow*. There were another five uniformed officers mooching around the site.

Nick caught his reflection in the back window of the car. He was dressed in a short-sleeved white shirt and dark-navy skinny tie. He turned away. He avoided looking at his own reflection anywhere if at all possible. It made him uncomfortable probably because he didn't think much of the person looking back at him. Taking in a breath of the warm air, he thanked God that no one could see behind his sunglasses. His eyes were bloodshot and his face was puffy. Approaching the uniform officer – twenties, male, athletic – by the police tape, he flashed his warrant card.

'DS Evans. Do you want to show me what we've got, Constable?'

They began to edge down the stony bank. Nick felt a little unsteady as he clambered down the steep stone-and-grass slope. His legs felt out of synch with his brain – that was the vodka.

'Unidentified male. Dog walker found him on that little stone beach there about two hours ago.' The uniform officer pointed down to an area of stones only about twelve feet by six feet where the river turned and began to head due east. It was now covered by a small white polyethylene scene-of-crime tent.

Nick began to clamber down the bank a little to where the SOCOs were working.

'Where's the dog walker?' Nick asked.

'Over there.' The uniform officer gestured to a diminutive middle-aged woman with a black Labrador. 'She's a bit shaken up.'

'Get her address and find out if she saw anyone around the area,' Nick said.

'Yes, sir …' The uniform officer nodded and walked away.

Nick scrambled down to river level and saw the chief SOCO, Tony Amis, bent over the body of what looked like a middle-aged man. Amis had skin the hue of skimmed milk and wore a wide-brimmed brown canvas hat that seemed incongruous with his white forensic overalls.

'Morning, Nicholas,' Amis said brightly with a half-smile. His accent was private school and educated.

'Morning. So, what can you tell us, Tony?'

'Male. Late forties. Slim, although the water has now bloated the face and body. Well dressed. Ralph Lauren. Unfortunately, no identification in the clothes.'

Amis removed his hat and fanned himself. Nick could see that his freckled skin and pale complexion were not designed for this heat.

'Drowned, suicide?' Nick asked.

'It's hard to tell. There is a contusion at the back of the head but I doubt that would have killed him. It also might have been caused post-mortem as the body came down the river. There are also scratch injuries on his arms. They could be defensive wounds or branches. Might be too deep for branches. The post-mortem should tell us a lot more,' Amis replied, sounding as though he was thinking out loud.

'How long has he been dead?' Nick was going through the motions. It was death by misadventure.

'At a guess, I'd say more than twenty-four hours, less than seventy-two, given the state of the body,' Amis explained.

Nick looked at the man's bloated, colourless face that was tinted blue and purple along the jawline. The light of life from the eyes was gone as they stared at nothing. They had the appearance of stone. He didn't know if being in the water did that to the eyes, but it made him shiver.

'Another thing,' Amis crouched and pointed to the

wrist where there was the white watch outline on the skin against the man's tan. 'He wore a watch. Again, it could have come off in the river.'

As Nick gazed at the man's hand, he noticed an ornate gold ring on the little finger of his left hand. It featured a compass and a manual square. He knew exactly what they were. 'Looks like our victim was "on the square".'

AMIS NODDED. 'HE WAS A MASON? I WONDERED WHAT that was.'

'My dad had one just like it.' As Nick said this, it occurred to him that he had used the past tense. His father might still wear the ring for all he knew.

'Can I move the body once the forensic photographer's finished? I don't want it to degrade any further before the post-mortem,' Amis asked.

Nick winked at him. 'Knock yourself out, boyo. We won't have much forensic evidence because of the water.'

Nick took out his phone. He took a few photos of the face, body and clothes.

'Given the strength of the river, I doubt that he went in anywhere near here,' Amis said.

Nick nodded. 'I'll get the tide times from the coast-guard.' Nick looked over at the detective constable. 'Right, Constable. I want you to start a crime-scene log and we need to sweep the riverbank for footprints or anything suspicious.'

Nick stood contemplating the scene in silence for a moment. The wind rushed along the bank and up into the trees. A tractor's engine started up somewhere in the distance. Life was carrying on as usual.

An hour later, Nick watched as the body was carefully placed in a thick black body bag and taken from the site. A team of uniformed officers then searched the bank. Due to the heatwave, the ground along the riverbank was rock hard so recent footprints would be very unlikely.

Nick had ordered other uniform officers to carry out a house-to-house of any properties overlooking the river. Both operations were a long shot. As Tony had said, it was unlikely that the victim had gone into the river anywhere near where they had found him.

An hour later, Nick got a call to say they had found nothing on the riverbank and no one had seen anything suspicious that was of any use.

It had death by misadventure written all over it.

RUTH WAS HEADING OUT WEST ON THE A4212 TOWARDS Harlech where she was due to meet Assistant Chief Constable Beth Davenport. Normally Ruth would put this type of missing-persons case to one side, knowing that in all probability the person would turn up having been on a business trip, golfing weekend or stag do that he'd forgotten to tell anyone about. But if ACC Davenport had worries, it needed to be looked at.

The road was banked with thick conifer trees and a continuous line of purple foxgloves that thrived in the acidic soil. To her right, Llyn Celyn, an enormous reservoir that had been constructed between 1960 and 1965 in the valley of the River Tryweryn. It was 140ft deep and two and a half miles long, and named originally *Llyn Tryweryn Mawr*, meaning Great Tryweryn Lake. However, the construction of the reservoir was highly controversial as it involved the deliberate flooding of the village of Capel Celyn and adjacent farmland. The village was a stronghold of Welsh culture and the Welsh language. Despite protest marches by locals in Liverpool, the valley was flooded in

1965 and the post office, school, chapel, cemetery and twelve farms were all submerged: eight hundred acres of land were lost.

Ruth had deliberately taken this route to see Llyn Celyn. She remembered it from her holidays as a child. She and her brother Chris were fascinated by the strange-looking turret that protruded from the water. They invented fanciful tales about mystical underwater creatures, which only came out at night, that inhabited the castle and the nearby village now hidden under the water.

RUTH HAD SEEN ON THE NEWS AND SOCIAL MEDIA THAT, because of the current heatwave in the country, the low water levels were beginning to reveal the deserted village of Capel Celyn.

The stones and gravel crunched as Ruth pulled the car over at the western end of the reservoir. To her left were the familiar tops of the straining towers that she loved as a child and that were visible all year round. She learnt years later that they silted debris and objects before the treatment plant cleaned the water on its way to Merseyside, which was far less romantic than her childhood theory of a submerged castle turret.

Buzzing down the window, she let the breeze tousle at her hair. A small line of cars had parked up as people gazed at where the sunlit water had receded nearly a hundred metres from where it normally lapped the grey stone banks. Now there was a strip of baked ground covered in dried sludge and rocks. *What was all the fuss about?*

Her phone buzzed. When she saw that the sender was Steven Flaherty, her liaison officer from the Missing Persons Unit at the London Met, she immediately knew it would be some kind of update on her partner Sarah, who had gone missing in 2013. 'Gone missing' didn't really do it justice. Sarah had got on a train and then vanished off the face of the earth. No note, no phone call, nothing. No clues to what had happened.

However, last April, just as the Dinas Padog murder case was coming to a close, Ruth had received an anonymous text that read: *Call me later, Sarah xxx.*

Ruth's head told her that it was someone's mistake, but her heart leapt at the possibility that it was Sarah getting in touch. She rang the number back a dozen times but it was switched off. Of course, she knew that if Sarah were to get in touch, a message of *Call me later, Sarah xxx* wouldn't really be likely or appropriate after four years of devastation. But those were the words that Sarah would use and she always signed off with three kisses. That irrational glimmer of hope was cruel but like an addict with a last fix, she clung onto it. By the time Ruth had surreptitiously checked the number at work, the phone had been off for two days. Its last GPS signal had been on Oxford Street in London.

Since then, Ruth was waiting to see if anything else could be uncovered about the phone or the message.

Taking her phone, Ruth dialled Steven Flaherty's direct line.

'Missing Persons Unit. Steven Flaherty speaking.'

'Steven, it's Ruth Hunter here,' Ruth said, trying not to sound too anxious.

They spent a few moments on pleasantries, as they always did. Flaherty was a lovely, caring man and Ruth knew she was lucky to have him continue to look after Sarah's case.

'The text from last April came from a Tesco Pay-As-You-Go phone,' Flaherty explained.

'Any details as to who registered it?' Ruth asked, fearing she knew the answer.

'Sorry, no. We've got no way of tracing the owner.'

Ruth's heart sank. 'Okay …'

'I'm sorry, Ruth. I know it's not the news that you wanted.'

'It's fine. We haven't had much to cling to in the last few years …'

'I know. And I'll be in touch as soon as anything else turns up. However small. Okay?' Steven said trying to reassure her.

'Thank you, Steven.'

RUTH WAS BACK TO SQUARE ONE WITH NO CLUES AS TO what had happened, treading the painful line between irrational hope and grief. She got out of the car and tried to compose herself. Smoking a cigarette, she leant back, slouched on the car's bonnet and looked out over the lake. She needed to banish all thoughts about Sarah from her mind now, or she might go mad.

As Ruth peered carefully, she could make out the distinct wooden line of a hedge row and the bricks of an old farm building. Further to her right, the access road that had led to the village and then, as she squinted, the distinctive rusted iron of tracks that were once part of the North Wales railway line. It was eerie but fascinating to think that all this had lain submerged under 1700 million litres of water for over fifty years. She would have to text her brother and tell him that their mystical ghost town was slowly rising from the dead.

By ten thirty, Ruth had arrived at Owen Ankers' luxurious home on the Harlech clifftops. A local uniform patrol had already parked outside beside a new white Audi that

Ruth assumed belonged to Assistant Chief Constable Davenport. She still couldn't understand the fashion for white cars. It wasn't long ago that white cars were the reserve of wide boys and page-three girls.

Before getting out of the car, Ruth checked herself in the sun-visor mirror. Every time, she was still surprised not to see her twenty-seven-year-old self looking back at her. That's how old she felt. But the lines and bags were there to prove otherwise. She touched up her make-up. *Need to make a good impression*, she thought to herself.

Slamming the car door behind her, Ruth let the warm sea breeze blow on her face and closed her eyes for a moment, allowing the sun to warm her skin. It was so bright that even when closing her eyes, she could see the sun's glare through the skin of her eyelids. *Be in the moment*, she told herself. She was never in the moment, never in the present, always in the past.

Ruth's momentary karmic peace was broken as the burly uniform officer approached. He was overweight and his hair shaved down to the bone.

'DI Hunter?' he asked.

Ruth blinked for a second, nodded and showed her warrant card. 'Yes. Have you been in yet?'

'Yes, ma'am. The assistant chief constable got here early so she had a quick scoot round, like. Nothing here that looks suspicious,' Yates explained.

'Good, thank you, Constable. Is the ACC inside?' Ruth asked.

'She's in the kitchen,' he explained.

As Ruth headed for the front door, something caught her eye. Someone peering at them from the small cottage across from them down the road. But the mystery voyeur had vanished by the time she took a full look.

Turning, Ruth gestured subtly to the cottage. 'Constable, could you have a word with some of the neighbours. See if they've seen Owen Ankers over the weekend at any point? Or anyone arriving or going from the property.'

'Ma'am …' The officer nodded and headed down the road towards the cottage. She suspected that he was one of those constables that had been doing the job forever and was rarely fazed by anything.

Ruth needed to focus on the case in hand. When a high-ranking and experienced police officer believed there was cause for concern, then it needed her full attention. She also needed to show Jones that she was more than capable of returning to active duty.

The Ankers' home inside was minimalist, high-end but bordering on both impersonal and a little pretentious.

Ruth headed to where she assumed the kitchen would be. The cream carpet in the hallway was thick under her shoes and she caught a waft of vanilla air freshener and freshly brewed coffee. Walls were tastefully decorated in a muted Farrow & Ball blue.

As Ruth entered, she spotted a tall, slim woman in her late forties with jet-black hair in a ponytail, no make-up and olive skin plunging a cafetière and seemingly making herself quite at home. She was in uniform – police-issue black formal jacket, white blouse.

Ruth supposed that the house had been Davenport's home for several years before the divorce.

'Ma'am? I'm Detective Inspector Hunter. I'm looking into your husband's disappearance.'

'Hello, Detective Hunter. Would you like coffee?' Her accent was soft with a trace of North Wales. Middle-class parents. Maybe even a private education?

'I'm fine, thank you,' Ruth said as she took a chair, sat down and then took out her notebook. 'Your husband has been missing since Saturday, is that correct?'

Davenport projected an aura of certainty and calm. 'Technically Sunday. There was a family gathering at the house in Abersoch for his brother Andrew. Owen never showed, or called, or made any contact.'

'And that's completely out of character?'

'Completely. One of the positives about my ex-husband was that he was dependable. Dependable and very predictable. He's incredibly close to his niece and nephew so he wouldn't have missed the chance to see them.' Ruth could see that there was a touch of anxiety as the ACC thought about her ex-husband.

'And there was some mention of Mr Ankers not arriving at work on Monday? Is that correct?' Ruth asked.

'Yes. Callum Webb called me to find out where he was. There were some financial papers he was due to sign,' Davenport explained.

'And that was, again, out of character?'

'Yes. That's why I'm worried. And I'm an experienced police officer so I'm not easily spooked.'

Ruth found Davenport disarmingly unruffled. She gestured to the interior of the house with her pen. 'Anything out of the ordinary as you looked around?'

'No, not really,' Davenport said with a hint of doubt.

Ruth picked up on her uncertainty. There was something amiss.

'If there's anything ...' Ruth probed gently.

Davenport nodded and motioned for Ruth to follow her. 'Just through here …'

Ruth followed her into an enormous living room with floor-to-ceiling windows that looked over the magnificent panorama of sea and mountains. The floors were wooden and the accent rugs and sofas neutral and elegant.

Davenport pointed to a low coffee table. 'Owen had been going through old photo albums. He doesn't do that very often.'

Ruth looked at about half a dozen thick photo albums that were all open. There were photos of Owen and Beth in happier times in places like New York or on the beach. Some were a lot older and featured family photos and children in the 1970s and 1980s.

'Do you have children, ma'am?' Ruth asked delicately.

Davenport baulked at the question for a second. 'No. We couldn't …' She corrected herself. 'Owen couldn't.'

RUTH WASN'T GOING TO DELVE INTO THAT ANY FURTHER. There was a slightly awkward silence as Ruth gazed around the room. It was minimalist and clutter free, like a museum or a show home.

Her eyes were drawn to an expensive Bang & Olsen turntable, amp and speakers. There were four or five vinyl albums that had been left untidily beside the turntable. Ruth felt they were out of keeping with the room.

'How did Owen seem recently?' Ruth asked as she wandered over to the stereo.

'Fine. More than fine. He'd just sold a stake in his company for millions. He didn't have a care in the world.'

Was that the cause of his disappearance? Owen Ankers had suddenly become a very rich man and then vanished? Coincidence?

Ruth looked at the albums beside the turntable – Dire Straits' 'Money For Nothing', Phil Collins, Queen. *Not a music fan then*, concluded Ruth as she gazed unimpressed at the eighties cover designs. It was the music that the second 'Summer of Love' of 1988 had strived to react against. The music of Yuppies. For a moment, she got a flash of dancing to 'Let The Music Use You' by Frankie Knuckles at Shoom at Busby's on the Charing Cross Road. It was a different lifetime.

'Owen's a bit of a vinyl bore as well,' Davenport said but she was clearly preoccupied. She came over and looked at the album sleeves.

'Seems like he was having a bit of a reminisce,' Ruth said, half to herself.

'Yes …' Davenport replied lost in her own thoughts.

Ruth's mobile phone rang. It was DS Nick Evans. She looked at Davenport and gestured to her phone as she walked away somewhere more discreet. 'Sergeant?'

'Boss?' Nick's voice was soft and possibly verging on slurred. She didn't want to think about him drinking on duty.

'I've got a body,' Nick said.

'That's nice for you,' quipped Ruth.

Nick laughed. 'Thank you, boss. What I mean is we've pulled a body out of the River Dwyryd.'

'Which is where?' Ruth asked.

'Tiny village of Maentwrog. You won't know it unless you look at a map, boss.'

'Try me.' Her geographical knowledge of the area was poor but it was improving.

'Vale of Ffestiniog just below Blaenau Ffestiniog,' Nick explained.

Nick was right. Ruth had no idea where it was. 'Okay, so that's …'

'Snowdonia National Park, boss.'

'Thanks, I'd gathered that much …'

'Missing Persons says that you're looking into the disappearance of an Owen Ankers who went missing over the weekend?' Nick asked.

'I'm at his home now. His ex-wife is here. ACC Davenport. Why, do you think it's him?' Ruth asked.

'Middle-aged man. Expensive clothes. About five foot eight.'

'Yeah, could be.'

'IF I SEND YOU A PHOTO, CAN YOU SEE IF IT'S A MATCH?' Nick asked.

'Of course, send away.'

'Thanks, boss.'

'Did he drown or something?'

'We're not sure yet. Nothing at the moment to indicate his death was suspicious. But the PM might throw up something,' Nick explained.

'Okay, leave it with me.' Ruth thought about the new information as she wandered back to the living area. Of course, if the body turned out to be Owen Ankers, she was now faced with having to break the news to ACC Davenport there and then. Even though she was experienced at breaking this type of devastating news, it was never easy. And it was particularly difficult when it was a fellow officer.

As she waited for Nick's text, she picked up a framed newspaper photo. It showed a middle-aged man shaking hands with another. The caption read: *Alan Gray, Secretary of State for Wales.* Owen Ankers was seriously well connected. Nearby was another photo, the same middle-aged man in ski gear with friends.

'Does your ex-husband have enemies, ma'am?' Ruth asked in an understated tone.

'Enemies? God, no. He sells organic fruit and veg. Tesco maybe.' Davenport then looked back at her. She looked a little embarrassed at having made a joke.

Ruth shrugged. 'He's also a very rich man. And that could make him a target.'

Davenport shook her head but she went and peered out of the doors that led onto the decking. Pausing for a second, she pulled a face, presumably having seen something outside. She unlocked the glass doors, opened them and went out onto the decking platform before Ruth had realised what she was doing.

'Ma'am?' Ruth said, following her out. *Where the hell is she off to?*

Davenport walked over to a long table and picked up an iPhone. 'It's Owen's phone.'

'Are you sure?' Ruth asked wondering how it had been missed earlier.

'Yes. Positive,' Davenport replied looking down at it in her hand.

'Can you put it back down on the table for me, please, ma'am? If it is evidence then I would like it to remain there,' Ruth asked lightly but underneath was now annoyed that uniformed officers had made such an omission.

'Of course. Sorry, I …' Davenport apologised. She clearly wasn't thinking straight.

At that moment, Ruth's phone pinged. It was the photos that Nick had forwarded over.

Ruth moved away and looked at the lifeless corpse that had been pulled from the river. Despite the bloated blueish features, there was little doubt that the dead man that Nick had seen earlier was Owen Ankers. The hair, though matted, the bone structure of the face and shape of the head was identical. Coppers had the skill to look at a dead body or face and then match what they saw to a living person they had known or a photograph very quickly. It wasn't a skill that Ruth enjoyed, but she knew she was good at it.

Ruth needed to think fast on her feet. 'Ma'am, I'm afraid I do have some bad news. A colleague of mine has just contacted me. Shall we go inside?'

'WHATEVER IT IS, YOU CAN TELL ME HERE,' DAVENPORT said, quietly preparing herself for the worst.

'A body's been found in the River Dwyryd.'

'Is it Owen?' Davenport asked.

'We suspect that it is your ex-husband,' Ruth said softly. 'I'm so sorry.'

'Oh God.' Davenport looked stunned. 'Are you certain?'

Ruth nodded. 'I've just seen some photos. I'm convinced it's Owen's body that's been recovered.'

A tear rolled down Davenport's face as she blinked it away. Ruth could see she was playing out the different questions that were now racing around her mind.

'Did he drown? He's a strong swimmer …'

'I'm afraid I can't discuss any of the details at the moment.' Ruth met Davenport's eyes with compassion. 'I'm so sorry. Do you want to sit down for second, ma'am?'

Davenport nodded as she followed Ruth back inside the house.

'I know it's silly. We were divorced. But we were still friends. Nothing horrible had happened, between us, you know?' Davenport explained and then took a deep breath trying to contain her emotions.

At that moment, the police constable who Ruth had met outside came in and immediately sensed the hushed tone.

'Constable?' Ruth said quizzically and they moved away so they were out of earshot.

'Ma'am.' Yates looked down at his notebook for a moment and said in a hushed tone, 'Neighbour, a Mr Alwyn Fields. Says he saw Mr Ankers walking the dog on Saturday afternoon.'

'It was definitely him?' Ruth asked.

'Yeah, he was certain it was him. Bit of a charmer is Mr Fields. He told me that he doesn't like the police as soon as he opened the door,' Yates said sarcastically.

'Nice. Bit of a curtain twitcher?' Ruth said with a smile.

'Yes, ma'am. Nosey bastards are the best source of intel sometimes.'

'And he didn't see Owen Ankers return?' Ruth asked.

'No, that's the last he saw of him. He thought it was strange as he normally sees him coming and going most days. They knew each other to say hello to,' explained Yates.

'Okay. Thank you. Is that everything?'

'No, ma'am. He's also sure he saw Owen Ankers leaving the house that afternoon with a man. Skinny, red baseball cap, grey hoodie maybe. Then they headed down to the beach together,' Yates said.

Ruth didn't like the sound of that one bit. Heading off to Harlech Beach with an unidentified man only to disappear and turn up dead in a river three days later.

Her instinct told her that there might be more to Owen Ankers' death. Until the post-mortem was carried out, she was going to be over-cautious.

Ruth led Yates away towards the front door. 'Constable, this house is now a possible scene of crime. I'm going to need the house taped off and a scene-of-crime log started. No one except CID or SOCO come in or out.'

Holyhead 2016

Even though it was dawn, the Port of Holyhead was busy with freight and tourists. The gigantic white Stena ferries dominated the port. Beyond that the darkness of the Irish Sea. It was fifty miles and three hours to Dublin.

Twin sisters, aged fifteen, were sitting together on the blue-patterned seats in the passenger lounge waiting for the first ferry. The one with blonde hair was asleep, her head resting on her sister's lap. It had always been like that. The sister with red hair had been born forty minutes before her twin. Ever since then, she had been looking out for her younger sibling. Protecting her from what had been a horrendous life so far.

Delving into her bag, the girl pulled out some Monster Munch. Not the pickled onion flavour that everyone seemed to rave about. No. The roast beef one. There was just about enough decent flavouring for it to remind her of a roast Sunday dinner. That was her favourite. It was also a rarity.

Pushing her white headphones back into her ears, the girl looked down at the playlist on her phone. 'Too Good' by Drake and Rihanna was playing. She checked the time. There was still half an hour before they had to board the ferry to what she hoped would be a new life for her and her sister.

When they had done a bunk from the care home in Llandudno for the third time, they had managed to hitch a lift to Holyhead with a lorry driver called Kev. He had bad breath but didn't try to shag them. That was a bonus. Men were animals. Maybe it was her limited experience of the opposite sex, because ever since she could remember, men just seemed to want sex with her. Sometimes her sister too. But mainly her. They told her she had 'a look'. A twinkle in her eye. She supposed it made them feel slightly better about what they were doing to her.

Over the past few months, she had made friends with some people online. They told her that if she and her sister came to Dublin, they *could find them jobs and a place to stay. Nothing much. Cleaning or a bit of bar work. But it would be a start. They told her that in the evenings they would have a wild time – drinking and partying all night. It sounded brilliant. No more school. No more interviews with care and social workers. No more abuse.*

She just wasn't sure how to break it to her sister that they weren't going to Dublin for the weekend. They were going there for good. She would probably freak when she found out. She would cross that bridge when she came to it. For now, it was enough to sit back with her Monster Munch, music and imagine a new start in a new country.

Chapter Five

E very available door and window was open in the small meeting room to the rear of the community centre. Despite it being nearly 8 p.m., the air was warm and thick. Pun-loving newspaper headline writers were having a field-day with the ongoing UK heatwave: 'Bake To The Future', 'Hazard Warming' and 'Let's go Loco – it's hotter than Acapulco!'.

Nick exchanged sweaty smiles and glances with other members of the AA meeting. Although it was fairly well-known that Nick had gone 'back out for some more research', they were glad to see him back. That's what AA was like. There was no judgement here. The only require-ment to go to an AA meeting was a desire to stop drinking. Most of the time that was Nick's aim. He just wasn't sure how or when.

Some of the regulars came and shook his hand and asked how he was with genuine concern. Nick knew that he probably stank of booze. The vodka was in the boot of his car. He admitted that he had 'slipped' but he knew he was in the right place. They nodded. 'Keep coming back' was the mantra. Keep coming back because it works.

Like a Scorsese-esque scene from *Goodfellas*, and to respect the anonymity of the fellowship, members of AA had codenames, often amusingly obtuse. Some were obvious. There was 'Scouse' Tony and 'Cockney' John. Then Chris 'Shorts' who wore shorts whatever the weather. Keith 'The Teeth' who had crooked teeth. However, there was Dave 'The Dog' who hadn't had a dog for over a decade. 'Sun Tan' Pam, who used to work in a sunbed shop in the nineties but had worked in the job centre since the millennium. 'Hairdresser' Andy was an IT consultant but always had flash white hairdresser-type cars. 'DJ' Mike had never been a DJ and no one knew why that was his name. 'Gwersylt' Dave, who had once lived in Gwersylt, but now lived near Oswestry. Nick was just 'Copper' for obvious reasons.

NICK SETTLED HIMSELF AND WAS FEELING POSITIVE TO BE surrounded by his tribe. He had agreed to meet his sponsor, Dundee Bill, and he knew that he was going to get a bollocking and some tough love. But that's what he needed.

Bill was a tough Scotsman with over thirty years' sobriety under his belt. He was the Don Corleone of the North Wales Fellowship and people referred to having the 'Bill Talk' with knowing grimaces. Yet Nick knew that was what he needed to hear. Not subtle suggestions but plain, direct orders of what to do. Nick's brain certainly wasn't fit for purpose and it was his sponsor's job to tell him what and how to think.

Sipping at the cheap coffee, Nick tried to get comfortable in the plastic chair. Crossing his legs, he still had the smell and image of Owen Ankers' face and corpse rattling around his head. It would go in a day or two. That's how it worked.

And then a figure appeared. Broken and shuffling, the old man took a seat on the opposite side of the room.

Nick couldn't believe his eyes as he took an almost cartoon-esque double take.

It was Nick's father, Rhys.

Despite being in his sixties, Rhys Evans had the look of a man ten, even twenty, years older. His skin was grey and pallid. His clothes hung off his skeletally thin frame.

Nick and his father hadn't spoken for over a year and they had no real relationship. As far as Nick knew, his father was drinking himself to death behind drawn curtains in a small cottage somewhere near Dinas Padog. And that suited Nick down to the ground. A slow, painful alcoholic suicide for a man that he hated and who on many occasions he had imagined murdering. Holding that kind of resentment was doing Nick no good. His sponsor Bill had told him to pray for his father. Nick had told him to piss off and stormed out of Bill's house.

THE PITIFUL WRECK OF A MAN THAT HAD JUST WALKED IN was a long way from the imposing, muscular sergeant of the Royal Welsh Fusiliers that Nick had known as a child. His father was a hard man and barely shed a tear when Nick's mother had died from cancer when he was eight. Maybe it was because he was the third son of a tough coal miner, Taid Evans. Not only were they men that did not show their emotions, they actively beat those that showed weakness. That included Nick and his mum on a regular basis.

After his mother's death, Nick went to live with Uncle Mike and Auntie Pat while Rhys Evans returned to active duty. His Uncle Mike, who had died the previous year, was like the father he never had. They were incredibly close as Nick grew up and he still missed Mike.

During the Bosnian War, Rhys Evans' regiment came under attack in 1995. His father was captured and tortured. Rhys got what Nick knew now to be PTSD but he didn't have any sympathy. His dad was a nasty bastard.

Nick had no idea what his father was doing there. As far as he knew, he had not stepped foot in an AA meeting in many years. And Nick resented the idea that his father had finally surrendered and wanted to get well. He didn't want him to get well. He wanted him to be in over-whelming pain.

Spotting him looking his way, Nick refused to meet his glance. *Who the hell does he think he is?* When Nick used to wet the bed, his father would slap his face and make him sleep in the damp sheets as a punishment.

And then a thought. What if his father got sober and stayed sober? It was something Nick hadn't managed – to stay stopped. What a kick in the nuts it would be if his old man managed to complete the programme before he did.

So, Nick did what he always did in these situations. Ran. He grabbed his mobile phone and clamped it to his ear. He got up, looked at his sponsor Bill and pointed to his phone to indicate he needed to take the call, and he left.

Nick knew that no one, especially Bill, was buying it. But he wasn't going to sit in an AA meeting with his father there. He would prefer to drink himself to death.

RUTH WAS LATE. IT FELT LIKE SHE WAS ALWAYS LATE. Running down endless corridors – dusty red carpets, flanked by dark wood-panelled walls and oil paintings that were centuries old. The air was musty and smelt of stale cigars.

The anxiety of being late to the meeting was overwhelming. However, she was lost and every corner she turned made her sense of disorientation worse. Dead ends, more corridors and locked doors.

And then she was tumbling back, waking and returning. Ruth turned over and the bed was refreshingly cold where she hadn't slept. She stretched out her leg and ran it over the cool material. There were the reassuring sounds of a bright, summer's morning. A radio burbled with chirpy intonation and upbeat pop songs.

The soft shutting of a cupboard door. The quiet clatter of plates being taken and put onto a work surface. The metallic spring of toast popping up and then the scraping of knife and butter.

Ruth came reluctantly out of that blissful slumber. A slumber in which Sarah still existed. A slumber where Sarah was still pottering around in the kitchen and would probably arrive with coffee and toast in the next few minutes.

But the noise was now gone. Only an uncomfortable, jarring silence.

Ruth had been dreaming and there was no one in the house. She was alone and there was that hollow hole in her stomach.

She had no control over when she woke but sometimes she wished that she wouldn't. That she would slip unnoticed from Earth, away from the pain and anguish that were often unbearably exhausting.

Her partner and love of her life, Sarah Goddard, had left their shared home in South East London on 5 November 2013 and boarded the 8.05 a.m. train from Crystal Palace to Victoria. It was her regular train into work. Sarah was an occupational health nurse at the Gordon Hospital.

But she never got off that train. She vanished off the face of the earth. No note, no phone call, no clues. Just like that. Disappeared.

The CCTV footage showed Sarah getting on the train, as she always did. But she did not get off. Not the 8.05 or anywhere else. CCTV at Victoria station was examined millisecond by millisecond. Every frame of CCTV on the line between Crystal Palace was scoured. Passengers remembered seeing her chatting to a man as commuters were squeezed together in compartments. He was tall, handsome, in his forties with glasses. Someone thought maybe a European accent. There was nothing sinister about what they had seen. No clues as to what they had talked about.

IT TOOK RUTH OVER A YEAR TO CHANGE ANYTHING IN THE flat. Another year before she could be persuaded to get rid of any of Sarah's possessions. Ruth still looked and hoped. What she could not do was grieve.

On the year anniversary of her disappearance there were news bulletins, reconstructions, posters. And again, nothing. And of course, Ruth became hyper-vigilant, seeing Sarah everywhere. Last year, she had chased someone she was convinced was Sarah through the back-streets of Conwy.

RUTH STILL FELT BROKEN AT THE THOUGHT OF SARAH, BUT also felt guilty if she didn't think about her daily. When her mind became consumed by worries of Sarah, over time she had become adept at putting the thought of her out of her head for fragments of time. And those fragments were precious.

RUTH SAT UP IN BED FOR A MOMENT AND TOOK A COUPLE of deep breaths. Flinging the duvet back, she forced herself to rise and confront the day with a brave face. She clicked on the radio, BBC 5 Live. Even though it wasn't even seven yet, she showered, ate some toast and dressed, all the while lost in the racing thoughts of her mind.

Her ears pricked up at a news story: *'North Wales Police have confirmed that a body found in the River Dwyryd in Snowdonia yesterday morning is that of local businessman Owen Ankers. His family have been informed and police are not releasing the cause of death but would like to speak to anyone who saw Mr Ankers last weekend.'*

As Ruth went to grab her coat and keys, her phone vibrated with a message. It was Steven Flaherty from the Met. However, it wasn't time for the annual review of Sarah's case. The fifth anniversary of Sarah's disappearance wasn't until November. Plus they'd only spoken the other day.

For a moment Ruth's stomach plunged like she had dropped down a sharp bend of a rollercoaster. She opened the message.

RUTH, I DON'T WANT YOU TO GET YOUR HOPES UP. I HAVE something, and it may be nothing, but I've been at a conference in Manchester. I could pop in around 9 a.m. on the way back to London. Would that be convenient? Steven.

Chapter Six

Drake and Nick walked into the mortuary where Tony Amis was in the middle of his preliminary post-mortem on Owen Ankers' body. Nick knew that Drake hated PMs. As a DCI, Drake rarely attended them but had been asked to accompany Nick by Jones as a courtesy to ACC Davenport. That's how the police worked. Having a higher rank present was a sign of respect and Drake wasn't in a position to say no.

On the way in, Drake and Nick had discussed this. Drunken misadventure seemed most likely. Their hypothesis had been that Owen had been celebrating his multi-million-pound capital investment and had ended up in the water somehow.

As an escape from the heat and bustle outside, Nick liked how the mortuary was silent, cold and still. There was the reassuring underlying hum of fans and the air conditioning plus the faint buzz of the enormous fridges at the other end of the room.

At first, it smelt sterile. Clinical disinfectants and other cleaning fluids. The lighting was cold and stark. Nick noticed the steel scales to one side for weighing internal organs. On the other side were hoses and steel drains to wash away blood and any other bodily fluids.

And then, as they approached, they were hit by the intense waft of Owen Ankers' cadaver, which was lying like a bloated porcelain doll on the gurney. A few days in the water did horrors to the human body and the smell of his rotting flesh, insides and escaping gases was thick and rancid. Drake took a breath, winced and gagged.

Amis noticed, took a small pot of Tiger Balm from the pocket of his green scrubs and offered it to Drake.

'Pretty ripe today, I'm afraid. Bodies from the water are the worst. Especially in the summer. It almost put me off my breakfast.'

Drake and Nick shared a look.

'Almost?' Drake said, raising his eyebrows sarcastically. He surreptitiously took an index finger of Tiger Balm and wiped it under his nostril.

Nick smirked.

Drake looked at him and growled, 'Oi, not a word to anyone at the station, Nick.'

DRAKE DIDN'T WANT TO BE THE BUTT OF ANY STATION humour or to have his tough Yorkshireman image tarnished but he needed the Tiger Balm to stop him gagging.

Nick smiled and shrugged as he waved away the Tiger Balm. 'Not for me, thanks. I didn't see anything, boss.' Nick would keep quiet and it would be a brownie point with Drake, which would count in his favour in the future.

'What have we got, Tony?' Drake asked, the Tiger Balm now easing his demeanour.

'Our victim died from a single wound to the thigh,

which hit the femoral artery and led him to bleed to death,' Amis explained.

Nick shot Drake a look of surprise – that's not what they were expecting. After seeing the body the previous day, Nick assumed it was a simple drowning.

'There are some defensive wounds to the hands and the forearms. A contusion to the back of his head.' Amis pointed to a cut about two inches in length on the front of the thigh. 'But this is what killed him. It was either a lucky shot or someone who knew what they were doing.'

'He was deliberately stabbed?' Drake asked to clarify what Amis was saying.

'Yes. The stab wound isn't that obvious, which is why I didn't see it yesterday. But the victim lost a lot of blood very quickly. He was dead before entering the water.'

'How long would death take?' Nick asked.

'Minutes. Victim would have been unconscious in less than a minute. Dead after two or three,' Amis explained clinically.

This wasn't a drowning. This was murder.

'Any clues as to who his attacker might have been?' Drake asked.

'The knife used had a serrated edge.'

'Hunting knife?' Nick suggested.

'Probably.' Amis pointed to the wound. 'As you can see, the wound has a linear bruise to either side of it. It was caused by the hilt guard of the weapon, which makes me think it might be military.'

'Anything else that might help us?' Drake asked, getting a little frustrated at Amis' vagueness.

'The killer also twisted the knife once it was in his thigh. That causes a lot of damage and shows a degree of knowledge.'

'What does that tell us?' Nick asked.

'Maybe military training. Or medical. If it was premeditated, you're looking for someone who is very cold and vengeful.'

Drake frowned. 'How do you mean?'

'If you really hate someone and want to watch them bleed to death, stab them in the femoral artery in the thigh. They can't walk and they bleed out in front of you. You can look them in the face as they die,' Amis explained with no hint of concern. In Nick's experience that's what all pathologists were like.

'Who wanted to see Ankers suffer and die? The man sold vegetables,' Nick asked out loud. He was struggling to match the severity of the attack to the victim.

'There was also sea water and sand in his lungs, which was a surprise,' Amis informed them.

'Sea water?' Nick was totally confused.

Amis nodded. 'This body has been in the sea in the last two days.'

FORTY MINUTES LATER, NICK ENTERED CID. THE morning sky was bright blue through the windows of Incident Room One, which was already feeling clammy and airless. He had managed a good lug of vodka in the toilets and was now feeling the first warmth and calm from the alcohol. He had dreamt of his father the night before and it had left him rattled. Even though every ounce of his will despised him, there was that nagging feeling that he was still his dad. Didn't that count for something? Nick just didn't want to entertain those thoughts.

. . .

THE ROOM WAS BUZZING WITH CHATTER AND THE ODD boom of male laughter. Despite his fuzzy head, Nick could sense there was more energy and anticipation than usual. Word had got around about Owen Ankers' PM and murder cases were rare in North Wales.

A large scene board had been set up. At its centre a large photo of Owen Ankers, sitting on a sea wall, looking away from the camera, carefree and smiling. His name and address were written in blue marker to one side, date of birth, plus the approximate time and location of his death – *North End, Harlech Beach 5.30 p.m.*

Nick looked over at the photo. Life was a bitch sometimes. Did Owen Ankers ever think he would one day be at the centre of a murder investigation? Of course not. It wasn't likely the thought ever entered his head. Why would it even be on the radar for any 'civilian' members of the population? Lives could be ruined or ended in a moment.

Nick took a breath, feeling the icy sensation of the strong mints he had just crunched on. He gave DCI Drake a nod as he manoeuvred across the floor to take a seat at the morning briefing. He could already feel a slight unsteadiness in his legs and feet. Maybe he had overdone it? A couple of strong coffees might level him out.

Drake gathered up his files, moved to the centre of the room and then casually put his left hand in his trouser pocket. His cobalt-blue shirt strained a little at the hard, muscular chest beneath. 'Good morning, everyone. I think some of you are already aware that as of this morning, we are now treating Owen Ankers' death as a murder.'

There were murmurs from the assembled detectives as the rumours were now confirmed. Drake walked over to the whiteboard and pointed to the photograph of Owen.

'Okay, I don't know if you've had a chance to see this photograph. This is our victim. Last seen late on Saturday afternoon, walking his dog with an unidentified person, possibly male, on Harlech Beach. There is no sighting of Owen after this point until his body was discovered in the River Dwyryd yesterday morning.'

Drake walked over to a map of North Wales and pointed to the coastal town of Harlech. 'It seems likely that Owen was attacked and died sometime late on Saturday afternoon or evening. The coroner can't give a very accurate time of death. The body was in the water for too long. There was sand and sea water in his lungs, which tells us that he died on the beach. The question is, how did his body end up being discovered thirty-seven miles away in this village here. Mac?'

Mac tried to tuck his shirt into his trousers as he approached the map and then gave up. That's what Nick loved about Mac. He didn't give a toss about protocol, manners or saying the right thing. He just cared about nicking the right people and getting the scumbags off the streets. Nick always teased Mac that he was Llancastell CID's version of Gene Hunt. A tough, ball-breaking throwback to policing in the seventies and eighties.

Mac sniffed and ran his hand through his cropped hair. Public speaking wasn't his thing. 'Nick and I talked to the coastguards about the tides off the coast at Harlech. If we think Owen was attacked and killed late afternoon on Saturday, then the tide would have been coming in. By seven o'clock most of the beach would have been covered in water and an undiscovered body in the dunes would eventually be dragged out to sea by the tidal currents. Given the northerly tides of the Irish Sea, the body could have travelled up the coast and then into the tributary of the River Dwyer. The body then lodged on the shallows here ...'

. . .

DRAKE MOVED BACK TO THE WHITEBOARD. 'GUYS, I WANT you to look at Owen. As far as we know he was a defence-less businessman walking his dog on the beach. He gave a lot to the community in Harlech. He raised money for local charities and funded all of the Harlech grassroots football teams. He was a mentor for young people in the Prince's Trust. I want it to be important to all of us that we get justice for him and his family. We need to be meticulous in everything we do. No mistakes. I want the person who did this.' Drake was calm but passionate. 'Okay, what have we got so far, Nick?'

NICK TRIED TO CLEAR HIS HEAD AS HE STOOD. HE PUSHED his feet into the floor to make sure that he was steady as he didn't want any tell-tale signs that his balance was off.

'Boss. Owen Ankers, aged forty-four. Born and bred in Snowdonia. Self-made millionaire through his organic food company Ankers and Webb, that he founded with an old school friend, Callum Webb. He was divorced from his wife, Assistant Chief Constable Beth Davenport, about a year ago. No children. She says that it wasn't acrimonious.'

'ACC Davenport?' Mac asked, just to clarify.

'Yes … Let's check her story out with solicitors and Owen's family to be on the safe side. What about the company? Any problems there?' Drake asked.

'Far from it. Owen had just sold a stake of his empire to the private equity firm TP Creed Global Management for forty-eight million pounds. Things couldn't have been better,' Nick explained as the vodka-induced haze started to clear.

'Business partner?' Drake asked.

'Callum Webb. They owned the company straight

down the middle. Fifty-fifty. At the moment, boss, there is nothing obvious that would make Owen Ankers a target for attack or murder,' Nick explained.

Drake paused for a moment. 'What about his house?'

Merringer looked over as he had been liaising with the scene of crime officers. 'Nothing, boss. SOCO are going through it. There's nothing out of the ordinary so far. His phone was discovered on a table on the deck. Tech are going to look through it for us. Neighbour says he saw Owen walking the dog on the beach late afternoon on Saturday with a young man. Skinny, grey hoodie or track-suit, red baseball cap.'

'And that was the last time he was seen until his body was discovered?'

'Yes, boss.' Merringer nodded.

'We need to find whoever Owen was with that after-noon. Mac, can you trawl CCTV in and around Harlech Beach?'

Mac nodded. 'Boss.'

'We need uniform to do a house-to-house. Anyone overlooking Harlech Beach or en route from Owen's house to the beach. Set up someone to be on the beach at around 5 p.m. Interview joggers, dog walkers. See what they saw if they were there,' Drake instructed. 'We need a fingertip search of the beach and the paths that lead down there.'

'His brother collected his effects when he identified the body. He seems to think that there is a gold Rolex watch missing,' Nick said. 'Although washing out to sea and then back down a river might explain that.'

'Okay. So where is the watch? It's valuable so was it taken? And we have no murder weapon at the moment,' Drake said.

'Where's the dog?' Merringer asked.

'What?' Mac asked in a disparaging tone. Mac didn't do pets and Nick knew that he had put a veto on his family ever getting something whose only supposed benefit was that it 'shits, stinks and costs a fortune'.

'Owen Ankers was walking his springer spaniel on the beach. Where is it now?' Merringer asked.

It was a fair point. Nick knew of two cases in the UK where a dog's DNA from hair and saliva had been used by the Prosecution.

Mac shrugged. 'It ran off. Who knows?'

Drake ignored Mac and nodded. 'Luke's right. Owen would have had his dog tagged and probably microchipped. Someone get onto local dog rescues and the RSPCA and see if the dog's been found.'

Merringer took notes and nodded. Nick couldn't remember a time when Merringer hadn't scribbled down every tiny detail.

Nick motioned to talk. 'Owen Ankers was stabbed with a serrated knife, possibly a hunting or military knife. The knife was also twisted so the attacker knew what they were doing. That could suggest military or medical training.'

Mac rolled his eyes. 'Or a bloody YouTube video.'

'The only time I've ever seen this sort of wound is in gang-related violence,' Drake said thinking out loud.

Nick knew of the rise in deliberate stabbings to inflict humiliation injuries on rival gang members in the north-west of England and North Wales. There was a practice among gang members known as 'drinking', where the victim would be stabbed in the rectum and could leave them needing a stoma bag for the rest of their lives. Other target areas were the groin and thigh, which lead to major problems. They were signs of a punishment stabbing. 'Bagging' was the less dangerous practice of stabbing rivals in the buttocks. Gang members played a game called 'Scores', where points were gained for each stabbing. However, Owen Ankers didn't fit that profile at all.

At that moment, Sian walked purposefully into the briefing, holding documents and headed for Drake.

'Boss, we solved the case of the vanishing drug dealer that was found unconscious in Harlech. He did regain some consciousness last night so was taken onto a ward from the ICU last night. While PC Chuckles was getting coffee, someone came in, put him in a wheelchair and took him away,' Sian said.

'CCTV?' Drake asked.

Sian put down some A4 printouts of the CCTV from the hospital and the car park. The images clearly show a figure in a dark tracksuit and red baseball cap pushing the unknown victim down a corridor and helping them into a small two-door car.

Drake came over and plucked a photo from the pile. 'Male, skinny, tracksuit and red baseball cap?'

'Same description as our suspect on the beach with Owen Ankers,' Nick said with a nod.

'Coincidence, boss?' Sian asked.

Drake muttered, still peering at the photo. 'I'm not sure this person *is* male.'

'We've got a reading of the car's plates. PNC has the car registered to a David Sabatini. Address in Rhyd in Llancastell. Suspended sentence for burglary. Several cautions for possession,' Sian revealed.

'Nick, go with Sian to Harlech with these photos and see if the eyewitness recognises this person from the hospital as the person he saw walking on the beach with Owen. Then go to Rhyd and see if you can find David Sabatini.'

'Boss.' Nick nodded and got up to go.

Chapter Seven

R uth was sitting with Steven Flaherty on the patio to the rear of her house. Adjusting her sunglasses, she pushed them back up the bridge of her nose as she took a cigarette and lit it. She took a long drag and blew out a satisfying plume of smoke. *That's better.*

She had explained to Drake and Jones why she was going to be late in and however hard-nosed they were, neither would have a problem when it came to Sarah's disappearance.

Ruth's skin was already tingling and warm from the morning sunlight. The sky loomed huge, blue, and clear over them. At the bottom of her garden, a simple fence separated the area from a handful of grazing Shetland ponies and then swathes of farmland into the distance, scorched shades of tan and brown by the summer heat-wave and no rain.

The squeaky sound of a meadow pipits that chirped nearby was undercut by a tractor trundling along the dry track of a nearby field. It was a stark contrast to the cramped terraced houses of Crystal Palace.

Steven Flaherty, balding with thin glasses, had a benign face that often looked like it was on the verge of breaking into a wry smile. White wispy chest hairs popped over his rust-coloured shirt. He put his coffee mug carefully down on the grey, wooden garden table as he scrolled thoughtfully through images on his laptop that he was showing to Ruth.

Steven stopped at a still photo from CCTV of commuters leaving a train and walking down the platform at Victoria station. A time-code at the bottom of the screen read 5 *November 2013, 08.28 a.m.* This was the train that Sarah had got on at Crystal Palace that day, twenty minutes earlier, but she had never arrived at Victoria station and not been seen ever since.

Steven shifted round so that he was in a thin slice of shade and then looked at Ruth. 'This is the footage of the train from Crystal Palace. And this is the man that we think Sarah might have been talking to on the journey.'

Steven pointed to the face of a smartly dressed man in his early forties. Fair hair, well-groomed, preppy glasses and an expensive charcoal-coloured suit and navy Crombie coat.

Ruth nodded. She had that image etched into her medial temporal lobe. It was the only clue that they seemed to have. Although the likelihood was that it was an innocent conversation on a train, Ruth couldn't shake the feeling that this man had something to do with Sarah's disappearance. However, they hadn't been able to trace the man since that day.

'The developments in biometric facial recognition have been vast since 2013. Last week, I had the technical forensic lab in Scotland Yard run this footage again and they created a 3D sensor capture of this man's face. Spacing of the eyes, bridge of the nose, contour of the lips, ears, chin, everything. Apparently, it then transforms it into digital data by applying an algorithm, before comparing the image captured to those held in a national database,' Steven explained.

'And?' Ruth wanted Steven to get to the point. The suspense of whether or not they had identified the man was killing her.

'Nothing on the UK database …' Steven said with a tone that suggested that there was more to come.

'Steven,' Ruth snapped impatiently.

'I got them to run it through Interpol and we got a match.'

'Shit! Who is he?' Ruth asked, her heart rate racing.

'Jurgen Kessler, a German investment banker who used to work for Commerzbank LDN in London.'

'Okay. Where is he now?' Ruth said feeling disappointed. He didn't sound like the kind of person to be mixed up in Sarah's disappearance.

'That's the thing. He left the firm in London in mid-November 2013 out of the blue. He said it was for "personal reasons",' Steven continued to explain.

Ruth looked wide-eyed. 'That's a week or two after Sarah disappeared.'

'In 2014, Kessler began to work for another bank in Berlin. He was then arrested for the kidnap and rape of a co-worker from the bank. It went to trial in 2015 but the case collapsed.'

'Jesus. Is he still in Berlin?' Ruth asked as she took a breath.

'Unfortunately, we don't know. In 2016, Jurgen Kessler seemed to vanish off the face of the earth. He hasn't been heard of since.'

Ruth's neurons were in overdrive. The last person that Sarah had been seen talking to had been charged with kidnap and rape. Taking a deeper breath, she held it for a moment. Ruth felt overwhelmed.

'You okay?' Steven asked, noticing that the colour had drained from her face and her hands trembled a little.

'Yeah. It just seems like a massive coincidence. And in twenty-five years as a copper, I've learnt not to believe in coincidences.'

Nick approached Drake's glass door, took a moment and knocked. Drake had asked to see him before he went with Sian to Harlech. His shirt was already a little damp under the arms from the growing heat of the day and he feared the sweat smelt of vodka.

Hoping he had been summoned to Drake's office for something positive, Nick always had a nagging doubt about everything. He would project into the future and, by his default setting, imagine the worst. That's what one of the therapists told him in a rehab in Flint. Apparently, Nick had 'a propensity to catastrophise everything'. The self-pitying voice in his head would immediately make excuses. Anyone who had lived a life like Nick's would bloody well have the right 'to catastrophise everything'. Imagine everything that could go wrong, and anything else was a bonus. It wasn't a healthy mindset.

That was why those in the fellowship suggested 'one day at a time'. There were only two days he couldn't do anything about – yesterday and tomorrow. Yet, however much Nick heard these little pearls of wisdom, something deep in his psyche stubbornly refused to adhere to them, knowing that in reality Nick knew better – even if the evidence strongly suggested otherwise.

Drake stood and waved Nick in with a serious look. Immediately Nick spotted two other detectives he didn't recognise sitting at the long meeting desk on the other side of Drake's office. He hoped they weren't from the Independent Office for Police Conduct.

'DS Evans. This is DI Choudry,' Drake said as a way of introduction.

Amir Choudry was British Indian, with dark, keen eyes that lit up as he nodded at Nick. His tie was loosened and top button undone.

'And DS Ryan.' Drake indicated a woman in her early forties, blonde, round attractive face with decent cheekbones and light-blue eyes. She didn't smile but Nick still did a double take. She was definitely fit, he thought. Immediately his gaze went down to her left hand. No ring. *Interesting.*

'They're officers from Operation Titan and with the North West Regional Organised Crime Unit operating out of Merseyside,' Drake explained.

'Nice to meet you,' Nick said and then took a seat at the table as directed by Drake. 'This to do with our OCU operation in Porthmadog and what happened in February?'

'NOT REALLY,' CHOUDRY REPLIED.

'We've been running surveillance on a company, Ankers & Webb,' Ryan explained, with a slightly sour look on her face.

Now Nick had Ryan pegged: uber professional and icy cold.

'Obviously now that Owen Anker's death is a murder case, we need to see if there is any link to Titan's ongoing investigation into Ankers & Webb,' Drake explained.

Nick was completely lost. How did someone like Owen Ankers get mixed up in a Merseyside county lines drug investigation? Why was there an ongoing investigation into an organic food company? He couldn't make the link.

Choudry took out some surveillance photos from a file and placed them on the desk. 'These are stills from surveillance footage taken in a car park at Cheshire Oaks Retail Park off the M53 last week.'

Nick looked at them. A tall man, in his late fifties, was standing casually beside a new white BMW. Another man, wearing a white baseball cap, was getting out of a black Range Rover with tinted windows.

Ryan indicated the man by the BMW in the photo. 'This is Callum Webb, Owen Ankers' business partner.'

The next photo showed the man in the baseball cap shaking Webb's hand beside the cars. His face was visible even at distance.

Curtis Blake.

'Jesus,' Nick said under his breath as his eyes widened.

'Nick, as you have a history with Curtis Blake, I thought you should see this intel. However, whatever we talk about in this room, stays in this room,' Drake said.

'We think someone either in Merseyside or North Wales Police is leaking intel to Blake. It's vital that officers have this information on a need-to-know basis,' Choudry explained.

Nick nodded, but he felt like swearing angrily. His stomach lurched at the thought that someone from inside the Force might be helping Blake. It did explain why Blake seemed to be permanently one step ahead of them.

'We've analysed the footage.' Ryan placed another document on the desk. 'They are clearly on friendly terms.'

Choudry showed a photo in which Webb and Blake were laughing mid-conversation.

Nick frowned. 'I don't understand. What's the connection?'

'Blake knows that we're watching his every move and that of his gang. He's got his county lines operations set up in North and West Wales. But we've intercepted three cars in the last two months and seized thirty-five thousand pounds of drugs and cash, along with firearms,' Ryan explained.

'So, getting the drugs from Merseyside to their destinations is proving costly. We have intelligence that suggests Blake wants to use Ankers & Webb vans to import drugs across the channel, and then deliver drugs to county lines gangs across Wales and the North West,' Choudry said.

Drake shook his head. 'And who is going to suspect an organic food delivery van of being cover for a drug gang?'

Thinking about it, Nick wasn't that surprised. Drug gangs could be pretty inventive. He had heard of gangs dissolving ketamine in Listerine bottles, moulding cocaine into the shape of individual Pringles and packaging them up in tubes. One gang in Kent even hid MDMA crystals inside live clams.

Nick remembered a case involving two gangs, one from Holland and the other from Cheshire, who posed as a flower wholesale business to smuggle drugs and large quantities of ecstasy, cocaine, MDMA and cannabis from Europe into the country. The drugs were smuggled across the Channel in huge lorries, which were also loaded with plants and flowers, before being dropped off and distributed from the gang's fake flower company in Altringham. When their premises were raided, officers found Glock pistols, submachine guns with laser sights, five hundred kilos of cannabis resin, one hundred and twenty-five litres of liquid amphetamine, fifteen kilos of coke, seven kilos of ecstasy and fifty kilos of amphetamine. In the old days, it used to be ice-cream vans that would rock up in winter in the deprived areas of North Wales selling drugs to users. It was all a lot subtler than that now, and a high-end organic fruit and veg company would be suitably obscure camouflage.

'How does Owen Ankers fit into this?' Nick asked.

Ryan looked up from her paperwork. 'Our hypothesis is that Owen Ankers didn't want to play ball. Possibly he was threatened. And then Blake dispatched someone from Liverpool to murder him in Harlech so that their operation wouldn't be jeopardised.'

Nick raised an eyebrow and said, 'Skinny man. Tracksuit and red baseball cap. Could be one of Blake's men?'

'Except the eyewitness seems to think that Owen went voluntarily for a walk with this person on Harlech Beach.' Drake glanced at Choudry and Ryan. 'It's also likely that this person helped an injured, small time dealer out of the hospital last night.'

Drake went over to the desk, got a photo from the hospital's CCTV footage, which showed the dealer in a wheelchair being pushed by the suspect in the red baseball cap. 'Best image we've got.'

'Fits the profile.' Ryan nodded and for the first time she made eye contact with Nick. He could get lost in those deep blue eyes.

'Webb was a very rich man. Why risk all that?' Drake asked, breaking Nick's train of thought.

'Two very expensive divorces. And Webb is a degenerate gambler. He flies to the Far East, Hong Kong, Macau. He's not poor. Not yet. But a lucrative, tax-free sideline in drug trafficking seems to appeal,' Ryan said.

Choudry nodded. 'From what we understand, it seems that Webb also gets a kick out of hanging out with gangsters. Helping them traffic drugs is part of the thrill for him.'

Webb sounds like a pathetic prick, Nick thought. But he was up for anything that could lead to a conviction against Blake. In terms of resentments, Blake was up there with his father. He'd imagined chasing Blake into an empty warehouse and beating and kicking him to death before anyone arrived to stop him. He could even picture Blake's pleading, bloody face and had worked out what he would say to him. Not healthy, but Nick didn't care. Blake was evil and that was that.

'At the moment, we need to keep Webb on the ground and close to Blake as we gather our evidence,' Ryan said.

'Nick, interview Webb after you've been to Rhyd. Routine questioning as you would normally. Nice and steady. Nothing that will spook him. And no one outside this room gets to know any of this.' Drake was clearly keen to make this point again.

'Nice to meet you both,' Nick said as he got up to go.

He had a sense of excitement that maybe, just maybe, they were going to get enough evidence to put Blake away this time.

NICK AND SIAN HAD DRIVEN ACROSS SNOWDONIA TO Harlech to interview Owen Ankers' neighbour Alwyn Fields. Begrudgingly, Fields had let them in, leaving them to follow and shut the front door as he walked into the living room. Alwyn, late sixties, had a shaved head, was thickset with a bulging belly and was wearing a vest and stained khaki shorts. His face was grey and drawn as he began to roll a cigarette. Nick noticed that his hand shook a little as he lit the match so he used two hands to keep it steady. *Withdrawals?* Nick wondered.

Nick and Sian exchanged a look, pulling a face at the state of the house before they looked at the dusty brown fabric sofa and decided to risk sitting down. *Hope we don't get bloody fleas.*

'Haven't much time for the police, like,' Alwyn mumbled in a thick North Wales accent as he blew a plume of blue-grey smoke up into the air. 'Of course, if they all looked like you, love …'

NICK SAW SIAN PULL A FACE AND SMIRKED AT HER. HE didn't know what the story was with Sian. She was a bit of a closed book. There had never been any mention of romantic connections.

'We'll try and make this as brief as we can, Mr Fields,' Sian said.

The thick smell of the tobacco was instantly redolent and took Nick right back to sitting watching television with his Uncle Mike, while his Auntie Pat pottered and brought them ham butties, cake and endless cups of tea. Although it was a morbid thought, he wondered if that had been the last time he was truly happy.

'We understand that you saw Mr Ankers on Saturday afternoon, Mr Fields?' Sian asked.

Nick gazed around the room and out at the hallway. His first impression had been that Fields was redecorating. Pots of paint were stacked haphazardly in the corner. A paint-flecked stepladder behind the door. The carpet had been ripped out of half the room and exposed grey, untreated floorboards. But the place smelt of damp and cigarette smoke. The walls definitely hadn't been painted in years and the ceiling had started to yellow from the tobacco that floated up continuously like an industrial chimney throughout the day. Nick's boots had left a pattern in the dust where he entered the room.

Nick was still sizing the place up. The tangerine

curtains were half drawn and sunlight came in like a thin shard. It had all the hallmarks of being the home of an alcoholic. He should know.

'Aye. Popped up to the Paki shop 'bout five. He was on the beach walking the dog, like,' Alwyn explained.

'We also understand that you saw someone with Mr Ankers on the beach?' Nick said, while rolling his eyes at Sian at Alwyn's casual racism.

'Oh aye. Skinny fella. Had a baseball cap.'

'And it was red, is that right?'

'Aye, red. Could see it even from up here. St Louis Cardinals maybe.'

'Sorry.' Nick frowned.

'St Louis Cardinals have a red baseball cap. Got into baseball in West Germany when we were in a base with the Yanks, see?'

'You were in the army then?' Nick asked, thinking momentarily of his father, who was also stationed in West Germany in the 1980s.

Alwyn rolled over his right forearm to reveal a dagger tattoo with the letters *R M* and *Commando* beside it.

'Royal Marines?' Nick asked.

'Aye. Four-five Commando, Arbroath,' Alwyn stated proudly.

There was a moment as Sian looked back down at her notes.

'And what was he wearing? The man in the baseball cap? Can you remember?' Sian asked.

'One of those hoodies,' Alwyn said, thinking aloud.

'And what colour was that?' Nick said.

'Think it were grey. Not dark like. And it had those white stripes down the arms.'

'Adidas?' Nick suggested.

'Aye. Adidas. That's right.'

'And what time did you return from the shop?' Sian asked.

''Bout twenty minutes after that.'

'So, about five twenty?'

'Suppose so. Something like that.'

'And was there anyone on the beach then?' Sian asked.

'No. Fella windsurfing. No one else,' Alwyn said and shook his head.

'You didn't see Mr Ankers or the person you saw with him?'

Alwyn was getting a little agitated. 'No. Like I say, the beach was empty.'

'Didn't you think that was strange? That Mr Ankers and this other person had vanished?' Nick said.

Alwyn shrugged. 'Nah. Once you get into the dunes down the other end, you can't see 'owt from up here like. That's where he goes every day, you know.'

'DID YOU SEE ANYONE SUSPICIOUS HANGING AROUND outside the house or in this area on Saturday afternoon?' Sian asked.

Alwyn shook his head and tapped his ash into a stained mug.

'What about in recent days? Anyone acting strangely or someone you didn't recognise?'

'YOU MEAN APART FROM ALL THE QUEER BOYFRIENDS HE brought home?' Alwyn sneered.

'You think Owen Ankers was homosexual?' Nick asked.

'He was a faggot, all right!' Alwyn virtually spat on the hard sound of his alliterative observation.

That doesn't make any sense, Nick thought. Owen Ankers

had been married to ACC Davenport. Or was that why they got divorced?

'How do you know that?' Sian asked.

'I seen them all at it. Benders. In the garden, parties till all hours. Not normal, all that carry-on, you know?'

FIELDS WAS SO UNAPOLOGETIC ABOUT HIS BLATANT RACISM and homophobia that Nick found it almost humorous.

'You do know that Mr Ankers had been married?' Sian asked.

'Right bloody sham, that marriage,' Fields said. 'That's who I thought the fella with the baseball cap was. Another one of his boyfriends. Or some rent boy. Thought they'd gone to the dunes for a bit of you know what.'

Nick shot Sian a look – they weren't expecting to uncover this side of Owen Ankers' life.

Chapter Eight

Still preoccupied by the new information she had received that morning about Sarah's disappearance and Jurgen Kessler, Ruth knocked at Jones's door and went in.

Jones was in shirtsleeves that were rolled up and there was a cold can of Coke Zero beside him. He was searching for something on his paper-strewn desk.

The heat of the day, as it approached twelve, covered the room like a thick blanket and made every movement uncomfortable. Ruth's trousers were sticking to her thighs and her feet felt like they were suffocating.

'Ruth? How did it go this morning?' Jones eventually met her eyes and beckoned for her to sit down. She could never tell whether he had any interest in Sarah's case or was just going through the motions. She assumed it was the latter because he was a self-absorbed prick.

'I'm not sure. The Met have identified the man talking to Sarah on the train the day she disappeared. Kessler, a German banker.'

. . .

Jones nodded and said, 'Good. Have they tracked him down?'

'No. He vanished from Berlin … but it's a start,' Ruth explained, realising that Jones was only half listening. There was little point in giving him the full details.

Jones looked back at his computer. 'Good. It's a lead of some sort. Keep me posted, Ruth.' His body language was a clear signal for her to go. She wished she could tell him what she really thought of him.

'That's not why I wanted to see you, sir,' Ruth said, a little tentatively. She needed to get back to CID. It was the only thing that kept her sane. And the phased reintroduction back to police work that Jones was providing was driving her mad.

'No? Okay.' Jones clicked his computer mouse and then leant back in his seat to give Ruth his full attention.

'I did some digging on Beth Davenport. She was very clear that she and Owen were still friends, that the divorce wasn't acrimonious and they were on good terms,' Ruth explained.

'Before you go any further, Ruth, you are aware that this is the assistant chief constable we're talking about?' Jones said with a frown. By investigating a senior officer off her own back, Ruth was treading on very thin ice. However, doing so was a clear nudge to Jones that she was ready to go back to CID.

'Yes, sir. But she is not above the law, is she?' She was steering a fine line.

'No … So, what she said about her divorce isn't true?' Jones asked.

'No. Far from it. I know someone at Brocklehurst Law in town. She says, off the record, that the divorce was very acrimonious. Especially when Beth went after Owen's pension pot, which was obviously worth millions. He tried to tie up everything off-shore to make sure she couldn't get anywhere near what she was due. She went to trial but lost.'

Jones took a moment. She could see this wasn't good news. She also knew that he would be assessing how to proceed while covering his own back. That was his MO.

'That puts us in a very awkward situation. Did she get any money from the divorce settlement?' Jones asked.

Ruth could see the thought of CID continuing to dig around in the private life of the ACC didn't sit comfortably with him.

'Yes. She's a very rich lady. And there may be nothing to this, but I would like to talk to her to clarify her version of the divorce,' Ruth explained.

'Before you do anything, does DCI Drake know any of this?' Jones asked.

Ruth knew it wasn't professional to begin investigating anyone, let alone the ACC, without running it past the SIO. But she wasn't officially on the case and DCI Drake could have handed that job to someone else in CID.

'Not yet, sir. I haven't seen him.'

'OKAY. WELL THAT CONFIRMS MY SUSPICION,' JONES SAID as he looked at her.

Ruth was lost now. 'Sorry, sir?'

'I suspect that we're not using you effectively in your phased return back to work. I need you back in CID,' Jones said. Without giving anything away, Ruth thought, *Thank God for that!*

'And that fits neatly with DCI Drake coming to see me today and asking for an experienced DI to step in as the SIO on the Owen Ankers' murder case. I need DCI Drake to keep more of an overview of our county lines operations.'

'That would be good, sir.' Ruth felt a flutter of excitement and relief at the thought of getting back to work as a detective. Of course, she knew that Jones might well be looking to save money by getting her back into CID, but she didn't care.

'And you're up to that now?' Jones asked. His tone was, for once, genuine.

Ruth nodded. 'Of course. I love the community and PR stuff I've been doing, but I need more and I'm ready.' Ruth was lying through her teeth. She hated everything that Jones had given her in recent months and Jones probably suspected as much.

'I'll tell DCI Drake. Good work, Ruth.' Jones's tone was a little pompous but Ruth could handle that if it meant she could get back to proper police work.

NICK AND SIAN SLOWED OPPOSITE AN EMPTY GARAGE forecourt and turned into Beech Road, a narrow street at the centre of Rhyd, a suburb of Llancastell. Originally a mining village, Rhyd grew up in the 1800s from a small settlement on the moorland and was originally written as *Rhyd Llanerchrugog*, translated as ford of the heather glade.

Even when Nick was growing up, the inhabitants of Rhyd were known as 'Jackos'. The term came from when Jacobites had settled in the area after being expelled from Llancastell in the eighteenth century during the Jacobite rebellion against the king. Nowadays, the term 'Jacko' meant little more than being different or in-bred but it was often used as a term of abuse for anyone from Rhyd.

'You think Sabatini was working as part of a county

lines gang run by Blake out of Liverpool?' Sian asked as she shifted uncomfortably in her seat.

'It would explain the drugs found on him. He could have been attacked in Harlech in a turf war?' Nick suggested.

'What about our unknown suspect in the red baseball cap?' Sian asked.

'Part of Blake's gang. Maybe he was sent to kill Owen Ankers over some dispute about using Ankers & Webb to transport drugs,' Nick said as his body relaxed from the vodka he had swigged fifteen minutes earlier. Getting the balance was so difficult. Too little and he would start to sweat and feel anxious. Too much and his speech and reactions would be impaired.

'So why did Owen Ankers go voluntarily for a walk with that person on Harlech Beach? He must have known him,' Sian said.

'That's the thing that doesn't quite fit,' Nick agreed. He wished it did. If they could implicate Curtis Blake in ordering Owen Ankers' murder, he would go down for conspiracy and serve life.

'Our suspect in the baseball cap took Sabatini from the hospital before we could question him. So where's Sabatini now?'

Despite the air conditioning, the heat in the car felt heavy, as Nick and Sian drove slowly down Beech Road, looking for number eight, the address that the PNC had recorded as David Sabatini's.

'Hopefully we'll find out down here.' Nick gestured to the road.

Beech Road was one way and narrow, only a car's width when cars were parked outside the houses. The scruffy, terraced, red-brick houses were on the left as Nick and Sian peered out at the house numbers. To the right was a long, red-brick wall that separated off the back gardens of the next road down.

Front gardens and brickwork had been colonised by weeds and straggly yellow shrubs, white paintwork was worn and the only symmetrical feature was a neat row of satellite dishes. *What a dump.* Nick looked ahead and saw the road ahead shimmering in the heat.

Three young girls, about ten, walked by wearing pastel shorts, vests and cheap sunglasses, giggling and screeching. One of them puffed on a cigarette and glared defiantly at Sian as her friends laughed at her bravado before she spat on the pavement.

'Welcome to downtown Rhyd, land of the Jackos,' Nick said sardonically as he watched the girls.

'Don't stand a chance, do they?' Sian said under her breath.

'We didn't all grow up in Chester,' Nick said teasingly in a slightly upper-crust accent.

'Piss off, Sarge. Blacon isn't Chester. Not by a long stretch,' Sian said with a defensive grin. 'Anyway, my mum was from Rhyd, thank you.'

Nick felt suitably awkward. 'Oh right. Didn't know. Sorry.'

Sian grinned. 'She's not really. But I did enjoy seeing your face, Sarge!'

Nick shook his head and said, 'Funny. Very funny, Sian.'

TWO WHEELIE BINS HAD THE NUMBER *8* PAINTED IN WHITE on them, indicating that this was Sabatini's house. Even though Nick had topped up his alcohol, his adrenaline started to pump as he wondered if they were going to find a group of young male Liverpudlian drug dealers behind the door of number eight.

A couple of months ago, CID officers had even found Brummie lads in a house in Callen Park with a stash of crack and weed. A house they raided in High Town had three Russian-made Baikal handguns, two silencers and seventy-five 9mm rounds. They never quite knew what they would find. And they couldn't afford to get armed response officers out every time they went into a suspicious premises.

Nick pulled the car over to the kerb. 'Here we go.' He could see that Sian was feeling tense. 'You okay?'

'Yes, Sarge. You take me to all the best places,' she replied, trying to hide her nerves.

As they got out of the car, the heat waves rose and smothered them. Nick drew breath, walked to the white tatty door and knocked. There was a plastic bag full of beer cans nearby and pizza boxes in a pile. A fly buzzed past his ear and he flicked it away.

After thirty seconds, Nick banged on the door again but there was still no reply. He listened. Nothing from inside – no voices, no movement.

Sian walked over to a ground-floor window but the curtains were pulled.

'Anything?' Nick asked.

'No, Sarge. Not a peep.'

NICK LEANT DOWN AND OPENED THE LETTER BOX TO SEE IF he could see or hear anything inside. The pungent smell of weed hit him as soon as he looked through the narrow gap.

Suddenly, the clattering noise of a gate. It came from the back of the house. Nick took a few quick steps to the left and glanced down the scruffy side passage and driveway.

Thirty yards down, a figure in a red T-shirt, black Adidas trousers and red baseball cap was already climbing onto a wheelie bin. They then jumped and pulled themselves up onto the flat roof of a single-storey garage in one move. Nick was annoyed but impressed. How was he going to do that?

'Stop! Police!' Nick bellowed as he broke into a run. 'Call it in, Sian!' he shouted.

Nick sprinted down the rickety, overgrown driveway. The figure stopped on the roof and then looked back at him.

It was a *girl*. He wasn't expecting that!

She was about seventeen or maybe eighteen years old. She was pretty and blonde hair hung down the side of her face.

'Stop, police!' Nick yelled but the girl turned, headed to the other side of the garage roof and disappeared down out of sight.

'Shit!' Nick growled. He had no choice but to follow. He wished he was sober as his heart was already starting to thud. Leaping onto the bin, he jumped and pulled himself up. At first, he thought he was never going to get there. It had been a long time since he pulled up his own body-weight with just his arms. He began to shake with the sheer effort. He clambered onto the garage roof, grazing the skin from his forearm on the mastic asphalt roof. It stung but he had no time to think about it.

Nick went to the other side of the roof. Below was an open area of concrete, with half a dozen parked cars, that backed on to two warehouses. A large white lorry was reversing up to some steel shutters, its reversing siren bleeping. It looked like a builders' yard.

The girl sprinted out of the yard through an opening in a brick wall and disappeared down Market Street.

Nick hesitated. It was high enough for him to break his ankle.

Sod it! he thought.

He jumped, hit the concrete with flat feet and felt a white-hot pain shoot up the outside of his right ankle.

Nick breathlessly clicked his radio. 'This is alpha-three-seven to control.'

'Go ahead, alpha-three-seven.'

'In pursuit of female suspect. Red T-shirt, red baseball cap. Suspect is heading west on Market Street, Rhyd, over.'

'Control received …'

Beginning to run flat out, Nick gritted his teeth and turned to follow the girl. As he got onto Market Street, there was a new, small, brick building directly in front of him – *Gorsaf Heddla.* It was Rhyd Police Station. The irony wasn't lost on him as he turned and saw the girl nearly a hundred yards away. *No time to pop in to ask for help now!*

Nick broke into a full sprint, pumping his fists as he went. He'd managed to run off the pain. To his left, the lurid green of Rhyd Kebabs, Pizzas & Burgers. On the right, the bright blue of Corbett's bookmakers. That said it all. A mother, holding the hands of two toddlers eating orange lollies in the sun, gave him a curious look as he thundered past.

The girl went left into Prince's Road and out of sight.

'Alpha-three-seven to control. Suspect now on Prince's Road. Heading north … I think,' Nick gasped into his radio.

The radio crackled, 'Be advised, alpha-three-seven. Uniform response vehicle is en route. ETA five minutes,' the female CAD operator told him.

By the time Nick got into Prince's Road, his feet were

numb and the sweat was running down his back and dropping from his forehead. He wiped his forehead on his shirt
sleeve as he glanced down the street.

The girl had gone.

Beginning to jog up Prince's Road, Nick was feeling
dizzy and shook his head to try and stabilise himself. The
sweaty material of his trousers now clung to his thighs.

Between houses were discarded garages, alleyways, flat
pieces of concrete peppered with weeds. It was quiet
except for the distant noise of children playing. There were
various side streets all the way up Prince's Road. It was
basically a maze from here on and the girl could have gone
anywhere.

A noise from the side of an old boarded-up house.
Slowing down cautiously, Nick jogged across the weeds to
take a look.

Then a clatter. Metallic maybe.

Nick moved slowly and put his back against the wall.
The brickwork felt rough against his back through his wet
shirt.

Another click. What the bloody hell was the girl doing?
Did she have a weapon?

Nick took a slow, quiet breath as his pulse thudded in
his eardrums. He didn't want to peer down the side of the
house only to get a blade shoved into his throat. The noise
stopped.

Nick moved his shoulder round, face touching the
brickwork and inched across to see.

Suddenly, out of nowhere, a cat sprang off an old,
stained mattress, yowled and bounded past him towards
the fence.

'Shit!' Nick blurted, jumping out of his skin. 'You
little—'

Knowing that the girl could be anywhere and probably

long gone, Nick cut his losses and walked back over to Prince's Road.

Nick clicked the hot plastic and metal of his radio. 'Control from alpha-three-seven. Suspect lost. Repeat, no visual on suspect.'

As he walked back, Nick redirected the uniform unit over to Beach Street and radioed for Sian to meet him back at Sabatini's house. His shirt was now sodden with sweat and it was more than hot – it was like the air had been heated by red, fiery coals. His pulse still thundered in his chest but it was slowing.

It had been a surprise to see that the assailant was a girl. Not necessarily because of her gender. Nick had seen plenty of teenage girls in gangs who were capable of violence, damage and threatening behaviour. Often groomed and victims of sexual violence, they were then used to carry drugs and weapons as they were far less likely to get searched, especially if they used their baby's buggy as a mode of transport.

The surprise had come from the expression on her face – the way she looked. Nick didn't even know quite how to define it. Girls that were in local gangs had a certain look. The way they wore their make-up and hair – sometimes it was just an expression. The girl he saw on the garage roof had nothing like that and that made her a curiosity.

Nick arrived at number eight Beech Road and saw that the uniform patrol had arrived, the front door was open and Sian was outside drinking from a bottle of water. That's what he really needed. A drink. Steady his nerves, his head. There was vodka in a Sprite bottle in the car boot and he would get it in a few minutes.

'Took your time, Sarge,' Sian teased as she drank more water.

'Funny. Why is the door open?' Nick asked.

'He left the patio doors open when he did a runner.' Sian pointed to the rear of the house.

'She,' Nick said, correcting her.

Sian frowned. 'She? Really?'

'Really.' Nick gestured inside the house, 'You had a look around?'

'Yeah, but don't we need a search warrant to be on the safe side?'

'We've entered the premises because we are concerned for the safety and welfare of the occupant David Sabatini. We have now established that it is also the possible address for a suspect in a murder case. We'll be fine,' Nick said. 'Why, is there something of interest?'

'You could say that.' Sian led the way through the house that was littered with junk mail, post and general rubbish. The place stank of weed and rotting food, the stench exacerbated by the heat.

Sian got to an old, battered washing machine. The door was open. Nick crouched down, took out a pen and prodded inside to get a better look. He flicked over a towel to reveal a grey Adidas hoodie damp from the wash.

'Bingo!' Nick said. He hoped it was the grey hoodie that had been seen at Harlech Beach on the day of Owen Ankers' murder.

'It's been washed, Sarge,' Sian said as she frowned.

'Doesn't matter. It's over an hour from Harlech to Rhyd. So, the blood will have dried into the fabric and so unless she soaked this in bleach first, there will still be traces of blood haemoglobin. And where there is haemoglobin, there's DNA,' Nick explained. It was an important find.

'All right, thanks for the lecture CSI Llancastell,' Sian quipped.

'Education, Sian. All part of the service,' Nick said with a grin. But he could start to feel his nerves jangle and his mind was now focussed on the vodka in the car.

'Smart arse,' Sian muttered under her breath and shook her head.

'I've got some gloves and evidence bags in the car. Back in a sec.' Nick got up to go, calm at the thought of booze getting in his bloodstream within minutes.

As he made it to the front door, Nick noticed several envelopes had become stuck under the mat. Flicking through them, he saw that a couple were addressed to a Miss Abi Mullen. Was that the girl he just chased?

He opened an official-looking letter. It was from Llancastell Sixth Form College regarding Abi Mullen's HND in hair and beauty. Putting the pieces together, it now made sense. The girl he had chased had only been seventeen or eighteen.

Why was a teenage girl like Abi Mullen mixed up in a case like this, and why had she run?

Chapter Nine

The early evening had a subtle, warm breeze and there was the smell of a barbeque from somewhere. Ruth took two gin and tonics from the bar, went out of the door, down some steep stone steps and onto the concrete terrace of the pub, which had magnificent views down the River Dee. She sat down at the corner table where Sian was sitting, sunglasses propped up on her hair, tapping at her phone. Further down the river, a man in waders was casting a line, trying to get brown trout or even salmon. The moving water glistened in the fading light of the day as it floated past and burbled on the rocks under a nearby bridge.

As a setting it was perfect, but Ruth was feeling like an anxious teenager. She told herself not to be ridiculous. They were having a quick drink after work. Sian was younger than her, attractive, probably straight. *Get a grip, Ruth. You're nearly fifty!*

Sian smiled at her as they clinked glasses and drank.

'*Iechyd Da!*' Ruth said with some hint of irony.

'*Saude!* I'm a quarter Portuguese,' Sian said.

'Very exotic … Hear it all went off in Rhyd today?' Ruth said.

'Nick did all the chasing. We found a grey Adidas hoodie that matches the description of our suspect in the red baseball cap, who turns out to be a teenage girl. Puts pay to the theory that it was one of Blake's gang,' Sian said.

'You don't think teenage girls are capable of stabbing someone?' Ruth asked dryly.

Sian shrugged. 'I've never heard of it but I guess anything's possible.'

And that is the difference between South London and North Wales right there, Ruth thought.

'Five years ago, I arrested a twelve-year-old girl in Camberwell who had stabbed someone at her school after an argument over Snapchat.'

'Bloody hell.' Sian shook her head and sipped her drink.

'Sian, I don't even know how long you've been in?'

'Five, nearly six years. Took me a while to work out what I wanted to do.'

'What about before this?' Ruth asked.

'Recruitment mainly.' Sian pulled a face to show that she found this embarrassing.

Ruth nodded. 'Big change. Well paid though, isn't it?'

'Yeah, it is. But I wasn't happy being little more than a glorified pimp for my clients. I was okay at it, but you spend all your working life being fake, selling, schmoozing.'

'So, this is it? North Wales Police, a dream come true?' Ruth was teasing her.

'Yeah, why not?'

'Must be the glamour.' Ruth looked at Sian and they smiled at each other for a moment longer than seemed natural.

'We do some good work. Sometimes we get people off the street that really damage other people's lives. You must think that?'

'I do, but it doesn't happen enough. Maybe I'm just old and disillusioned.'

Sian looked at her with a bemused smile. 'First, you're not old. Second, you've wanted to do this all your life, haven't you?'

Ruth glowed inside from the comment about her not being old, even if Sian was just being polite.

'Have I?' Ruth sipped her drink. 'It comes and goes. Days when you feel like you've done something really important. And days when you just want to quit there and then.'

'Never boring though?' Sian pointed out.

'Nope, never boring. Something different every day.'

Sian looked at Ruth's left hand resting on the wooden table. A six-inch scar ran from the palm round to the back. 'How did you get that?' Before Ruth had time to answer, Sian had taken her hand in hers and turned it over to look at her palm. 'Looks nasty.'

Ruth was taken aback for a moment by Sian's intimacy, and even thought she would jerk her hand away. She was turned on and uncomfortable at the same time. No one had held her hand for years. It felt comforting.

'Streatham High Street. There had been a stabbing. I went over with a DC and a kid of fourteen came at both of us with a machete. I put my hand up to protect my face and got that.'

'What did he get?'

'Five years in a young offenders' unit.'

Sian held her hand for a second longer and let it go softly. 'One of the reasons you came up here, I guess?'

'One of them.' Ruth nodded and smiled. There was

something between them, wasn't there? Or was she just imagining it? It had been a long time since she had been in the situation of having to read the signals.

'Mind if I smoke?' Ruth asked.

'Only if you give me one,' Sian said.

'You smoke? I didn't think anyone smoked anymore?' Ruth remarked.

'I've given up every month or two. But life's too short to worry.'

'It's even shorter with these bloody things,' Ruth joked, gesturing to the cigarette.

Ruth leant across the table and clicked her lighter as Sian moved to light her cigarette. The wind picked up and blew out the flame.

'Bit windy,' Sian said with a laugh and then cupped her hands around the lighter. Her hands pushed against Ruth's wrist, skin on skin. Ruth felt her pulse quicken.

Sian gave her a knowing smile as she left her hands there for just a second too long. Ruth met her gaze as she leant back and took a long deep drag of her cigarette. They were definitely flirting and she loved it.

HAVING HAD A VERY BRIEF MEETING WITH DRAKE, RUTH told him she would like to interview ACC Davenport. Drake told her to go carefully, but agreed, reluctantly. So, it was nearly ten o'clock the following morning when Ruth came over the brow of the hill on the A497 from Porthmadog and saw before her the enormous marina at Hafan Pwllheli. The town dated back to the thirteenth century and under Edward I, fishing and boatbuilding were recorded as the town's main trades.

The new marina swept in an impressive long arc away from the mainland. It housed over two hundred yachts and boats at this time of year, although there were berths for nearly four hundred.

With the Snowdonia mountains as a backdrop, Ruth had to admit that this part of the Llyn Peninsula was near perfect. She pulled into the marina and headed for the boat yard at the south end where Davenport's boat was being serviced and cleaned.

Ruth parked up, took out a cigarette and lit it, giving herself a moment before trying to find Beth Davenport. Ruth wondered if the Beth Davenport she had spoken to at Ankers' house in Harlech was in fact real or pretence? Ruth normally had a good bullshit detector and Davenport seemed genuinely upset about his disappearance and death. She seemed soft and kind underneath her professional veneer.

However, Davenport had lied about the divorce, which Ruth now knew had been a bloody, bitter affair. Although she still received some money from Owen in the settlement, according to the solicitors, it was nowhere near what she had expected and she was furious about that. She had still managed to clear over two million pounds but that was peanuts compared to Owen Ankers' net worth.

Ruth stubbed out the cigarette and let the cool sea air wash over her face. The previous night she had had a dream that featured both Sian and Sarah. It had left her confused and anxious. George Michael's 'Waiting For That Day' was playing on the radio. It was one of her favourites and Sarah used to tease her about how 'sad' it was to be into George Michael. Since then the lyrics had taken on a poignancy of their own as they talked about never seeing your face again.

A few times a day, the image of Jurgen Kessler flashed through Ruth's mind. The blue eyes behind the designer glasses, the blond hair and the expressionless face haunted her. Ruth took a breath and refused to let the tears come but a few drops escaped. She turned off the radio, wiped her make-up in the sun-visor mirror and got out of the car.

Ruth fully expected to find the yacht club full of snooty sailing types. No doubt they would have a strict dress code and there wouldn't be an ethnic face anywhere in sight. As she wandered along the quayside, her suspicions were confirmed.

When Ruth eventually found Davenport, who was dressed in expensive-looking Bretton sailing clothes and black wellies, she was fully composed and back in professional copper mode. Davenport was spraying the sleek white hull of her Jeanneau Leader 33 Motor Cruiser with a high-powered hose. The boat had a huge glass cockpit that sparkled like cut gems; it slept six and retailed for just under a quarter of a million pounds.

'Ma'am?' Ruth said loudly over the noise of the hose. As she approached, the wind picked up some of the spray from the power hose and flung it her way. In this heat, it was refreshing and Ruth could have quite easily stood in its cold jets and cooled off.

'Sorry, I'll just turn this off!' Davenport yelled and turned off the hose while a handsome, Mediterranean-looking man scrubbed the hull with a huge brush. Ruth wondered if he was Davenport's new 'man'. *So, what first attracted you to millionaire and older divorcee, Beth Davenport?* Ruth thought acerbically.

'Nice boat,' Ruth said, thinking it was actually the showy toy of someone with too much money. She didn't get boats. The only boat she was ever attached to was the one her and her grandad sailed on the pond on Clapham Common when she was little.

Davenport's hair was pinned back and she looked prettier than Ruth remembered, but not her type. Too pointy.

She also looked tired, but Ruth didn't yet know if that was just grief or something darker.

'Thanks for meeting me here. I might take this over to France next week once she's had a few repairs. I just need to … get away. You know?' Davenport explained, her voice getting increasingly uncertain and quiet.

Ruth nodded with an understanding expression but registered that Davenport was leaving the country. She wasn't a meaningful suspect by any means, but Ruth didn't want her disappearing into mainland Europe any time soon. She would mention it to Drake.

'Any word on when there can be a funeral?' Davenport asked, sounding more like a concerned relative than a high-ranking police officer.

'As you know, I think it will be some time yet. It's down to the coroner. The family liaison officer might give you a better idea, if you talk to her,' Ruth said, realising that she was needlessly giving Davenport her well-rehearsed answers to bereaved families. 'But you know all that, ma'am.'

'Yes. Any developments that I should be aware of?' Davenport asked, becoming more professional.

'Not at the moment. Just a couple of things I want to clarify, if you don't mind?' Ruth said in her usual gentle tone. Everything about Davenport seemed to suggest that she was upset and struggling with Owen's death. She was also a high-ranking police officer that Ruth admired, so she needed to tread cautiously.

'Of course.' Davenport nodded with a serious expression. 'How can I help?'

'When was the last time you saw Owen?'

'LAST MONTH, I THINK. MIGHT HAVE BEEN MAY.'

.   .   .

'DID YOU NOTICE ANYTHING STRANGE IN HIS BEHAVIOUR? Anything different?'

'No. He was his usual chirpy self,' Davenport said with a shrug.

'You told me that you were on good terms, even after the divorce. Is that right?' Ruth's tone was innocent, allowing Davenport to confirm again what Ruth knew to be a lie.

'Yes. Fine. By the end of our marriage we were like friends. We'd … grown apart,' Davenport explained as she took the sunglasses from on top of her hair and put them on. She shook her head sadly. 'Doesn't feel real, you know? That I won't see him again. What a … waste.'

Ruth waited, giving her next comment the significance that comes with a pregnant pause. 'You see, ma'am, this is where I'm getting confused. We have information that your divorce from Owen was, in fact, acrimonious and that you went to trial.'

Davenport took a moment to compose herself. Ruth wasn't sure if she was getting angry but instead, she just shrugged. 'No. Not at all. I was just doing what my solicitors advised me to do. What do I know about divorce law?' Davenport then frowned slightly as she dried her hands on her sides slightly nervously.

'You've told me on two occasions now that you and Owen were on good terms. "Like friends", I think you said. And yet you went to trial over your divorce settlement?' As the question settled, Ruth worried that she had pushed too far, even though technically she was well within her rights to ask.

Davenport's face and body language changed. She wasn't used to being challenged, especially by a lower-

ranking police officer. 'I know how it might look, DI
Hunter. Owen treated it like a game. His solicitors against
mine. To him, it was just business, not personal.'

Ruth had picked up on Davenport's anger and decided
to leave it at that. 'Thank you, ma'am.'

Davenport shook her head. 'I'm a very rich woman. I
never need to work again. Owen was a really nice human
being. Kind, generous, funny. We don't meet many of
those in our line of work, do we?'

'No, ma'am. That's true. And you remained friends?'
Ruth asked.

'I think "friends" might be stretching it. But there was
no malice. I was invited to his brother's birthday celebrations in Abersoch with the rest of Owen's family. That's
when we all started to worry because he didn't show up.'
Davenport's tone was convincingly confident.

Ruth realised that Davenport wasn't going to change
her version of the divorce or her fairly amicable relationship with Owen. And to be honest, her account of what
had happened and her relationship with Owen seemed to
be genuine.

'Sorry to ask, ma'am, but just so I can eliminate you
from the investigation, can you tell me where you were on
Saturday afternoon. Around five?' Ruth asked.

'Sitting in the garden at home,' the ACC replied,
clearly starting to lose patience.

'Can anyone verify that?'

Davenport snorted. 'Am I now a suspect? Is that what's
going on here, DI Hunter?'

'No, ma'am. I just need to tell my DCI that we've had
the conversation and you've given me all the information I
need,' Ruth said, now squirming at the direction the interview was going in.

'No. I was on my own. I went out later with friends,'

Davenport explained, her temper shortening and emotions beginning to fray a little.

'And what time was that?'

'Around seven. Maybe later.'

'And your friends will verify that?' Ruth asked.

'Yes … Of course.'

Ruth nodded as she wrote the details down in her notebook.

'And you can't think of anyone that might wish to harm Owen?' Ruth asked.

Davenport was starting to fidget and answering questions she had already been asked wasn't helping. 'No. No one. Owen was a gentle man.' Davenport was clearly getting emotional. 'He didn't deserve to … Why would anyone do that?'

Ruth gave Davenport a sympathetic smile. 'We're going to find that out. I promise you. That's all I need at the moment, ma'am. Sorry for the intrusion.'

Davenport gave Ruth a meaningful look. 'DI Hunter?'

'Yes, ma'am.'

'Can you keep me in the loop of developments? I know it's not terribly professional, but Owen meant a lot to me,' Davenport said.

Ruth nodded. 'Yes, of course.'

The blazing sun had at last begun to lower and the heat lessen by the time Nick left the A55. North Wales' picturesque main coastal road, which had originally been built by the Romans, went directly west and started in Chester. The sweeping expanse of the Irish Sea, a mixture of bottle-green and dark inky blue, bordered the road for much of the journey.

Nick was on the way to visit his Auntie Pat and his cousin Cerys. It had been a couple of weeks, so he had picked up a new baby grow for his cousin Alex, who was now six months old. It had the Welsh red dragon flag on it and the slogan *Not only perfect, but Welsh too!* Nick smiled to himself as he looked over at it on the passenger seat. Alex felt like a little ray of light and innocence for what was left of the family. They had been through so much. Too much.

After Uncle Mike had died, Pat and Cerys had decided to move over to Llanberis to be closer to Pat's mother, Anne, who was well into her nineties. They also desperately needed a new start after the trauma and pain of what had happened. Anyone would.

Llanberis was a small town on the southern bank of the lake Llyn Padarn, at the foot of Snowdon and somewhere where hopefully no one knew their business or history. The town was busy all year around with tourists as it was a centre for walking, mountaineering, climbing and mountain biking.

As Nick arrived, the huge expanse of Llyn Padarn, a glacially formed lake that was over two miles long, shimmered to his left in the late-afternoon sun. It looked invitingly cool, Nick thought, as he remembered swimming in it as a child.

He parked beside the Llanberis Art & Craft and Coffee Pot Centre where Pat and Cerys now both worked. 'Nina Cried Power' by Hozier was playing from Nick's phone via Bluetooth.

Nick pushed his tortoiseshell Ray-Bans back up the

bridge of his nose and then leant over, opened the glove box and pulled out a litre-bottle of Coke. Having become bored of vodka, Nick had bought a litre of Aldi Napoleon Brandy, abv 37%. He poured out most of the coke onto Llancastell Police Station's car park that morning, and then expertly decanted in the brandy. He took a swig. And then another longer glug. The fumes of ethanol went up his nose, his eyes watered a little and he shuddered. And then that lovely sweep of calm and contentment that all alcoholics get almost immediately. Back in the game. Absurd as it seemed to anyone without the condition, he now felt 'normal'.

Nick returned the bottle, grabbed the baby grow, sniffed to clear his head and climbed out of the car. Stepping out of the cool air conditioning still felt like walking into a sheet of warm air, even in the early evening. The whole area was enclosed by the purples and greens of peaks and mountains, and only their very tops had any hint of cloud cover. It was stunning. There was the babble of foreign accents as seasoned walkers from around Europe congregated to start their ascent of Snowdon.

As Nick wandered towards the centre, wasps buzzed around the bin and birds chattered high in the trees as they prepared for dusk. He got a waft of homemade cooking and coffee from the café. However, the brandy and Coke had ruined his desire for either.

Opening the heavy wooden door to the Coffee Pot Café – *Crefftau*, Nick wandered in. It was functional. Four wooden chairs at each symmetrically square wooden table. There were some attempts at hip modernity. The menu was in chalk on a blackboard behind the serving counter and till. Wooden spoons with numbers on at the middle of each table. A French coffee advert framed on the wall.

In the corner, Nick spotted his cousin Cerys sitting at a

table feeding Alex. She had lost weight since the birth and was wearing the blue café uniform. After Nick's mum had died when he was eight, he had grown up with Cerys and she was effectively his sister.

Looking up as he approached, she gave him a sarcastic smile. 'Christ! Don't tell me. It's … Uncle Neil, Nigel. Something like that.' Whatever had happened, Cerys never lost her sense of humour.

Nick rolled his eyes. 'You're a funny twat. It's only been two weeks.'

'Nearly three. Look Alex, it's your Uncle Rick with a silence P,' Cerys said pointing at Nick. 'I would kiss you, but I don't want to catch anything.'

'No chance of that,' Nick said and handed over the baby grow. 'I bought this for him.'

'Ta.' She held Alex high and sniffed his nappy. 'Might need a change, mind.'

'In a café. Nice.'

'Hold him for a sec, will you?' Cerys said, passing Alex over to Nick.

Nick tentatively took his little cousin and looked at him. 'Here you go, mate.' Alex gurgled noisily and blew bubbles in his saliva. He wondered if he would ever have his own children. At the moment, he was struggling to look after himself.

Cerys gave him a look and raised a pierced eyebrow. 'You had a drink?'

'No,' Nick replied, pulling a face as if that was a ridiculous question.

'No? You sure?' Cerys looked at his eyes which were always a giveaway.

'Can you lower your voice? No. No, I haven't had a drink.' Nick hated himself for lying to her. Unfortunately, all alcoholics were professional liars. It was the only way they could protect their drinking.

'Hold him properly, Nick! He's not made from Semtex!' Cerys said a little too loudly. He knew she suspected he was drinking again and was now clearly annoyed.

'All right. Calm down, will you?' Nick mumbled as his guilt grew.

Cerys looked at her watch. 'Break's over. Hold him while I get Mum. She should be finished now. You're staying for tea, aren't you?'

'Yes, course.'

Cerys went to say something to him, thought better of it, got up and walked away. Nick knew she was angry at him. He didn't blame her. She had seen the devastation that alcohol could bring.

Within a minute or two, Auntie Pat came over and Nick handed Alex to her. Pat gave Nick a kiss on his forehead as though he was still ten years old. He hoped she couldn't smell the alcohol that was probably seeping out of his pores as he sweated in the heat of the evening.

'Sight for sore eyes,' she said, slightly out of breath as she sat down.

'Bloody hell. You two would think that you hadn't seen me in a year!'

'WE LIKE SEEING YOU. AND SO DOES ALEX,' PAT SAID, bouncing Alex on her knee.

'All right working here, is it?' Nick asked gesturing to the centre.

'Yeah. Pays the bills. Staff are nice, you know.' Pat took a swig of water from a bottle she was holding. There was a moment before Pat looked over at him with a slightly awkward expression. 'Rhys … your dad's been in contact.'

NICK FROWNED AND THEN GREW ANGRY. 'WHAT THE bloody hell for?' His father and Auntie Pat had hardly spoken since his mother's funeral, except to exchange information about Nick when he was growing up. Pat knew just what kind of man his father was and what kind of toxic marriage her sister had become trapped in.

'I don't know. Something about old photos of the family.'

'Was he drunk?' Nick snapped. Part of him was hoping that he had relapsed.

'No. He sounded clear and calm. He was asking me about my parents and my grandparents. Where they lived and worked.'

'What for?' Nick was feeling very uncomfortable.

'He said he's looking into the family tree online.'

Nick shook his head. Now he had heard it all.

As he drove home, Nick tried to second guess what his father was doing. He was getting sober. He was doing some family research. Maybe he had been taking stock of his life and regretting the man he had been? Nick thought that was too much to hope for. All that redemptive nonsense was for Hollywood films. They were in North Wales for God's sake.

As the car turned, its full-beam headlights swept across the curved, steel speed barriers and revealed a country road stretching out into the blackness. Ruth squinted. Everything looked out of focus. The rising fog edged ominously from the dense conifer forest that lined both sides of the road. Slowing to about five miles per hour, she steered carefully down a steep dip and almost immediately the beams of the headlights softened and seemed to be swallowed in the thick white haze. For a moment, she stopped and wondered if she should head back. Visibility was down to about six feet and her anxiety was growing. A moment of slight claustrophobia. This was ridiculous. She reached the bottom of the dip and the road began to climb.

Ruth buzzed down her window as the windscreen was fogging over from the inside. A blast of clean, fresh air. There was the distinct smell of pine, spruce and fir. It was damp and thick. Sharp and sweet. Then refreshing, which was the limonene with its citrus odour.

The white light of her beams carved a cone out of the gloom. Then up ahead, the flashing orange of lights spilled through the darkness of the trees. The fog began to thin. Ruth slowed even more, squinted and peered ahead, waiting for her headlights to reveal where the orange lights were coming from.

As she rounded the bend, she saw a new white Mercedes-Benz s-class coupe, which had pulled over on a gravel clearing on the road. A figure in a smart overcoat, fashionable ski hat and glasses stood at the side of the road holding a red petrol can. It looked like a woman. She waved enthusiastically.

For a moment, Ruth thought about driving past. Picking up a stranger on a foggy country road. It was the stuff of horror films. Then she had a word with herself. She was an experienced police officer. A woman needed her help. She had just run out of petrol. What was she going to do? Leave her stranded there? Not really in the spirit of female solidarity.

Ruth half-smiled to herself as she pushed the brakes and slowed. She'd watched too many spooky, late-night films. The person came over and opened the door.

'Thanks.'

. . .

RUTH DETECTED AN ACCENT. 'NO PROBLEM. CAN'T LEAVE YOU out here on your own.'

The figure turned. Ruth instantly recognised the face. The steel blue eyes, the designer glasses. The cold, detached look.

It was Kessler. Jurgen Kessler.

'So where is the nearest garage, Ruth?' he asked.

Ruth woke on her sofa with a start. Her pulse was racing and stomach knotted. She sucked in air as if she was almost drowning. And then she burst into tears.

After a moment, she reached for her handbag and plucked out some prescription co-codamol. Thirty milligrams of codeine and a stiff gin and tonic was enough to take the edge off her nerves. She worried how much she now depended on the pills and it was rare for her to go a week without taking them.

The phone rang and it was her daughter Ella. It was a lovely distraction to hear her voice.

'You okay, Mum?' Ella asked.

'Fine. I just dozed off on the sofa,' Ruth explained.

'Sign of getting old, that's what that is,' Ella teased.

'Cheeky bugger,' Ruth said with a laugh.

'You're okay though?' Ella asked.

Often it felt as though the parenting roles were reversed. Ella had seen the devastation that Sarah's disappearance had inflicted on her mother. In fact, she had seen too much for a teenage girl. And Ella had her own issues to deal with. Absent father that she never heard from, confusion about her own sexuality and the chaotic life of someone in their early twenties in 2018.

'I'm fine, darling. Fine,' Ruth reassured her.

They spent the next half an hour chatting and laughing. Then Ruth had a hot bath, a large gin, another pill and drifted into a dreamless sleep.

Chapter Ten

R uth looked up from the PM report as Drake came in. Taking off his jacket, he sipped his water bottle as he headed for the white board, which now not only featured a photo of Owen Ankers, but also the CCTV stills from the hospital. Next to it a close-up PM photo of the red wound on his thigh and various other bits of information, maps etc …

An hour earlier, Drake and Ruth had met in his office to discuss her role as SIO and to get her up to speed with the case. Although he was clear and even friendly, he made sure that Ruth knew that he would oversee the case. But then again, that's what male dogs do, Ruth thought to herself. Piss on the ground to mark their territory. And to be honest, Drake seemed all right.

As they chatted, they realised that they had both attended the Accelerated Detective Constable Training Course at Hendon at the same time in 1997. However, neither of them could remember the other. That was a particular relief to Drake who admitted that, on a drunken night out, he had slept with one of the female trainees. He hardly remembered a thing, her name or what she looked like.

As Ruth walked down the sixth-floor corridor towards CID, she began to feel anxious. It had been nearly three months since she had worked there and she wondered how her return might be received by some officers.

Turning into the office, Ruth saw Merringer coming the other way.

'Hiya, Luke,' Ruth said as he approached.

'You look really well, boss,' Merringer said with an immediate smile. He was a big softy.

'Thanks, Luke. It's good to see you,' Ruth said.

'I'm glad you're back. You've been missed around here,' Luke said.

It gave Ruth a real lift to hear that.

'How do you know I'm coming back to CID?' Ruth asked.

'Boss, I know I'm not the best detective in the world, but you're walking in here before briefing, with a load of case files and heading for the DI's office,' Luke explained with a friendly grin.

Within ten minutes, Ruth had been welcomed back to Llancastell CID with open arms. Whatever had happened in Dinas Padog was long forgotten.

Closing the glass door to her office, Ruth flopped into her soft office chair with a smile and sigh of relief. She was raring to get stuck into the investigation. Logging onto her CID computer for the first time in months, she typed up her notes on her interview with Davenport.

She was back. And it was good to be back.

At 9 a.m., CID assembled for their briefing. Drake went to the scene board purposefully. 'Okay, good morning. Listen up everyone ...' He waited for everyone in CID to settle. 'Now this is a full-blown murder case, Detective Inspector Ruth Hunter is coming on board and will be acting as the senior investigating officer. I know that many of you have worked with her before. She is a very experienced detective and is a great addition to our team.'

Ruth glanced around the room furtively. If anyone had a problem with that, they weren't showing it. It was a relief. CID officers were a tough crowd. Nick caught Ruth's eye, giving her a friendly wink. She smiled back. Nick would be an outstanding copper if he didn't spend so much time battling his demons.

Ruth got up and gathered her thoughts for a moment. She hadn't run a briefing for a while. *Here we go*, she thought. Pointing to the CCTV still from the university hospital of the teenage female suspect in the red baseball cap pushing David Sabatini out of the hospital in a wheel-chair, she said, 'For those of you who don't know, Nick and Sian went to an address in Rhyd where we believed David Sabatini was living. Sabatini wasn't there but our female suspect from both Harlech Beach and the hospital was. She did a runner and managed to escape. We're still trying to locate her.'

'Bit embarrassing that, Nick. Left for dead by a teenage girl,' Mac said, mocking Nick with a tut.

A few chortles of laughter as Nick gave him the finger. 'Bloody hell, Mac. If you'd gone after her in that heat, you'd be lying next to Owen Ankers in the basement morgue.'

Ruth couldn't help but laugh with everyone else as Mac shook his head with a grin. 'Such a twat,' he muttered.

That was one thing that Ruth had missed about not being in CID. The dark humour and the camaraderie. She was back where she belonged. CID officers were her tribe and had been for decades.

Rolling her eyes, Ruth continued. 'All right, Cannon and Ball. Nick, what have we got?'

Nick grinned at her as he moved to the scene board. 'Cannon and Ball, boss? Showing your age.'

She let it go. It was time to get on with the investigation.

Nick pointed to a detailed road map of Llancastell. 'We looked at the post at Sabatini's home and talked to neighbours. We believe that our female suspect is an Abi Mullen. The person in this CCTV looks very much like the girl – who was incredibly fast might I add – that I pursued from David Sabatini's home yesterday afternoon. There's no record of a driving licence or passport in her name, so no photograph.'

Ruth saw Sian looking her way. There was a little moment between them before Sian glanced down at her notes and said, 'Boss, we ran Abi Mullen's details through PNC. She is eighteen and well-known to social services. Fostered when she was younger but ran away on several occasions. She was a 'looked after child' through Llancastell Council but now she is eighteen, she's no longer their problem. Seems she was living with David Sabatini.'

'Abi has also been under the Children and Adolescent Mental Health Service for ongoing mental health issues but we don't have any more details on that,' Nick explained, looking at his notes. 'She's enrolled at Llancastell Sixth Form College and doing a HND in hair and beauty. Her attendance is terrible. Except for Wednesdays when she does work experience at a salon in Newtown. Apparently, she likes that but she's always late.'

'Mac, go over to the college and see what you can find. Did Abi Mullen have friends on the course or in the college? Talk to the special needs or wellbeing team. Were they aware of Abi's mental health and social services?' Ruth said.

Mac nodded. 'Boss.'

'Why was a girl like Abi Mullen on a beach with a man like Owen Ankers?' Ruth asked rhetorically. The pieces of the case felt very fragmented at the moment.

Drake, who had been perching casually on the table, stood up with his hands in his pockets and looked out at the room. 'I want this girl in custody here by the end of the day, please.' Then he refocussed. 'Any other lines of enquiry?'

'I spoke to ACC Davenport yesterday,' Ruth said.

Merringer frowned. 'ACC Davenport is a suspect? Bloody hell!'

That was the problem with Merringer, Ruth thought. He was a conformist who believed in the sanctity of the police force. And sometimes that made him naïve.

'Not really, Luke. But as she's the victim's ex-wife, and they're recently divorced, we have to look at her,' Ruth explained, unable to hide her frustration.

'Bet she loved that,' Mac said sardonically.

'She was okay. Bit spiky. She claims that despite what her solicitor's firm told me, her divorce to Owen was not acrimonious.'

'You believe her?' Drake asked.

'Not sure, boss. But instinct tells me she's not hiding anything,' Ruth said.

'Does she have an alibi?' Nick asked.

'No. Sunbathing in her garden on her own,' Ruth said shaking her head.

'Anyone got anything else?' Drake asked the assembled detectives.

Nick nodded. 'Sian and I spoke to our only eyewitness, Alwyn Fields, yesterday. He is certain that he saw Owen Ankers on the beach with this person in a red baseball cap and a grey Adidas hoodie, which matches the one we found in the washing machine at Sabatini's house.'

'Anything back on that yet?' Ruth asked.

'No. Forensics said they would fast-track it,' Nick replied. 'Fields is also convinced that Owen Ankers was a homosexual and that there were frequent male visitors and parties.'

'Is there anything in that?' Drake asked.

'Don't know, boss. Fields seemed pretty disgusted by Owen's lifestyle.'

'ENOUGH TO ATTACK HIM?'

'I don't think so, but the word "faggot" was used. This doesn't feel like a hate crime and Fields has got an alibi,' Nick explained.

Ruth bristled with Fields' unashamed homophobia. People said that attitudes were changing, but sometimes she couldn't see it in places like North Wales.

'Okay. Anyone spoken to Callum Webb yet?' Ruth asked.

Merringer looked over and said, 'Hard man to track down, boss.'

'NICK, CAN YOU GO INTERVIEW CALLUM WEBB?' DRAKE said and gave Nick a subtle but meaningful look. Nick knew what it meant – the ongoing Operation Titan.

Ruth knew it was time to try and finish off the briefing.

Everyone was raring to go. 'Sian, speak to Davenport's neighbours. See if anyone can confirm her alibi for Saturday, just so we can eliminate her. Luke, I want to know how Abi Mullen got to Harlech. Did she go with David Sabatini? Does she have a car? Look at ANPR. Or did they come by train? Okay, thank you, everyone.'

Taking her folders, Ruth headed for her office with a growing sense of satisfaction.

Back in the game.

It was two o'clock by the time Ruth and Nick got to the Llancastell Police Station car park. They had tracked down Callum Webb through the offices of Ankers & Webb. He was playing golf at Royal St David's Golf Club in Harlech in a charity competition.

'Just like old times,' Ruth said after a moment of silence that bordered on awkward.

Nick indicated his car and smiled. 'I know the routine. You smoke, I'll drive.'

'If you don't mind,' Ruth said remembering their uncomfortable start when she first arrived in Llancastell CID. They had come a long way since then.

'Why would I mind having tar clogging up my lungs?' Nick quipped.

They headed out of Llancastell on the A5 towards Llangollen. The overhead branches dappled the bright sunlight on the windscreen as they made their way along the winding road that went east to west across Snowdonia Park. The A5 was congested with caravans and Ruth had forgotten what an impatient driver Nick was.

'Owen Ankers. What do you think?' Ruth asked, having failed again to find a decent hypothesis in her head.

Something didn't feel right. Maybe the answer was somewhere in his personal life?

Nick replied slowly, almost as if talking to himself. 'What do I think?'

'Something wrong?' Ruth asked him. Instinct told her he was hiding something.

Nick pulled a face and then shot Ruth a meaningful look.

'I'm not meant to say,' he said.

'What? What aren't you meant to say?' Ruth asked, now lost. *What the hell is he talking about?*

'This is strictly on a need-to-know basis, boss,' Nick said.

'What is? Now you're worrying me, Nick. Spit it out!' Ruth growled.

'I have been told to go very gently on Callum Webb today. Very routine questioning. Nothing that might spook him,' Nick explained.

'Why's that?' Ruth was now frustrated that she had been left out of the loop on something.

'I had a "special" briefing with Drake and two officers from Operation Titan being run out of Merseyside Police. They're looking at county lines drug gangs infiltrating areas in Cheshire and North Wales.'

'How is someone like Callum Webb on their radar? And I'm now SIO, so why the bloody hell wasn't I there, and why can't you tell me?' Ruth could feel the anger rising. She had had enough of internal politics and secrecy when she was in the Met.

'They have run surveillance on Webb for months and have intel that he is negotiating with Curtis Blake to transport drugs out of Europe and then Merseyside on Ankers & Webb delivery vans,' Nick explained.

'And this is on a need-to-know basis because …?' Ruth asked.

'Merseyside Police think Blake has someone in their force or our force feeding him intel. They're paranoid.'

'What? And you and Drake think I might be on the take?' Ruth barked. She was now fuming.

'No, of course not. I'm assuming that Drake was going to tell you today at some point,' Nick said. 'You're the SIO. You can't run the investigation without knowing this. I just didn't want to talk to Webb without you knowing.'

Nick's logical explanation calmed her. She had probably over-reacted.

'Have they got any ideas?' Ruth asked.

Nick shook his head grimly. 'Not that they told me.'

RUTH LIT A CIGARETTE AND BLEW SMOKE OUT OF THE window. 'You think someone in our CID is bent?'

'No. Who?' Nick asked with a sense of indignation.

Ruth held her cigarette out of the window and let the oncoming breeze take away the ash. Casting her mind around their team, she agreed with Nick. No one was on her radar as being suspicious – but you never knew.

'Blake using Ankers & Webb vans doesn't make any sense. Webb's minted.'

'He's also a gambling addict and has lost a fortune. He fancies himself as a bit of a gangster. I've seen the photos of one of their meetings,' Nick explained.

'Did Owen Ankers know about it?'

'NOT SURE. THE THEORY IS THAT ANKERS EITHER DIDN'T know, or he wasn't happy about it. Either way, it looked like Ankers was going to get in the way of Blake and Webb's deal.'

'And so they kill him just like that?' Ruth asked.

'A grass on Merseyside claims that in recent weeks Ankers made life difficult for Webb. Possibly said he'll involve the police. Blake isn't going to risk that and so sends someone to murder Ankers on Harlech Beach. Now the deal can go through with no hitches.'

Ruth took this in as she flicked her cigarette stub out of the window. That did start to make more sense in terms of motive.

'That's pretty ruthless, even by drug-dealer standards,' Ruth said.

'Blake's a sociopath. He doesn't have feelings,' Nick sneered.

'How does that fit in with Abi Mullen?' Ruth asked.

'Not sure. Her boyfriend Sabatini is a low-level dealer so there might be a connection there. Of course, we don't know that Abi Mullen had anything to do with Owen Ankers' death.'

'You don't believe in coincidences do you, Nick?'

'No. Abi Mullen might be involved somewhere but she doesn't seem like a person Blake would hire to top Ankers.'

'What about Webb as our killer?'

'I doubt it. No criminal record. I can't see him popping up on Harlech Beach to stab his business partner and supposed oldest friend to death.'

'So, we just leave Webb in place while Merseyside build a case against him and more importantly Blake?'

'Merseyside Police have spent the last fifteen years trying to mount a case against Blake and get it to stick. This could be it.'

. . .

Ruth could see that Nick couldn't hide his excitement at the thought of Blake going down.

In the glorious summer sun, the pristine greens and fairways of the Royal St David's Golf Club – *Clwb Golff Brenhinol Dewi Sant* – were stunning. The uneven line of Snowdonia mountains traversed the skyline in all directions. Far closer, the brooding presence of Harlech Castle, which overlooked the course a couple of miles away.

As Ruth and Nick circled to the back of the clubhouse, Callum Webb was milling around talking to other golfers in his party. There was a burst of laughter and back-slapping.

'Mr Webb?' Ruth asked, as she approached and showed her warrant card.

'Can I help?' Webb gave a confident smile.

'Detective Inspector Hunter. This is DS Evans. We're with Llancastell CID, sir.'

Webb beckoned them away from the other golfers to a more discreet area and said, 'I guess you've come about Owen. Bloody horrible. I can't believe it.'

'We understand that you've known Owen Ankers for a long time?'

'We went to school together. Set up our business together. Everything.' Webb shook his head and swallowed as though he was holding back his emotions. 'I don't know what I'm going to do without him …'

Webb put his thumb and forefinger to his eyes for a moment. He then took a dramatic deep breath to show that he was trying to compose himself.

Ruth shot Nick a look through the gritted teeth of her

sympathetic smile. To give him credit, Webb might have been a two-faced wanker, but his acting could have won him a BAFTA.

Ruth nodded with her best compassionate expression. 'We're very sorry for your loss.'

The next ten minutes were spent establishing that Webb was at Bangor-On-Dee races on Saturday afternoon. Webb had a half-share of the racehorse Laughing Policeman running in the 12.30. The irony wasn't lost on any of them. It also wasn't a big surprise to Ruth or Nick that Webb had been at the races. They knew from the intel that Webb was a gambling addict and if he had anything to do with Owen Ankers' murder, he wouldn't have done it himself.

Webb casually threw in that having won the race, Laughing Policeman was now worth in excess of seventy thousand pounds. He chortled that they had already got back fifteen thousand in prize money in his first race.

Ruth had taken an instant dislike to Webb. He was a man clearly uncomfortable in his own skin who bragged about his wealth with no self-awareness.

However, she was relieved that they now had a viable motive for Owen's murder.

Chapter Eleven

Ruth and Nick made their way over to Owen Ankers' home. Ahead of them, the *Moel Hebog* – Bare Hill of the Hawk – mountain dominated the view. It gave its name to the range of plum coloured peaks in the north-western ridges of Snowdonia, and *Mynydd Mawr*, which simply meant big mountain.

Moel Hebog lay on the margins of one of the major eruptive centres within the Caradoc Series of North Wales. With a series of dangerous rocky slopes, it had a distinctive pointed, snow-dusted summit. From the north side, the peak appeared gentler and more rounded. Much of the mountain consisted of a connected series of rhyolitic domes and sills and basaltic magmas from the volcanic eruptions of the Ordovician period, over four hundred million years ago. The only time the mountain had been inhabited was during the Bronze Age when it was used for mining copper.

When they arrived at Owen Ankers' home, the SOCO forensics van was still outside. A female SOCO, in a white forensic suit, hood and mask, came out of the house with a labelled evidence bag.

Ruth flashed her warrant card. 'DI Hunter. This is DS Evans. What have we got?'

The SOCO showed them the clear polythene bag that had a delicate silver crucifix inside. 'We found this between the boards of the decking. The clasp at the back is broken.'

Ruth nodded. 'Anything else?'

'Nothing at the moment, ma'am.'

'Thank you,' Ruth said as she and Nick headed inside.

Now that she was the SIO, Ruth wanted to take another look at Owen Ankers' home. As an experienced detective, she wanted to see if anything struck her that might help the case. Was there anything that CID had missed first time around?

Even though the upstairs of the house had been meticu-lously examined by forensics, Ruth and Nick were still advised to wear forensic suits, shoes and gloves. They climbed the designer 'floating' staircase that was made of dark wood, glass and brushed steel. On the top landing, there were a series of professional studio photographs, two of which featured Owen with his nephew and niece, both about ten years old. With beaming smiles, the first photo showed Owen with his arms around them both, his eyes sparkling with sheer joy. In the second, the boy and girl were a little older but the pose was almost identical, as was the look on Owen's face. Ruth hurt seeing those expressions, those faces so full of joy and life, knowing the light had now permanently gone from Owen's eyes. She wondered how Owen's nephew and niece were dealing with his death.

Ruth found such unnatural sadness in the homes of victims. Frozen in time, homes left with the full expectation that life would carry on as always. Ruth had seen homes where meals were half eaten, televisions still blaring, a washing machine cleaning clothes that would never be worn again.

It was the children's bedrooms that Ruth found the most difficult. She remembered a case on a North Peckham estate where a four-year-old boy had been smothered and strangled by his mother for being 'too noisy' while she and her boyfriend were smoking crack and trying to watch television. Even now she could recall the details of little Alfie's room. The small single bed with a Spiderman duvet cover. The crayon drawings stuck to the wall with Sellotape. The toy cars lined up neatly that he would never touch or play with again. And the fancy-dress costume that was going to be worn to a friend's party the following day.

Other officers seemed to be able to detach themselves and be objective. They were there to do a job, to solve a crime, to find evidence. Getting emotionally involved clouded their judgement. Ruth didn't know how to do that. Whether that made her a better or worse copper, she didn't know. And she didn't care. That was the way she felt.

As she moved along the landing, there were some tasteful prints and paintings on the wall. And then a door that led into Owen's office. The room was stacked floor to ceiling with hardback books in fitted, dark-wood bookshelves.

A plush leather office chair sat in front of an oak desk that had papers neatly stacked on it. Everything was ordered and pristine. On the walls, a series of photos that showed Owen's extensive charity work. One showed him shaking hands with Prince Charles with an oversized cheque. There were photos of the local football team that he had sponsored with *Ankers & Webb* printed on their purple shirts. Letters of thanks were framed at the other end of the room. *The man was a bloody saint,* she thought.

Ruth wondered how someone who had done such magnanimous, selfless work both in the local community and for the country as a whole, had created any enemies. What had Owen Ankers done to make someone target and kill him in cold blood? Was Curtis Blake the key to this?

Ruth moved on to the large dressing room. Everything was as she expected – tidy, ordered and expensive. Opening the doors, she saw around forty designer suits of every shade hanging neatly. It reminded her of a scene from *Goodfellas*.

A full-length mirror hung on the left-hand wall. Ruth looked at it for a moment. There was something slightly off with it. At first, she wasn't sure what it was. Then she realised it was something she had seen before.

Approaching the wall, she looked at where the mirror joined the wall. It seemed to be part of the wall rather than fixed to it. Pressing her face against the cool glass, she cupped her hands to block out as much light as she could and peered ahead. Her breath made a neat circular pattern on its surface.

Standing back for a moment, Ruth could hear that Nick was in the bedroom next door.

'Nick, can you put the lights on in that bedroom?' she shouted.

'Erm … Yes, boss.' Nick sounded confused.

Going back to the mirror, she cupped her hands again and then as the light went on, she could see the bedroom.

It was a two-way mirror.

Nick came in and looked at her. 'Everything all right, boss?'

Ruth gestured to the wall. 'It's a two-way mirror.'

Nick raised an eyebrow. 'Kinky.'

For Ruth it posed the question, why did someone like Owen Ankers feel the need to have a two-way mirror in his dressing room to look at what was going on in the master bedroom? In her decades as a copper, Ruth had seen all sorts of weird sexual practices and was shocked by little. However, it did reveal a darker, more clandestine side to Ankers' character that might give them a clue to his death.

It was midday by the time Mac and Sian arrived in Harlech. They parked close to St David's Catholic Church that was now criss-crossed in lines of shadows from the huge trees that surrounded it. The streets were busy with tourists and day-trippers. Sian was trying to avoid talking to Mac, who had spent the journey in an interminable groan about Llancastell CID and everyone in it. For Sian, Mac represented all the old-fashioned and outdated attitudes of a police force from decades ago.

Sian spotted and pointed to the discoloured yellow sign for J&B Newsagents where Alwyn Fields claimed that he had gone last Saturday afternoon at the time of Owen Ankers' murder. They needed to verify Fields' alibi. The sign read *Stationery, Confectionery, Off-Licence.* Another sign advertised Western Union money transfers from anywhere in the world.

Sian went in first. The shop was quiet and smelt slightly of air freshener. Pachai Patel, the owner of the shop, nodded a hello. He was tall and thin to the point of skinny. His forehead was furrowed, eyes light and kind, and his hair silver.

'Mr Patel?'

He smiled. 'Yes. Can I help?'

'DC Macdonald and DC Hockney, North Wales Police. Could we have a quick word?'

Pachai looked naturally concerned. 'Of course. If I can help?'

Mac fished out a photo of Alwyn Fields from his pocket and showed it to Pachai. 'Do you recognise this man, sir?'

Pachai's expression immediately darkened. 'Yes.'

'Mr Fields?' Mac asked.

'I don't know.' Pachai's tone was verging on hostile.

'Mr Fields claims that he was in this shop at around five o'clock on Saturday afternoon. Is that correct?' Sian asked.

'That is impossible. This man is banned from this shop.'

Mac frowned. 'Banned?'

'A very bad, horrible man. He is a racist. He is not welcome in my shop and he knows it,' explained Pachai.

'So, you didn't see Mr Fields on Saturday afternoon?'

'No. No, I most definitely did not! That man has not been in here for over a year.'

Mac and Sian exchanged a look.

So much for Fields' alibi.

'Thank you, Mr Patel.'

More importantly, Fields had lied when there was no good reason to. And that was highly suspicious.

NICK AND RUTH HAD PARKED ON THE HIGH STREET AND were heading for Cut Above Hairdressers where they knew that Abi Mullen did work experience for college. It was a long shot given that Abi now knew the police were on to her. But you never knew and Nick agreed it was worth a try. They might get some information on Abi anyway.

They arrived at the shop with its black and silver frontage that Ruth thought looked like an eighties throwback.

'I'll go in. If she sees you, she's likely to run. You go around the back,' Ruth suggested.

'Good idea, boss. Oh, and while you're in there, make an appointment for yourself,' Nick said with a grin.

Ruth rolled her eyes, gave him the finger and muttered, 'Twat,' as she headed for the door. She opened the door and saw that one woman was having her hair coloured. On the other side, another woman was having her wet, black hair cut. Pop music was playing from a tinny radio somewhere.

The receptionist looked up and smiled. 'Can I help?' she asked in her well-rehearsed sing-song voice.

'Yes,' Ruth said looking around and stalling for time. 'I'm looking for my niece, Abi. She does work experience here, I think?'

'She does sometimes,' the receptionist said with a sardonic tone and then gestured. 'She's out the back, sweeping up.'

Walking through the shop that smelt heavily of hair-dyeing chemicals, Ruth came out into the back where there was a small kitchen and storeroom.

A blonde girl was obliviously sweeping the floor.

She looked up. It was Abi Mullen.

'Abi Mullen?' Ruth asked.

However, before Ruth had got any other words out, Abi had bolted for the back door, opened it and was gone.

Bloody hell, she's like a whippet, thought Ruth, as she chased her outside.

By the time Ruth had looked around the rear of the building, Abi was climbing up the back wall.

'Abi! Stop! Police!' Ruth shouted as Abi got to the top of the wall.

Nick came jogging up the rear alleyway and saw that Abi was now on top of the wall.

'Where are you going, Abi?' he asked calmly.

At that moment, Abi turned to look at him, lost her footing and fell down into an enormous industrial bin, which Nick could smell from where he was standing.

It was nearly an hour later when Nick and Ruth came into Interview Room Two. After falling into the rancid bin, Abi had been allowed to have a shower and was now wearing the standard grey tracksuit. The magnolia room was brightly lit and smelt of cheap shower gel.

Beside Abi sat her legal-aid solicitor, a small, bespectacled man with a greying beard.

Ruth could now see Abi clearly for the first time without the baseball cap and hoodie. She was about five foot four and she cut a surprisingly diminutive figure. Almost child-like.

At first, Ruth only gave her a cursory glance as she sat down and put the case papers on a grey plastic table.

'Hello, Abi.' Ruth reached over and clicked the tape machine. 'For the purposes of the tape, I'm Detective Inspector Hunter. This is my colleague Detective Sergeant Evans. Present as well are Abi Mullen and the duty solicitor, Peter Barnes. I need to read you your rights under caution. You do not have to say anything but it may harm your defence if you do not mention when questioned something which you later rely on in court. Anything you do say may be given in evidence.'

It was only then that Ruth really looked at Abi's

face. It was soft and slightly rounded. Her cheekbones were high and rosy. The rest of her skin was milky and flawless, straight nose and a full, heart-shaped mouth. Her soft-brown eyes were striking in their gentleness, like those of a puppy. Her blonde-auburn hair was still a little wet from the shower and hung in curled tresses.

My God, Ruth thought to herself, *she is stunning.* Somewhere between a cherubic angel and the subject of a Pre-Raphaelite painting. Ruth was completely taken aback, as was Nick. This is not the girl he had pictured when legging after her through the side alleys of Rhyd.

Abi just stared at the floor and as she looked up at them, she looked confused and afraid.

'Did you understand what I said to you, Abi?' Ruth asked.

Abi nodded. 'Yeah. It wasn't … me though.' Her voice was soft, with a hint of North Wales but not much. However, she also sounded a little childish in her immediate response as though she was a pupil at a primary school.

Nick smiled at her. 'Let's take this one step at a time, eh?'

Abi began to bite the skin from around her thumb as she moved awkwardly on the chair. There was no attitude, no surly looks – none of the unpleasant and sometimes threatening behaviour the police got from many teenagers that were interviewed in the station.

'Do you know why you're here, Abi?' Ruth asked in a gentle tone that invited immediate reassurance.

Pursing her lips, Abi gave the slightest of nods. She looked scared and completely out of her comfort zone.

'For the purposes of the tape, the suspect has nodded her head to that question.' Nick's voice was low. They had both immediately sensed Abi's fragility and wanted the interview to be as calm and quiet as possible.

'Abi, could you tell us where you were last Saturday afternoon, about five o'clock?' Ruth asked.

Abi shot a glance to her solicitor who gave her a nod to say it was okay for her to answer. 'I was on the beach … at Harlech.'

'Okay. Could you tell us what you were doing there?'

'I'd … I'd gone to see Owen.'

'Owen Ankers is that?' Ruth asked, feeling relieved that Abi wasn't going to lie about her whereabouts.

'Yes, miss.'

Ruth gave her a kind smile. 'It's okay, Abi, you don't have to call me "miss". Could you tell us why you had gone to see Owen Ankers that afternoon?'

'Erm … He ran this charity for young people. That's how I met him, see?' Abi explained with a nod.

'So, you had met Owen Ankers before Saturday?'

'Oh yeah, miss— Sorry … yeah, a couple of times. He came to speak at my college. He worked with the Prince's Trust. As a m-mentor … is that the right word?'

Ruth nodded reassuringly, 'Yes, mentor … Okay. So why did you go out to Harlech to see him?'

'He was going to help me finance my hair and beauty course. I want to run my own hairdressing shop eventually, you know?' Abi explained.

Nick looked up from his notes and frowned. 'Not sure that explains why you were on the beach with him on Saturday afternoon.'

'We had sent some texts. I told him I wanted to go to college but I couldn't afford the fees and everything. Then he said he wanted to see me, have a chat and meet face to face. He said he'd like to help me. We went on the beach to walk the dog and talk about my future …'

'Did anything happen while you were on the beach?' Ruth asked.

Abi looked at them like a startled rabbit and then eventually nodded.

'Abi, do you think you could tell us what happened while you were on the beach with Owen?'

NICK WAS STILL IMPRESSED BY HOW RUTH COULD CREATE such a calm, close bond with someone in an interview so quickly. She could read people fast and then work out how to put them at their ease and get them to talk. It was a real gift, he thought to himself.

'We was walking along … Owen called for the dog … then someone came towards us … and … we got … a-a-attacked …' Abi's voice trailed off as she relived what had happened and began to cry.

Ruth nodded. 'You were attacked?'

'Yeah …' Abi gave her solicitor a look of panic. 'Of course.'

Nick and Ruth exchanged a glance. From what they had seen of Abi, that made more sense than her carrying out a motiveless attack on Owen.

Abi continued. 'I didn't hurt him … You don't think I …'

Abi looked at her nails and her hands were shaking. She looked at the floor, wiped the tears from her face with her sweatshirt and sniffed.

'Do you need to stop for a bit, Abi?' Ruth asked quietly.

Abi shook her head. 'No. No … it's fine.'

Ruth nodded. 'Okay. Tell me if you want to stop though. Do you think you could describe the person who attacked you, Abi?'

Abi composed herself. 'A man. I think. He was quite big. He came out from behind the sand dunes. He … he hit Owen on the back of his head. It happened really quickly …'

'Where were you when this happened?' Nick asked.

'I screamed and ran away at first. I didn't see everything. Then I screamed again and the man ran away into the sand dunes. I kept thinking he would come back to get me,' Abi explained, clearly terrified at having to relive the attack.

'Did you see the man that attacked you, Abi?'

'Yeah. He had one of those things, like a hat, but over his face.'

'A balaclava?' Nick suggested.

'Yeah, that's it.' Abi looked at Nick and nodded.

'And it was a man?' Ruth asked.

'Yeah. It had slipped and I could see his nose and eyes. Sorry … tha-that's all I saw.'

Ruth looked at Nick. Everything about Abi seemed to point to the fact that she had been an innocent bystander. 'That's all right. And this attacker stabbed Owen?'

'Yeah. I think so …'

'You think so?'

'I'm not really sure. But yeah, he did …'

'So, you saw it happen? You saw Owen getting stabbed, Abi?'

Abi seemed to be panicking as she looked at the duty solicitor. She then whispered something to him and he gave her some advice. Abi looked at Ruth again. 'No … I didn't. I can't … seem to remember.'

'I'm confused. This was only a week ago, Abi?' Ruth said.

'Sometimes … I get this thing where I can't remember stuff. Like a blackout where my memory goes. And then

I'm all right again, you know what I mean?' Abi was clearly embarrassed at admitting this and went back to chewing her nails.

'I think so ...' Ruth said. It wasn't clear to her if Abi was describing a mental health condition to them.

Nick clicked the nib on his pen. 'A significant amount of Owen's DNA and blood was found on the grey hoodie top that we found in the washing machine at your home in Rhyd. Do you know why that is?'

'I went over to help him. At first, I-I thought it was just a little cut ... but, but the blood kept flowing down his leg. I couldn't get it to stop. It went all over my hands.'

'Why didn't you call for an ambulance?'

A moment hung in the air as Abi thought about how to answer this question.

'My phone was dead. Owen had left his at his house. I screamed for someone to come and help us. No one came. No one. It felt like I was there forever.' Abi began to cry again, her shoulders juddering.

'It's all right, Abi. Just take your time,' Ruth reassured her.

'And then ... and then he just died in front of me ... I was there on my own with him ...' Abi sobbed into her hands which covered her face.

Ruth looked over at Nick. She knew they were both thinking that this fragile teenage girl wasn't their killer. Instead she had witnessed a brutal murder.

'Abi, why didn't you go and get help after that?' Ruth asked softly.

Abi looked up and wiped her face on her sleeve. 'I was covered in blood. I thought I would get into trouble. I thought that if I went to the police, the person who had murdered Owen would come back and kill me. I was scared.'

Ruth nodded. 'Thank you, Abi. You've been very brave telling us what you saw last Saturday. And you're not going to be in danger again from the man who attacked you, okay?'

Abi nodded. 'Will I get into trouble?'

'No. Not at all.' Ruth shook her head.

'I have some mental health things going on. People don't take me seriously you know?'

'I don't want you to worry about any of that at the moment, okay?'

'You're nice, you know that? I thought coppers were …' Abi decided not to finish her sentence.

'Do you think if you spoke to one of my colleagues, you could describe the man, or what you could see of him? He can use a computer and we can try and build up a picture of the man.'

Abi nodded. 'Yeah. I could try.'

'Good girl. That would really help us.' Ruth looked at Abi and she nodded. They had made a connection and Ruth promised herself that she would make sure that this vulnerable young girl was going to be okay through all this.

Chapter Twelve

Pulling the car onto the dark-grey pavement, Mac parked outside Alwyn Fields' small stone cottage. It was on the roadside, fifty yards before the left-hand fork with a sign that read *Harlech canol-y-dref* – Harlech town centre. Most of the houses further along the A496, away from Harlech, were large detached houses, with long drives and expensive cars.

As Mac and Sian got out, the afternoon sun bore down on their backs. The smell of the sea was in the air that blew across them. Mac wiped his forehead with his hairy forearm, a habit that irritated Sian. But then again, most things about Mac irritated Sian.

'Here we go,' Mac said as he hoisted up his sweaty trousers. He rapped on the door and they waited. Nothing.

Sian blinked as her eye caught a tiny movement behind a net curtain at a side window of the cottage. It looked like Fields was inside.

'He's in …' Sian said quietly as she gestured to the window.

From somewhere close by, a dog started to bark and whine.

Sian frowned, looked over at Mac and then made her way down the side of the house.

'Why don't you stay at the front?' Sian suggested in a hushed voice.

Wondering if she would be able to spot Fields through a window or doors at the back of the house, Sian stepped over a tiny six-inch stone border.

The side of the house was flat brick, with a small frosted glass window that she guessed was a downstairs toilet. Flies buzzed and swooped around a small mountain of black bin bags that were stacked by the back door. As she passed, she was hit by a thick, pungent waft of decay that made her wince. *What a shit tip.*

A noise came from the interior again. Someone was moving around. Why wasn't he answering the door?

Sian looked at Mac and gestured to him that someone was definitely inside. Mac nodded and went and rapped on the front door again.

There was the urgent, clattering sound on the wood as the dog scraped its claws against the fence and door. Its barking was getting incessant now that it realised that someone was nearby.

There was a wooden slatted door sandwiched between a stone wall and the house. The dog was now going crazy. Sian certainly wasn't going to go into the garden. She wondered if she went up onto the wall, she could get a better view of the back of the house.

The sound of Mac banging on the front door again stopped her for a moment. She leant and peered through a two-centimetre crack in the garden gate.

A springer spaniel jumped up and then backed away

from the gate before sniffing vigorously at the ground beneath the door, trying to get Sian's scent.

Turning on her heels, Sian returned down the side of the house.

Mac looked over. 'Anything?'

'Someone's in there. And there's a springer spaniel going nuts in the garden.' Sian had a thought. 'Anyone found Owen Ankers' dog yet?'

Mac shook his head. 'No. Not that I'm aware of. Why?'

'Owen Ankers had a springer spaniel. And we haven't managed to find it yet.'

'DOES ALWYN FIELDS STRIKE YOU AS THE DOG-LOVING, springer-spaniel type of man?' Mac said sarcastically.

'Definitely not. It looks like Owen Ankers' dog from the photos.' Sian nodded at the door. 'I'll call for back-up.'

Then a more metallic noise came from the front door, as if it was finally being unlocked.

'Mr Fields. It's DC Sian Hockney. I was here two days go,' Sian said trying to reassure Fields.

The door then clicked and opened about six inches and Fields' unshaven, drawn face appeared.

'What do you want?' he demanded.

'Mr Fields, can we come in for a minute? We just want to clarify a few things with you.' Sian's tone was upbeat, trying to convince him that their visit was purely routine.

Mac made a slight move towards the door.

Fields shook his head. 'No. I've got nothing to say to you. Unless you have a warrant?'

Sian flashed a smile at him. 'It'll only take a moment.' What she really wanted to say was, *Open the bloody door!*

'No. Go on, piss off will ya?'

'We can do this down at the station if you want?' Mac's tone was now stern.

'I'm not going anywhere.' Fields went to close the door in their faces.

'Mr Fields, can you tell us how long you've had your dog? The springer spaniel in your back garden?' Sian asked.

She could see that the question had clearly rattled him.

Then suddenly the front door swung open. Before Sian and Mac could react, Fields had pointed the two steel barrels of a shotgun into Sian's face.

Sian felt Fields grab her by the hair, pull her towards him turning her as she went. She felt his arm go around her in a neck lock. She was struggling to breathe. Her head was spinning. *What the hell is happening?*

Fields might have been old but his movements were swift – you never lost the muscle memory of being a Royal Marines Commando.

'Get back!' Fields moved back and then waved the gun at Mac.

Sian was relieved for a moment not to be looking down the barrels of the gun.

'I can't breathe …' Sian spluttered. The lack of air was making her feel dizzy.

Mac raised his hands as if to pacify Fields. 'Okay, okay. Take it easy, Mr Fields. No one wants anyone to get hurt here. Put the gun down.'

Fields snorted. 'If you come any closer, I'll blow your bloody face off. Then I'll break her neck. That's what I was trained to do, see?'

'Mr Fields, whatever it is, I'm sure we can sort it out.' Sian could feel her voice rasp under the tension of his forearm against her throat. The whole thing had escalated so quickly. It didn't feel real.

'No. No one can.'

SIAN FELT HERSELF BEING USED AS A SHIELD AS FIELDS backed into the house.

Sian watched as Mac moved forwards. *Stay where you are, you moron, or you'll get us both killed.*

'I meant what I said!' Fields bellowed at Mac.

Sian could see Mac's face full of concern. 'It's all right, Mac. I'll be all right.' She was still trying to draw breath in as Fields' forearm locked again against her windpipe.

Fields kicked the front door closed with a noisy slam.

DRAKE, RUTH AND NICK WALKED INTO THE EMPTY canteen. In the background, there was the clatter of cutlery as the kitchen staff prepared for the lunchtime rush.

Ruth spotted Drake as he looked up at the silent television screen that was showing the BBC News feed and shake his head.

'Problem, sir?' Ruth asked.

'Yorkshire are all out for a hundred and eighty,' Drake explained.

'You've lost me,' Ruth said.

'Cricket,' Nick explained to her.

'No. Not just cricket. It's a one-day match against Lancashire,' Drake said sourly.

Ruth was totally lost. 'And that's bad, is it?'

'The Wars of the Roses, boss,' Nick clarified.

Drake raised his eyebrow – he was impressed. 'Know your history, Nick?'

'He's a total history nerd, boss,' Ruth said with a grin.

Nick gave her a sarcastic smile as he reached and got a brown plastic tray for their coffees.

'Nick tells me that he's filled you in with the details of Operation Titan and our suspicions about Callum Webb?' Drake said.

Ruth shot Nick a look. 'I understood that the information was on a need-to-know basis?'

'As SIO, you need to know, Ruth,' Drake said. 'It was my mistake not to give you the intel as soon as you joined the investigation.'

That's what impressed her about Drake. He had the balls to acknowledge mistakes. There weren't many male officers in CID that would ever do that.

'What about Blake having someone on the inside?' Ruth asked.

'There's nothing concrete on that,' Drake said as they stopped by the coffee machine. 'How was Abi Mullen?'

'Abi says she was on the beach with Ankers and they were attacked by a man in a balaclava,' Nick explained.

'What was she doing there?' Drake asked.

'She met Ankers when he gave a talk at her college. He has a charitable foundation for teenagers and is a mentor for the Prince's Trust. She spoke to him afterwards and he promised to help her out. She says they exchanged a few texts. He invited her out to Harlech to have a coffee and a chat about her future plans. They took the dog for a walk.'

Drake nodded and then pointed at the machine. 'What can I get you two?'

'Two coffees, one white, one black, no sugar,' Ruth

replied, giving Nick a look. She had known him long enough to know what he really wanted.

Drake pushed a button on the coffee maker. 'Sounds plausible. Let's check their phones for those texts.'

'Yes, boss.' Ruth nodded.

'What did you think of her?' Drake asked as he watched the coffee draining from the machine into the plastic cups.

'I don't think she's our killer, boss. In fact, I'm certain she's not,' Nick replied.

'What's she like?' Drake seemed intrigued by Nick's answer.

Nick looked to Ruth as he searched for the right words. 'If she had a halo, she would look like …

'A cherub?' Ruth filled in the blank. God, they could even finish each other's sentences.

'Yeah, like a cherub.' Nick nodded but then his eye was drawn away to the flat screen on the wall that was showing the BBC News Channel with no sound.

'Boss, she's very sweet. Not the brightest teenager I've ever met. But she's had a horrible life up until now, and I think she thought Owen Ankers could help her. That's it.' Ruth shrugged. At the moment, they had no reason to doubt what Abi had told them about being attacked.

'Yeah, you could see her in the Girl Guides or something. And there's no viable motive for Abi Mullen to murder Owen Ankers,' Nick explained.

Ruth knew that Nick was keen for them to pursue the hypothesis that Blake had hired a killer to attack Owen Ankers on the beach and hadn't counted on Abi Mullen being there. It was definitely the most viable lead.

Drake thought for a moment. 'What about her relationship with David Sabatini?'

'She admits she's his girlfriend. So far, all we've got is

that Sabatini peddles a bit of weed here and there. He is plankton when it comes to the drugs food chain,' Ruth said.

Nick's eye had been drawn to the television again. However, this time he stayed glued to the set as a banner appeared on the screen: *BREAKING NEWS – Police officer has been taken hostage in Harlech, West Wales.*

'Boss!' Nick pointed to the screen.

BY THE TIME DRAKE, RUTH AND NICK ARRIVED AT Harlech, the circus that sets up when an armed suspect has taken a police officer hostage was in full swing. The whole area was on lock-down and a police helicopter circled noisily overhead. High-powered cameras were being used to try and see into Fields' house. The same would be true of the officers who were now positioned in surrounding houses. Any advantage in terms of where Fields and Sian were situated in the house could be vital if they decided to go in.

About ten yards to the right of the building, Ruth could see a six-man tactical firearms squad that were hunkered silently against the wall. They were ready to breach the door and go in at a second's notice. Looking at all that firepower, Ruth couldn't help but feel frightened for Sian.

Drake, Ruth and Nick approached the tapestry of blue and yellow. The squad cars, police officers and tape were all there to make sure that no one could get near. They flashed warrant cards and ducked under the tape.

Drake approached Inspector Morton, the most senior uniform officer at the scene.

'What have we got, Inspector?' Drake asked, heading closer to the house.

'DC Hockney is inside with Alwyn Fields. He has a shotgun. There are two main points of entry at the front and back.'

'What does he want?' Ruth asked.

'We don't know,' Morton said.

'Any contact?' Drake asked.

'He does have a mobile phone, which he picked up. I spoke to him for a few seconds and then he hung up,' Morton explained.

Mac hurried over clearly concerned.

'Any idea what sparked this off, Mac?' Drake asked him.

'There's a Springer Spaniel in Fields' back garden. According to the neighbours, Fields hasn't got a dog and never has done. When Sian asked him about it, he flipped and came out with the gun. Then he forced her inside. There was nothing I could do.' Mac was clearly feeling guilty that he had allowed a female police officer to be taken hostage in front of him.

'He had a shotgun, Mac. There was nothing you could do,' Ruth reassured him.

Drake nodded. 'So, it could be Owen Ankers' missing dog?'

'Could be. Same breed. Looks like the photos,' Mac confirmed.

'Where is the hostage negotiator?' Drake asked.

'They're en route but it could take an hour or longer,' Morton said.

'An hour!' Ruth exclaimed. What were they meant to do for *an hour*?

'We haven't got a bloody hour. I've got an officer in

there with a gun to her head, for Christ's sake!' Drake boomed.

'Boss, if it helps, I've done the police negotiator's course at Hendon. It was years ago,' Ruth suggested. If she was honest, she could only remember the basics.

'Ever done anything like this, Ruth?' Drake asked.

Ruth pulled a face. 'Not really.'

'Think you can give it a crack?'

'Yes. The longer we wait, the more agitated he'll get, and the more danger Sian is in.'

'Get me the phone. Now,' Drake said.

Ruth nervously ran through the negotiating basics in her head as she waited to be handed the mobile phone. Active listening. Using open-ended questions, emotional labelling, mirroring and reflecting, silence and paraphrasing. She needed to make Fields feel that she heard what he was saying and was empathetic. Time was the negotiator's greatest ally. Slow things down and don't look for a quick resolution. Allow Fields to feel that he is part of the decision-making process, which might lead to gaining his voluntary compliance. That was her goal.

Ruth was handed the mobile phone, which was now calling Fields. He answered in a gruff voice.

Ruth's tone was quiet and soothing. 'Mr Fields, my name is Ruth. I'm wondering how you are.' There was silence. 'I've been asked to talk to you. Is that going to be okay?'

There was another long silence and Ruth looked at the other officers. Then Fields muttered, 'I suppose so.'

'The officer you have with you is called Sian. Is she okay?' Ruth asked.

'Yeah, she's fine … I didn't do it, all right? I had nothing to do with that man's death.' Fields' voice was jittery but also slurred as if he had been drinking.

'Well that's good for us to know, isn't it?'

'You've got to believe me about that …' Field was starting to sound desperate.

'I do believe you … So, why don't we start with you letting Sian go. Then when you're ready, you can come out, and me and you can have a chat about it? You can tell me exactly what happened. How does that sound?' Ruth's tone and pace was friendly and calm. It sounded like she had known Fields for years.

'I've got his dog, see? Found it roaming around outside his house so I took it in. Thought I would take it back when he came home. Except he didn't, like, you know?'

'Well that's something you and me could talk about, isn't it? You could tell me about Owen's dog and how you got it, if you want?'

There was another long silence and Fields coughed. Ruth looked at the others as the silence continued.

'You one of them negotiators, aren't you?'

RUTH SHOT A LOOK AT DRAKE. 'NO. ACTUALLY, I'M JUST A police officer. Sian is a good friend of mine. I want to make sure that she's all right, that's all. And I want to make sure that nothing happens to you, Mr—'

'Not from round here are you?' Fields said interrupting her.

'No. No. I'm from the South. London … Can I call you *Alwyn*, Mr Fields?'

A long pause. 'Yeah.'

'Are you married, Alwyn?'

Fields snorted. 'Not anymore. Bitch left me. Don't blame her, mind.'

'I'm sorry to hear that, Alwyn.'

'Years ago, it was. Ancient history.'

. . .

'Have you got any children, Alwyn?'

'I'm not bloody daft you know. I know what you're trying to do here like. All these questions. What about you? You married? Do you have children, do you? All sitting at home nicely, waiting for you to get back. Must be nice for you,' Alwyn said starting to sound irritated.

'Not really … Yeah, I was married. Same as you, it didn't work out. I have a daughter Ella. She's twenty and lives over in Liverpool. And she's the best thing I ever did with my life. Sometimes I think she's the only good thing I did in my life. I live on my own like you do. Sometimes it gets a bit lonely, if I'm honest.' Ruth looked over at Drake who looked a little surprised at her honesty. 'What's your child's name, Alwyn?'

'My son, Steven … He doesn't want nothing to do with me.'

'That's a shame,' Ruth said hoping the thought of his son would have an emotional effect on Fields.

'Yeah …' Fields' voice was breaking a little.

'It sounds like not seeing Steven makes you very sad?' Ruth was labelling his underlying emotion.

'I wasn't around, see? In the Royal Marines. All over the world. West Germany, the Falklands.'

'You were in the Falklands?'

'Aye, we were down there. Landed on Ajax Bay in the war.'

'Right …'

'Yomped all the bloody way across to Port Stanley. Then pepper-potted our way up Two Sisters and through the Argy lines. Lost eight men down there, we did. It still haunts me …'

'You must be very proud of what you did for your country though?'

'Maybe … Yeah. But no one gives a shit these days, do they?'

'And that makes you angry, Alwyn? That people don't think about what veterans have been through.'

'It's all bloody well and good honouring the dead of the First World War, don't get me wrong. But what about the living, eh? I still have bloody nightmares about that shit. Mate's brains shot all over my face. Wake up in a sweat, you know?'

'I'm sorry to hear that. What about your son or your grandchildren? Aren't they interested in what you did?'

'Dunno … Never spoke to them about it really.'

This was all taking time and distracting Fields from why they were really there. The more time they talked about other things, the more the heat would be taken out of the situation.

Ruth couldn't bear to think of Sian and how frightened she would be. There hadn't been a waking hour since their cosy drink where Sian hadn't passed through her thoughts. She had got to her and it was such an exciting, warm and lovely feeling.

'You know, I didn't get on with my father. We were very different. We didn't speak from one month to the next because we were too bloody stubborn. And then on my twenty-first birthday, he had a stroke and dropped dead in Northcote Road market in South London.' Ruth's voice broke a little as she told the story. She looked at Drake who encouraged her to continue. 'And I would give anything now to have an hour with him. Anything. A few minutes. To tell him that I loved him. He never met my daughter, his granddaughter. He would have loved her. She's just like him – head-strong. And there were things about him, wonderful things about him that I discovered after he had died that I never knew about. Things that he'd never talked to me about. What a waste that was. Don't let that be you, Alwyn.'

There was a tense, deafening silence of about ten seconds. Then twenty. Ruth wondered if the next thing that she heard would be the metallic unlocking of the front door or something far more sinister like a gunshot.

To her slight relief, there came movement from behind the front door. On the phone, the sound of feet on a mat.

Drake motioned for two of the authorised firearms officers to come over and cover the door in case Fields opened the front door and came out firing.

The AFOs, dressed in their black Nomex, boots, gloves, Kevlar helmet over a balaclava, had nothing to distinguish them as human. Their goggles and ballistic body armour added to the slightly sci-fi look. They were carrying Glock 17 9mm pistols, the most common firearms employed by British armed units. It carried ten rounds of ammunition.

For the next few moments, there was stillness. Ruth's heart was pounding in her ear as adrenaline pumped round her body. She knew that some of the sieges ended with 'suicide by police officer', which would see Fields come out brandishing his shotgun and go down in a hail of 9mm bullets travelling at a velocity of 1250 ft per second. It would be a bloody mess, literally. He could also choose to shoot Sian and then himself inside. The only thing that mattered now was Sian's safety.

And then it happened. The front door opened about a foot and Sian came out, gingerly at first.

'Police officer! Hold your fire!' Drake bellowed.

Sian looked dazed and shaken. She locked eyes with

Ruth, jogged over, hugged her. Ruth could feel her shaking in her arms as she pulled her away from the house and out of danger.

'Come on, over here. You okay?' Ruth asked. Sian nodded. 'You need to see a paramedic,' Ruth said urgently. 'You sure you're okay?'

SIAN NODDED BUT RUTH COULD IMAGINE THAT EVERYTHING in her head felt surreal and dream-like.

'Mr Fields. I need you to come out nice and slowly now,' Drake commanded.

There was more silence and many now expected the sound of a shotgun as Fields ended his own life. However, the front door opened slowly and Fields walked forwards with his hands in the air, just like in the movies.

The two AFOs moved in quickly and aggressively, coming towards him, Glocks pointed and ready to fire.

'Armed police! Get down on the ground! Get down on the ground!' the AFO roared.

'Hands behind your head, now!'

Fields dropped to his knees and the AFOs moved in to handcuff him.

Chapter Thirteen

R uth's nerves had finally calmed by the time she left
Llancastell nick three hours later. She was giving
Sian a lift home after the paramedics advised that Sian
would be shaken up for a few hours and it might be
dangerous for her to drive. Ruth jumped at the chance to
help. However stupid it sounded in her head, she had
nearly lost Sian that afternoon.

As they chatted quietly, they agreed it had been a hell
of a day. They had stopped at Bargain Booze in High
Town and stocked up on mini bottles of prosecco and
premixed cans of gin and tonic.

Sian had then gone from being quiet, subdued and in
shock for the past hour, to what could only be termed
'laughter-shock'. Being held at gunpoint had caused her
body to be flooded with adrenaline, her pupils to dilate and
for her to now be as high as a kite.

Sian cracked open another mini-bottle of prosecco and
swigged at it hard. 'Bloody hell, it's good to be alive!'

'Well remember that the next time you moan about
Mac's personal hygiene,' Ruth said with a smile.

'My heart is still racing a bit.' Sian put her hand to her chest and then looked at Ruth with a grin and turned her chest towards her. 'Feel here.'

'I'm driving, you twit.' Ruth laughed, not sure what to make of the comment.

They slowed in traffic in High Town beside the IMO Car Wash – white lettering on a bright green background.

'Go in here,' Sian commanded a little hysterically and pointed. 'Come on.'

'What?'

'You do know that if you go in here, this car will magically go back to its original factory colour,' Sian explained with deep sarcasm.

'Cheeky bitch. It's not that bad.'

'Is that why someone's written "I wish my girlfriend was as dirty as this" on the back of the car?' Sian teased.

'Ha, ha, you're hilarious … Come on then.' Ruth pulled the car left and into the yellow-painted lane that led up to the car wash. The noise of the rollers and spraying water got louder.

A tall, muscular Polish man in his twenties, blue overalls rolled up past the elbow revealing tattoo sleeves, came over. Ruth handed him a five-pound note.

'Thank you,' he said in a thick accent. He smiled at them with his twinkly blue eyes as he waved the car forwards.

'Cute,' Sian said looking the man up and down as he walked away.

'Not my type.'

Sian looked Ruth directly in the eye. 'Oh, I know that, trust me.' They held their gaze for a second or two longer than they should have. Ruth could feel her pulse quicken.

Sian smirked, swigged back and finished the next prosecco mini. 'Boom.' She reached into the bag for another.

'Careful.'

'Sorry, Mum. I nearly died today. I need to embrace life.'

Ruth clicked her fingers and gestured to the bag. *If you can't beat them* ... Sian fished out a can of gin and tonic, cracked it open and handed it to her.

'Cheers,' Ruth said as they clinked their drinks.

'Earned it' by The Weekend came onto the radio and Sian immediately turned it up. 'I bloody love this. It's in *Fifty Shades*, isn't it?'

'Is it? No idea.'

'Oh, prefer your porn a bit harder, do you?'

'Of course.' Ruth's heart was now beating faster as she sipped her can quickly. Her head was swimming a bit.

Sian began to sing along to the song as Ruth followed the man's directions to line up her wheels so that her car would be pulled automatically into the car wash. Ruth joined in with a grin as they sang together.

The machine pulled the car forwards with a jolt that made them both jerk forwards.

They shared another look and laughed.

The car was pulled out of sight and under the huge, blue rollers that covered the windscreen and windows in soapy lather.

Sian looked over, the tension inside the car starting to heighten. 'How long do these things take?'

Ruth looked at her. 'I dunno. Five or six minutes, I guess.'

'Oh, so there's time.'

'Time for what?'

. . .

Sian leaned in and kissed Ruth softly on the lips. And then again, longer and harder. Ruth responded, putting her hand to Sian's face.

There was part of Ruth that was giddy, even over-whelmed. Was this really happening?

'Time for this ...'

Sian moved herself closer as they began a sensuous but urgent dance of tongue and lips. Her mouth latched on to Ruth's like there was nothing else she needed in the world.

Ruth's hands roamed over Sian's back and then down low on her hips, pressing down onto her inner thigh.

Then for a moment, they stopped for breath. They looked at each other, eyes sparkling with joy and sexual longing. Close enough to feel the heat of breath. Ruth swept a strand of hair from Sian's face.

'I want you,' Ruth gasped as her chest heaved up and then down.

'Like you wouldn't believe,' Sian whispered as they kissed again and the mechanical heaters descended and began to dry the drops of water from the windscreen.

Drake and Nick got down to the interview room to talk to Alwyn Fields just before seven. The dog in his back garden had been identified as Hector, the missing springer spaniel that belonged to Owen Ankers. It had been taken to a local Harlech vet where the embedded microchip it had implanted as a puppy had been read. This was then cross-referenced with the UK Pet Microchip Database.

Mac's description of Fields' reaction to being asked about the dog seemed extreme unless he was guilty of Owen Ankers' murder. Nick's closer examination of Fields' records, however, did give some clue as to why he might have reacted in such a way.

In the winter of 1985, 45 Commando were in Norway, protecting NATO's northern flank. While on a night out in Oslo, Fields had got into a bar brawl with American sailors and one was killed in a nearby alleyway beside Oslo Cathedral. Fields was found guilty in Norway of manslaughter and sentenced to fifteen years, which were to be served in Britain. After serving five, a local man, Jorgen Johannsen, finally admitted that he had in fact killed the sailor and Fields was released with an honourable discharge.

However, as Drake pointed out, Fields might well believe that this incident in Norway might count against him as well as giving him little faith in getting a fair trial. He had, after all, lost five years of his life for something he hadn't done.

As Nick sat down, Fields looked drawn and his skin was grey. He was lost in thought. His legal-aid solicitor, a young man in his thirties, short slightly spiked hair and glasses, sat beside him making notes.

Nick leant across and pressed the button to start the recording of the interview.

'Mr Fields, I do need to recaution you at this time. You are being charged with the abduction of a police officer and the threatening use of a firearm. We are also going to arrest you on suspicion of the murder of Owen Ankers,' Nick said calmly.

'Do you understand all that, Mr Fields?' Drake asked.

'Of course. I'm not daft, lad.' Fields sniffed and ran his hand over the stubble of his chin.

Nick and Drake had already played the hypothesis through on the way to the interview room. Alwyn Fields, a loner, watches Owen Ankers' homosexual lifestyle with growing anger. When he spots Owen on the beach, with what he assumes is a boyfriend, Fields decides to take his chance and attack them on the beach. Maybe he is thrown by the sight of Abi Mullen. Maybe the dog follows him back and he decides to keep it, not having the heart to kill it.

'Mr Fields, can you tell us why you had Owen Ankers' dog in your garden?' Drake asked him.

'I found him.' Fields sat back in his seat, looking conceited.

'Found him where?' Drake asked.

'He was scratching around the house. Seemed lost, see? So, I took him in. Thought I'd take him back when Ankers came home.'

'You told officers that you saw Owen Ankers with someone on the beach walking his dog,' Nick said.

'I assumed he was walking his dog,' Fields snapped.

Nick looked over at him. 'So being a dutiful neighbour, you took his dog in to look after it until his return?' His tone was sarcastic. Nick didn't think Fields had a charitable bone in his body.

'Yeah. What's wrong with that? Is that against the law?'

Drake flicked through his notes. 'Mr Fields, why did you lie about your whereabouts around five last Saturday afternoon?'

'I don't understand.' Fields shot his solicitor a look and they whispered for a moment. 'I was confused.'

Nick snorted. 'You were confused so you claimed to have walked to a shop that you have been banned from for the last year?'

Fields talked in a low voice with his solicitor again.

'Okay, I didn't go to the shop. It was hot and I had my windows open. I heard someone talking loudly. I thought they were arguing. I looked out and then I saw Owen and someone else walking towards the beach.'

'And were they the ones that were arguing?'

'I dunno. They were on their way to the beach by the time I went outside.'

'And then what happened?' Drake asked.

Fields hesitated for a few seconds. 'I followed them. Eventually they were out of sight so I went home. About half an hour after that, I saw that the dog was outside his house.'

'You followed them?' Nick said with a frown. This was quite a departure from popping to the shop.

'Yeah. Just wanted to see what they was up to. What all the rowing was about.'

'You followed them down to the beach and then you stabbed and killed Owen Ankers. Is that right?' Nick asked.

'No, no. 'Course not.'

'You don't like homosexuals, do you, Mr Fields?' Drake asked.

Fields didn't answer and looked away to avoid Drake's eye contact.

Drake looked at his notes. 'Or "faggots" as you refer to them. You didn't like Owen Ankers flaunting his lifestyle across the road. That made you angry, didn't it? So, you thought you'd take matters into your own hands? Is that what happened?'

'No.' Fields' voice was now breaking a little. 'No …'

'You didn't go onto the beach last Saturday?' Nick asked.

Fields shook his head. 'No.'

'And when our forensic team go through your house, your clothes, your shoes, they're not going to find anything to link you to Owen Ankers?'

Fields hesitated, puffed his cheeks and sighed. 'No. I didn't know about any of this till it was on the news. I didn't have anything to do with it, all right? I knew there was something up when your lot arrived later but I didn't know what.'

Drake looked over at Nick.

'Sorry, "your lot"?' Drake asked, now confused. No one had been alerted to Owen Ankers' disappearance until the Monday, over forty-eight hours later.

'Yeah, coppers. Across the road, at the top of the path down to the beach.'

There was a moment as they took this in without wanting to alert Fields that they knew nothing about this.

'How did you know they were police officers, Mr Fields?' Drake asked.

'They were in a police car.'

'They were uniformed officers, were they?'

'One was. The other was in a shirt and tie. Guess he was plain clothes, you know, detective.'

Nick didn't like the sound of what Fields was describing. The pairing of a single uniformed officer with a CID detective was unusual. And as far as he knew, no one from CID had been at Harlech Beach that afternoon.

'Could you describe them for us, Mr Fields?'

'Bloody hell, don't you know what each other are doing? They were a few hundred yards away. Plain clothes bloke was middle-aged, bit stocky maybe. The other copper, the one in uniform, he was tall, young lad, like.'

'What were these officers doing?'

Fields snorted. 'They were checking the beach, weren't they? With their binoculars.'

The enormous Anglican church seemed out of proportion in the tiny rural village of Rhydmedre. The church dated back to the 1840s. It was also the meeting place for the Friday-night meeting of AA.

Nick had gone early to meet with his sponsor, Dundee Bill, and discuss why he was still 'in the shit'.

Bill was a tough-looking Scotsman in his late sixties, with decades of sobriety behind him. Well-built, handsome, with an air of don't-fuck-with-me. His main share told of street homelessness in North London in the 1970s, prison and fights. He had stopped drinking on 8th June 1977, the day after the Queen's Silver Jubilee, a date he would never forget. Last year he had been forty years sober.

Bill had already bollocked Nick on the phone. They now sat on an old wooden bench to the side of the church. It was time for Nick to listen and be told about where his thinking was going wrong, rather than relying on his own scrambled brain to make sense of the world.

The grass around the flowerbeds was beige and brown, and the leaves on the flowers looked parched. There was the humming of bumble bees and the laughter of children playing in a garden.

Bill's tone was no-nonsense and no bullshit. This was a killer illness.

'How are you doing, fella?' Bill asked with a wry smile. He had seen and heard it all before.

'Shit. Again.'

'AGAIN. WE'VE BEEN HERE BEFORE, NICK, YOU AND I.' BILL shrugged. 'Steps One and Two, you get. You know that once you start drinking, you can't stop. You're powerless? You're screwed.'

Nick nodded. 'Yeah. I have no control once I start.'

'That's right. And you know and accept that. And you also know that it's ruining your life. And you know that what is on offer at AA can save your life, am I right?'

Nick nodded and even though he had heard it before, he felt desperate and emotional. He swallowed back a wave of sadness that he feared would leave him crying.

'But when it comes to Step Three, you mess it up every time.'

'I know, I know. I'm sorry.'

'I'm not interested in apologies and self-pity. You cannot recover from alcoholism on your own, with no help or guidance. So, when are you going to get the idea that you don't know what you're doing? Do you know how many drunks I've had tell me they can "beat this thing" or they'll "take it seriously this time"? Dozens. And do you know where the ones that never got past that point are now?'

Nick nodded and pointed out to the graveyard they were sitting in that now took on a more powerful poignancy.

'Yeah, exactly right. They all ended up in a box, in a place like this.' A moment as Nick took this in and looked at the ground. 'You have tried to do this on your own on too many occasions. And how has that gone for you? Shit, right? You're in the shit right now. It's not going to change.'

Nick's previous sponsor, Tony, had been far more compassionate and kinder to him. But Nick had just used that to lie and manipulate their relationship. He needed some tough love but it was hard to hear and added to his current feeling of self-loathing.

Bill wasn't for stopping yet. 'Addiction is lonely. Get to the meetings, I've told you that. You need to make connections with people in AA. Talk to them. Talk about how you feel. It's about fellowship. Because I tell you what, there is a lot of love in these rooms. There is a lot of hope and compassion in the rooms too. And if you cut yourself off from that by sitting on the outside with your pride and your ego, you're not going to recover. Never, Nick. And you'll die, plain and simple.'

'I want what's on offer so much. But then something seems to stop me, I press the fuck-it button and I'm back to square one,' Nick said miserably.

Bill stabbed his forefinger in the direction of Nick's forehead. 'This. This is what stops you. Your head is a mess and it will con you. That's why I'm your sponsor. You run stuff past me because at the moment, your first thought might often be wrong. You said your last relapse was triggered by being with a dying man. I'm not saying that's an easy thing to go through. It isn't. But there are thousands of people out there who go through awful and traumatic things in their jobs and in their lives, and they don't go on a three-month alcoholic bender. My wife, Brenda, is a midwife. She's seen still-births, full-term births of dead babies, mothers dying in childbirth. And you know what she does? She comes home, has a large glass of wine and a fag on the patio. She puts the rest of the wine in the fridge. Doesn't touch it for a day, a week, whatever. It's your alcoholic brain that tricks you into thinking you've had a traumatic day and so you deserve to drink to black out. And as an alcoholic, that's insanity.'

Nick nodded. 'I know.'

Bill put his arm on his shoulder. 'Just pick up the sodding phone, Nick. Ask for help. Put your pride and ego to one side.'

Nick nodded again. 'I will do.'

'Good. I do not want to come to your funeral.'

They sat in silence.

Nick sat forwards. 'My dad came to the Monday-night meeting this week.'

'Yeah, I heard. It's been a long while since I've seen Rhys at a meeting.'

'I didn't know he'd ever been.' Nick frowned.

'Yeah. He was in and out of the rooms for a bit. Talking twenty years ago mind.'

Nick was a little taken aback by this revelation. He had no idea that his father had ever been to an AA meeting. For some reason, it annoyed him.

'This thing with your father, it's not good you know. It'll eat you up.'

'He was a bastard. When my mum died, he didn't give a toss.'

'And you're still carrying all that around like a rucksack of bricks on your back. You need to let it go.'

'I can't just forgive him.'

'Why not?' Bill looked at Nick who had no answer. 'Tell you what you're going to do. You're going to pray for your father.'

'What? No bloody way!'

'You'll pray for him every night, to whatever your higher power is, and then you'll text or ring me to say that you've done it,' Bill said sternly.

'I can't do that,' Nick muttered.

'You want my help or not?' Bill asked angrily.

Nick desperately wanted Bill's help and however much it angered him, he would take his advice.

'You still don't get it, Nick. You're not praying for your father because it will help him. You're praying for your father because it will help you.'

Nick nodded. He knew what he was being told made sense. He just had to do it.

Libby and Abi Mullen had been on the ferry for about an hour. They were sitting at a corner table in the ferry bar with two lads from Dublin who were plying them with drinks.

Libby wasn't happy. Abs was acting like a little bitch and being her usual quiet, stammering self. She was an embarrassment sometimes. Sod her, *Libby thought. She was getting nicely smashed for free and both lads were good-looking. Jet-black hair, blue eyes and soft accents. She might shag one of them later in their car on the car deck below. They were giving her and Abi a lift to Dublin and Libby knew exactly how to repay free drinks and a free car ride. It was nothing to her.*

'Here you go, ladies,' the taller lad said as he brought over a round of drinks. Pints for the boys and large vodkas for the girls.

'Cheers, boys,' Libby said clinking their glasses.

'Thanks,' Abi mumbled into her glass.

'Don't mind her. She takes a while to warm up. But when she does, bloody hell, all bets are off like …' Libby said loudly. She didn't care that people at the table next to them looked over. Sod them.

The boys laughed as they swigged back their beers.

'You're eighteen then?' the smaller lad asked.

'Why? Don't I look it?' Libby said, taking mock offence.

'Hey, as long as you're sixteen, I'm not fussed,' the tall lad said, flirtatiously raising an eyebrow.

Libby hit his arm playfully. 'You cheeky bastard. We're not like that, are we, Abs?'

Abi smiled and shook her head. 'I'm not.'

The two lads roared with laughter as Libby's eyes widened.

'What does dat mean, Abs?' Libby said but she liked the attention, the booze, the flirting and the laughter. It beat double science at that shitty school they had sent them to in Llandudno.

'Oh, I think we know what Abi means,' the small one laughed.

'Feckin' saying that about your own sister,' Libby said, grinning as she swigged her drink hard. The room was going a bit fuzzy.

'So if you're twins, why do you sound like a Scouser, and she sounds Welsh?' the tall lad asked.

'When we was little, we had to go to two different foster families. Got split up, you know. I ended up in Liverpool, Abs was in Mold, weren't you, kid?'

'Yeah.'

'Then we ran away and they put us both in the same care home,' Libby explained.

'Christ, I can't believe they split you up in the first place,' the smaller boy said.

'So, bit of a holiday is it, ladies? See the sights of Dublin?' the tall one said trying to lighten the mood.

'Actually we've got some work out there, so we're staying there for a while,' Libby said and then regretted it. Abi said nothing but her face was telling a different story.

'Christ, we'd better warn Dublin that you're coming then!'

They all laughed.

'Well, ladies, we're off for a slash, get some ciggies and we'll be back in a minute,' the taller lad said as they got up from the table.

The smaller lad pointed at them. 'You two beautiful girls don't go anywhere, okay? Promise?'

'Promise,' Libby said with a flirty grin.

As soon as they had gone out of earshot, Libby saw Abi turn to her and glare.

'You … said … we w-w-were going for a couple of days,' Abi protested.

'You want to go back to Llandudno?' Libby asked.

'I don't want to live in Dublin, Libs. We're f-fifteen years old!' Abi said getting upset.

'Well it's settled. I've got us jobs, a place to stay. It's all sorted,' Libby said. She was getting angry at her sister's selfishness.

'I-I'm not staying …' Abi said taking a breath.

'What? What does that mean? We'll be free in Dublin. No one knows who we are.'

'I'll g-get the first ferry back. And I'll tell everyone where you are. They'll come and get you back—' Abi said, tears in her eyes.

'Don't be a little bitch, Abi. You'll ruin everything,' Libby said as she stood up. 'I'll get us another drink. Maybe that will make you see sense!'

She wasn't going to allow her sister to dictate how she lived the rest of her life.

Chapter Fourteen

By nine thirty, Ruth had already completed the morning briefing. She was keeping the information about the two unidentified police officers at Harlech Beach to herself while it was being investigated. Fields didn't seem to have anything to gain by lying about what he had seen, and that was worrying.

Having checked with the duty log and the CAD operators, Ruth was confident that she knew of all police activities in and around Harlech. CAD stood for Computer-aided Dispatch and the operators knew where every uniform and CID officer was at any time of the day.

Nothing matched. No one from CID or uniform had been asked to carry out surveillance on Harlech Beach, let alone last Saturday. She had even checked with private security firms in the area. Given the timing and the delay in the discovery of Owen Ankers' body, Ruth had to conclude that the police officers that Fields saw were somehow connected to the murder. The very idea made her feel sick to her stomach, but Nick agreed that they needed to keep this to themselves.

With fifteen minutes spare before her next meeting, Ruth decided to do some surreptitious digging of her own. She wanted to know more about Kessler. She had already put out some feelers to old contacts in Interpol. Jurgen Kessler had a couple of sexual harassment allegations from his time at the London School of Economics, which he attended in 1996. Unfortunately, it was something Ruth had seen in sexual predators before. The escalation of violence. Sexual harassment, assault, rape and then some-times murder. It sent a shiver down her spine. She wanted to know how someone like Kessler could have vanished off the face of the earth for two years. Had there been any sightings? Had there been any unsolved attacks on women?

Ruth grabbed a coffee and a ciggie before making her way over to the Tech Crime Unit – or as it was now called, *Digital Forensics*. It was mainly staffed by casually dressed civilians. With its modern and airy decor, chrome chairs, dark-grey carpets, and state-of-the-art monitors and computers, Ruth thought it looked like a business hotel.

Ruth peered over a bank of powerful Apple computers as Anthony Cahill, known as 'Tech Tony', thirties, jeans and old school trainers, was explaining to her the prefer-ence for Macs over PC. With sex crimes, Macs allowed them to preview for pics quicker than disassembling a machine, pulling the hard drive out and then using a true forensic tool to find out what's there. Ruth didn't really care but Tech Tony was invaluable and she needed to keep him onside. She knew Cahill from a couple of cases she had worked. He was amiable, funny and just this side of camp. He had, as she remembered from the sitcom *Friends*, 'a quality'. She supposed that was totally politically incor-rect and Tech Tony should be referred to as 'gender fluid' or something like that.

Nick and Merringer had been in the Digital Forensics

Unit all day sifting through data. The first thing that the team had done was a backwards plot on Owen Ankers' movements and phone calls in the past ten days to see if there were any unusual patterns. As far as Merringer was concerned, there weren't any, but he would let Ruth have a look.

She was keen to see what had been found on Owen Ankers' mobile phone. They had his contacts, chats – Facebook, Twitter, WhatsApp, instant message, MMS – call logs, calendar, cell towers, passwords, unlock pattern, device locations, wireless networks. They also had access to thousands of deleted items including browsing history, photos and even messages shared in the Signal app, which could give information on end-to-end encryption.

Cahill looked up at them and explained. 'What we've done is looped in and on it with all the phone companies. We've now got the cell-site analysis back as well. And we're checking for geo-mapping too.'

'That's good. Great.' Ruth nodded, completely lost by what he had just said.

'You don't know what that means do you?' Anthony leant back on his swivel chair and smiled.

'Not a clue, Einstein,' Ruth admitted with a grin and looked in Merringer's direction. 'Luke, anything Earth shattering?'

'Sort of, boss. The first, most obvious thing we found on the victim's phone was a series of messages from Abi Mullen via WhatsApp.' Luke's tone suggested that there was something untoward about them.

'We know they had some contact from our interview with Abi,' Ruth said – it wasn't a surprise.

'But the content of them is weird,' Merringer said as he hunted through the pages that he had printed out.

'Define "weird", Luke.' Ruth frowned.

'Over-familiar. Look …' Merringer flicked through the print-out of Owen Ankers' text messages before handing them to Ruth.

I'VE LEFT A LONG MESSAGE ON YOUR PHONE BUT YOU HAVEN'T got back to me. Why not? Can you message me to say you've got it? A x.

HI. YEAH, GOT YOUR MESSAGE. I DID SAY I WAS GOING TO London for a few days. You ok? X

YEAH. SORRY. MY HEAD'S ALL OVER THE PLACE AT THE moment. It means a lot to me when you message, that's all. A x

LUKE POINTED TO THE LAST MESSAGE IN THE conversation, later that day sent by Owen: *Of course. I need a bit of time. I've got to talk to Beth at some point and that's not going to be easy X.*

Ruth thought out loud as she sat forwards on her swivel chair. 'That definitely doesn't sound like they just met through a charity foundation and the Prince's Trust.'

'Was he shagging her?' Nick asked, pulling a questioning face.

'Delicately put, Nicholas,' Ruth groaned, rolling her eyes at him. He rarely gilded his thoughts but at least he wasn't as vulgar as Mac.

'You should be grateful I didn't ask if he was knocking the back out of her.'

. . .

'Lovely, Nick ... I just can't put the two of them together,' Ruth said.

'I've dealt with stranger matches,' Nick recounted. 'Seventeen-year-old boy and a seventy-five-year-old piano teacher. Caught them going at it on a garden swing seat. Took me a while to get over that mental image, I can tell you.'

Merringer looked up. 'Boss, I also did some digging into Owen Ankers' financial affairs. He deposited ten thousand pounds into Abi Mullen's bank account two weeks ago.'

The others now shared a look. Abi hadn't mentioned anything about Owen Ankers giving her money. Why?

'Really? What the bloody hell's that about?' Nick asked.

'We also discovered a series of far more threatening texts that Owen had deleted. They are all within the last ten weeks and they're all anonymous,' Merringer said as he began to read: '"You're a selfish bastard, Owen. You'll get what's coming to you", or "Ignore what I've asked you to do and you'll regret it." Stuff like that.'

'Did he reply to them?' Ruth asked.

'No. Just deleted them. It's all in there, boss.'

It seemed that whoever had sent the texts was their prime suspect.

'Any leads on tracking down who sent them?' Ruth asked.

'Definitely sent from a burner,' Merringer explained.

Many criminals used disposable pay-as-you-go mobile

phones or 'burners' because they were confident they could never be traced.

'But these lovely guys here' – Merringer gestured to the Techs working around the room – 'got the IMEI code from Owen Ankers' phone.'

Nick nodded and said, 'Nice one.'

EVERY MOBILE PHONE IN THE UK HAS A UNIQUE FIFTEEN-digit code, called an IMEI number. You could use it to unlock your device to use with other networks, or for some insurance policies. An IMEI code could be found by entering '*#06#' on the phone's call screen. More importantly, it could give you previous owners if they had been registered.

'Gotta love a digital forensic geek.' Ruth grinned. Cahill gave her the middle finger with a grin.

Nick's mind was already running away. He was still convinced that Owen Ankers had been killed by one of Curtis Blake's gang. These texts could have easily been sent by Callum Webb as a way of warning him or bullying him to take the deal that Blake was offering them. From the texts, it would appear that Owen wasn't ready to work with a violent Scouse gangster. Owen was a very rich man so why would he risk all that?

'Bad news. There is no history or details of the owner of that IMEI code. The phone has either been destroyed or the battery taken out so we can't trace its location,' Cahill explained.

'Bollocks. Could be Callum Webb from the content of the texts?' Nick ventured.

Ruth nodded. 'That would make sense.'

. . .

'OUR CELL-SITE ANALYSIS CAN TELL US WHEN AND WHERE the phone was used. Its transmitter can be seen by two or more base stations at the same time, signal levels plus time delays allow for a relatively precise positioning of the phone.'

Merringer brought up a map of North Wales and north-west England on a large screen on the wall and walked over. 'The phone and its SIM card have only been used seven times. Twice in Liverpool, here and here.'

Nick's ears pricked up. 'Where is that?'

'BOOTLE AND KNOWSLEY. PRIVATE HOUSES WE THINK.'

Nick zipped around the map of Liverpool in his head. Knowsley was a stone's throw across the M57 from Croxteth, which was Curtis Blake's hunting ground. *Bingo.*

Merringer continued to point to the map. 'Twice in Rhyl, up here on the coast.' He moved his finger down the map. 'Once in Harlech, five days before Owen Ankers was murdered. And then over here, twice in Llancastell. One in the shopping centre. And then this one.'

Ruth looked at where Merringer was pointing. 'So where's that one?'

'That's the thing, boss. That's here. That location is Llancastell Police Station.'

NICK HAD BEEN SUMMONED TO DRAKE'S OFFICE AGAIN. Beforehand, he had made his way swiftly to the toilets where he had swigged down two inches of vodka to get back to the kind of blood alcohol level that made him feel normal. Nick knew he needed to be on top form as it was likely that there had been developments in the ongoing Titan operation. The vodka had given him a much needed boost, and he began chewing gum to hide the smell. There wasn't much he could do about it seeping out in his sweat in the growing heat of the day.

As Nick arrived at Drake's office, he saw that Choudry and Ryan were already there, poring over files, photos and some surveillance footage. Even though he knew that he was only a DS, it still bothered him that he hadn't been in on the meeting from the start.

As he came in, Choudry looked up and gave him a nod. Ryan gave him half a look and no acknowledgement. *Fuck her*, Nick thought to himself, in both senses of the word. He checked out her left hand again. Definitely no ring, but she had the air of someone who had been married, maybe even a couple of times. No kids though, Nick guessed. She wasn't the nurturing kind.

'Nick, we've had a development in Operation Titan,' Drake explained coming towards him. 'Come and sit down.'

Nick went over to a computer screen, which was showing surveillance footage that was marked *Deeside truck stop – 22.59.* There were around fifteen enormous articulated lorries parked up in the bays of the park. Deeside was an industrial area of Flintshire on the Wales-England borders.

'This footage was taken at the Deeside truck stop at twenty-three hundred hours the night before last,' Drake said.

As the footage and time-code rolled on, a white BMW X6 parked up and the tall man that Nick now knew was Callum Webb got out. A moment later, Curtis Blake's black Range Rover Evoque SD4 pulled in. Blake clambered out the back and another man got out of the passenger side.

'Because this footage is clear and relatively close, we

passed it on to a company we use that have professional lip readers. They've supplied us with a transcript of what Blake and Webb talk about.' Choudry indicated a typed document which he opened on the screen. 'I won't read it all. But Blake does say "Now our friend's out of the way, we can get the stuff moving with no hassle, all right, Cal?" Webb tells him: "Yeah. The police were sniffing around but I assume it was just routine." Then Blake tells him: "Don't worry about that, la. Our fella on the inside will let us know if there's any sniff from those 'jack cunts'. Osprey got it sorted, okay?" At this point, Webb laughs.'

'Hilarious,' Nick muttered sardonically.

'And very worrying.' Drake looked at Choudry and Ryan. 'Nothing yet on the identity of this "Osprey"?'

'No, sir. The only thing we know is that he is a serving police officer,' Ryan replied.

'Blake and Webb then confirm that if all goes well, the first shipment using Ankers & Webb vans would start on Saturday the sixth of August. But we don't have any details. They have a fleet of around seventy commercial vans serving our target area.'

Nick looked disappointed. 'So it's essentially a needle in a haystack.'

IT WAS EARLY EVENING, AND THE SUN WAS BEGINNING TO set. It poured an orange glow through Ruth's open bedroom window. From outside, the sound of wood pigeons nearby, and further away children playing, laughing and someone cutting their grass.

Ruth and Sian were breathless in bed, a white sheet draped across their legs. Ruth rolled over and reached for her cigarettes.

'I thought they only did that in films?' Sian said teasingly.

'Want one?' Ruth asked.

'No, I like my arteries the way they are.' Sian smiled. 'Oh, go on then.'

Sian took a cigarette and Ruth lit it. They lay in each other's arms and for the first time in years, Ruth felt a little inner peace. She clicked the remote for her Bluetooth speaker and 'God Is A Woman' by Arianna Grande started to play.

'Bloody feminist,' Sian said with a half-laugh.

'It's not feminist. It's just about a woman being brilliant at sex. She's so good at sex that "You'll believe God is a woman".'

'Okay. So, does that make you a God then?' Sian smiled.

Ruth pulled her a little closer. 'I don't know, does it?'

'Fishing?' Sian jabbed her gently in the ribs.

'Me? Never.'

They lay, their breathing synchronised, their minds clear and connected in every way.

After a while, Ruth turned and leant her head on her elbow. 'When did you know you were gay?'

Sian thought for a moment. 'I think it was when I saw Madonna at Wembley in about 1992. I just fell in love with her … You?'

'I dunno. I fancied John Taylor from Duran Duran and Madonna, so that was all a bit confusing,' Ruth explained.

'And you got married and had a daughter,' Sian said, raising her eyebrow with a knowing smile.

'Yeah. What was that about?' Ruth asked, feeling a little embarrassed.

'I remember my dad going mental,' Sian explained. 'Actually, he didn't go mental, he just didn't talk to me.'

'How long for?' Ruth asked, seeing that Sian was feeling a little emotional.

'Years ... and then he died before we ever had a conversation about it,' Sian explained taking a breath.

'I'm sorry. That must be hard?' Ruth said.

'Different generation, I suppose,' Sian said with a shrug. 'Sorry, I didn't want to do the whole let's-share-our-sad-stories thing tonight.'

'Hey, I haven't even started on my sad stories. They go on forever,' Ruth said with a kind smile.

They lay back in a blissful, comfortable silence.

Chapter Fifteen

R uth sat opposite Abi Mullen and her legal-aid solicitor. Nick reached over and pressed record on the tape.

'Interview: Llancastell Police Station. Present in the room are DI Hunter, DS Evans, Abi Mullen and duty solicitor, Kate Trigg,' Nick said.

Ruth took a moment so Abi could settle herself as she looked very agitated. They needed to get the truth about her relationship with Owen, but they also needed to tread carefully.

'Abi, we would like to go through a few things that you told us in your last interview. Is that okay?' Ruth asked quietly.

Abi didn't make eye contact as she jigged her legs nervously and nodded almost imperceptibly. *God, she really is fragile,* Ruth thought to herself.

'For the purposes of the tape, Abi Mullen has confirmed that she understands the purpose of today's interview,' Nick said.

'You confirmed that David Sabatini was your boyfriend, is that right?'

Abi nodded and then looked up slowly. 'Yes, miss.'

'You took him out of the university hospital but someone came to pick him up early the next morning?' Ruth asked.

Abi nodded again. 'Yeah. I was still asleep.'

'Have you had any contact with David Sabatini since then?'

'No. Nothing … I swear…'

'David Sabatini's bank card was used at an ATM in Glasgow two days ago. Do you know if that's where he might be?' Nick said, looking at his notes.

'Sorry … I dunno. I'd tell you if I did, like.'

Ruth flicked through her own notes. 'If I remember correctly, you said you met Owen Ankers after he gave a speech at your college? Is that correct?'

'Yeah …' Abi's voice was virtually a whisper.

'He was speaking to students because he ran a charitable foundation and worked as a mentor with the Prince's Trust. Is that right?' Ruth continued reading from her notes.

'Yeah … that's, that's how I knew him, miss.' Abi was relaxing a little.

Ruth gave Abi a smile. She wasn't going to correct her endearing use of the word *miss*.

'And you exchanged a few text messages? Owen suggested he might help you finance your HND course?' Ruth asked.

'Yes …'

'And then he suggested you come and meet him for coffee and a chat to see how he might help you?'

'Yeah. That's what happened.' Abi made eye contact with Ruth for the first time. She wanted to be believed.

'Abi, can I read you some exchanges that we have downloaded from Owen's phone?' Ruth asked.

Abi didn't respond, but she shifted noticeably in her seat and looked down at the floor. It was clear she did not want to hear her texts.

Ruth flicked through the print-out. 'Here we go. So this is a message from you to Owen on the twentieth of July at around eight in the morning. "I've left a long message on your phone but you haven't got back to me. Why not? Can you message me to say you've got it? A x." And then Owen messages you back: "Hi. Yeah, got your message. I did say I was going to London for a few days. You ok? X." You reply later that day at eighteen hundred hours: "Yeah. Sorry. My head's all over the place at the moment. It means a lot to me when you message, that's all. A x." Could you tell us about those texts please, Abi?'

Abi went from biting her nails to rubbing her hands on her trousers. Her breathing was becoming shallow as if she was panicking.

Ruth noticed and smiled at her. 'It's okay, Abi. Whatever it is, please, just tell us the truth.'

'We were just friends. That's all. You're making it sound weird,' Abi said as she started to sound upset.

'Abi, I need to read you another text please.'

The legal-aid solicitor glanced at Ruth. 'I think my client needs a break.'

Nick leaned forward and said quietly, 'She can have a break in five minutes. Okay?'

Ruth spoke as though talking to a child. 'Abi, this is the text Owen sent you that evening: "Of course. I need a bit of time. I've got to talk to Beth at some point and that's not going to be easy. X." Please be honest with us. What did Owen need to tell Beth?'

'I dunno. I didn't know … know what he meant.'

Nick looked over at her. 'Abi, we know Owen transferred ten thousand pounds into your bank account on the twenty-fourth of July. Can you tell us what that was for?'

'For my course.'

Ruth waited a moment as the pressure built. 'Abi, we've checked. The course fees for an HND in hair and beauty are two thousand five hundred pounds.'

Abi was now desperate. She started to sit upright in her chair.

'Abi, were you having a relationship with Owen? Were you sleeping with him?' Ruth asked aware that the pressure of the interview was building.

Abi's arms stiffened. 'No, no. Don't be disgusting.'

'Then what? Tell us. Because these texts don't make any sense, do they?'

'IF YOU WERE HAVING A RELATIONSHIP WITH OWEN, YOU need to tell us, Abi,' Nick said.

Her eyes narrowed for a moment as though she was trying to focus on an object behind them. 'He's my dad. Owen was my dad, okay?'

'I don't understand.' Ruth frowned. Wow, she wasn't expecting that.

'My biological father. I tracked him down …' Abi continued to stare at something behind them so much so that Nick and Ruth looked around. There was nothing there. And then Abi's eyes glazed slightly. She looked up and sat back in her chair.

'Abi?' Ruth said with concern.

There was nothing. Abi didn't seem aware of anything around her. It was as if she had fallen into a trance.

The solicitor put her hand on Abi's arm. 'Abi, are you all right?'

There was no response for a good five seconds and then Abi began to blink and look around at everyone.

'Sorry … sorry …' Abi mumbled looking thoroughly confused.

'Abi?' Ruth asked in a worried voice.

'I just …' Abi blinked. 'Did you ask me a question?'

IT WAS NOW THREE DAYS SINCE OWEN ANKERS' MURDER and as Ruth made her way along the corridor, she couldn't help but think about Abi Mullen. She had had a shitty, horrible life. Abandoned by both parents, abused in foster care and with ongoing psychological damage. And then when she finds and reconnects with her birth father, and there is a glimmer of something good in her life, he is brutally murdered in front of her.

Ruth sighed as she sat down and took a sip from her flat white. It was still too hot. Earlier that morning, she had woken next to Sian and for a good two minutes in half-sleep believed that she was next to Sarah. She even thought she had muttered Sarah's name under her breath but she wasn't sure if that was a dream or not.

The burgeoning relationship with Sian was lovely, exciting and thrilling, as any good relationship should be in that honeymoon period. But the ghost of Sarah wandered through her thoughts and she suspected that Sian knew that. The subject had been broached very tentatively, but it still felt like the proverbial elephant in the room.

Sitting back on her high-backed office chair, Ruth absorbed the peace of the office while it was still empty and smelling clean and freshly hoovered. She stared at the carpet, lost in thought as the early morning light was split by the long vertical window frame.

There was a buzz from her phone and she saw that

Nick had sent her a text with an attachment from the *Llangollen Leader*:

ANKERS' KILLER HAS STRUCK BEFORE!

Daniel Warburton, Lyn Povall and now Owen Ankers – how three horrific murders could be linked to one coastal path in West Wales and possibly one killer.

As North Wales detectives launch an appeal today into the murder of a Welsh businessman, Owen Ankers, who was stabbed to death on Harlech Beach last Saturday, a retired detective says he believes his murder could be linked to two unsolved stabbings, including the death of Barmouth schoolboy Daniel Warburton. The fourteen-year-old was brutally murdered in 1996 while dog-walking on the coastal path close to Shell Island, only five miles from the site of Owen Ankers' murder. Three years later in 1999, mother of three Lyn Povall was also stabbed to death on the beach at Borth-y-Gest while walking her dog, around four miles north of Harlech.

The retired detective believes there are too many similarities between these unsolved murders for it to be a coincidence. They were all viciously stabbed to death while dog-walking in isolated areas within a ten-mile stretch of the same coastline.

Four years ago, police revealed that thanks to modern DNA testing they had a partial match to Lyn Povall's murderer. There was an appeal for anybody with suspicions to come forward. Two years ago, they launched a twenty-year anniversary appeal to find Daniel Warburton's killer. To date, both murders remain unsolved.

North Wales CID haven't officially linked the three cases at this stage.

As Ruth came out of the office an hour later, she saw that Drake was pinning photographs of Owen Ankers' bloated blue body to the incident board next to the image of him smiling on the beach. An uneasy silence fell across CID. There were some DCIs, in the modern era, who believed that such photos should be kept in the files and out of sight. They believed that the constant images of the dead created a difficult working environment. There was also the possibility of someone being questioned or even a relative seeing them, although that was unlikely.

However, Drake was from the old school of detective thinking. He wanted everyone that worked on the case to understand what had happened to Owen Ankers. He was an innocent man who had helped and supported his community and raised thousands of pounds for those less fortunate than himself. He wanted everyone to remember that they needed to do their best work for Owen Ankers and his family. Getting his family justice and some semblance of closure was paramount, and so they needed to find the person who killed him. The photos were there as a stark reminder of what had been done to him and their duty to him.

Gathering up her files, Ruth walked to the front of Incident Room One. 'Okay, morning, everyone. We've got a lot to get through this morning, so if we can get going, please? DCI Drake has something to say to you first.'

The room quietened as Drake looked out at the CID team.

'Thanks, Ruth. As you know, we had a serious incident yesterday involving one of our team. It's good to see you here this morning, Sian, safe and sound. But if you need time off, you come and find me,' Drake said. Ruth knew that he meant it and she had told Sian the same thing earlier that morning.

'I'm fine, boss. But thank you,' Sian said, looking awkward at having the attention of the whole room.

Drake put his right hand in his pocket. 'Guys, I just

want us to remember that we do put our lives on the line in this job. Sometimes it's easy to forget that. But it only takes a split second for that to change and I think yesterday was a timely reminder that we need to be careful out there and watch each other's backs. So have a productive and a safe day.'

Drake looked at Ruth to indicate that he had finished and turned to leave the room.

Picking up a copy of a newspaper, Ruth said, 'Right. If you haven't seen the *Leader* already, there is an article that alleges that there might be a link between Ankers' murder and two unsolved historic murder cases in the same area. We've been swamped this morning with phone calls and the media desk down at St Asaph has been inundated. We will have to hold a press conference this morning just so we can keep control of the story.' She couldn't hide the fact that she was fuming that an ex-police officer had deemed it okay to give his theories to the press before coming to them.

'Is there anything in the story, boss?' Mac asked as he loosened his tie.

'No, Mac. As far as I'm concerned, Owen Ankers was targeted and murdered by someone who knew him. The idea that someone, who had committed two murders decades ago, has reappeared and murdered Ankers in a motiveless attack doesn't seem likely,' Ruth explained.

'So our focus is on the current suspects and lines of enquiry?' Nick asked.

'Yes. However, Sian and Mac, I do need you to dig out these old case files and speak to this …'

'Ian Sayle. Retired DS,' Sian said.

'I don't know what ex-DS Sayle is doing. Maybe he's bored and wants a bit of attention. I just need to know the details of the previous cases so we've covered ourselves.'

The briefing continued as the team ran through the various lines of enquiry around Owen Ankers' murder. Ruth knew that Nick was frustrated that what he thought the most likely line of enquiry – Webb and Blake protecting their drugs trafficking – couldn't be discussed within the room because of the fears that there was a corrupt officer on Blake's payroll somewhere in the investigation.

Ruth explained that other lines of enquiry needed following. Elimination was the backbone of any decent investigation. However, Nick was desperate for Blake to be convicted and he was worried that their covert operation with Merseyside was under-resourced and understaffed due to the fears of a leak.

Ruth moved swiftly through their suspects and pointed to a photo of Fields on the incident board.

'Fields is now on remand since the siege. Except for having Owen Ankers' dog, there's little else concrete to tie him to the attack.'

'SOCO are in his house today, boss,' Merringer explained.

'Good. Let's see what they dig up.'

Sian looked over. 'Boss, Fields is a lonely old man who feels bitter at the world. But he doesn't seem like someone who would follow Owen Ankers to the beach and stab him in cold blood because he was homosexual.'

'This is a man who held you hostage with a shotgun!' Mac snorted. Sian bristled at Mac's comment.

'See what SOCO find today but I tend to think that Sian's instincts are right.'

RUTH SHOT SIAN A QUICK LOOK AS IF TO SAY, *GOOD WORK*. She smiled back. 'I want to know who the police officers are that Fields claims to have seen on the day of Owen Ankers' murder. It seems a strange story to have made up.'

'It doesn't make him any more or less guilty,' Nick said.

Merringer looked over. 'Boss, I've been through the duty roster for that day. There were no units from uniform or CID assigned to go to Harlech Beach for any reason.'

'Who were they and are they even police officers? Luke can you recheck the ANPR cameras on both routes to Harlech for that afternoon. Let's match all plates of any North Wales Police cars that afternoon.'

Merringer nodded. 'Boss.'

RUTH POINTED AT A PHOTO OF ABI MULLEN. 'WE'VE discovered that Owen Ankers is Abi Mullen's biological father.'

'Bloody hell,' Mac spluttered in a surprised tone.

'When he found out Abi's mother, Lynn Stevens, was pregnant, Owen wanted nothing to do with them. Abi, and her sister Libby, were taken into care in 2001 and then went to a foster family.'

'Does she blame Owen for abandoning her? Is that motive?' Mac asked.

'Not according to Abi. She had made contact on her eighteenth birthday through the UK Adoption Contact Register. Owen responded, and they met up for the first time three months ago. He gave her some money to help her out. From the outside, it looks like their relationship was going well. Certainly, no clear motive for murder. In fact, it looked like Owen and Abi had been looking through old photos before they went on their walk … Any trace on the whereabouts of David Sabatini?'

Nick shook his head. 'No, boss. His cash card was used

in Glasgow but the CCTV from that was inconclusive. Otherwise, he seems to have vanished.'

Ruth gathered her things together. 'Okay, everyone. As the boss said earlier, have a safe day out there.'

It was nearly lunchtime when Ruth sat down at a white plastic table in the cafeteria at Llancastell. Having had a cigarette, she was drinking hot white coffee despite the heat. She hadn't slept well and needed some caffeine.

Ruth felt yet another guilty pang at the enjoyment she was getting from her relationship with Sian. However mad it sounded, she felt twinges of disloyalty towards Sarah. She was getting on with her life – new job, new home and now a new relationship. Was that okay? Would Sarah have done the same in her situation? Or was it a sign that Ruth was moving slowly towards the uncomfortable acceptance that Sarah might have gone forever? She drummed her fingers on her thigh as the weight of that thought circled.

'Mind if I sit down?'

Ruth was lurched out of deep thought and looked up. ACC Davenport was holding a bottle of mineral water. She was in shirtsleeves and her hair was scraped back.

Ruth indicated the seat opposite. 'Of course not, ma'am.'

Davenport sat down and let out a sigh – she was hot.

'How are you doing, ma'am?' Ruth asked.

'Okay. Grief is a strange thing, isn't it?' Davenport shifted slightly in her chair as she opened her water. Maybe she was being too open.

'Losing anyone close is difficult.' Ruth nodded, thinking how she wished for some kind of closure with Sarah. 'And in these circumstances, it's also such a shock.'

Davenport nodded and drank her water. Ruth noticed

a delicate silver crucifix hanging around Davenport's neck. It was identical to the one that the SOCO had found at Owen Ankers' house.

'I like your necklace,' Ruth said.

'Thank you. I've always worn one. I know it's silly, but I used to think that it would somehow protect me.'

'That doesn't sound silly at all. Actually, we found one just like that under a board on the decking at the house,' Ruth said. It was probably nothing, but she wanted to flag it up.

Davenport took a moment. 'I lost one a year or two ago. It's probably mine.'

'Could you have a look at it for us at some point?' Ruth asked, uncertain if the question had thrown Davenport. She seemed a bit flustered.

'Of course … I'm assuming you've seen the historic-crime story in the press this morning?' Davenport asked, trying to regain a more professional tone and change the subject.

'Yes. We've all seen it in CID,' Ruth said.

'What do you think? Anything in it?'

'Not sure. It seems like such a long time ago.'

'My thoughts precisely.' Davenport paused and considered her next comment. 'I don't want to step on any toes, but I really don't think any crime from twenty-five years ago is relevant to your investigation.'

'That's my feeling, ma'am.' Ruth was pleased that Davenport was on the same page.

'Good. I remember both the cases vaguely. When I first joined. I think I was still on probation.' Davenport smiled at the recollection.

'I didn't realise you had been in the North Wales Police before?'

'It's where I started. When did you join the force, Ruth?'

'1993,' Ruth said and got a flash of her first day on the force. Lavender Hill Police Station in Battersea. She was so scared and so incredibly young and naïve.

'Me too!' Davenport exclaimed with a grin, and for a moment Ruth saw behind the veneer of professionalism.

'Bit different in those days, eh? Christ, "Get me a cup of tea, Plonk."' Ruth shook her head.

'Those bloody skirts, shoes and hats. It was the dark ages.'

'And the tights! Don't forget the bloody tights!' Ruth chortled. 'How long were you in the force here?'

'Three years. Then the Met for a while. That's where you joined us from, isn't it?'

'I did twenty-five years in the Met.'

'That's impressive. I don't know how you survived. Where were you stationed?'

'South London mainly.'

'Ever come across DCI Terry Harrison?'

'Uncle Terry? Bloody hell.' Ruth laughed. 'He was my first guvnor at Lavender Hill. Funny as hell.'

Davenport chuckled. 'What did he used to say …?'

'*Deprehendo Deprehensio Vitum*,' Ruth and Davenport said in unison and laughed. 'Overtime solves crime!'

'Or he would say, "You have nothing to fear …"' Davenport recalled.

Ruth finished the saying. '"… Except fear itself."'

Davenport continued. 'And then he would say, "Except for that bastard coming at us with that hammer, of course!" It was always something like that.' Davenport shook her head and then looked at Ruth. 'We've done all right, Ruth, me and you.'

'For two dorises? Yeah, I suppose we have.'

'God, I haven't thought about those days for a while. We'll have to go for a drink sometime and reminisce about the old days.' Davenport took her bottle of water from the table and got up.

'Yeah, I'd like that.'

'Thanks, Ruth.'

Ruth watched as Davenport walked away. This was a very different side to the ACC and Ruth had warmed to her.

Chapter Sixteen

The operations room in the basement of Llancastell nick was buzzing with chatter as nearly forty uniformed and CID officers from both the North Wales and Merseyside Forces mingled. Nick had been told by Drake that there had been a significant development in Operation Titan. Merseyside CID had intercepted information that a delivery of drugs was coming that afternoon from Merseyside across to North Wales, heading for Rhyl, Porthmadog and Colwyn Bay. Nick's pulse quickened – he had never seen such a big briefing, nor experienced the palpable sense of tension and anticipation in the room. This was going to be huge.

Choudry came towards Nick and handed him the detailed briefing notes. 'You'll need these.'

'Thanks.' Nick began to flick through notes, maps and images of men from Blake's gang.

'You're in alpha-delta-three vehicle with DCI Drake,' Choudry told him.

Nick nodded and went over to take a seat next to Drake, who was looking at his phone.

'You all right, boss?' Nick said as he sat down.

Drake nodded and said, 'Yeah. Just checking exactly where we're going today. I'm still getting my bearings in North Wales.'

As Drake went to close his phone, Nick saw the screen-saver of two young girls.

'Are those your daughters?' Nick asked, hoping he wasn't crossing the line of appropriate conversation.

'Yeah, Jasmine and Ruby,' Drake said and smiled.

'They're beautiful. How old are they?' Nick asked, seeing how much joy the thought of them had brought to Drake.

'Jasmine is six, and Ruby is nine,' Drake said as he pointed to the photo.

'So you're outnumbered at home then?' Nick said with a grin.

'Completely.' Drake nodded with a smile.

The lights in the room had dimmed slightly and up on the wall a map of North Wales was projected. Three red routes and circles were marked on the map to indicate where each van would be travelling and then intercepted by members of the Armed Response Unit and detectives.

Chief Superintendent Andy Rourke from Merseyside Police came to the front of the room with purpose. The room began to fall silent. Rourke signalled with his hand for everyone to sit down. 'Okay, thank you ... As you know, Operation Titan is an ongoing investigation between the Merseyside and the North Wales Police Forces aimed at the detection and prevention of the county lines supply of drugs across the North West and North Wales.'

Rourke clicked the projector and an image of Curtis Blake appeared on the wall. Nick tensed a little.

'Many of you will be familiar with Curtis Blake. He is a known criminal from Liverpool and our primary target.

We have intelligence sources that indicate that large quantities of cocaine, heroin, ecstasy and crack cocaine will be leaving an unknown location in Merseyside at fifteen hundred hours today.'

The projector clicked again to show one of Ankers & Webb's delivery vans. 'The suspects will be using three of this type of van to transport the drugs.'

Another image showing three tough-looking men from surveillance photos appeared.

'These three men are part of Curtis Blake's criminal gang. Tony Bilkin, Steve Pennell and John Maloney. Each one of them is expected to be onboard one of the vans. They all have extensive records of extreme violence and they are expected to be armed. My opinion is that they should be designated as extremely dangerous.'

Nick started to feel anxious with both excitement and fear. His adrenaline pumped and his head cleared.

Rourke pointed to an authorised firearms officer, Gary Langton, who stood up briefly so that everyone could see him. 'Our senior AFO today is Inspector Langton. You will be operating out of six vehicles. Each vehicle will be positioned at the interception points indicated in your briefing notes. You will await Gold Command's orders before you intercept. Anything to add, Gary?'

Nick turned as Langton stood up again, dressed in his black, armoured firearms uniform. He was short and muscular with a goatee beard. He looked like he could handle himself.

Langton cleared his throat. 'I need all AFOs to sign the FFC paperwork on the legal use of force before you leave.'

Drake turned to Nick. 'Are you firearm trained, Nick?'

'No, boss.'

'Okay. Just be careful today, all right?' Drake said looking directly at him and with genuine concern.

The gravity of the operation hit Nick.

'Boss,' Nick replied with a nod of his head. He was tingling all over with fear and adrenaline.

Nick needed to get more alcohol in his system before the operation. He wasn't sure, once they started, when he would next have the chance to top up his blood alcohol level and he certainly didn't want to be having any withdrawal symptoms that afternoon.

Nick made his excuses, hurried to the toilets on the fifth floor, got into a cubicle and finished the vodka that he had in the jacket. His body relaxed, and he took a deep breath of relief. *Right, let's do this,* he thought to himself. *Let's get that bastard Blake and put him away for a long time.*

Full of energy and excitement, Nick came flying out of the toilet. As he turned, he nearly knocked Sian coming the other way.

'Where's the fire, Nick?'

'Sorry. In a bit of a rush.'

'Lots of unfamiliar faces around. Something to do with this Merseyside operation and Webb?'

Nick frowned. 'How the hell do you know about that?'

'You know what it's like in the department. Hard to keep secrets from anyone.'

Even though he could trust Sian, the intel was classified for a reason.

'I know, Nick. You could tell me but you'd then have to kill me, right?'

Nick laughed. 'Something like that. All I'll say is that as of tomorrow, I think we should be able to go after Webb properly.'

. . .

Nick turned to head back to the briefing and Sian watched him go.

Mac and Sian were heading west on the North Wales Expressway towards Rhyl-on-Sea. They were going to have a chat with Ian Sayle, the retired detective who had claimed that Owen Ankers' murder was linked to two historic cases. Sian wasn't impressed that an ex-copper had gone to the press before running his theories past the force first. What was that about? Maybe Sayle had some grievance against Llancastell CID? She had asked around and most of the old-timers remembered Sayle as a decent copper.

Pulling down the sun visor, Sian tried to block out the sun, which glared down at them. She was driving and Mac had insisted on having the AC belting out, so she was actually cold.

Mac had been his usual judgemental self all journey, picking holes in members of the department and generally being critical of the way the Owen Ankers case was being handled. She had heard it all and she put it down to the fact that Mac liked to have a moan about most things.

Mac looked down at his phone. 'How many kisses on a text?'

Sian shrugged. 'Depends. Who's it to?'

The thought of Mac sending anyone a text with kisses made her feel slightly queasy.

'There's this woman I've been sort of seeing,' Mac explained.

'I thought you were married,' Sian said in a surprised tone.

'Oh no. The wife moved out a few months ago,' Mac stated in a very matter-of-fact way.

Sian wasn't surprised. She didn't know how anyone could be married to Mac. *Imagine what he must look like naked,* she thought to herself. *Yuck!*

'Two kisses then. One isn't enough. Three is a bit needy. So two,' Sian informed him trying to get the mental image of a naked Mac out of her mind.

Mac nodded and went back to his phone. 'Thanks.'

Sian took a turning from the A55 and began to follow the signs for Rhyl-on-Sea, which was a small seaside resort just along the North Wales coastline from Colwyn Bay. It was named after the Welsh kingdom of Rhyl, which was established there in late Roman times and was part of the county of Gwynedd.

Sian remembered a story that her nain had told her as a girl about a Welsh prince, Madoc Owain Gwynedd, who had set sail for America in the twelfth century from Rhyl-on-Sea. Nain Thomas said that Prince Madoc had crossed the Atlantic and discovered the United States several hundred years before Christopher Columbus. Apparently, Prince Madoc had landed in what was now Mobile Bay in Alabama.

It was reported that the Welshman tracked up the Tennessee and Missouri rivers and encountered and even befriended local native Cherokee Americans. There were believed to be several stone forts, said by the local Cherokee tribes to have been constructed by 'White People' – they were the same design as Dolwyddelan Castle in North Wales.

By the eighteenth century, a Native American tribe called the Mandans was discovered that seemed different from any other. They lived in towns and permanent villages that were built on streets and squares. They spoke

a language remarkably similar to Welsh, fished from cora-
cles and grew white-haired when old. Nain Thomas said it
was typical of life that the Welsh had been forgotten in the
founding of the most powerful nation on earth.

Turning onto Llandudno Road, Sian noticed the small
detached houses that bordered the pavement.

Mac looked up from his mobile phone. 'What's the
score with Callum Webb?'

'How do you mean?' Sian asked.

'Come on. Why is Webb untouchable?'

'My guess is as good as yours, Mac,' Sian said sharply,
although instinctively she also suspected that they weren't
being told everything.

'Come on. You and DI Hunter are ... you know?' Mac
said with a knowing gesture.

Sian felt immediately defensive. Mac was such a prick!
She wasn't aware that anyone knew about her relationship
with Ruth. 'Don't know what you're on about. What I do
outside of the station is nothing to do with you, anyway.'

'All right, none of my business,' Mac laughed and put
his hands up in mock defensiveness.

'You're right, it's not. And I don't know anything,' Sian
snapped. She wanted to punch him in the face.

There was an awkward silence and Sian wondered who
would be the first to break it.

'Sorry ... come on, Sian. It's me. I just want to know
how viable Webb is as a suspect in this case, that's all.
We're working our balls off here ...'

'Or tits, thank you,' Sian said with a wry smile. She was
thankful to break the tension that had quickly developed in
the car.

Mac laughed. 'Or tits. It's hard to do this without the
full picture.'

'I really don't know much. Some big operation with

Merseyside Police today. They were all over the third floor in the station. I saw an AFO. Nick seems to think that we can have the full picture on Webb from tomorrow.'

Mac nodded. 'Okay. That would be helpful.' He pointed at a house and Sian pulled the car up outside.

Chapter Seventeen

R uth was running late when she arrived at the Child and Adolescent Mental Health Service, CAMHS, at the Paediatric Health Centre in the university hospital in Llancastell.

She knew that Abi Mullen had a history of mental health issues. If she was going to be a witness in any trial over Owen Ankers' death, then she needed to be assessed. Abi was already under the care of a clinical psychologist at the service, Dr Charles Maitland. There were standard guidelines that needed to be addressed by Maitland, the police and the CPS. Maitland needed to comment on Abi's credibility and reliability as a witness. He needed to explain the nature or extent of Abi's mental health condition and how that would affect understanding, perception or recollection of the incident. Maitland would also have to discuss with the CPS in particular about how Abi's mental health would affect her ability to give evidence and withstand cross-examination. Finally, Maitland would need to confirm and sign a disclosure test with regards to Abi in line with the Criminal Procedure and Investigations Act of 1996.

Ruth's preliminary meeting with Maitland was to discuss what Abi had told the police up to this point. Ruth also wanted to check that everything possible was being done to help Abi after what had been a horrific few days for her. Abi was only a few years younger than Ruth's own daughter and had had a horrendous life so far. Ruth wanted to know that there was support for Abi now that she had turned eighteen and was technically an adult.

Weaving her way through the corridors of CAMHS, Ruth couldn't help wondering what damage she had done to her daughter, Ella. First the break-up with Ella's father when she was only young. Being brought up first by Ruth as a single mum. Then as a teenager having to deal with having 'two mums' when Sarah moved in. Finally, Ella had had to deal with her own trauma with Sarah's disappearance, as well as supporting Ruth who had gone to pieces. How Ella ever passed her GCSEs, A-levels and got a place at university was a miracle and testament to her incredible resilience and maturity.

As Ruth rounded the corner, she spotted Abi sitting on some seats. She was curled up on the seat looking at her phone. She looked tired.

Ruth smiled as she approached. 'Hi, Abi.'

'Oh … hiya,' Abi replied and immediately looked awkward.

'Mind if I sit down here?' Ruth asked.

Abi shook her head almost imperceptibly.

'I spoke to your college and they told me that you've moved into student accommodation in town.'

'Yeah. Last night,' Abi answered, not looking up.

'That's good. What's it like?'

'Okay, yeah,' she mumbled.

Ruth remembered dropping Ella off at her halls of residence in Fairfield in Liverpool and crying on the drive back to London. However, she guessed that Ella had been glad to get away from the terrible cloud that had hung over Ruth since Sarah's disappearance.

'I'm going to have a quick chat with Dr Maitland. And then you're going to see him and he'll explain everything,' Ruth said, aware that she was starting to sound like she was talking to an infant.

'Okay.' Abi nodded and pursed her lip.

'I'm really sorry you've been through such a horrible experience, Abi. I'm going to do all I can to make sure that you're looked after and that you get any help or support you need, okay?' Ruth said kindly.

Abi nodded and at that moment, the receptionist looked over and caught Ruth's eye.

'Dr Maitland is ready to see you.'

Ruth went to put a reassuring hand on Abi's arm but she flinched suddenly, as if Ruth was about to hit her. *God, she really is damaged.*

'Sorry ...' Ruth murmured quietly, waited a moment and smiled. 'I'll see you soon, Abi. And remember, if there's anything you need, just give me a call.'

Abi looked up and, for a moment, she made direct eye contact with Ruth. It was the first time Abi had ever really looked at Ruth, and the power of that expression twisted and pulled at Ruth's insides, almost overwhelming her. It was an expression of loss, fragility and deep hurt. She just wanted to take her home and look after her.

Ruth took a breath and composed herself. She made her way over to Maitland's office, knocked and went in.

'Detective Inspector Hunter, is that right?' Maitland came over and shook her hand firmly. He had thick, greying hair and wore a chalk-striped navy suit.

'Hi there,' Ruth said with a smile.

'Please, have a seat.' Maitland's accent was cut glass and his voice soft.

After the preliminaries, Maitland looked down at Abi's file and began to tell Ruth about her life.

'I've got Abi's file so I'll go through the major events for you. Abi and her sister, Libby, were born in Liverpool Women's Hospital. Their mother, Kim Goodman, was only seventeen and had had a one-night-stand with a Welsh businessman, Owen Ankers. He told her to have an abortion and when she told him she intended to keep the babies, he cut off all contact.

'Abi and Libby were adopted a few months later by a Welsh couple, Nick and Rachel Mullen. The girls were brought up in the small village of Beddgelert. However, Nick Mullen sexually abused both girls from an early age, something that was missed by social services, who were called by a concerned neighbour and the local primary school.

'In 2010, Nick Mullen's violence and alcoholism reached its peak and he murdered Rachel Mullen in front of the girls. He was sentenced at Mold Court to life imprisonment in 2011.'

Taking a moment, Ruth couldn't imagine the kind of pain and anguish that Abi and Libby had suffered. She wondered how the sisters had survived.

Maitland continued. 'The girls were fostered to various families but Libby's behaviour, in particular, was found to be challenging and violent. The girls refused to be fostered separately and so lived in several local authority children's homes.

'Libby was constantly running away and in her early teens was involved with drugs and petty crime. Abi was the polar opposite. She was quiet, polite and well behaved.'

Closing the file, Maitland pursed his lips and looked over at Ruth. 'It makes for pretty grim reading, doesn't it?'

Ruth nodded. 'It's horrendous. How has that affected Abi in the long term?'

'I've been Abi's clinical psychologist for seven years. She has developed PTSD and a dissociative disorder. When faced with the overwhelmingly traumatic abuse from which she has no physical escape, Abi may resort to "going away" in her head. This type of "disassociation" is an extremely effective defence against acute physical and emotional pain. Or the anticipation of pain. That means that Abi's thoughts, feelings, memories and perceptions of traumatic experiences can be separated off psychologically, allowing her to function as if the trauma had never occurred. For a childlike Abi, who was repeatedly sexually abused, her defensive dissociation would have become reinforced and conditioned.'

'As you know, we think that Abi may have witnessed the murder of her birth father,' Ruth said.

'Yes. I think it likely that Abi can automatically use dissociation whenever she feels threatened or anxious – even if the anxiety-producing situation isn't abusive.'

'Would that explain Abi's description of some kind of "blackout" on the beach when she and Owen Ankers were attacked?' Ruth asked.

Maitland nodded. 'It sounds like Abi's brain went into an automatic disassociation pattern.'

'Something similar happened when I interviewed her,' Ruth said.

'If she felt under great stress there would be a smaller, less severe "blackout". This does suggest there might be many issues if Abi needed to take the stand in a murder trial and appear as a competent witness. The Prosecution would make it difficult for her because, however sympathetic they were to her mental health, they could make a strong case that her memory of the attack was not reliable.'

'Where does that leave us?' Ruth asked, predicting in her own head that Maitland's recommendation would not be what they needed. She didn't blame him. And she didn't really want to see Abi on the witness stand.

'I'm afraid that my recommendation to the CPS would be that Abi could not stand as a witness in any trial regarding Owen Ankers,' Maitland said.

As a police officer, Ruth knew that this was a frustrating turn of events. Abi had seen the partial face of the man that attacked Owen, and yet that evidence could never be used in a murder trial. However, as a mother and caring human being, there was part of Ruth that was glad that Abi wouldn't have to go through the ordeal of appearing at a murder trial and face cross-examination.

SIAN AND MAC WALKED THROUGH THE SIDE DOOR TO IAN Sayle's ramshackle cottage. They came through the sparse kitchen that was clearly a modern extension. If she stretched out both arms, Sian calculated she could probably touch both sides of the room. A blue Calor gas canister was attached to an old rusty cooker.

Sayle ushered them into a living area. There was an old sofa and armchair that were both covered in bottle-green bedspreads.

'Sit down, sit down.' Sayle's manner was chirpy and upbeat. Sian wondered if he was just glad of the company and the attention.

Sian looked around, spotting some old books that had

been damaged with mildew. There was an old Welsh dresser that had a mish-mash of china cups and plates. Even though it was burning hot outside, the room felt cold and damp.

'You've come about the newspaper article, no doubt?' Sayles asked as he lowered himself gingerly into the armchair. He seemed pleased to see them.

'Yes. We'd like to go through a few details with you if that's all right, Mr Sayle?' Mac said turning the pages of an old case folder.

'Fire away, fire away.' Sayle's tone was strangely jovial given the subject matter.

Mac gave Sian a quick glance, acknowledging that Sayle's behaviour was a little on the odd side.

'Mr Sayle, we understand that you believe that Owen Ankers' murder is in some way linked to two historic murder cases that you worked on while a detective sergeant in the North Wales Police,' Sian clarified.

'Please call me *Ian*. Erm … yes, from what I've read, the MO of Owen Ankers' murder matches the murders of Daniel Warburton and Lyn Povall. Dog-walking on an isolated beach in this area,' Sayle explained.

Mac looked up from the paperwork. 'Daniel Warburton was only fourteen when he was murdered in 1996, is that right?'

'Yes. Horrible. Twelve stab wounds to his neck and chest. I understand that Owen Ankers was also stabbed to death?'

Mac and Sian shared another look. That kind of frenzied attack didn't match the attack on Owen Ankers in any way. It wasn't something they were going to share with Sayle though.

'Yes … Did you ever have a prime suspect? It says here

that you arrested Steven Pritchard two days later?' Mac asked.

'Pritchard was his stepfather. Nasty piece of work. Smackhead. But it wasn't him. He had a solid alibi and there was no real evidence except that he had been violent towards Daniel before. We had to let him go. A few others were questioned but no one else was really in the frame, so we had to conclude that the attack had probably been random.'

'And Lyn Povall?' Mac said scribbling in his notepad.

'Three years later. Same MO. She was out walking her dog on the beach up at Borth-y-Gest. We found her body in the dunes up there. Stabbed and strangled.'

There was a moment as Sian frowned and turned to Sayle. 'Sorry. Did you say strangled?'

'Yeah. Some kind of ligature. Rope maybe. But she was stabbed too. Like the attack last week.'

Mac looked up. 'Any sexual motive element to the attack?'

'Her underwear had been removed. And she had bruising around her genitalia.'

Sian was starting to get irritated. The MOs for both historic murders were different. And it was clear to her that it was very unlikely they were connected to Owen Ankers. How did an experienced detective like Sayle not realise that? Did he not realise that he was wasting their time and hampering the investigation?

Mac looked at the file. 'I can't see any mention of suspects in the file?'

Sayle shook his head. 'No. No one saw anything and we couldn't find anyone who had any motive to kill her. A few people were questioned but that came to nothing. It was the same killer. I could tell when I saw the body.'

Sian frowned. 'Even though she had been strangled and sexually assaulted?'

'Lyn Povall was stabbed in the chest and neck too. The killer was just escalating the violence of the attacks.'

Mac closed the file and looked at Sian. They both knew that although there were similarities, the MOs were different enough to make a link unlikely. If they added the fact that they had happened twenty years ago, with no other obvious attacks in the interim, Sayle's theory didn't hold water.

'Thank you, Ian. You've been very helpful,' Sian said in a tone intended to indicate that he had been wasting their time. She shifted on the lumpy sofa and went to stand.

'Yes. If we need anything else, we know where to find you,' Mac said.

'Don't bullshit me. You don't think there's a link, but you're wrong,' Sayle said with a sneer.

'Thank you for your time,' Sian said with a forced smile. He was a lonely, retired policeman looking for the thrill of seeing his name in print. And that made him a sad prick.

'Where's the dog?' Sayle asked.

Sian frowned. 'How do you mean?'

'Owen Ankers' dog. Where is it?'

'Why do you ask that?' Sian asked. How did Sayle know about the dog?

'Because we never found Daniel Warburton or Lyn Povall's dog. They disappeared and were never found. They both had clear identity tags but never turned up as strays and we never found the remains of those dogs.'

Sian looked at Mac and then sat back on the sofa. Fields had taken Owen Ankers' dog and kept it in his garden.

Sayle looked at them. 'I can tell, you haven't found the dog, have you?'

'Did you ever question an Alwyn Fields when investigating the two murders?'

Sayle let out a snort and said, 'Alwyn Fields? Yeah, we did. Why, has he got something to do with your case?'

SAYLE'S EYES WIDENED — HE KNEW HE HAD STRUCK A chord.

'We can't discuss the details of the case with you, you know that,' Sian said, now feeling unsettled by what Sayle was telling them.

'Yeah. We interviewed Alwyn Fields for both the murders. Several times. Couldn't find anything to take it any further but his name seemed to hang around both investigations like a bad smell.'

Chapter Eighteen

The press conference started at 3 p.m. and the room bustled with local and national journalists from newspapers, radio and television. Ruth had popped a couple of painkillers so the codeine would take the edge off the fluttering nerves in her stomach. Although she had held press conferences in the Met and while running the Dinas Padog case, her confidence had been damaged in recent months and she was still being troubled by self-doubt.

Sitting next to her was Kerry Mahoney, a chief corporate communications officer who had come up from the main press office in Colwyn Bay. They had chatted briefly before going into the conference room. Ruth had taken an instant dislike to Mahoney who had been incredibly patronising when explaining the new media guidelines published by the College of Policing that aimed to impose a number of new controls on police contact with journalists. She said her role was to make sure that the media received the 'key messages' that the North Wales Police wanted to communicate.

Ruth explained calmly to Mahoney that she was well aware of the changes and that off-the-record conversations between police officers and journalists should only happen in 'exceptional circumstances'. It was clear that Mahoney's agenda was to control, and therefore censor, all contact between the North Wales Police Force and the media. She implied that there should be virtually no direct contact and clearly saw the media as the enemy, something that Ruth thought was naïve.

Ruth knew how the Leveson Report of December 2012 had recommended a clamp down on police and journalist relationships which were branded as 'too close.' However, Ruth believed it ignored two key reasons why they should keep the media informed. First, the public had a right to know what was happening in their communities, especially if there was any threat to their safety. Second, it was a fact that the police stood a better chance of catching criminals if they used the media to appeal for witnesses.

Ruth reached over, took the jug and poured herself a glass of water, without offering to do the same for Mahoney. She could go and screw herself. The codeine had made Ruth's mouth dry. Someone approached and Ruth looked up to see ACC Davenport approaching.

'Everything okay?' Davenport asked.

'Yes, ma'am. We just need to make it clear that at the moment we don't believe there's any connection between the historic cases and Owen's,' Ruth clarified. She knew that was what Davenport wanted to hear.

Davenport nodded. 'Great. Glad we're all on the same page, Ruth. Good job.'

Ruth watched Davenport head to the back of the room. Although Ruth had caught a glimpse behind the professional veneer, she hadn't made her mind up about her yet.

Looking out at the journalists, Ruth knew it was time to start. Behind her was a banner on the wall, *Heddlu Gogledd Cymru: Gogledd Cymru diogelach – North Wales Police: A Safer North Wales*, and beside this the North Wales Police badge. There was also a large map of North Wales with the location of Owen Ankers' murder on Harlech Beach marked with a red plastic pin.

On the table in front of Ruth were several small tape recorders and microphones that had been placed there by journalists. She took a moment to focus herself. *Come on, you've done this before.*

'Good afternoon, I'm Detective Inspector Ruth Hunter and I am the senior investigating officer for the investigation into Owen Ankers' murder. Beside me is Kerry Mahoney, our chief corporate communications officer. This press conference is to update you on the case and appeal to the public for any information regarding the murder of Owen Ankers last week. This is a dreadful tragedy and Owen Ankers' friends and family have been devastated by this loss.

'At this stage in the investigation, we know that Owen was walking his dog along Harlech Beach at around five p.m. when he was attacked. The beach had been busy earlier in the day, so if you saw anything out of the ordinary, however insignificant you think it might be, please contact us so we can come and talk to you.'

Ruth spent the next fifteen minutes fielding questions about the investigation. There were several questions about the speculation in the press linking Owen Ankers' murder to the historic crimes in the past. Ruth assured them that all lines of enquiry would be looked at. However, she had made it clear that they were convinced that Owen Ankers had been targeted, that the attack was not random and therefore they gave little credence to former Detective

Inspector Sayle's recent allegations in the press. Ruth also made it clear that as far as they were concerned, there was no immediate danger to the local community in Harlech. She finished the conference by reiterating their need for information about anything suspicious that was seen or noticed on the night.

Ruth felt some self-satisfaction on handling the press conference professionally. Davenport gave her a nod and a thumbs-up to reinforce her feeling that it had gone well.

Ruth sat back for a moment and believed that at last she was getting her confidence back. It was a good feeling.

By the time the Armed Response vehicle had turned off the A55 onto the A525 heading for Rhyl, Nick was ringing with sweat.

They had begun to follow the Ankers & Webb delivery van on the A55 just past St Asaph. There were eight officers in the large black Mercedes Vito, which had sliding doors and blacked-out windows. The heat and the tension inside the vehicle was intense.

Nick and Drake were both wearing Mehler covert bulletproof vests, which were heavy and tight. However, compared to the equipment, vests and helmets of the six AFOs, Nick knew he had little to complain about. A bead of sweat ran from his forehead down the length of his nose and fell onto his lap. Sardonically he wondered what alcohol percentage his sweat was.

There had been virtually no conversation in the Mercedes Vito since they left Llancastell. Officers knew that they were likely to encounter one, if not more, armed criminals and that meant that it would be a highly dangerous operation.

The sign to Rhyl read twelve miles. Rhyl was a Victorian seaside resort popular with visitors from Liverpool and Manchester in the post-war era. However, cheap package holidays had lured holidaymakers abroad and the town had declined ever since. Despite regeneration, Rhyl was still deprived and Rhyl West was the poorest district in Wales. A third of all crime in Denbighshire was committed in Rhyl. It was an obvious target for county lines drug dealing, and crime in Rhyl had doubled in two years.

The vehicle's radio crackled with a female voice from CAD. 'Alpha-delta three, radio check, over.'

Nick's adrenaline was now pumping and he could feel the tension in his stomach. This was his chance to get Blake. The surveillance, the evidence, the drugs on the vans. It would all lead to a conviction to supply class-A drugs and Blake going to prison for a hefty sentence. He deserved more. He deserved to hang as far as Nick was concerned. However, this would be a start and anything to get Blake off the streets and stop him destroying the lives of the vulnerable was a good thing in Nick's eyes.

Sensing that Drake was looking at him, he turned to look back. The collar of Drake's light-blue shirt was now dark with sweat.

'You okay?' Drake asked.

'Yeah, boss. Bring it on,' Nick said quietly. The combination of alcohol and adrenaline had given him a self-assurance bordering on bravado.

The AFO in the passenger seat clicked the radio. 'Alpha-delta-three received. Target vehicle three hundred yards on sierra route. Target is travelling north on A-five-two-five, over.'

Nick had his sunglasses resting on the bridge of his nose. Even though it wasn't bright in the Vito, he wanted them on as he left the vehicle as the sun was dazzling outside.

The CAD operator spoke again. 'Alpha-delta-three, Gold Command instruction. Continue visual on target, maintain obs, over.'

'Alpha-delta-three, received.'

The silence and growing tension in the van was intense as it ran through the whole of Nick's body.

The timing of the interception of the vans was crucial. The operation needed to be synchronised perfectly otherwise it was likely that they could warn each other of the police sting and take evasive action.

The area on both sides was now residential. Nick knew that they had to stop the van before it got into Rhyl town centre. A single-decker blue Arriva bus pulled out suddenly. The Vito swung hard right to go past it even though it was a manoeuvre that might alert the van driver and its occupants that they were being followed.

Nick's breathing was getting faster now. He took a deep breath to calm himself. He knew they were going to stop the van any moment now.

The radio crackled again. 'Alpha-delta-three, Gold Command order is promenade. Repeat, order is promenade.'

'Alpha-delta-three, order received.' The AFO then boomed to the driver, 'Go! Go! Go!'

Suddenly the Vito accelerated. Nick felt himself pushed back in his seat by the velocity, like on a roller-coaster ride.

A burst of noise and colour as the blues and twos sounded and flashed. They were in full operational mode.

The Ankers & Webb van sped up and pulled out to the middle of the road.

'Alpha-delta-three to Gold Command. Request a hard stop of target vehicle, over.'

· · ·

As the van quickly took a left, the Vito followed, turning hard.

Nick found himself flung against the AFO next to him. His cuffs dug into his thigh. His pulse was banging in his ear drum.

'Left, left, left. Alpha-delta-three. In pursuit of suspect, up to fifty miles an hour, over,' the AFO thundered.

'Alpha-delta-three, received. Hard stop as soon as possible, over.'

'Received. Hard stop now!'

The Mercedes engine roared. The Vito sped alongside the delivery van, which was no match for its speed. The van began to slow. The driver's face was one of panic.

The Vito pulled in front to force it to stop. There was the squeal of brakes.

Drake looked at Nick and gave him a caustic smile. 'Here we go.'

The side doors hurtled open and the AFOs leapt from the vehicle with their automatic weapons trained on the van driver.

'Stop! Armed police! Put your hands where I can see them!'

Nick could smell burnt rubber. Noticing the passenger door was open, he spotted a shaven-headed man running away from the van.

'Oi! Stop! Police,' Nick yelled as he went after him.

The heat was oppressive as Nick chased him along the road. The man vaulted the metal pedestrian guardrail and raced along the pavement.

Nick followed, starting to gasp. There was little oxygen in the hot air.

'DS Evans to Control, in pursuit of suspect, over,' he shouted into his radio.

Cutting left, the man raced down Cefn Road, his feet clattering noisily on the tarmac.

'Stop! Police!' Nick hollered through sharp intakes of breath as he followed. He didn't know why he bothered. He wasn't going to stop.

Scuttling right, the man disappeared out of sight. A moment later, Nick arrived and saw that the man had gone into a huge builders' merchants' yard, Roger Evans and Sons.

'Shit!' Nick muttered. *Where the bloody hell is he?*

The yard was full of piles of timber, stacked pallets and fence panels. There was a vast sky-blue warehouse to one side. There were lots of places to hide but Nick was focussed. *This man might be the key to getting Blake,* he thought to himself. *He's not getting away.*

Nick panted into his radio, 'DS Evans to Control. I have followed suspect into Roger Evans builders' merchants. Request back-up, over.'

His radio crackled. 'DS Evans, received. Will advise.'

Cautiously, Nick made his way into the yard. A forklift rattled as it came out of the warehouse. Nick scanned left and then right. The yard was surrounded by high fences and CCTV cameras. The man was going nowhere. He was trapped. The smell of wood and chemical treatments was particularly pungent in the summer heat.

Out of the corner of his eye, Nick glimpsed the man running from behind a pile of roofing timber.

'Stop! Police!' Nick thundered.

The man dashed for the warehouse. Nick lurched left and then sprinted close behind him. He was fifty yards away but Nick was closing in. Then thirty yards. Twenty. It wouldn't be long before Nick could tackle him to the ground. Then from out of nowhere, a yellow forklift truck appeared in front of him. It blocked his way. *Bollocks!* He was losing valuable seconds.

Nick jumped onto a pile of wooden flooring tiles and leapt down the other side. He pumped his arms, the lactic acid burning in his legs, and came into the warehouse.

Several men in work overalls stopped work and looked at him with confused expressions.

'What the bloody hell is going on, mate?' the skinny teenager asked.

Nick flashed his warrant card. 'Police. I'm chasing someone. He came in here.'

'He went over there.' The skinny teenager pointed.

'Thanks.'

Looking up, Nick spotted the man climbing a long metal ladder that stretched to the top of the warehouse roof. Where the bloody hell was he going now?

'Great!' Nick muttered under his breath.

Pivoting, Nick ran across the concrete floor, gripped the ladder and followed. The metal was cold against his palms. He scrambled up the ladder as fast as he could, his legs shaking with the effort. He was exhausted. His muscles were tiring.

Nick paused a second and looked up again.

The man looked back at him and their eyes met. The man glared at him with contempt but no fear. Nick didn't recognise him as anyone he had seen at that morning's briefing.

Clambering upwards, rung after rung, Nick pulled with his arms and pushed hard with his legs. He paused again and looked up. The man had reached the top of the ladder and the roof, which was vaulted with dark steel girders. He had nowhere to go.

Nick was trying to calculate what he would do when he got to the top. He didn't want to fight the man forty feet from the ground.

Nick stopped and gazed up. The man reached for the metal handle on a huge open skylight. It was too far surely? The man looked down again, then stepped up and balanced on the top rung of the ladder. It was then that Nick realised that the man was going to try to leap and pull himself out of the skylight and make his way onto the roof. It was too far.

'Wait there!' Nick shouted. He wasn't going to make it. No way.

The man crouched and then jumped out with his hands stretched. His left hand clasped the skylight handle for a second.

Then he lost his grip.

Nick watched in horror as the man plummeted past him, his body horizontal. He made no sound.

Then a sickening crack as his body hit the concrete floor below.

'Jesus!' Nick was dazed by what he had just seen.

The noise of shouting from below as Drake arrived with two AFOs. They went over to the body of the man. He was stone-cold dead. A pool of dark blood had seeped out of his cracked skull over the concrete.

Nick moved slowly down the ladder. Was the dead man part of Blake's gang? If he had been armed, why hadn't he used a weapon? Nick consoled himself that at least they had stopped the van. They would have enough to convict Blake and Webb. That would be a more than decent result.

Walking over to where the two AFOs were checking over the dead man's body, Nick still felt detached through shock and exhaustion.

Drake looked at him. 'You okay, Nick?'

Nick nodded as he tried to suck in air. 'Sir … I didn't think he would jump.'

'No. Not your fault, though,' Drake reassured him.

'Have you searched the van yet?' Nick asked. Finding the drugs was all that mattered.

Drake nodded but his face revealed his disappointment. 'It's not good news, Nick. There's nothing there.'

Nick felt as if he had been elbowed in the stomach. 'What? How is that possible?'

Drake shook his head. 'They were tipped off. It's the only way they could have known. And the thought of that makes me feel sick.'

Closing his eyes, Nick felt overwhelmed. He needed to get home and drink himself to black out. It was the only way to deal with the day.

Chapter Nineteen

The craft shop at the centre of Chester was bustling with tourists. The shop was a welcome respite from the airless heat outside. Ruth watched a parent fuss over a small child eating an ice cream, getting most of it on her face. She smiled at them as she fished through some over-priced handmade greetings cards. Looking up, she spotted Ella and Sian sifting through bags and scarfs together. It was a moment that lifted her heart. They had all spent the last hour wandering around the Roman walls of Chester in the evening sun. It had been the perfect antidote to the stress of the day.

Ruth hadn't seen Ella for over a month and she wanted her to meet Sian. She knew deep down it was too soon, but Sian thought it was a lovely idea. Naturally, Ella had jumped at the chance because she was nosey. Ruth hadn't had any form of relationship since Sarah's disappearance.

Ruth watched Sian and Ella laughing together, and glowed with warmth and love. She wandered over.

Ella had put a white, floppy seventies boho hat on and paraded it with a silly grin.

'I saw this, and I thought, you know what I don't have?' Ella asked.

'A mirror?' teased Ruth.

'Oh piss off, Mum.'

'She looks lovely. Who's that actress that was in *Charlie's Angels*?' asked Sian.

'Cameron Diaz?' Ella suggested.

'She means the original, you dope. Farah Fawcett.'

Sian nodded. 'Farah Fawcett, that's it. You must have the men falling at your feet?'

Ella grinned. 'Or women.'

Sian shared a look with Ruth, who shrugged. 'Don't ask me. I can't keep up with Ella's preferences.'

Ella wandered away to put the hat back.

'I need you to help me find something for my mum. It's her birthday next week,' Sian said, grabbing Ruth's hand.

'What does she like?' Ruth asked.

'George Clooney, gin and romance novels,' Sian quipped.

'Helpful,' Ruth said rolling her eyes.

'She has early onset Alzheimer's so sometimes she doesn't know what she likes,' Sian said.

'I'm sorry. You never said … you should have told me,' Ruth said putting her hand on her arm.

'I don't like talking about it. It's fine. You can hardly notice it at the moment,' Sian said awkwardly.

Ruth's phone rang. She gave Sian a smile, gestured to the phone and walked away to a quieter part of the shop.

It was Nick and he explained all that had happened.

It was a bitter blow for everyone in Operation Titan that there had been no drugs on any of the vans. But it was more concerning that someone was feeding Blake intel from somewhere inside the force.

It was a dark note on what had been a lovely evening.

SLIM SHARDS OF LIGHT CAME THROUGH THE GLASS OF THE windscreen. Nick squinted from the car over at the church hall where the AA meeting was taking place. The smokers were standing by the steps as always. He had promised his sponsor, Bill, the evening before that he would attend. That was before the empty Ankers & Webb vans, the tip off and watching a man fall to his death. Now he was in two minds about going in. What was the point?

Sitting outside in the car park, Nick swigged from the bottle of vodka again. It stung the back of his throat before hitting his stomach. He was becoming nicely numb. But he was also getting to the point where he was too drunk to go in. He already stank of booze and his voice would now slur. Bill might sack him as his sponsee – he wouldn't blame him. Nick had been sacked by two sponsors before. They had grown tired of his dishonesty, his inability to do what he was told and his constant disappearing acts.

The illuminated end of a cigarette caught Nick's eye as a man came around the corner of the hall. It was his father. Even in the small amount of time his father had been coming to the rooms of AA, Nick had seen the improvement. He looked better. He had put on weight so his clothes now fitted him properly.

That made Nick's mind up for him. There was no way he was going into the same meeting as his father, drunk. *No. Bloody. Way. Jose!*

The self-pity and anger began to take hold. How dare his father get sober? It was his cold, violent behaviour and neglect that had shaped Nick as a boy. He needed to take responsibility for that behaviour.

And then Nick's thoughts turned to Curtis Blake. The man had done a deal with the Devil. He feared that Blake would never pay for what he had done.

Swigging heavily again from the vodka, Nick adjusted the driver's seat so that it reclined a little. He put the radio on and drank more.

Finishing the bottle, he let it drop to the floor beside his feet as he closed his eyes and drifted away.

It was 3 a.m. by the time Nick came to. Rubbing his eyes, he started the engine and drove home via the twenty-four hour petrol station for some beers.

Chapter Twenty

The murmuring in the incident room slowly quietened as Drake and Ruth entered and headed for the front and the two evidence white boards.

'Good morning, everyone,' Ruth said. She wasn't looking forward to her and Drake having to break the news about possible corruption within the department. An effective CID relied upon trust and transparency. She had seen departments in the Met paralysed by suspicion and secrecy.

Everyone stopped talking and shifted where they were sitting to focus. The previous evening news had given some details of the police operation against the Ankers & Webb vans, and that a man had died in Rhyl while being pursued by officers. The details in the news were vague but officers in CID knew that something somewhere had gone wrong.

Ruth looked across at Drake. 'Boss?'

'Thanks, Ruth. Yesterday afternoon, Nick and I were involved in an operation in conjunction with Merseyside Police and Operation Titan. We had intel that in the lead-up to Owen Ankers' murder, Callum Webb and Curtis

Blake had made a deal to transport drugs from Europe to Merseyside, and then to county lines operations in Cheshire and North Wales on the delivery vans of Ankers & Webb.'

Ruth saw several CID officers exchange looks. Merringer pulled an astonished face at Mac and then looked over at Drake. 'You're kidding, boss?'

'No, I wish I was,' Drake replied.

Mac looked angry. 'Why didn't we know any of this? We're investigating a murder without vital information. That's a total joke!'

Ruth glanced at him, raised her hand and said, 'Let's be calm, Mac. We were asked by Merseyside to keep this information to ourselves until there was enough evidence to arrest Webb and Blake.'

Drake nodded and pursed his lips. 'Merseyside Police also had good reason to believe that there was an officer or officers either in Merseyside or in North Wales that was feeding information back to Blake about the operation against him.'

'Great!' Mac thundered.

'This officer is known to Webb and Blake as "Osprey".' Drake took a sip of water. 'We had good information that the first shipments of drugs were leaving on vans yesterday. Nick and I were part of an armed-police operation on one of those vans. However, they were tipped off and there were no drugs or anything of interest found on those vans.'

Sian shook her head and muttered, 'Bastard.'

RUTH COULD SEE IT WAS HARD TO TAKE THAT ONE OF THEIR own was corrupt and being paid for information or worse.

Drake took a moment. 'We are now convinced that the corrupt officer is working out of Merseyside Police Force and they will be dealing with that. I need a debriefing with officers from Merseyside and Titan about how we proceed with our investigation of Callum Webb. We have to talk to IOPC investigators too. Nick, you'll need to go through your statement from yesterday.'

Nick nodded. 'Boss.'

Drake looked over at Ruth. 'Ruth, what have we got?'

Ruth held up a copy of the *Mirror*. The headline read: *Ankers' Killer May Have Struck Before!*

'This is not great bloody news. The article claims that if Owen Ankers' killer isn't the same person as the murders from years ago, the murder could even be a copycat killing.'

'That's the problem with the summer. Silly season and no proper news,' grumbled Merringer.

'Anything in the story?' Drake asked.

'Boss, Sayle gave us the details and the MOs are completely different.' Sian flicked over her notebook. 'Daniel Warburton's murder was frenzied. Yes, he was stabbed while walking a dog in that area, but the killer stabbed Warburton repeatedly in the chest and throat. It was frenzied and out of control. Lyn Povall was stabbed and then strangled, but she was also viciously sexually assaulted.'

Mac looked at Ruth and shifted in his chair, the sweat already staining his blue shirt, and frowned. 'Boss, I know the MOs are different in particular details. But are we then saying that three people were stabbed to death while walking their dogs on a ten-mile stretch of coastline by three different and unknown attackers?'

RUTH NODDED. 'YEAH, THAT DOESN'T SIT COMFORTABLY with me in any way. Did he come up with anything else?'

Mac nodded. 'They interviewed Alwyn Fields for both crimes. Sayle also said that the dogs for the previous two murders had disappeared.'

Nick glanced over. 'Like the killer took the dogs with them? As trophies?'

'That puts Fields in the frame. Mac and Sian, reinterview Fields about his movements that day. Also check the case files for his whereabouts for the other two murders. See if there's a pattern or if anything was missed in the original investigation,' Ruth said.

She moved to the large screen on the wall, clicked a mouse and put up a computer facial composite, which in the old days was known as an artist's impression. However, North Wales Police now used EFIT-V, which had been developed by the University of Kent. The progressive system tried to create a likeness to a suspect through a developmental process in which a witness selects the closest complete faces, and not just individual features, and this created an increasingly accurate final image. Ruth had been impressed by what she had seen of EFIT-V.

Abi Mullen had spent several hours in the Tech Unit and the face that looked out at them was what Abi thought the man who attacked Owen Ankers looked like. It was the rounded face of a man in his fifties or early sixties. He was slightly unshaven, balding, and with a flat nose that looked like that of a boxer.

'This is the man that Abi Mullen says was the attacker on the beach,' Ruth said, gazing up at the image.

'Does that look like Alwyn Fields?' Drake asked.

Sian shrugged. 'Not a million miles away, boss.'

Mac nodded more positively. 'Yeah, it could easily be him.'

'The problem we have is that Abi Mullen is an unreliable witness. Her clinical psychologist will not sign the paperwork for the CPS that would allow her to act as a witness at trial. Added to that, Abi has a dissociative mental disorder that sees her prone to blackouts under extreme stress. We're not even sure she saw the murder happen,' Ruth explained.

'Right. So, this composite is only useful to us to give us an idea of what the suspect looked like?' Nick asked.

'Exactly. It could never be used as evidence in a trial.' Ruth nodded.

Drake stood again as Ruth moved away from the screen and asked, 'Anything on the missing watch or the murder weapon?'

'Fingertip search of the beach found nothing. SOCO went through Fields' house and found nothing there either,' Merringer explained.

'They've got to be somewhere,' Drake said. 'Right, let's get going on this. I'm starting to get pressure from upstairs and I need to give them something. Thank you, everyone.'

NICK AND RUTH HAD BEEN SUMMONED INTO DRAKE'S office. They were both still reeling from the developments outlined in the morning briefing.

Nick had made it clear to Ruth that he was seething that they had lost their chance to get a conviction against Blake. He was still convinced that Blake and Webb had contrived to have Owen Ankers killed. The balaclava man on the beach that Abi Mullen had seen had been one of Blake's gang, but it looked like they would never be able to link either of them to the murder.

Drake was sitting at his desk with a middle-aged woman with bobbed black hair and wearing a smart suit.

Drake stood as they came in. 'Hi there. Catrin, this is Detective Inspector Ruth Hunter and Detective Sergeant

Nick Evans. Guys, this is Catrin Jones, who is a senior investigator with the IOPC.'

'Nice to meet you both,' Jones said as she shook their hands confidently.

Ruth knew the Independent Office for Police Conduct. She had had several dealings with them when she was in the Met. In those days, it was known as the Police Complaints Authority. Old-timers just called it the Rat Squad.

Ruth remembered the fall-out from Operation Tiberius. It was an official internal Metropolitan Police investigation between 2001 and 2002. It was the year she moved to Peckham CID. Allegations had been made that certain crime families had been able to manipulate and bribe officers in the Met. According to the *Independent* newspaper, gangsters had used connections made inside Freemasonry to recruit corrupted officers. There were allegations of evidence tampering, jury intimidation, tip-offs and, most worryingly, senior police officers and criminals working together for a split of the proceeds.

The mention of the IOPC immediately struck fear into most officers.

'Don't worry, it's nothing to do with you.' Drake then pointed for them to sit down.

Jones shifted forward in her seat and opened the yellow file in front of her.

'Okay. The IOPC has been running Operation Neptune for the past six months in conjunction with Merseyside Police. We received intel in January that Curtis Blake, whom you will both be aware of, had bragged that he had a corrupt police officer feeding him information.'

'Osprey?' Nick asked.

Jones rolled her eyes. 'I think Curtis Blake watches too much television. But yes, Osprey.'

Ruth looked at Drake. 'Boss, I thought this was now exclusively a Merseyside issue?'

'Quite the opposite, I'm afraid. The latest intel we have is that Blake's rogue officer is in the North Wales Police Force.'

'Shit!' Nick said.

'You think this is coming from inside Llancastell nick?' Ruth asked.

'Could be. It was where yesterday's operation was run from. Unfortunately, no one is above suspicion at the moment. And nothing about this goes outside these four walls.' Drake looked at them sternly. 'That's understood, isn't it?'

They nodded. 'Boss.'

An hour later, Nick and Ruth were hammering along the A5 towards Harlech. Merringer and uniformed officers had checked out Fields' allotment and shed. Merringer had then radioed in to say that he had found something of significant interest: an expensive watch.

Drake immediately told Merringer to get uniform to tape the area off and informed Ruth of the development. As SIO, Ruth needed to get to Harlech as soon as possible. The SOCO Unit in St Asaph had told her they could be in Harlech within the hour and so Ruth assumed they were already there setting up.

As Nick drove along the main road, Ruth lit a cigarette. Summers seemed to have a logic all of their own. And the summer was a sensual, redolent overload. Even cigarette smoke smelt better in the heat of a warm breeze. It was a season of freedom, youth and no school. Adventure. Ruth had lost all that in recent years but her growing relationship with Sian seemed to promise that some of those feelings would return. And yet that also made her feel guilty. What if Sarah was still being held somewhere? What if she had been in an accident and was suffering from amnesia? How would she understand that Ruth had just got on with her life? Sometimes the *what-if*s drove Ruth mad as they churned around her head like a washing machine on an endless cycle.

As if psychic, Ruth's phone buzzed with a text. It was one of her old contacts who worked at the International Crime Coordination Centre in London.

RUTH, I HAVE DONE SOME DIGGING AROUND FOR YOU. BERLIN police have a suspect that they are watching in the Neukölln district of Berlin. They're being very cagey about saying anything else at the moment. I'll get back to you when I get more info.

Regards, Dave x

RUTH WONDERED WHAT THAT MEANT. SHE WAS LOST IN thought as the flashing light of the sun flicked dappled patterns of white on the water to the left. The air smelt of salt and seaweed. A gull wailed rhythmically until another joined in.

Nick parked next to the white SOCO van. As he and Ruth got out of the car, they were hit by the heat, as though someone had turned on a giant hairdryer right next to them.

Ruth looked at Nick and blew out her cheeks. 'Bloody hell.'

'Mad dogs and Welshmen?'

There was a dry, narrow path that led up to the allotments, which were just north of Harlech Cemetery. A moment later, they came across a uniformed police officer and behind him were symmetrical, square plots of the allotments. They were virtually all the same size but what the owners had decided to grow varied wildly. Spring onions to broad beans and courgettes. In the far corner there was an old greenhouse. Closer by were around four to five wooden sheds.

One of the sheds had yellow police evidence tape around it. The square patch of bare earth that was beside it was dotted with weeds and conspicuous by its lack of plants and vegetables.

'DI Hunter and DS Evans, Llancastell CID,' Ruth said as she flashed her warrant card to the uniformed officers who were trying to keep nosey neighbours at a relative distance.

Ruth looked over as three SOCO officers in their distinctive white suits and purple latex gloves busied themselves.

'Doesn't look like Alwyn Fields has particularly green fingers,' Nick commented on the barren plot.

'It's not been used in ages,' Ruth observed.

Another uniformed officer approached them.

'Ma'am, we've spoken to a Mrs Cartwright.' The uniformed officer pointed to a small new-build house that backed onto the allotments. 'She lives over there. She says that Alwyn Fields has had this allotment as long as she can remember, and she's lived in that house for over twenty years.'

'It doesn't look like he uses it,' Ruth said.

'That's the weird thing. He used it for a few years at the end of the nineties. After the millennium, he completely stopped. Came up here once a year, if that. The Allotment Association tried on several occasions to get Fields to give up the plot as there were others who would have used it. Apparently, he refused and as long as he paid the annual twenty-five-pound membership fee, there was nothing they could do.'

Nick frowned. 'Strange. And a waste of bloody money.'

'And Fields is not someone who looks like he can afford to,' Ruth said, thinking aloud.

The constable then flicked over the page of his notebook. 'Also, ma'am, Fields was up here in the early hours of last Sunday.'

Ruth felt a shiver run down her back and up her neck. 'What? Is she sure?'

'Full moon and the sun starts to come up before five, ma'am. He was around the plot for about an hour. He then came back on Sunday afternoon.'

'What was he doing?' Ruth asked, realising that given the timing, this was very suspicious behaviour.

'She couldn't see. She thought he was in the shed for most of the time.'

Ruth nodded. 'That's great work, Constable. Thank you.'

Ruth turned to Nick as they began to walk towards the SOCOs. 'Right, let's see this watch.'

Alexander Travis, the chief SOCO, headed their way holding an evidence bag. He had a confident, public-school manner and Ruth thought he had a handsome face, in an old-fashioned sense.

'Ruth, good to see you again,' Travis boomed with a smile as though they were meeting outside a pub. 'Nick.'

'What have you got for us?' Ruth asked.

Travis held up the evidence bag that contained a gold watch with a gold metal strap. 'Uniform boys found this while rummaging around. Apparently, it was hidden at the back of a drawer.'

Ruth took the bag and looked at it carefully. 'Rolex?

Very smart.' Ruth experienced that quick surge of excitement she always got when a significant piece of evidence was found.

'I'm not sure Alwyn Fields is a Rolex kind of person,' Nick quipped sardonically.

'No. I'm pretty sure he's not,' Ruth replied, realising that this might be the key to Owen Ankers' murder.

'I'd like to see how he's going to explain this, boss,' Nick said, although he was now realising that if Fields had murdered Owen Ankers, that moved the spotlight away from Webb and Blake. Nick knew that he should be pleased that they had made a significant breakthrough in the case, but there was part of him that was also disappointed.

At that moment, one of the SOCOs looked over and shouted, 'Alex! We've got something else in here.'

Travis looked at them and gestured. 'We'd better go and take a look.'

As Ruth followed him up the allotment, she looked at the dry earth square. Why did Fields use the allotment at the end of the nineties? Why hadn't he used it since and kept paying for it? What was he doing last Saturday and Sunday? Was there anything buried under that weed-strewn earth?

The SOCO, a young Asian woman, came over to them with a grave expression. 'I think you all need to see this.'

Ruth, Nick and Alex went into the shed, even though there was barely enough room for them all to fit. It was dark and smelt of earth and wood. The uneven wooden flooring creaked a little under their weight.

On the dark potting table was an old-fashioned, red steel safety box that was about two feet long and a foot wide. An old brass padlock hung from the lock but it wasn't secured.

The box was open. Ruth and Nick peered inside.

There was an assortment of objects. There was a button badge that had *Oasis – Wonderwall* in white lettering on a Union-Flag background. A screwdriver. A woman's silver hair clip. Something that looked like a multi-coloured festival wristband.

'What's that?' Ruth asked.

Alex carefully moved the wristband with his purple latex fingers. The wristband read: *Glastonbury 1995.*

'What the hell is he doing with all this?' Nick said under his breath.

They both knew that none of these objects were likely to be Alwyn Fields' possessions. In fact, they seemed totally incongruous.

As Alex moved the other objects, both their eyes were drawn to some material. It was bubble-pink in colour. As Alex moved them a little, it was clear that it was a pair of women's knickers.

There was a moment as they took in the significance of what they had found.

Ruth looked at Nick. 'You know what all this stuff looks like?'

'Trophies,' Nick said.

Two hours later, Nick arrived at HMP Berwyn to interview Fields under caution. Fields was being held there on remand after the siege at his home.

Looking tired and drawn, Fields was led in by one of the prison officers. He sat down next to his duty solicitor.

The room was plain with simple chairs and a table. From outside, there was the noise of men shouting during recreation time.

Nick cautioned Fields, who stared defiantly at the floor, and explained the reason for the interview.

'Mr Fields, I'd like you to look at this watch that we found in the shed that you own on Harlech allotments,' Nick said as he put down the evidence bag that contained the gold Rolex watch.

Fields looked confused at Nick and then moved the bag closer to have a look. Nick noticed that he had *CATH* tattooed in blue ink at the base of the fingers of his right hand. He looked to his left hand where the letters *ANDY* were tattooed in the same way. Nick assumed they were the names of his ex-wife and son. It reminded him of his own father's tattoos that he had on his shoulder with Nick and his late mother's names on. Nick thought they had been done for show rather than any true feelings of sentiment. Maybe it had been a tough, unemotional man's version of love?

As Fields shifted on his chair, it broke Nick's train of thought.

'You look confused, Mr Fields?' Nick said.

'I am,' Fields replied with a wry smile.

'Is that your watch?' Nick asked.

'Yes. Of course.' Fields looked at Nick with a smirk growing across his face. He was starting to really annoy Nick.

'You own a vintage Rolex watch, do you?' Nick couldn't hide the tone of contempt.

Field smiled and snorted in a laugh. 'It's not a vintage Rolex watch. Well, it's not a real one.'

'What do you mean?'

'I bought this watch in Bangkok about fifteen years go. I think it cost me about three hundred Thai baht. That's about eight quid. Is that why you've dragged me in here?'

Fields grinned and shook his head. 'Bloody coppers. Haven't got a brain cell between you, have you?'

'Can you tell us why it was hidden in the shed at your allotment?' Nick wasn't having any of it.

'It wasn't hidden. It doesn't work. It stopped working on the plane home. I took it up there thinking that one day I would have a go at fixing it. But I never did, see?' Fields leaned forward in a slightly aggressive manner. 'Can I go now?'

'No.' Nick leant and took another evidence bag. 'Could you tell me why these items were in a box in your shed?'

Nick slid over the evidence bag, which contained the coloured Glastonbury 1995 wristband and the Oasis badge. Fields took them for a moment, looked at them and then put the bag back on the table slowly.

'Is it illegal to have these in my shed?' Fields sneered.

'Mr Fields, we are investigating a number of very serious crimes. I would like you to tell me why these objects were in your possession,' Nick growled.

'They're my son's,' Fields said with a nonchalant shrug.

'Your son's?' Nick was getting worried at Fields' confidence. Nothing he had shown him so far had rattled him one bit. That suggested that he was either innocent or a deluded sociopath.

'Yeah. I took my son down to Glastonbury in 1995. He was meeting his mates there, like. Went to see Oasis play.'

'And you kept his wristband?' Nick's tone was incredulous.

Fields shrugged. 'No. I found it when I cleared out his

room when he moved out a few years ago, like. It was a good trip, you know. We didn't have many. I just kept it.'

'AND IF WE TALK TO YOUR SON, HE'LL CONFIRM ALL THAT, will he?'

'If you can find him, then yeah he will.' Fields nodded with total self-assurance.

'And if we test that wristband for DNA, it will be a positive match for your son and no one else?'

Fields gave him a withering look. 'Dunno. How does any of this have anything to do with Owen Ankers?'

Fields sat back in his chair and sipped his tea. His face betrayed the fact that he had understood what the connection might now be.

'You're investigating the two murders from all those years back, aren't you?'

'I can't tell you any details of our investigation at the moment, Mr Fields,' Nick said, annoyed that Fields now understood why he was being questioned.

'Bloody hell. They talked to me about both those murders at the time. You know that, right? 'Course you do. That's why you're here. Just 'cos I live overlooking the beach. Nothing to do with me.'

'I'm just here to ask you a few questions and for you to tell us about what we found at your allotment.'

'Find anything else?' Fields looked Nick directly in the eyes, challenging him.

Nick reached for another evidence bag which contained the silver hair clip and bright pink knickers.

'What about these?' Nick asked.

Fields rolled his eyes. 'What about them?'

'Any idea why they're in a metal box in your shed?'

. . .

'IT'S JUST CRAP THAT I'VE PICKED UP ALONG THE WAY. How do I know?' Fields replied.

Fields didn't seem rattled by being shown either of the bags of evidence. There was no trace of any nerves or surprise that Nick would have expected if he was trying to hide something.

'It doesn't look like crap to us. It's a woman's hair clip and knickers.'

'All right. I used to meet a woman up there. Few years ago, mind. We'd shag in that shed and she left stuff there once in a while. I just shoved it in that box. I don't think that's against the law.'

'And you never thought to return them?' Nick asked.

'She was married, so, no.'

'And she'll verify this story, will she? If you give us her name?'

'I doubt it.' Fields glared directly at Nick.

'And why's that?' Nick asked returning the glare.

'She died five years ago,' Fields replied with a dark grin. 'Is there anything else, or can I go now?'

RUTH HAD SPENT THE LAST TWENTY MINUTES TALKING TO the North Wales Communications and Media Department. Two major national tabloid papers had latched onto Owen's case and the arrest of Alwyn Fields. The summer was always slow for news and so this made perfect copy.

Murder Suspect Is Falklands Hero. The article detailed Fields' arrest and the brief siege that took place at his house. The police activity at his allotment was also discussed, with one local saying that 'police took away several key pieces of evidence'.

Harlech killer suspect linked to more murders! read the other tabloid. They had used the information in Ian Sayle's interview with the local media to link Fields to the historic murders in the 1990s. An old neighbour of Fields had told the paper, 'He has these eyes. They had no colour, and his expression was so blank. There was nothing there. I felt scared, but never threatened enough to go to the police. Seeing him on TV was a shock because it brought it all back.'

The media speculation was getting worse on a daily basis and it was hindering the investigation.

ACC Davenport's temporary office was upstairs on the ninth floor, and by the time Ruth got up there, she wished she had gone for a cigarette break before going.

There was something different about Davenport, Ruth thought, as she sat down opposite her. She had done her hair differently or was wearing a touch of make-up. She couldn't put her finger on it but there was something different about her appearance.

The air smelt light and perfumed. Ruth recognised the scent from somewhere and wondered if it was the Marc Jacobs that Sian wore.

'I heard about the covert operation from yesterday. DCI Drake keeps me up to speed with some of what is going on in Owen's case,' Davenport said as she relaxed a little in her chair.

'Yes, Ma'am. It was a bit of a disaster to say the least.'

'Please call me Beth, Ruth. Unless we're in front of some stuffy old senior copper.'

Ruth smiled at her and nodded. She had never had a senior officer say that to her and was pleasantly surprised at Davenport's humility, which was rare in the senior ranks. Humility didn't get you far in the police force.

'You said you had something to show me?' Davenport asked.

'Yes. We've been looking at an Alwyn Fields. You heard he took DC Hockney at gunpoint?'

'Of course. Horrible. How is she?' Davenport nodded.

'She's okay. Well, she says she's okay and she wants to keep busy.'

'Alwyn Fields? I only know the name from what I've read in the papers this morning. A Falklands hero but also a slightly strange loner now?'

'Fields admitted to following Owen on the day of the attack. We found Hector, Owen's dog, in his garden. We know that he was interviewed in 1996 and 1999 in connection with both of the previous attacks on the coastline.'

'You think he carried out all three attacks?'

'We don't know yet. We didn't have anything to link him to any of the attacks until SOCO took a look at the shed he has on his allotment. And he had this watch hidden away.'

'What did Fields say?'

'He said it was a fake.'

Ruth passed the evidence bag containing the gold Rolex for Davenport to look at.

Ruth continued. 'We know that Owen was missing an expensive watch. Alwyn Fields is not someone you would expect to have a vintage Rolex watch in their possession.'

Davenport looked at the watch for less than a second. 'It's not Owen's. Sorry.'

'You're sure?' Ruth said with a frown.

'Owen couldn't wear metal watchstraps. It gave him an allergic rash. Every watch he owned had a leather strap,' Davenport explained.

Ruth felt a little deflated at the news. In recent hours, she had become increasingly convinced that Fields was their man.

'And it's a fake,' Davenport said.

Ruth took a moment. 'How do you know it's a fake? Out of interest.'

Davenport moved forward to show Ruth the watch inside the bag. For a moment, their hands touched and it seemed as if Davenport had done it on purpose.

'Look at the second hand,' Davenport said to Ruth.

'Okay.'

'You see how it moves forward a click at a time for every second and then stops.'

'Yeah.'

'A real Rolex's second hand is a continuous movement. It doesn't click around, it's smooth. Owen told me that. Sorry, but it's not Owen's watch. Do you think Fields had anything to do with Owen's death?'

'I'm not sure. My instinct says that there's something not quite right about him.'

Davenport nodded and looked slightly emotional. 'It would be good for us to find Owen's murderer as soon as possible. For everyone's sake.'

Chapter Twenty-One

R uth and Nick were sitting in Drake's office. The white plastic fan whirred but it was essentially blowing warm air around the clammy room. Drake went over to a mini-fridge and opened it.

'I didn't have one of these in Manchester,' Drake said and looked at them. 'I've got Diet Coke and water.'

''I'll take a Diet Coke, boss,' Nick said.

Drake threw it across the room and Nick caught it.

'Good catch,' Drake said with a smile.

'I didn't play rugby for North Wales for nothing,' Nick quipped.

'Impressive … Ruth?' Drake asked.

'I'm fine, boss,' Ruth said, thinking that Drake's laid-back style was such a breath of fresh air in Llancastell CID. She was glad he had made the move.

Ruth looked down at the case folder that she was holding and said, 'We need to show the items we found at the allotment to the families of Daniel Warburton and Lyn Povall as soon as possible. If there's any kind of recognition, we can test for evidence of Fields' and the victims' DNA.'

Having been here before, Ruth wasn't looking forward to those meetings with the victims' families. First, it stirred up all the pain and hurt of losing that person in such a hideous and unbearable way. It was likely that the newspaper stories of recent days had started that process already.

Second, it gave the families hope of the one thing that could make their grief and pain a little more bearable. Finding the person who had taken away their loved one. It gave them some sense of resolution to their loss – or what the Americans called *closure*. It was a word Ruth disliked, especially now it had found its way into the British vernacular. Finding the murderer would give them some kind of 'closure'.

'Even if the DNA matches, it might not be enough to meet the threshold for the CPS to sanction charging Fields with anything,' Drake said.

'The Defence could easily point out that the shed was on a public allotment. Anyone could have put those items there,' Nick pointed out. 'They're completely different MOs. As far as I can see, Owen Ankers was targeted and killed deliberately. My instinct is that Webb and Blake are at the centre of it.'

Ruth watched as Drake thought for a moment. Nick had a good point but she was convinced that Fields was hiding something. She also knew that Nick was like a dog with a bone when it came to Blake.

'My instinct is the same as yours, Nick. Especially now we know that the Rolex doesn't belong to Owen. The gaps between the murders just don't feel right,' Drake said. 'I would have expected to see female victims and a sexual element to the attacks if it was the same killer.'

'And if it wasn't a targeted attack, then why was Abi Mullen not attacked too?' Ruth said.

Drake took a pen drive from his pocket, went to the computer and found an image that he wanted to show Nick and Ruth.

A man's face came up on the screen. He was around fifty, shaved head, broken nose and tough-looking.

'Tony Downes. He's a member of Blake's gang. Suspected of the murder of a member of a rival drugs gang, in Amsterdam, in 2015. Also wanted in connection with several attacks on members of the Speke gang in Marbella in 2016 that left one in a coma and one paralysed.'

'Nice,' Nick muttered.

'In the past, Downes basically acted as a hitman for Blake.'

Drake pulled another image up onto the screen. It was the composite of the man that Abi Mullen said she had seen on the beach that afternoon.

The two faces weren't identical but they were very close. Close enough to be non-identical twins, Nick thought.

'Downes has been missing off Merseyside's radar since 2016. However, he flew to Dublin last week. Then got the ferry from Dublin to Holyhead and arrived back in Liverpool.'

'Just before Owen Ankers' murder.'

'Exactly.' Drake nodded. 'I strongly suspect that Downes is our killer.'

Nick rubbed his face. This was just the sort of intel he wanted to hear. It put Blake right in the middle of Ankers' murder.

Ruth was less happy with the shift in the investigation.

She trusted her instinct and there was something about Fields that bothered her.

'Boss, are we putting Fields out of the running? He had motive and opportunity. He had Owen Ankers' dog in his garden. He took Sian hostage when challenged. Despite what he says, he had a Rolex watch in his garden shed, which we haven't actually verified as a fake.'

Drake looked at Ruth. 'Fields remains a suspect while we examine the evidence we found. My instinct is still that Blake's at the centre of Owen's murder. And that is our main line of enquiry.'

'What are we doing about Webb, boss?' Nick asked.

'Blake now knows that using Ankers & Webb vans to transport drugs out of Merseyside is a non-starter, which puts Webb in a dangerous position,' Drake explained.

'Are we bringing him in?' Ruth asked.

'Yes. Surveillance shows that Webb and Blake have been spending time together in the last twenty-four hours. My guess is that Blake is evaluating whether Webb will talk to us if he's arrested. My worry is that Blake decides not to take the chance. Webb gets killed rather than risk him providing evidence in return for a reduced sentence.'

Drake went to the computer and opened up another photo. It showed Blake, Webb and some other men sitting at a table at a club. Ruth could see from the young women wearing revealing underwear, it was a lap-dancing club.

'Blake owns a lap-dancing club in Southport called The Platinum Lounge. He and Webb were there last night. My guess is that Blake was sounding him out.'

Drake approached the screen and pointed to a man sitting on the far right of the booth.

'And sitting just here, is our friend Tony Downes. And that doesn't bode well for Webb, I'm afraid. Ruth, I want you and Nick to track Webb down and bring him in. I spoke to the CPS. We have enough to charge him with conspiracy to supply class-A drugs.'

However, Ruth's eye had been caught by something else on the photo.

When she didn't respond, Drake frowned at her. 'Ruth?'

Ruth approached the photo. 'Sorry, boss. I've just noticed something.' Ruth pointed to the mirrors that were behind the men in the club. 'Can you make the image any bigger?'

Drake nodded, walked over and zoomed in on the image.

Ruth pointed at the girl that was lap-dancing one of the men in the booth. 'This girl here,' she said.

At first, Drake and Nick only noticed the back of the girl's head. Ruth pointed on the wall to the reflection in the mirror behind where the men were sitting. And in the mirror, they could all now clearly see the girl's face.

'That's Abi Mullen,' Ruth said in a confused voice. But there was no way that the Abi Mullen she had met could be working as a lap dancer. It just wasn't possible.

Nick frowned. 'What? It can't be.'

Nick and Drake went a little closer. There was the face of the blonde girl in the mirror. There was no doubt about it.

It was Abi Mullen.

RUTH HAD PICKED ABI UP AT THE HALLS OF RESIDENCE around 3 p.m. Abi had seemed her usual timid, fragile self and Ruth found it difficult to marry the idea of the young girl she had driven back to Llancastell nick with the half-naked girl lap-dancing Liverpudlian gangsters in the surveillance photo.

On the way through Llancastell town centre, Ruth tried to strike up a conversation but Abi was fairly monosyllabic. There was part of Ruth that felt let down. She had developed a fondness for Abi and felt great empathy for her. Her traumatic upbringing and her mental health issues made her vulnerable and Ruth had felt a nurturing instinct towards her. Abi looked like she needed looking after. There were moments when Ruth wondered how Ella would have turned out with all that baggage. Having seen the photo, most of that was gone. It was likely that Abi had lied about knowing Curtis Blake and possibly Callum Webb. It seemed that she was somehow mixed up in the Liverpool underworld, but Ruth didn't know yet to what extent. Either way, Abi being the witness to Owen Ankers' murder, and being photographed with two major suspects, put a very different slant on her as a witness.

When Abi arrived at the station, Ruth made it clear that it was a voluntary interview to clarify some of the things she had told them previously. Ruth knew that once Abi was charged, she would need a solicitor with her.

Entering Interview Room Two, Ruth sat down. In her long cardigan, black jeans and blue Converse, Abi looked like any other eighteen-year-old student.

Ruth began the interview by cautioning Abi, reading her rights.

'You understand what I've said to you, Abi?' Ruth asked lightly.

'Yes … m … miss.' Abi shifted in her chair awkwardly.

'When you were last here, Abi, you said that you didn't know anyone by the name of Curtis Blake or Callum Webb? Is that right?' Ruth's tone was harder than usual.

Abi nodded but she was clearly flustered by Ruth's direct tone. 'Yeah. I mean, no, I don't.'

Ruth looked at her directly. 'You don't know those men? Have you ever heard their names before?'

'No. Never,' Abi whispered.

Reaching for a file, Ruth pulled out the photo from The Platinum Lounge club that showed both Webb and Blake, and someone identical to Abi lap-dancing one of the men.

'Could you take a look at this photo, please, Abi?' Ruth asked.

Ruth slid the photograph around on the table for Abi to look at. Abi leant forward and frowned as though she had no idea of what she was looking at.

'Do you recognise where that photograph was taken?'

Abi shrugged. 'No. Sorry. I ...'

Ruth leant forward and pointed. 'This man here is Curtis Blake. And this one is Callum Webb. And we think that this girl here, is you, Abi.'

Abi moved away from the table as her arms stiffened a little and she blinked. 'No, n-no.'

Ruth took out another photograph, which was a blown up and enhanced image of the girl's face reflected in the mirror. There was no doubt it was Abi.

'Abi, I want you to think very carefully about this. You're saying that this girl is not you?' Ruth asked, trying to make direct eye contact with her.

Abi continued to look at the floor, her shoulders hunched. 'No ...'

'No? Really, Abi? Come on,' Ruth said.

Abi's face was full of panic and then a tear came. 'No. Why are you saying that?'

Abi's eyes flicked back and forth as she tried to process what she had been shown. Then she leant forward, looked again at the face in the reflection and then over at Ruth. 'It's ... my sister.'

'Your sister?' Ruth was confused.

'It must be Libby. It's not me, I swear. It must be Libby.'

And then the penny dropped. 'Libby is your twin sister, Abi?'

Abi nodded almost imperceptibly. 'Yeah.'

'Is Libby your *identical* twin sister, Abi?' Ruth asked.

Abi looked up and her eyes had glazed over as if she was in a trance. Then she looked at the floor. Tapping her fingertips together rhythmically, she seemed as if she was lost in a daydream.

'Abi …?' Ruth said, seeing that she seemed to be lost in thought.

Sitting up suddenly, Abi pushed her shoulders back and pushed her hair back. She narrowed her eyes in disgust.

'Who the hell are you lookin' at, bitch?' she hissed.

Suddenly the room seemed to have changed. The air different. The light. Ruth felt a chill. The back of her neck tingled and the hairs stood on end as she realised she was looking at a completely different person.

'Oi, I'm talking to you, you sketty bitch!' There was no trace now of the North Wales accent. It had been replaced by a thick Liverpudlian twang.

Abi looked older. Maybe three or four years. Her eyes were tighter. Lips were thinner. Her body was fuller, chest and shoulders forward. As she moved her head, she frowned at Ruth aggressively.

Ruth tried not to show her shock at seeing this transformation in front of her. But if she was honest, it had struck terror into her. And she wasn't easily spooked.

The girl, whoever she was, sat back in the chair,

plonked her feet up on the table noisily and pushed the chair back on two legs and rocked. She smiled.

'Have we met? What's you name again?'

'Detective Inspector Hunter,' Ruth replied keeping calm.

'Bugger off, Bizzy. What's your first name?'

Ruth had no idea what was going on but knew she had to play along, at least for a while.

'Ruth. My name's Ruth,' she said.

'Nice to meet you, Ruthzie. Have you got a ciggie? Hey, rhymes dat, don't it?'

Ruth smiled and nodded. 'Yeah. Actually, I have.'

DELVING INTO HER BLOUSE POCKET, RUTH PULLED OUT A packet of Marlborough and offered one to the girl.

'Ta. You're a total belter, Ruthzie.'

Leaning across the table, Ruth lit the cigarette and said, 'Sorry. I can't remember your name?'

'Libby. Yeah, thought it was time we met. Before me dickhead of a sister gets herself into a loada trouble, you know?'

Ruth nodded. 'Oh right. You're Abi's sister.'

Libby snorted. 'Yeah. Quick on the uptake, love. Thought you detectives were meant to be smart?'

'So, why are you here, Libby?'

'I just told you! You stupid or summit? Abi's messing everything up. All that bloody crying. Soft bitch.'

'You and Abi don't get on?' Ruth asked gently.

'We're sisters. I love the bones of her. But she does me bloody 'ead in,' – now mimicking Abi's soft voice and North Wales accent – '"Sorry, m-miss. Owen said he wanted to-to … see me, have a ch-chat and meet face to face. We went on the beach to walk the dog and talk about my future." The hell they did!'

Is Abi faking it? Ruth wondered. She had heard of murderers inventing voices or other personalities to cover their crimes. Peter Sutcliffe, the Yorkshire Ripper, claimed that the voice of God had told him to go out and kill prostitutes.

But Ruth also knew the transformation she had just witnessed was staggering and utterly convincing. Her instinct told her that Abi had indeed changed. She didn't know what to think. It was surreal. At this stage, Ruth knew she had to play along. She thought multiple personalities was the stuff of the movies or TV dramas.

'Libby, do you think you could tell me what actually happened to Owen on that afternoon?'

'Eh, that little prick. He 'ad it comin'. Thought he could buy me and Abi off like. Yeah, mate. You sod off when we was born. Not a word. It was our Abi's idea to track him down. We go and meet him. Then the prick doesn't wanna know us. Blocks calls. Cancels at the last minute. Who does dat to their own daughters? Sacks them off twice!' Libby couldn't hide her fury.

'And that made you and Abi angry?'

'Not little Abi. Always sees the good in everyone, that one. Says we can't blame 'im cos he's busy. Tried to buy us off with ten grand. But me? Me? Yeah, I was fumin', mate. He left us, we got fostered and we was abused day and night for years. He left us and didn't give a toss.'

'And then what happened, Libby?'

'I THOUGHT, SCREW HIM. NOW HE STILL WANTS TO JIB US off, like. What kind of bastard doesn't wanna know his own daughters?'

'Libby, can you tell me what happened on the beach that day?'

'Yeah, I can tell ya. I showed him. I shanked 'im. Gutted him like a pig.' Libby smiled and shook her head at the memory of it.

'So, you stabbed Owen on Harlech Beach on that Saturday afternoon?'

'That's what I just said. Bloody 'ell love. I carved 'im up. Tried to cut off his prick. Must have shanked 'im twenty times. Don't need to tell you that, you saw the body.' Libby's tone was full of conceit, proud of what she had done.

'You stabbed Owen twenty times, Libby? You're sure about that?' Ruth asked.

Now there was confusion. Ruth knew full well that Owen had died from a single stab wound to the thigh. There was no frenzied attack. Why was she lying?

'Eh? Am I sure? There was blood everywhere. Nearly cut off one of his fingers. He was trying to protect himself.' She then mimics Owen's voice. '"No, no. Why are you doing this to me?"' Libby was now virtually spitting with fury. 'I'll tell you why, Daddy. 'Cos you left us, we got adopted and we was fucked in every orifice by some sick evil bastard. You should have been protecting us. Where the hell were yous?'

There was a moment's silence as Ruth looked at Libby who had crouched over on the chair with her head in her hands. She was breathing deeply.

'Libby?' Ruth got up and put her hand on her shoulder to see if she was all right.

Libby was rocking back and forwards in the chair, her hands covering her face.

'Libby?'

The rocking slowed and slowed and the girl looked up as though she had been in a long, deep sleep.

The girl looked up at Ruth. All the anger, bravado and confidence had gone.

'Abi?' Ruth asked uncertainly.

'Yeah. What did you ask me? Sorry,' Abi said quietly.

Chapter Twenty-Two

Nick arrived at the stylish building that housed the head office of Ankers & Webb. He had Merringer, two young DCs and four uniform officers in tow. Traversing the cool, air-conditioned corridors, Nick smelt new carpets and paintwork. They hadn't been in these offices for long.

An hour earlier, a magistrate had issued Llancastell CID with an arrest warrant for Callum Webb on suspicion of intent to supply class-A drugs. Section 18 search warrants had also been issued to search both the offices of Ankers & Webb and Webb's home.

Now that Webb's dealings with Blake were at an end, Webb needed to be taken into protective custody before Blake got to him. Or before Webb decided to go into hiding or do a runner abroad.

Nick marched into the smart reception area where the orange Ankers & Webb logo was blazoned in sharply designed ten-foot letters on the wall. A receptionist looked up as she answered the phone. Her eyes widened as she hung up immediately.

Nick flashed his warrant card briskly and said, 'Detective Sergeant Evans, North Wales Police. Is Mr Webb in?'

The receptionist seemed slightly overwhelmed. 'I … I'm … Can you tell me what this is concerning?'

Moving closer, Nick spoke in a lower tone. 'I have a warrant here for his arrest. If he's here, I would like to talk to him discreetly first.' Nick gestured to all the office workers who were clamouring to see the sudden arrival of police officers.

'Yes, of course. But I'm sorry. He isn't in,' the receptionist explained.

Nick couldn't tell if she was lying and covering for him. 'You understand that this is very serious? And we will check the premises?'

'No, I'm not lying. He left about an hour ago,' she said nervously.

The receptionist looked over at her colleague who nodded at Nick to confirm that Webb had left.

Nick looked at his watch. Only 2 p.m. 'Bit early. Is that usual for Mr Webb?'

'No. But he said he wasn't feeling well. And he asked me to cancel a meeting he had booked for this afternoon.'

Nick had to think quickly. It sounded like Webb knew they were coming. Where was the leak coming from? Who kept tipping Webb and Blake off? If he found the bastard, he would remove their testicles, slowly, painfully and individually.

If Webb was in fact heading home, was he grabbing clothes and passport, before fleeing the country? Did Nick need to put out an all-ports alert, which covered airports too. But to do that he would need a court order and they didn't have time for that now.

Nick wondered if Blake was tailing Webb to see if he

was talking to the police or if he was acting like a man about to run or talk.

'Anyone hanging around here today that you don't recognise? Or anything out of the ordinary?' Nick asked.

The receptionist shook her head. 'No. Nothing I can think of.' And then a thought appeared to come to her. 'Except …'

Nick spotted it. 'Anything might help us, however small.'

'Our head of accounts, Janet. She said that someone had parked in her parking space today. That's a bit strange because it's clearly marked. We're in a business park so we don't ever really get that happening.'

'Did she say what kind of car?' Nick asked as he got a nasty feeling about what he had just been told.

'No. But she did say there were people sitting in it.'

'Can I talk to Janet now?' Nick said with a sense of urgency.

'She's out at a meeting.'

'Can you show me her parking space?'

The receptionist went over to the window and pointed down into the car park. 'It's over there. Oh, it's empty now. They must have gone.'

Nick went over to have a look. 'What about CCTV? Can I look at the CCTV for the car park?'

'The security office is on the ground floor, by the building's reception,' the receptionist explained.

Nick nodded and got out a piece of paper. 'We have a Section 18 search warrant for these premises. Could you show these men to Mr Webb's office now?'

The receptionist nodded, came out from behind the reception desk and showed the way.

Ten minutes later, Nick was in the small CCTV monitoring room on the ground floor of the building. A security officer was trawling backwards through the footage for the particular camera that covered that part of the car park. He was more than happy to help and seemed excited at the prospect of police involvement. Nick assumed he spent most days doing very little.

The time code went back as they watched.

Nick peered closely to see who had been waiting in the car park and when they had left. 'It's going to be about an hour ago.'

The security guard pointed to the screen. 'There you go. That car is parked in Miss Hennessey's parking space. And then just under an hour ago it leaves.'

Nick's stomach dropped. The car leaving the space was a black Range Rover Evoque with blacked-out windows.

It was Blake. And he was following Webb home.

NICK HAD DRIVEN AT HIGH SPEED TOWARDS LLANGOLLEN, hoping to get to Webb before Blake did. Units were on their way from Llancastell but Nick had a head start.

As Nick arrived, he saw that Webb lived in a beautifully converted Grade-II listed Victorian mansion townhouse, which sat above the River Dee just outside Llangollen. Nick was already anxious. Webb's Audi was parked out the front of the enormous in-out gravel driveway. The electronic gates were open. Why weren't they closed? Where was Webb?

Gulping some vodka from the Sprite bottle, Nick took a moment and then got out of the car. *That's better*, he thought to himself.

He crouched for a moment beside the open gates. Within the gravel were large fragments of white and orange glass. It had clearly come from a car hitting something. The gate was missing paint from the black metal at one end.

Approaching the front door, his feet crunched on the gravel. Nick stopped. There were dark spots on the grey flagstones by the door. Blood. It was congealed a little but it was recent. Minutes or an hour, no longer.

Now fearing that someone had got to Webb before he had, Nick pushed the heavy dark oak front door. It had a small square of opaque glass and dark metal handle and knocker.

The door opened. It swung on its own weight. There was an oriental rug in the hallway that had been ruffled and moved so it was out of place. A small table and lamp had been knocked over, the lamp's china base smashed to pieces.

The house was silent. It smelt of furniture polish.

With his heart banging, Nick moved into the hallway. He had no idea if Webb was still there or if those who had come to take him were either. The PNC had showed that Webb had several cars so the fact that his Audi was on the drive didn't necessarily indicate that he was home.

A noise of movement from upstairs. Someone was in the house. Nick felt his stomach tighten as his pulse thudded faster. The vodka wasn't going to take the edge off that amount of adrenaline.

Treading his way across the polished block-wood floor and into the living room, he stopped. The room was enormous with white sofas, a rug and a giant screen at the far end.

Another noise. From the blood outside and smashed lamp, Nick knew there had been a struggle. Webb could be either kidnapped or dead. Maybe his attackers had left someone behind to clean up? Maybe he even managed to escape in another car.

Then the slow sound of footsteps on the stairs. Someone was moving casually from the sound of it and it didn't seem that they were aware of his presence. Spotting a brass poker by the fireplace, Nick crept towards the doors to the living room. He held his breath.

Someone was looking around the hall. They were now heading for the doors to come in. Nick's pulse was racing. What if they had a gun? He needed to attack swiftly and brutally. He would go for the head to start with. A clean blow to the head would stun them whatever happened.

'Hello?' A deep voice broke the tension. 'Anyone there?'

Nick frowned. It was a voice he knew. It was Mac. What the bloody hell was he doing there?

'Mac?' Nick appeared from behind the door.

'All right, Nick. You bloody scared me there, lad,' Mac said.

'Scared me? For fuck's sake,' Nick said startled. He was relieved to see a familiar face and not have to tackle anyone with a gun.

Mac gestured to the heavy metal poker. 'Glad you knew it was me before you hit me with that bloody thing.'

'What the hell are you doing here?' Nick asked. Now he'd had a few seconds to think, Mac's presence in Webb's house was unsettling.

'Heard the shout from Dispatch go out on my way home. I was only a mile or two away. I missed whatever happened here,' Mac said and gestured to the mess and blood.

'Any sign of Webb?' Nick asked as he looked around the hallway.

Nick's gut told him that this wasn't right. Mac in Webb's house on his own. Creeping about. Did he really hear the shout from Dispatch even though he was officially off duty and on his way home? He'd forgotten where Mac lived but he was sure it wasn't close. If it wasn't for the fact that other officers were going to be arriving in the next few minutes, Nick might even fear for his own safety.

Did this mean that Mac was the leak? Nick's mind was racing but he knew that he had to hide what he was thinking.

'No. I've checked the rooms upstairs. Front door was open. Blood outside. It doesn't look good, does it?' Mac said.

Nick looked at Mac trying to suss him out. Was he a rat for Blake? Had he been on the take for the past three years and feeding intel back to Liverpool?

Mac spotted Nick's face. 'You all right, Nick?'

'What? Yeah. Have you checked out the back yet?' Nick asked, his mind still occupied with what the hell Mac was up to.

'No. Didn't have time. If you check out the back, I'll have a scoot round the rest of the ground floor, okay?'

Nick suspected Mac was stalling for time. His voice and manner gave his anxiety away. Mac could have used his warrant card to gain access through the security gates and intercom to Webb's house. Once in, he could have let in whoever Blake had sent to do their dirty work.

Nick looked at Mac again. 'Where is he, Mac?'

There was a moment between them. Nick's question had two meanings.

'How the hell do I know?' Mac barked defensively.

'You got here very quickly after the shout went out.' Nick looked at him again.

Mac moved towards Nick in a threatening way. Nick wasn't bothered. Mac was overweight and out of shape.

'You got something to say, Nick, you'd better get on and say it, all right?'

At that moment, the sound of gravel crunching and the blue strobe of a police light came through a ground-floor window.

Nick looked at Mac with no expression.

There was the thud of car doors closing and a moment later, Merringer and a female DC came through the door.

'Where's Webb?' Merringer asked urgently.

'Gone,' Nick said darkly.

Chapter Twenty-Three

The remand wing at HMP Rhoswen, which was close to the North Wales coast, wasn't busy. Many of the prisoners, who were awaiting trial, were watching television, playing pool and in the prison gym.

Fields came down the green steel stairs and onto the area of the second floor. There was a strip of light-green right through the middle of the floor all the way along the wing. Everything else was various shades of grey – the doors, the walls, the ceilings.

A moment later, Fields was in the small neat cell that he shared with Ethan Williams, a young man who had been convicted of selling drugs and assaulting a police officer in Llandudno.

The cell was basic. A single bed against each of the opposing walls, with a blue blanket and green pillowcase. Between the two beds there was a table where there was a television, blue plastic bowls, and a knife, fork and spoon each.

Fields thought it was a hell of a lot nicer than the barracks he had spent many years living in with the 45

Commando at the Royal Marines base near Arbroath in East Angus, Scotland. That was cold and uncomfortable, with ten men to a room in bunks. The idea of prison cells with televisions and PlayStations made Fields laugh. He had heard some of the younger prisoners moaning about Wi-Fi. They didn't have a bloody clue.

Fields was still in the middle of his week-long induction process for new prisoners. Then he would be given a job in the prison in the lead-up to his sentencing for the kidnapping by force of Detective Constable Sian Hockney. He had pleaded guilty. There was no point pleading anything else.

What was worrying Fields were the unpleasant comments that had been directed at him in the past twenty-four hours since the news had broken about the historic murders in Harlech. Several tabloids had linked Fields to them and the papers had made it clear that Daniel Warburton was a teenager and Lyn Povall's murder in 1999 was sexually motivated. And that made Fields a target. However, he wasn't sure that it constituted enough for protective custody. He would have a quick word with one of the screws later.

Gazing out of the window, Fields caught the smell from outside the kitchens below. Someone was smoking, and the mixture of tobacco and fish from the kitchen took him back to a cold, icy beach in the southern Antarctic nearly forty years ago.

It was dawn when his unit of Commandos had landed on the wet, shale beach on the west coast of the Falklands. The far end of the beach was a mass of seals, which is where the pungent smell of fish came from. They spotted an elephant seal closer by, which was enormous. It must have been twenty feet long and Fields estimated it must weigh in at three to four tonnes. It made a strange deep bleating sound. He hadn't thought of that for many years.

Fields sat on his bed. He took out his packet of cigarette papers and began to pre-roll a cigarette. Even the action of rolling calmed his nerves. He had planned to go and watch the nine-o'clock film in the television room.

Suddenly, the light in the cell darkened.

Two men moved slowly and quietly into his cell. A third stood outside and pushed the door so that it closed as much as it would.

So, this is it, thought Fields. He knew that he deserved what was coming. There was a law of balance and redress somewhere in the universe and it was his time. Everything seemed to slow as he looked down at the floor and prepared himself.

It was nearly eight when Nick pulled up into the car park of the Ramada Hotel in Llancastell. The exterior was well lit and looked smart. Everything you would expect from a decent conference or business-hotel chain. The red lettering of *Ramada Plaza* looked almost oriental in design.

Nick swigged the vodka that was in the glove compartment. He had missed the AA meeting at the Llancastell detox unit. He had been in two minds about going. Part of him didn't want to see his father. And yet part of him hoped to see his father there sober. It was confusing but the latter thought was a bloody miracle.

Nick finished the vodka and made a mental note to get more on the way home. He was meeting Drake in the bar, so that would keep him going. However, the anxiety of not having booze stored safely away in the car worried him.

Even though it was late, the night air was hot and reminded him of being on Mediterranean holidays when he was younger. He didn't like to go on holiday anymore. Gone were the days where he could go on 'lads' tours and go on the piss for a week. Nick's drinking had gone past that and he would end up in a blackout, fighting, threatening bouncers, being sick and generally pissing everyone off. Anyway, blokes his age were starting to get married, have kids and generally calm down a bit. His drinking was done in secret now and that's how he liked it. When he went drinking in public, all bets were off.

Making his way into the bar, Nick was relieved to see that Drake had a pint in front of him. *Licence to drink*, he thought.

Drake looked up and moved a dark mauve-patterned stool for Nick to sit down at the bar with him. 'Need a drink?'

'That's an understatement,' Nick gasped. The irony that he drank continuously, all day, every day, wasn't lost on him.

'Pint?'

'Great,' Nick replied, thinking that he would need a large whisky chaser at some point.

'This is all very clandestine, Nick. Hotel bar out of town. You're not really my type, Nick,' Drake quipped.

Nick smiled and shook his head. 'No … but I'm not sure who to trust anymore, boss.'

Drake caught the barman's eye, pointed at his own drink and gestured to bring one for Nick.

'Listen, I've spoken to the commander. Merseyside and the NCA are aware that we think that Webb might be on the run or he might have been taken by force by Blake. Merseyside are on to every informant they've got on the ground.'

'If they took him, I don't think they took him for a chat.'

'Neither do I. But whatever happens to Webb, he's had it coming to him. What's that saying? "If you decide to eat with the Devil, then make sure you use a long spoon."'

'Very profound, boss.' Nick smiled dryly.

'I passed my eleven plus,' Drake said.

Nick knew Webb was a prick. He was completely out of his depth when it came to Blake. He had been seduced by what he perceived as the glamour of crime and gangsters. Now he was paying the ultimate price.

'If he's on the run, I've got an all-ports out, so he won't get very far,' Drake said.

'Maybe he'll contact us and make a deal?' Nick speculated hopefully. It was Webb's only real option. Even with his wealth, a man like Webb wouldn't know how to go on the run successfully.

'Now that would be ideal.' Drake sipped an inch from his pint. 'So, Mac was there when you arrived?'

Nick looked at Drake. 'Massive coincidence that he was nearby and heard the shout.' Nick's tone was darkly sardonic.

'You don't buy it?' Drake asked.

'Do you? Neither of us are great believers in coincidence. And I've been thinking over a few things this year that don't add up.'

Drake took a quick look around the bar. 'Fire away.'

'Mark Ferguson's murder last February. We know that was down to Blake because I saw him there. But how did Blake know where Ferguson was in Porthmadog? He knew the precise location of where Ferguson had been seen by our informant. And the only people that had that information was us. Mac was out with me that night. Maybe he got that information to Blake? Doesn't take more than a text while we're on the way. I wouldn't even notice,' Nick explained grimly.

Drake nodded and drank his drink for a moment as he thought. 'It didn't add up at the time, did it?'

'Fields saw an overweight, middle-aged detective watching Harlech Beach with binoculars on the afternoon of Owen's murder. Who was that? Failing that, the photofit that Abi Mullen came up with even looks like Mac. Maybe he did it? Maybe Mac murdered Owen Ankers for Blake?' Nick's face fell as he said this out loud.

'If that's all true, then Mac is Osprey.' Drake shook his head with the gravity of what they were suggesting. 'Jesus … We have to tread very carefully at the moment. All of this is circumstantial and that's exactly what the IOPC will say.'

Nick nodded as he gulped at his pint. 'I know, I know. There were police from Merseyside buzzing around the station yesterday. It wouldn't take a genius to work out there was a joint operation taking place within Titan. Mac tips off Blake that there is something big going on at the station, even though he doesn't exactly know what. Blake knows that's the day the drugs are going out on the vans. He knows it's no coincidence and takes all the drugs off the vans.'

'My instinct says you're right but there's no evidence. We have to flag this up to the ACU and the IOPC first. We cannot be seen to investigate our own officer in any way. Clear?' Drake said.

'I let something slip at Webb's house. I confronted him. I couldn't help it, but he might think I'm on to him,' Nick explained.

Drake's phone buzzed, he looked at it and answered. 'DCI Drake. Yes …'

As Drake wandered away for some privacy, Nick's

anxiety got the better of him and he signalled to the barman. 'Double Jack Daniels. Sorry, treble.'

Nick spun around and watched Drake on the phone. The barman returned with the drink. Nick took it, moved out of view of Drake and gulped it down in one. *Phew.* Instant relief throughout his body. *Nice one.*

Drake returned and gestured to his phone. 'That was the NCA. Webb has made contact.'

That was good news. Webb was no good to them in a case against Blake if he was dead. 'So, at least he's not at the bottom of the Mersey,' Nick said dryly.

'Not yet. He's in hiding and won't say where. But he does want to make a deal for intel on Blake,' Drake said.

This was news that Nick wanted to hear and, with the whisky now in his system, he was buzzing.

An oyster catcher, black and white with a distinctive orange bill, flapped noisily on the uneven rocks as an incoming tide approached ominously. However, the bird had a nylon fishing line wrapped tight around its neck and the other end was trapped under an enormous boulder. Every time it attempted to fly away, the line went taut and the bird crashed to the ground.

Ruth yanked the line, seeing if she could free it from under the seaweed-strewn rock but it wasn't budging. The more she pulled, the more the line cut into the palms of her hands. She urged the frantic bird to stop flying – it was making it more difficult to pull the line clear.

A spray of sea water splashed into the air close by. Ruth could smell and taste the salt. She looked at the approaching sea, which was now about ten feet away. If she didn't free the oyster catcher, it would drown and time was running out.

A figure appeared above Ruth, standing high on some rocks. The figure had their back to Ruth and was dressed in the brown robes of a monk. They turned and pulled the hood down from their head. It was Sarah. Her eyes were glazed, black and dead like that of a shark.

Sea water crashed over Ruth and she was helplessly swept away, dragged back by the tide and then sucked under the sea. She couldn't breathe. She was gasping and drowning.

Then a swollen face appeared in the sea. The face of someone drowning beside her. It was Abi Mullen. She was dying.

Ruth woke with a start. Another anxiety dream. Her pulse was racing and she could feel her heart thudding against her rib cage. She took a deep breath and let it out slowly before checking her phone, but there were no text messages. It took several minutes for her to compose herself.

Ruth glanced over at where the photo of Sarah used to sit. She had forgotten that she had moved it now that Sian stayed over on a regular basis. She knew that Sian wouldn't mind but it was such an emotive subject. It was just prudent not to have a permanent visual reminder next to them.

Sian stirred a little and moved her head on the pillow. She opened her eyes and looked blearily up at Ruth who was now sitting up in bed.

'You okay?' Sian asked in a croaky voice.

'Yeah.' Ruth's response was unconvincing.

Sian gave her a look to say that she didn't believe her.

Ruth shrugged. 'Just a dream. That's all. It scared me.'

'Yesterday was a strange day. Just your subconscious making sense of it all.'

'Thank you, Dr Freud.' Ruth smiled back at her. God, Sian was so sensible and wise. So much more so than her. Ruth still felt like an infant in her presence sometimes.

'Who was in your dream. That girl, Abi?' Sian asked as she yawned and sat up.

Ruth nodded. 'Yeah. Some of it.'

'I can't imagine that. Having another personality that can just take you over and you have no choice. It must be terrifying.'

'Self-protection. Anyone subjected to that much fear and trauma, their only option is to not be there. I guess it's that or go mad or just die from the experience. The brain finds its own way of surviving.'

Sian nodded, her face thoughtful and compassionate. 'Christ, poor Abi. You going for a ciggie?'

Ruth shook her head. 'No. They're very bad for you.'

'Quick brew? Come on, you stay there and I'll go and make it.'

'No, it's fine.' Ruth seemed lost in thought. For a moment, she was overwhelmed. The emotions from her dream were still being held physically by her body. And then what she had seen in Abi Mullen.

Ruth looked over at Sian who watched her. 'I've never felt anything like it. The room seemed to go cold. Completely spooked me. And I've seen some bloody awful things.'

'COME HERE.' SIAN PULLED THE SHEET BACK AND beckoned for Ruth to come over.

Ruth shifted over, curled so that Sian was behind her and they were spooning. Sian stroked her head.

Ruth felt safe and content for the first time in years. It was a blissful feeling.

She was falling in love with Sian.

IT WAS GONE MIDNIGHT. NICK HAD BEEN SITTING OPPOSITE Mac's house, just outside the village of Trevor, for nearly an hour. He wasn't sure what he expected to see but he couldn't sleep yet. There was too much going around in his head to go home and relax.

Nick had checked that Mac was in when he arrived at 9.30 p.m. After that there was nothing. No one came or went from the house.

Nick gave it another half an hour and then made the long drive out to a village near Corwen where his father lived in a ramshackle bungalow. Sitting in the car, Nick was drunk and was feeling increasingly maudlin. Neil Diamond sang out in the car. It was his classic go-to album for self-pity. 'I Am, I Said' played its mournful, sombre tone.

Nick dug deep, recalling memories that made him feel emotional. It was only when he drank like this that he ever felt any emotion. It allowed him to tap into that part of himself that seemed to be lacking when he was sober.

When Nick reflected back on his life, he wondered sometimes if he had been a sociopath. There was a distinct lack of empathy and emotion.

In his twenties and early thirties, he had jumped from one relationship to the next in true serial-monogamist style. However, there was always a crossover and sporadic infidelity, so the 'monogamous' part wasn't strictly true. Each relationship lasted between nine months to a year, basically until the buzz of the honeymoon period had gone. And once the girl he had chosen to deceive and manipulate into loving him no longer produced the endorphin highs that he needed to fix himself, he moved onto the next. It was classic addict behaviour. Trying to fix the internal pain and void with external doses of manufactured 'love', until it no longer worked.

The relationships played on a loop. Nick would say the same well-rehearsed lines, play out the same studied scenes, go on the same practised romantic trips to the same picturesque places. And the results were the same. The girl would fall for him and for a while Nick bathed in those blissful and exciting surges of phenylethylamine that his brain produced. The chemical was a stimulant, much like an amphetamine, that caused the release of the feel-good highs of norepinephrine and dopamine. And like any addict, when those chemicals ran out, he needed to move onto a new relationship that could elicit the same rush of euphoria. It was like being on a low dose of ecstasy or MDMA powder for weeks on end.

However, when Nick knew it was time for the relationship to end, he engineered it with silences and calculated emotional distance that made it clear, in a non-verbal way, that something was seriously wrong. Things would come to a head. There would be a discussion. Nick could even elicit appropriate tears and even a sob. And when the girl had left, he felt nothing but a twinge of relief that he could soon find a new fix. No loss, no pain, no emotion. Nothing. And it scared him if he was honest.

Sociopath. Nick had looked it up. Someone who had no conscience. Someone who would lie, cheat, manipulate and hurt others with no understanding or thought of the other person or how they were feeling. And that was Nick down to a tee.

Swigging hard at the vodka, Nick got out of the car and let the cool night air wash over his face. The night sky was clear and the blackness was studded with sparkling flecks light years away. It was a relief to feel this small. This insignificant. If only he could get that kind of perspective when he was sober.

Wandering slowly over to his father's home, Nick realised that he didn't know what he was going to do. Was he going to knock and say hello? Was he there to confront him? Something in his mind had told him to go there. Now, in his drunkenness, he didn't know why.

The garden outside had been tidied. Actually, it was much more than just tidied. What had once been a mixture of rubble, weeds and cracked paving stones, was now a neat, colourful garden with a new brick patio.

At first, Nick wondered if his father had moved. The more he looked, the more he could see that the front of the house had been transformed. The door had been repainted in an olive green and the exterior cleaned and repointed.

There was a car on the drive and Nick knew his father hadn't driven for several years. Maybe now he was sober, he was driving again?

Moving closely towards the front of the house, Nick glanced around to make sure that no one was watching him. To say that he was acting suspiciously was a huge understatement. And if there were new occupants, it wouldn't look good for a police officer to be snooping around. A drunk police officer.

There was a dim light coming from the downstairs window that Nick knew was the living room. Inching down the path, Nick slowly peered into the room. The dark, black silence of the night rang in his ears.

His father, in a dressing gown, was sitting on the sofa watching the television. In front of him was a cup of tea and biscuits. The room was softly lit with a couple of lamps that gave out a vanilla glow.

Nick watched him. His father's face was different. It wasn't that it was clean-shaven and no longer grey and sullen – in fact there was even a hint of tanned skin on his forehead. It was more a glint of life or hope in his eyes, possibly. Nick didn't believe in auras, but he would swear that the light around his father had changed colour. Maybe it was just the vodka in Nick's system?

And then his father leant forward, took the mug of tea

and sipped it. He took a pack of tobacco out of his pocket and began to roll a cigarette.

Pushing his teeth together, Nick thought that tears were going to come but he managed to swallow them back down. He took a deep breath to compose himself. *Booze.* It made him emotional and vulnerable, and there was a good deal of self-pity in there as well.

He watched as his father chortled at something he was watching on the television. And then he boomed laughter and sat back on the sofa with utter delight, shaking his head. It was like the moment when you watch a child and they don't know you're watching them. There was something quite magical in that feeling.

Nick couldn't believe this was the same man whom he had seen, only two years ago, collapsed on the floor in this house, urine-soaked jeans around his ankles. That was the day that Nick thought enough was enough. He only saw his father every couple of months, but he had cut off contact after that. The hypocrisy of this wasn't lost on him either. Nick was looking for an excuse to hurt him. To signal to him that he wasn't forgiven for how he had been when Nick was a kid. Sod him. Let him die in alcoholic squalor.

And now there he was. There in front of him, looking like he had been reborn. Laughing. Smiling. And sober. The capacity the human body and mind has to repair itself staggered him.

Nick looked at him again and realised suddenly that he was pleased for his father. He was glad that he looked this well. And it was a treat to see him laughing.

Chapter Twenty-Four

It was mid-morning and Ruth was still trawling through endless paperwork. Anxious to get on with some real work, Ruth reminded herself of some of the menial tasks she had been doing a couple of weeks ago during her "phased" return. It was good to be back in CID, getting to grips with a proper case and making a difference. She also felt that she was lucky to be working with DCI Drake. He had all the qualities needed for a good guvnor. And Ruth had worked with some right wankers in the Met.

As Ruth saw it, an effective guv'nor was dependent upon a combination of management skills, investigative ability and relevant knowledge across the entire investigative process. Drake knew exactly what he was doing at every point; from the initial crime-scene assessment onwards.

Ruth glanced at her watch. It was 9 am and she was due to meet with Daniel Warburton's mother in Interview Room One. She had travelled up from Kent the day before to look at the items that the SOCO had found in Fields' allotment shed.

Belting down the corridor, Ruth composed herself and entered. Daniella Warburton was sitting at the table with a WPC, who left now that Ruth had arrived.

Daniella Warburton had remarried and was now Daniella Lensky. However, a new name couldn't hide the fact that time hadn't been kind to her. Her face was pinched. Her eyes were sullen and her hair badly dyed blonde.

Ruth had seen it before. The death of a child has a profound and catastrophic effect on any family. When the murder is not solved, the pain seems never-ending. There was no way of hiding the long-term physical damage and wear that type of mental trauma and agony would bring.

Daniella Lensky was sitting quietly at the desk. Ruth knew that their call had given Daniella hope that they had found Daniel's killer. It would be no consolation for his death. But it would bring some kind of natural conclusion for her if his murderer could be found and convicted so that there was some semblance of justice.

'Hi Daniella. I'm Detective Inspector Ruth Hunter,' she said, offering her hand and sitting down opposite.

Ruth didn't want to prolong the agony.

'Thank you so much for coming to see me today. I know it must be difficult for you,' Ruth said.

'No, it's fine,' Daniella said.

'I'm going to show you a couple of things we have discovered. If you can look at them and tell me if they belonged to Daniel,' Ruth explained.

Ruth carefully lay the evidence bag down onto the table in front of her. Inside were the Glastonbury wristband and the Oasis pin badge. Ruth calculated that these items were more likely to be Daniel's than the other evidence.

Daniella's hands shook as she looked at the bag and then she put it down.

'No. They're not Daniel's,' she said. She blinked and Ruth could see how overwhelmed she was.

'Okay, thank you. I'm going to show you another bag, so if you could look at that for me,' Ruth said.

Daniella nodded as Ruth put the bag in front of her. It contained the hairclips, knickers.

Daniella shook her head. 'I'm really sorry …' Her voice began to break.

'Thank you. I'm afraid that's everything,' Ruth explained and she saw the look of devastation that came over Daniella's face.

'I'm sorry to have got your hopes up but I did think there was a chance these things could have belonged to Daniel,' Ruth said.

But Daniella wasn't listening. Tears welled and then fell down her face as she began to shake. And then she let out a wail and hugged herself to stop the pain.

The phone call had stirred up all that loss and all that agony. It was too much to bear.

Ruth comforted her and after a few minutes, Daniella began to compose herself. There were minutes, and even sometimes hours, where she forgot what had happened to her son, she told Ruth. Yet her memory would default back to that day and the aftermath still on a daily basis.

The station's family liaison officer took Daniella to have a cup of tea and to make sure she knew how and when she was going to return to Kent.

THE SUN WAS BEGINNING TO SET WITH PINK AND PURPLE hues when Ruth came into the lounge. The case was running merrily around her head with hypothesis after hypothesis. Her instinct was that Fields was guilty of something. He had a darkness that she had rarely seen.

For a few moments, Ruth watched Sian sleeping on the sofa. Her face looked perfectly symmetrical. That perfect, flawless and innocent face almost like a child asleep. In that moment, there was such rapture in her. Joy. She never thought for one moment that she would find it again. And of course, now Ruth worried about it being taken away. Nagging thoughts of self-doubt. What the hell did someone like Sian see in her? Why hadn't she gone for someone her own age?

Ruth caught herself wallowing deeply in negativity and wandered quietly to the kitchen. Glass of wine and a fag. That's what she needed. The solution to most problems lay in that combo.

Ruth ambled out to the patio and sat down at the table and chairs. Looking out across the countryside, the air was still warm but it was thick and heavy. She could feel the pressure growing. Forecasts had said that the summer heatwave was going to break with a series of heavy thunderstorms and she could sense them coming. In fact, as she looked at the horizon, the burnt-orange glow was tinged with the ominous battleship grey of storm clouds.

Her phone buzzed and rattled for a second on the table. Taking a deep drag of her fag, Ruth checked. A text from her daughter Ella. *I'm dropping Charlotte in Chester tomorrow afternoon. Thought I'd pop in or go for a drink? You okay? Love E xx.*

A little warmth glowed inside Ruth. She texted back, thinking how lovely it would be for her, Sian and Ella to sit by the Dee in the sunshine and put the world to rights.

Ruth sipped her wine and stubbed out her cigarette. In the next field, that backed onto her garden, a neighbour kept two horses. They were both palomino and beautiful.

For several seconds, the horses were still and didn't move. It was as though Ruth was looking at a photo. And then a tail swished, manes shook and they moved off together.

Another buzz on her phone. Probably Ella confirming tomorrow with an emoji. It wasn't though. It was Steven Flaherty.

HI RUTH. SORRY FOR TEXTING SO LATE. THERE'S BEEN A development with Jurgen Kessler in Germany. I'll send you a BBC link. I didn't want you to see it without me giving you a heads up. I will call you later. Steven.

THE BOTTOM OF RUTH'S STOMACH ROLLED AND PITCHED. What was he talking about? She was angry. Why was he being so vague? Her anxiety went through the roof and she started to feel sick.

Ruth quickly clicked the link.

GERMAN BANKER WANTED BY POLICE IN CONNECTION with Double Murder.

The BBC understands that police in Berlin are beginning to mount a manhunt in their search for Jurgen Kessler, a forty-year-old banker, who they want to question in connection with two murders in the capital city in the last week. On Friday, Eva Schurrle, a twenty-three-year-old waitress, was found murdered in the Mitte district. Then on Monday, the body of Nina Kohlsberg, a twenty-nine-year-old nurse, was discovered in the Neukölln district of the city. Police are appealing for any witnesses who think they saw anything to contact them.

. . .

RUTH RAN INSIDE, JUST REACHED THE TOILET AND WAS physically sick. She took a breath and she could feel tears coming. He was the last person that anyone had seen with Sarah. Various witnesses had confirmed that. The CCTV showed it was him. Now he was wanted in connection with the murder of two young women. There was no coincidence that he was on that train with Sarah and that she had disappeared. Her head was spinning.

She went outside and taking another cigarette with her shaking hand, Ruth lit it and checked various other news sites. Sky, Fox News and Reuters all had similar stories, clearly based on the press release that police in Berlin had released. There was also an English language news website for Germany called *The Local*, but again the information it had was the same as the BBC.

Sian came out half an hour later but Ruth didn't really want to talk about what she had learnt about Kessler. She said that there had been a development in Sarah's case and she would talk to Sian about it later. The whole thing was already complicating their relationship. She didn't want her to have to deal with even more turbulent emotional baggage.

Sian brought out more wine. Ruth wasn't looking forward to the following morning as she had to meet with Lyn Povall's family and go through the suspicious items from Fields' allotment shed. When she added in the news about Kessler, her mind was a bloody mess.

'You sure you're okay?' Sian asked after another pregnant pause.

'What? Yeah … fine. Work stuff.'

'Hard to switch off. I dreamt I was trapped in Fields' house. Except it wasn't Fields' house, it was a holiday cottage we used to go to near Abersoch.'

Ruth sipped from her wine, took a cigarette and lit it.

Sian wagged her finger playfully. 'Hey, I thought you were going to cut down?'

'What are you. My bloody mother?' Ruth snapped and regretted it as soon as she had.

'Wow. You're a little ray of sunshine this evening.'

'Sorry. Lot of stuff going on.'

Sian was trawling through some social media on her phone. 'Sorry to talk shop but any word from Merseyside on a possible leak?'

'No. Nothing.'

'Christ, you're hard work sometimes, aren't you?' Sian said, still looking at her phone.

'Just piss off and grow up, Sian. I've got a lot on my plate!'

'Don't we know it,' Sian muttered putting her phone down and getting angry.

'What's that supposed to mean?'

'Hasn't anyone told you, self-pity isn't an attractive quality,' Sian said.

'It's not self-pity. But sometimes life is serious and not everything in the world can be made into a joke,' Ruth growled.

'Life's too short to be miserable about what's happened in the past.'

'My past. You're talking about my past,' Ruth said. She was feeling angry about being judged.

'Do you want to talk about your past?'

'No, not really,' Ruth said.

'Well that makes you emotionally unavailable,' Sian said.

'Does it? Really?' Ruth sneered but she feared that Sian was probably right.

'And I'm fed up of sharing you with a bloody ghost that I can't compete with.'

'I want you to go.' Ruth glared at her. 'Now!'

'Read my mind. I'll leave you to your wallowing,' Sian sneered, getting up and heading inside.

Ruth got her wine glass and hurled it at the back wall where it smashed.

Chapter Twenty-Five

Outside, the summer heatwave had broken and the sound of rain started against the large windows. Then a rumble of distant thunder.

As Drake got up to address the waiting detectives for morning briefing, the strain of recent days showed on his face. He looked uncharacteristically tired and his usually pristine clothes appeared a little thrown together.

Sian had already seen Ruth when she arrived in CID and made a good job of blanking her immediately. Ruth hoped that no one noticed. She couldn't handle any speculation or humorous comments today. She already felt emotionally exhausted.

'Okay, listen up, everyone. I need us to run through all our lines of enquiry on this case. And then we need to get out there and find something solid.' Drake gulped at his black coffee and looked over at Ruth. 'Ruth will update us on Abi Mullen.'

Ruth pointed to the photo of Abi Mullen that was pinned to one of the case boards. 'As most of you know, we brought Abi Mullen in yesterday to explain why she – or someone looking identical to her – was photographed in Curtis Blake's lap-dancing club in Southport. Abi claimed that the girl in the photo' – Ruth walked over to the screen where the photo was now being projected – 'was in fact her identical twin sister, Libby. We knew from social services that Abi Mullen had a sister but we didn't know that she was an identical twin. However, as an explanation that does seem plausible. If you've ever met Abi, she is nervous, very shy and suffers from several mental health issues. I would suggest it would be impossible for her to work as a dancer in a lap-dancing club. We are now waiting to hear from births, deaths and marriages to confirm that Libby Mullen is Abi's twin sister. I've checked council tax and Inland Revenue. Libby Mullen has never paid tax or council tax in her life. However, she does have a NatWest bank account with several thousand pounds in it.'

Ruth moved back across the room and sipped some water. 'I've spoken to Abi's clinical psychologist. She suffers from a disassociate personality disorder. It was a coping mechanism she developed when she was abused by her foster father. It manifests itself in blackouts and memory loss at times of high stress. It can also manifest itself in fantasy and even multiple personalities.'

Merringer looked dubious. 'And have you seen one of these "personalities"?'

Ruth nodded. 'Yes. Yesterday, Abi went into a blackout and a different personality – claiming to be her sister Libby – appeared.'

'I thought the twin sister Libby worked in Blake's lap-dancing club?' Merringer said.

'I don't know. Look, what I do know is that I used to think this was the stuff of films and TV. But either Abi Mullen is an Oscar-winning actress, or she is a very damaged, very sick young lady. My instinct says it is the latter.'

There was a moment when everyone in CID took it all in. It was definitely a first for most of them.

'And I know what I saw in there. They were two different people. Same body but two different people. And I've had my share of the weird and creepy as a police officer. And it was as creepy as it gets,' Ruth said.

Ruth accidentally caught Sian's eye for a second. Sian looked away. Ruth didn't have time for juvenile behaviour at that moment.

Ruth continued. 'This other personality – Libby, or whoever she was – had everything wrong. She described a ferocious sustained attack of over twenty wounds. She said she cut at Owen's genitals and virtually cut off one of his fingers. It's pure fantasy. Maybe that's what she wanted to do to him. And according to her clinical psychologist, this exaggeration or fantasy about actual events is symptomatic of this type of personality disorder.'

As the thunder rumbled outside, Drake got up and looked out at everyone. 'Okay. My gut tells me that Abi Mullen was there, but nothing more. She is not a viable line of enquiry, and we have several others that are.' Drake frowned as he looked out across the assembled detectives. 'Where's Mac this morning?'

Merringer shifted forward. 'Just had a text from him to say he's got car trouble and that he'll be in later.'

Drake nodded and then shot a meaningful look at Nick and Ruth. They knew that news could be a problem. If Mac had any idea that anyone was on to him, he could disappear. 'Nick, can you fill us in where we're at with Callum Webb and Curtis Blake?'

Nick nodded and stood up. 'Boss.' Nick went over to the board and pointed to some photos of Webb's house.

'Now that the deal between Blake and Webb to use his vans is redundant, it looks like Blake has decided it's too risky to allow Webb to talk to the police. Webb was followed home yesterday but managed to escape. He is now in hiding. He has contacted the NCA and confirmed that he will do a deal in return for giving evidence against Blake. We're waiting for a phone call this morning to arrange where and how we are going to meet Webb.' Nick looked at Drake. 'I'm also confirming how many AFOs we can have for that meeting.'

Drake nodded. 'Good. As far as I'm concerned, this is our most viable line of enquiry. What about Tony Downes?'

'Nothing, boss. He seems to have vanished too.'

'I will liaise with the NCA and Merseyside. As soon as we have Webb in custody, I want Blake taken off the streets before he can disappear too.' Drake walked over to the photo of Fields on the case board. 'Other lines of enquiry?'

'Fields was stabbed last night in his cell. Reports from the ICU aren't hopeful,' Ruth explained.

'What about the evidence we took from his allotment?'

Ruth looked up from her notes. 'I met with Daniella Lensky, Daniel Warburton's mother, but unfortunately there was nothing there that she could identify as having belonged to Daniel. Lyn Povall's husband is arriving in a couple of hours, so we'll see what he says.'

'Instinct?' Drake asked.

'I still think Fields is a genuine line of enquiry, boss. He hated Owen Ankers. His money, his sexuality. He admits he followed him and Abi Mullen that afternoon. He has no alibi. He had Ankers' dog on his property. He could fit Abi's composite of the man she saw that day. He's an ex-paratrooper so stabbing someone isn't something that would phase him. Motive, means and opportunity,' Ruth explained clearly.

Drake nodded. 'Okay. Wait to see what Lyn Povall's husband says.'

'Something bothers me about the unused allotment too. It doesn't add up,' Ruth said thinking aloud. 'My fear is that Fields will die and then we find out that he has something to do with these deaths. The families would never see him brought to justice.'

Sɪᴀɴ ᴘᴜᴛ ᴅᴏᴡɴ ᴛʜᴇ ᴘʜᴏɴᴇ ᴛʜᴀᴛ sʜᴇ ʜᴀᴅ ᴊᴜsᴛ ᴀɴsᴡᴇʀᴇᴅ on the other side of the incident room. She looked straight past Ruth at Drake. 'We might not need to worry, boss. ICU from the hospital report that Fields is making some progress this morning. Not out of danger but not critical.'

Drake nodded. 'Right. I want CID officers over to take a statement from Fields as soon as he can speak. I'm not interested in what the medical staff tell you. If Fields has any compulsion to confess or give us any evidence, I want one of us to be there.'

Tʜᴇ ᴡᴇᴀᴛʜᴇʀ ᴏᴜᴛsɪᴅᴇ ᴡᴀs ᴅᴀʀᴋ ᴀɴᴅ ᴛʜᴇ ʀᴀɪɴ ʟᴀsʜᴇᴅ against the windows of the corridor. Ruth was running late and she knew that Mr Povall was waiting for her in the family room. As her heart thumped, she admonished herself for not having done a run in months. She would have to start again. She could feel the heat under her hair-line as she sprinted the last few yards along the corridor, stopped, took a couple of deep breaths and composed herself and went in.

Geoff Povall was sitting at the table. Overweight and a little scruffy, he looked up at her awkwardly. Having spent twenty years waiting for the police to come up with a decent lead for his wife's murderer, Ruth couldn't imagine how or what he felt at this precise moment.

Ruth approached with her best empathetic smile, shook his hand firmly and sat down. 'Mr Povall. It's really good of you to come here today. I know it can't be easy for you.'

'Geoff, it's Geoff.' He thought for a moment about what Ruth had said. 'No. I've wanted justice for Lyn for twenty years now. There's been nothing. I don't suppose this will be anything, will it?' He sounded emotionally exhausted.

'We don't know, Geoff. We hope it is something so that we can get some kind of justice for Lyn, you and your family. I cannot imagine how hard it has been,' Ruth said, but in reality, she did know. She knew what it was like to lose a loved one and have no idea about what had happened to them. The destructive nature of false hope. The only difference was that Geoff Povall knew that his wife was never going to walk through their front door because she was gone. He needed to know why and who was responsible. Was it better to have that certainty? Or was it better to have hope that there had been an accident, a crime or a medical issue and that that person was still somewhere out there?

'Okay. I'm going to show you some items that we believe might have belonged to your wife. Now, take your time, and if it gets too much for you, let me know and we can take a break,' Ruth said.

Geoff took a breath and then swallowed. He appeared to be struggling with the hope that he would find out what had happened to his beloved, beautiful Lyn and that the person who had stolen her away could be brought to justice. It was almost unbearable.

Quietly, Ruth took the first evidence bag and placed it

carefully in front of him. It contained the large silver hairclip.

After a moment, Geoff allowed himself to look down at it. He pursed his lips tight and shook his head. It wasn't anything like Lyn would wear. His sense of deflation was inexplicable.

'No, I'm sorry …' he murmured.

Ruth nodded. 'It's okay. I'm going to show you the next piece of evidence.'

Ruth placed the next evidence bag, which contained the pink knickers, on the table. Geoff looked again and shook his head.

'No. No … I'm so sorry. I thought there might be something …' Geoff said.

Ruth had hoped that either of these items would have sparked some recognition as they clearly belonged to a woman. Now all she had was the Glastonbury wristband and the Oasis pin badge. She wasn't holding out much hope.

'Okay, Geoff, could you look at these two items for us?' Ruth's voice was now virtually a whisper.

Geoff looked at the multi-coloured Glastonbury '95 wristband and his face drained of colour. Then he noticed the Oasis button badge.

'Oh my God.' He mouthed the words to himself before creasing up his eyes.

'Geoff?' Ruth could see that he was suddenly over-whelmed.

Geoff took a deep breath. 'Yeah. They're hers. Oh God … I …'

'That's all right, Geoff. Take your time,' Ruth said.

'That's where we went for her twenty-first birthday. We drove to Glastonbury in 1995.'

Ruth nodded but then frowned. 'And she still wore the wristband in 1999?'

Geoff's hands shook as he held the bag and gazed at it. 'We went with her sister Emma. We had such an amazing time there. Emma died from breast cancer the following year, and Lyn wore the wristband, you know, to remember her by.'

'Okay, thank you, Geoff. I can't imagine how difficult that was for you … What about the badge?' Ruth asked.

Geoff nodded. 'Yeah, the badge was hers … I can't believe they're just here in front of me.' The tears rolled down his face. His shoulders juddered as he began to sob. 'I miss her so much. I miss her voice. We had so many things we were going to do together.'

Ruth nodded at him and put her hand on his shoulder.

DRAKE LOOKED UP FROM HIS DESK AS RUTH BANGED urgently on the door. 'Geoff Povall just identified the wristband and badge as belonging to Lyn Povall.'

Drake took this in for second. Fields murdered Lyn Povall twenty years ago. How then did Fields fit in with Owen Ankers' murder? Did Fields have anything to do with it? Were they separate murders and not linked except by location?

'How sure was he?' Drake asked urgently.

'One hundred per cent. There was no doubt in his mind. They belonged to Lyn Povall,' Ruth replied gravely.

Drake shook his head. 'Let's get that allotment dug up today.'

Ruth nodded. 'Yes, boss. I'll call SOCO.'

'We need another officer down at the hospital. I want that bastard Fields read his rights and arrested even if he's half dead,' Drake growled.

'Boss. I pray that the bastard survives. If you had seen Geoff Povall's face when he saw those things ...' Ruth couldn't hide her emotion.

'All that waiting. Twenty years. I cannot imagine how that feels.'

'If there is a God, he needs to get Fields to recover so he can stand trial. So that Geoff Povall and the rest of her family can have justice and a little bit of peace in the rest of their lives,' Ruth said looking at Drake.

Chapter Twenty-Six

R uth and Nick had been ushered into Drake's office. It was littered with paperwork and used coffee mugs. It was unusual for Drake, thought Ruth. He was usually fastidious in having order and tidiness. Ruth assumed it was a sign that the stress of having someone in the department on Blake's payroll was taking its toll.

The IOPC Senior Investigator, Catrin Jones, was sitting at the table on the other side of the room.

Drake beckoned them over. 'Nick, Ruth. Come and sit down for a second.'

Ruth and Nick sat down. On the computer monitor, there was CCTV footage. Ruth immediately assumed that this was connected with the IOPC's investigation into Mac and links to Blake and Webb.

'We have put in place surveillance on DC McDonald from last night. He was followed to a retail park where he met this man. I am reliably informed that this is Jason Penn, his brother-in-law, who owns a local building contractors,' Drake said.

Ruth and Nick looked at the footage, which showed

Jason Penn handing over shopping bags to Mac, who then placed them into the boot of his car.

'What's in the bags?' Nick asked.

'Our investigator on the ground went into the hardware and camping outlet that Jason Penn had visited. On DC Macdonald's shopping list was industrial gaffer tape, dust masks, a balaclava, plastic ties and industrial ear protectors,' Drake explained darkly.

'Bloody hell,' Ruth muttered under her breath. It had been a long time since she had been in a police station where there had been a corrupt officer.

'Not decorating the spare room then?' quipped Nick sardonically.

'We assume that this is equipment to be used in the hunt for Callum Webb,' Drake said.

Drake looked at Ruth. 'Go with Nick to Mac's home right now. Uniform have already been past and reported that he's there. I want us to pick him up and then we can let the ACU and IOPC handle the rest.'

As Nick and Ruth slowed in the lunchtime traffic out of Llancastell, thick, black clouds sprawled across the sky, rolling slowly in from the Irish Sea to the west.

Rain started to patter again on the windscreen. Ruth wound up her window. Outside, the colour of houses, trees and cars drained away in the darkening light. It was such a contrast to the colours that she had grown used to during the summer heatwave. The signs of the weather breaking had threatened ominously all morning. The air was uncomfortably heavy again. The humidity still pushed down. The scent of rain was heady and under its growing volume, the low boom of thunder juddered.

Knowing that Mac would recognise his car, Nick had

signed out a silver, unmarked BMW Series 3 from the carpool. As an unmarked car, the windscreen had been treated to give it a slightly smoked or oily effect, which meant its occupants were unrecognisable even from a short distance.

As they took the A487, the main road out of Llancastell towards Llangollen, Ruth saw the signs to Cefn, pronounced Kevin, and Trevor. As a Londoner of a certain age, having two places called 'Kevin' and 'Trevor' next to each other was strangely amusing to her when she first arrived.

On her lap were the old case files for the murders of Daniel Warburton and Lyn Povall. They were still in the old cardboard folders from the nineties and looked worn. Ruth wanted to check some of the initial statements and interviews to see if anything had been missed. She also wanted to see when and how Fields' name cropped up in the original investigation.

The sound of the rain amplified and accentuated the silence in the car.

'You're very quiet.' Nick's tone was one of concern. It wasn't the actual silence that concerned him, it was the sense he got that Ruth was struggling with something.

Ruth thought for a moment. It was the news about Kessler, the meeting with Geoff Povall, the row with Sian. Everything. Everything was getting to her and she couldn't shake it off. Maybe it was being with Geoff Povall who had at last found some resolution. 'I do wonder how long I can keep doing this job for. Maybe moving up here should have been the chance for a new start doing something else.'

'You don't mean that. I've seen how much you care about the people you help,' Nick said forcefully.

Ruth felt a little glow from the compliment. 'Yeah, but that can take its toll.'

'Come on. There is nothing else like this job. Helping people when they are at their lowest ebb of despair. Saving lives. Stopping those who cause misery and suffering to others.'

Ruth smiled, nodded and pulled out a cigarette.

'Driving really fast with blue lights and sirens,' Nick joked with a smile.

Ruth let out a dry laugh and smiled back. There was a warmth between them, despite them being essentially chalk and cheese.

'You've never told me why you became a copper,' Nick said.

Ruth hesitated. 'My old man, I suppose.'

Nick frowned. 'Didn't know your dad was a copper.'

'Oh, he wasn't. He was as bent as a nine-bob note.'

Nick raised his eyebrows. 'Now you've lost me. I'm pretty sure you're not saying he was gay.'

'No. He was a petty crook. Into everything. Stolen goods. Everything in our house came off the back of a lorry. Every time there was a knock at the door, we had to hide. Or he'd get me to answer the door and say he was out. Then one day, someone who he owed money to decided to take a baseball bat to him as he and my mum were packing shopping into our car.'

'Christ,' Nick exclaimed.

'Mum went to the hospital with him. He was in intensive care for a day or two but made a full recovery. I just remember this WPC coming around to talk to me and my brother while we were waiting for our gran to come over. I suppose I was about ten. And this WPC was so kind, and I thought that's what I want to do when I grow up.'

'Makes sense.' Nick nodded.

'I used to lay in bed and wonder what it would be like to live in a house where no one worried about the police or a local thug knocking on the door all day, every day. We lived on our nerves. My mates at school thought my dad was a real character.'

'And you?'

'He was my dad. I loved him. But he could be a pain in the arse.'

'Is he still around?'

Ruth shook her head. 'He dropped dead from a stroke in the Northcote Road market on my twenty-first birthday.'

'I'm sorry to hear that.'

'Oh, listen to me rattling on.'

Ruth looked back at the files for a moment. She flicked through a couple of pages and then began to read.

'Do you miss him?' Nick asked.

Ruth thought about this for a moment and nodded. 'Every day. I was his little girl, and whatever he did, he did his best. Parents are only human after all. And I didn't realise how difficult that is until I became one. And I've made so many mistakes, I can't stand in judgement of my father. Not now. I guess that's what you realise as you get older.'

Nick took these words in thoughtfully. Ruth was right. Nick had made a mess of his life, and for him to sit in judgement of anyone was complete hypocrisy. It had only taken him thirty-six years to come to that conclusion.

Nick's train of thought was broken by Ruth's face looking very perturbed by what she was reading in the old case files. She looked over at Nick.

'What's wrong?'

'This is the crime-scene log for Daniel Warburton's murder. It has a PC Davenport's name on it, which means the officer was present when Daniel Warburton's body was discovered. And then the initial interview with Povall's family has a PC Davenport down as being present for the first ten minutes.'

'Davenport? The ACC?' Nick frowned.

Ruth shrugged and nodded. 'It must be. She told me she started off working in North Wales. There can't have been many PC Davenports working in the North Wales Police Force in the late 1990s. But when I talked to her about Warburton and Povall's links to Owen's death, she said she vaguely remembered the cases. She certainly didn't say that she had worked on those cases. Why wouldn't she mention that?' Ruth asked. 'In fact, why would she hide the fact she had been on those cases?'

By the time Drake had arrived at the Harlech allotments, he had taken an accidental detour through Ffestiniog. It had been the first time he had managed to get into the centre of Snowdonia and the views of the countryside and mountains were breath-taking. It confirmed that their move from Manchester to North Wales was the right thing to have done, especially for the girls.

As Drake arrived at the allotments, the parched earth was darkening like gravy from the incessant rain of the thunderstorm. Some of it was starting to turn to surface mud. However, streams seemed to be running off along the surface of the ground, still hard and dry for many metres down. The air was full of the thick smells of dehydrated flowers, plants and undergrowth receiving their first rain in weeks.

Drake had spotted the SOCO forensics van on the other side of the allotments. Two SOCO officers, decked out in white forensic suits, waited and watched as the driver of the bright yellow JCB mini-excavator struggled to cut into the barren earth of Fields' allotment plot. The engine roared and juddered as it moved back a few yards.

On the drive to Harlech, Drake had gone through the hypotheses around Owen Ankers' murder again. It was rare not to have some kind of concrete lead by this point in a murder investigation. Usually there would be a prime suspect and their time would be spent building a case against that suspect. Sometimes there was very little. However, this case was just confusing.

His gut instinct was still that Owen's murder was likely to be linked to Callum Webb's dealings with Curtis Blake. The composite that Abi Mullen had created – the man in the balaclava – looked like Terry Downes. Blake had a history of maiming or killing anyone who stood in the way of him making money or expanding his empire. It was likely that Owen Ankers had done just that.

Where Fields fitted in, Drake didn't know, although it did look very likely that he attacked and killed Lyn Povall in 1999. However, that murder seemed to have a sexual element so did that rule Fields out of Owen's murder?

Drake saw one of the SOCOs wave and come to greet him. It was Jim Crozier. Drake knew him from a couple of old cases back in the day.

'DCI Drake,' Crozier said with a winning smile. He looked up at the sky. It was starting to rain again. 'Hottest, driest summer on record, and you pick today to dig up this bloody allotment.'

Drake shrugged. 'How we doing?'

'Not good, I'm afraid. Despite the rain, the earth is really dry and hard. It's all the sand and it's on a slope. It's really difficult to dig out.'

'GPR?' Drake asked. Ground Penetrating Radar was standard equipment for any police excavation now, but Drake hoped it would be a godsend today.

'Nothing, I'm afraid.'

DRAKE NODDED. HE WONDERED HOW FIELDS WAS DOING IN hospital. If he knew they were digging up his allotment, it might just finish him off. He agreed with Ruth. He wanted Fields to make a full recovery so that he could stand trial for at least Lyn Povall's murder. It would make all the difference to how her family dealt with her murder. Sometimes it gave them a little more peace to know what had happened and that justice was being served.

'What are we looking for? Bodies, I'm assuming?' Crozier's tone was matter of fact, even upbeat, as always. Drake did wonder if some of the SOCOs enjoyed their work a little too much. Maybe because they never really dealt with victims or families directly. For them, it was an intellectual exercise, like a puzzle.

'I'm not sure yet. Fields seemed to come up here every few years in the dead of night and do some digging around. I want to know why,' Drake explained.

'Might take us a while.' Crozier gestured to the digger.

'I haven't got a while.' Drake's voice bordered on withering.

Suddenly there was a shout from the other SOCO who waved them over. 'Got something, sir!'

Drake followed Crozier around the yellow evidence tape that fluttered noisily in the wind and the drizzle.

The other SOCO was crouched down using a small trowel and brushes on the earth. As she continued, what was being revealed were clearly bones.

They were small but they were intact. Drake's immediate thought was that they belonged to a child.

He crouched down to get a closer look. 'Human?'

'At first I thought they were,' the SOCO replied and

then tapped a large bone that she had just cleaned. 'It's a femur. In a human, even a child, it would be a lot longer than the other bones we've got here. This is a similar size.'

'And that means what?' Drake was getting impatient.

'An animal. From the look of some of the loose teeth here, I would say it's the remains of a dog.'

It had started to rain as Libby and Abi reached the outside deck for a quick fag. They were both hammered but it was only forty-five minutes before they pulled into Dublin.

'D'you wanna shag the little one?' Libby asked and then started to giggle. Abi wasn't a virgin but she had only been with a couple of men.

'I think I'm gonna shag the tall one,' Libby said as she blew a plume of smoke and watched it blow away in the sea wind.

That's what she liked about drunken sex. She didn't have to think about anything. She didn't have to be herself. It was an escape. And she felt wanted.

'You don't h-have to shag anyone, Libs,' Abi said.

Libby put her arm around her sister. 'You are funny, Abs, you know that?'

'When are we going back, Libs?' Abi asked cautiously.

'We're not even there yet, you stupid cow,' Libby growled.

And that's when she knew. Abi wasn't going to stop pestering her until they came back from Dublin.

Grabbing her phone, Libby switched it onto camera mode.

'Come on, Abs. Let's take some selfies, girl!' Libby yelled. She was drunk and she wanted to have some fun.

Libby grabbed Abi and they ran down the ferry deck towards the back of the boat. The rain was now falling hard, passengers were heading inside and the decks at the back were deserted.

With the wind lashing at their hair, Libby took a few selfies with Abi and they looked back at them giggling at how windswept they looked.

Libby gestured to the railings at the back of the ferry.

'Stand there, Abs. Like they do on Titanic,' Libby yelled.

She took a photo and came over to show her. It hadn't taken properly.

'I look a mess!' Abi giggled.

'We'll take it again.' Libby smiled at Abi. 'Don't worry, Abs.

We'll go to Dublin for a few days. Have a laugh. And then we'll come home. All right, kid?'

Abi nodded and Libby could see the relief in her face.

'Yeah, okay …'

'Right go back against those railings and put your arms out like Kate Winslet!' Libby shouted. 'That's it, Abs. "Near, far, wherever you are …"'

Libby sang at the top of her voice as she took more photographs.

Chapter Twenty-Seven

By the time Ruth and Nick pulled up just down from Mac's house, the thunder had started again even though the rain had stopped. The air was still muggy and the building pressure palpable.

There was a moment of quiet. Ruth and Nick's minds were focussed on taking a fellow police officer to their own station to face charges of corruption. It didn't sit well for either of them. They both felt an overwhelming sense of disappointment and anger.

Ruth wondered where it had all gone so wrong for Mac. No one joins the force without the moral conviction that they want to make the world a better place and help people. It's not a job you fall into because you don't know what else to do. So, at what point did Mac become so disillusioned that he was willing to risk everything for a low-life like Blake? She knew that Nick's view of the world was less curious about human nature – he had already made his opinion on Mac abundantly clear. He was a bent copper and that made him despicable. She suspected that Nick felt very betrayed as he and Mac had once been close.

Nick took off his seatbelt. 'Ready for this, boss?'

Ruth nodded as she shifted in her seat and went to open the door.

'Hang on,' Nick gestured to the house, stopping her in her track. That's when Ruth spotted him.

There was movement further up the street as Mac's front door opened and Mac appeared in a baseball cap and sunglasses.

Mac made his way to his silver Audi parked on the drive. He got in and quickly started the engine.

'Doesn't seem to be much car trouble. Where the hell is he going?' Nick asked.

'Are we bringing him in or following?' Ruth said, half to herself. She got her phone and rang Drake.

Nick clipped his seatbelt back in and started the engine. Mac's car began to reverse slowly off the drive.

'Boss, target is in his car and starting to leave. What do you want us to do?' Ruth asked with a sense of urgency.

'Follow him. See where he's going,' Drake replied.

'Yes, boss,' Ruth said and reached over to turn on the police TETRA radio that would allow her, Drake and any other response units to talk together.

However, Mac parked his car in a space on the road outside his house and got out again.

'I'll send another car as back-up. I don't want to lose him. Switch to TETRA and I'll inform Dispatch that's what we're doing,' Drake said.

'What the hell is he doing now?' Nick asked quietly as they watched.

Mac went to the boot, opened it and took out some shopping bags. It was the bags that they had seen his brother-in-law hand him at the retail-park car park the night before. The bags that Ruth knew contained bala-clavas, industrial tape, plastic ties and gloves.

Mac went to the side of the house and pulled the up-and-over metal garage door. Parked inside they could see a new black Toyota Hilux, which was essentially an expensive pickup truck with a flat back. Even from where they were, the number plate was visible.

'Switching cars. Not suspicious. And that's thirty-five thousand pounds worth of new car right there,' Nick said sarcastically. 'If there was any doubt he was on the take, there isn't any now.'

'Dispatch, this is three-six. I need a PNC check on a number plate. Foxtrot-charlie-seven-nine. Victor-oscar-whisky,' Ruth said.

Mac returned to the car and the parking lights glowed red and white as he reversed slowly out of the garage.

Nick had already started to edge the BMW out of the parking space. They needed as much evidence as they could get that Mac was corrupt to build a solid case; following him could give them what they needed.

'Three-six from Dispatch. Car is a black Toyota Hilux. Registered to a James McGill in Edinburgh.'

'Three-six received.'

Ruth shot Nick a look. 'Number plate's been cloned.'

Ruth wasn't surprised. Number plate cloning was endemic in the UK and loopholes were being exploited by criminals and unscrupulous garages who asked no questions for those requiring a 'new number plate' for one that had been 'damaged' or 'lost'. Technically, garages or companies that produced number plates were meant to check the logbooks for the cars they were providing new number plates for. However, there were many who didn't bother or were paid not to carry out the checks.

Mac pulled away and headed off down the quiet residential street. Nick followed, keeping a decent distance to avoid suspicion.

Ruth spoke into the radio as her pulse started to quicken. 'Dispatch, this is three-six. We have visual contact with target.'

The radio crackled a little. 'Three-six received.'

'Target heading east on Charles Avenue,' Ruth informed them.

Ruth looked out at the drab semi-detached houses that lined both sides of the road. The metallic grey sky was now darkening to the west with black clouds like those from the fire of oil or tar. The rain began again and Ruth was relieved. Mac would be hypervigilant at the moment of being followed, or anything that didn't feel quite right. The rain and thunder would provide a useful distraction for them, especially as they followed him on these quiet residential roads where there wasn't much traffic to mask them.

The road curved to the right slowly.

'Three-six. Target heading south-east on George Avenue.'

As Mac slowed to turn right, the red of his brake lights bled into the raindrops of the BMW's windscreen.

'Three-six. Target turning right onto B-five-four-three-four,' Ruth informed them.

'If he's not going to the main road, where is he going?' Nick asked.

A minute later, they saw exactly where Mac was going. The visitors' car park for the Pontcysyllte Aqueduct. Built in 1800, it was a spectacular one hundred and thirty-foot Victorian construction that carried the Llangollen Canal across the River Dee in the Vale of Llangollen.

However, Mac stopped without pulling into a space. He wasn't there to sightsee. Nick and Ruth watched and spotted another man get out of a white Cherokee 4x4 with a large, navy gym bag. The man walked swiftly around the car, looking around as he jumped purposefully into the passenger seat.

The man was stocky with a shaved head. They both recognised him straight away.

It was Tony Downes, Blake's executioner-in-chief.

'Shit,' Nick muttered.

'Where the hell are they going?' Ruth asked no one in particular.

'I don't know, but I'm guessing that's not Downes' trackies and trainers in that bag.'

'Three-six. Target has picked up a passenger. Possibly one Tony Downes, known associate of Curtis Blake. Be advised, target and Downes might be armed.'

Mac swept around the car park in an arc, gravel crunching under the Toyota's large tyres. Nick swiftly reversed to keep out of sight and then pulled out behind them.

Drake's voice came onto the radio. 'Three-six. Armed Response Unit contacted and dispatched. Do not, repeat, *do not* engage with target until ARU arrives.'

'Three-six received,' Ruth replied.

Mac then turned left and Nick followed as the rain started to fall heavily. It made a metallic drumming on the car roof.

'Target turning north on Station Road.'

Nick looked over at Ruth. They were both thinking the same thing. 'They know where Webb is, don't they?'

'Yeah, that does seem a distinct possibility.'

'Don't lose them then,' Ruth said seriously.

Mac got to the top of the road and indicated to turn right onto the A539, which was the busy main road that led from Llangollen back to Llancastell.

'Three-six. Target turning east on A-five-three-nine, heading to Llancastell.'

As Nick slowed, there was now a small red Polo between him and Mac as they waited to turn right.

After about thirty seconds, Mac pulled out, turned right and headed away down the A539 and out of sight.

Rather than pulling forward, the passenger door of the small Polo in front opened and a middle-aged man got out, smiled and gave them a wave.

'What the hell are you doing? Get out of the way!' Nick bellowed.

The driver door opened and a teenage girl scurried around the back looking very self-conscious and swapped with her father who mouthed *sorry* at them with a broad smile.

'Bloody hell!' Ruth yelled.

After even more time, the car pulled forward and indicated left.

'Three-six. We have lost visual contact with target. Repeat, we have lost visual contact with target,' Ruth informed Dispatch and Drake.

'Shit!' Nick shouted and hit the steering wheel.

The Polo eventually pulled out and went left. However, as Nick glanced right there was a long stream of traffic behind a huge articulated lorry coming the other way.

They were losing Mac and they knew it. Nick nudged the car forward in frustration. 'Come on, come on.' Nick had the clutch and accelerator poised under his feet ready.

'Three-six. Still no visual contact with target.'

Then a gap came and Nick shot out onto the A549 with a screech of tyres before slowing down behind a car pulling a caravan. A minute later, Nick managed to find a gap in the oncoming traffic and overtake.

However, it was too little, too late.

For the next ten minutes, Nick drove at speed back along the A539, overtaking where he could. The ARU came the other way. Neither of them could see Mac or his vehicle. They had lost him.

NICK AND RUTH DROVE IN VIRTUAL SILENCE BACK TO Llancastell.

The radio buzzed with various bits of intel. North Wales Police were now out in force looking for the Toyota that contained Mac and Downes. Cheshire and Merseyside Police had been put on alert in case they headed over the border into England.

Drake told Ruth and Nick to leave the hunt for Mac and Downes to the Armed Response Units, some of whom had been drafted over from Liverpool. Drake wanted them to go to the hospital and make sure that a full statement had been taken from Fields and that he had been read his rights. Fields was being kept in a single room on a rehabilitation ward.

As Nick and Ruth made their way along the complex hospital corridors, Drake rang Ruth.

'Boss?' Ruth said as they walked.

'Still no sightings of Mac or Downes,' Drake explained. 'We've got the helicopter assisting the ARUs. I need you back here as soon as you're done with Fields.'

'WHAT ABOUT WEBB?' RUTH ASKED.

'He's playing silly buggers and won't commit to a location to be picked up.'

'Does he know that there are people out there that want him dead?' Ruth said in disbelief.

'If he does, he's being very relaxed about it. However,

Tech seem to think that they might be able to get a triangulation on his mobile signal. He left it on for ten minutes after he spoke to me, and that might be enough to pinpoint a location,' Drake explained.

'Okay, boss. I'll let you know what happens with Fields.'

Ruth hung up as she and Nick got into the large, metallic lift to go up to the first floor.

'Remember the last time we were in here?' Nick asked Ruth.

She thought for a moment and nodded. 'I think I caught you flirting with a nurse who was taking a shotgun pellet out of your thigh?'

'And then you tried to poison me with hospital tea.'

THIRTY SECONDS LATER, THE DOORS OPENED. 'HERE WE go,' Ruth said.

They walked along the wide corridor that smelt of hospital food and detergent. Nick glanced out of the large windows that looked over the car park. There was no let-up in the weather. It was grey and gloomy.

Several nurses were gathered around the nurses' station inside the ward. Patients names were on a chart with the bed numbers beside them. An old woman in a pink dressing gown shuffled past them and gave a smile.

Ruth got out her warrant card and showed it. 'We're looking for Alwyn Fields. There should be a police officer with him?'

Before the nurse could say anything, a young, male constable approached, looking troubled.

Ruth showed her warrant card. 'DI Hunter. Can you show us where Alwyn Fields is please, Constable?'

'You haven't heard?' the constable replied.

'Heard what?' Nick asked anxiously.

'Mr Fields died ten minutes ago.'

'What? How?' Ruth asked.

'He had a heart attack. They got a crash team up here. Then they took him down to ICU but it was too late.'

Chapter Twenty-Eight

R uth sat in the car smoking a cigarette, the window wound down even though it was raining. Nick had gone to get coffee. Fields' death had been a blow. Everything was pointing to his guilt. And now he would never stand trial and face what he had done. The Povall family would never get the justice they had craved for two decades.

Ruth's phone rang and broke her train of thought. Drake.

Drake sounded serious. 'Ruth, we've triangulated Webb's phone again. We've got him located at Tesco's supermarket in the middle of Llancastell. Uniform patrols are on their way. There are two Armed Response units on standby. I want you and Nick to see if you can arrest Webb and bring him in without any fuss.'

'Yes, boss,' Ruth replied as she flicked her cigarette away into the rain.

'And Ruth,' Drake said. 'Be careful. Don't take any risks.'

'Boss.' Ruth hung up.

Nick returned with their coffees but there was no time to drink them. Nick and Ruth left immediately and a few minutes later they had parked. They scouted the supermarket car park and Mac's Toyota pickup truck was nowhere to be seen. That, of course, didn't mean he and Downes weren't there.

Nick radioed the two Armed Response units that were being positioned at the entrance and exit of the supermarket car park. The hope was that Webb would come quietly with Ruth and Nick into protective police custody. Why Webb had been stupid enough to go out into public in the first place, God only knew.

In Nick's mind, getting Webb into protective custody and doing a deal for a reduced sentence meant they were one step closer to getting Blake behind bars. And that's all Nick wanted.

The clouds overhead were black and portentous but the rain had now stopped. Nick got out, went to the boot of the BMW and grabbed two ballistic and stab proof vests that had *Police* and *Heddlu* printed on them. He turned and handed one to Ruth.

Putting on the jackets, they both looked around the car park. Nothing out of the ordinary. The wind was picking up.

'You okay?' Ruth asked.

'Fine. Let's get the bastard.'

They turned and began to walk purposefully towards the supermarket where Webb had been spotted and where his mobile phone had been triangulated.

Ruth clicked her radio. 'DI Hunter. All units, we are approaching the supermarket.'

Her radio buzzed. 'Received.'

A young mother with her daughter in the trolley seat rattled past them and gave them a quizzical look.

As they entered, Ruth noticed the smell of fresh fruit and the cool air conditioning. She flashed her warrant card at the security guard at the entrance and he nodded but looked worried.

They moved forward, scanning left and right for a sign of someone who could be Webb. The tension in both of them was growing. Thankfully the supermarket wasn't busy and a few of the aisles were even empty.

However, some shoppers seemed a little alarmed at their presence and moved away or changed course when they saw them. To those who were absorbed in their weekly shopping, they were completely invisible.

Something in the corner of Ruth's eye caught her attention. She spun around but saw it was just a middle-aged customer talking loudly on his mobile phone.

'Anything?' Ruth asked.

'Nothing. Where is he?' Nick replied, looking the other way at the tills and waiting queues, praying that they hadn't missed him.

As they moved closer to the far end of the supermarket, they were becoming despondent. Maybe the tip off was wrong. Maybe the triangulation of Webb's mobile was wrong.

They turned and spotted a figure casually looking at the shelves of wine. Even though the person was wearing a grey tracksuit, baseball cap and sunglasses, they knew immediately it was Webb. It wasn't a great disguise.

Ruth said quietly into her radio as they inched forward, 'DI Hunter. All units. We have visual on target. Repeat, we have visual on target.'

'Received.'

'I need uniformed officers in position on both exit doors. No one comes in. Armed Response units, standby.'

'Received, ma'am,' the ARU confirmed.

Ruth could feel the adrenaline starting to pump. Get hold of Webb, get the cuffs on him and get him out of there as fast as possible.

When they got about twenty yards away, Nick took the handcuffs from his belt.

'DI Hunter. Could you come with us please, Mr Webb?' Ruth said in a confident tone as she showed her warrant card.

Webb turned, dipped his sunglasses and looked at them. He gestured to the handcuffs witheringly. 'Do I need to wear those? I'm not going to run off anywhere. Not with my heart.'

'Just do it.' Nick wasn't in the mood for any of Webb's nonsense or arrogance.

Suddenly there was a sharp noise. Webb's attention was drawn to the left to something or someone along the wine aisle. Neither Nick or Ruth could see – their view was blocked by a ten-foot shelf of beer and cider.

Webb looked startled and moved backwards.

'Shit …' he muttered.

Nick glanced up to a curved security mirror mounted high on the wall. Coming up the aisle was a man wearing a black motorbike helmet holding a handgun which was pointed directly in Webb's direction.

'Shit!' Nick said and instinctively ran towards Webb to grab him and get him out of the way.

Crack! A bullet smashed into a row of bottles that were six inches from Webb's head, and wine and glass splintered everywhere.

Webb ducked and cowered as he backed away, not daring to turn his back on the gunman.

Ruth's head was spinning as her adrenaline pumped in shock. She needed to remain as clear and calm as humanly possible with a gunman heading their way.

There were screams from nearby shoppers who scattered and shielded children.

'Police! Everyone get down!' Ruth bellowed back at them.

Webb turned and came sprinting towards Nick, sunglasses falling to the floor, face full of utter terror.

Nick was now wondering whether to make a run with Webb or tackle the gunman. Either way he could get shot.

Crack! Another bullet shattered the doors of the freezer section and shards of glass smashed to the floor. There were more screams.

Webb tripped, fell to the ground and skidded along the tiles for a few inches before coming to a rest about six feet from where Nick was standing.

However, Nick looked past him as the gunman came out from behind the shelving.

The helmet visor was tinted black, like an alien from a sci-fi film.

'Help me!' Webb yelled in panic, trying to get up.

Ruth busied herself with getting shoppers out of the way and into some kind of safety. She couldn't believe that some were peering down the aisle, trying to get a look.

'Police! Get back or get down, now!' she hollered at the top of her voice as she took cover behind a freezer cabinet. Her stomach was knotted tight as she radioed. 'DI Hunter. Shots fired. One gunman. Request back-up! We need AROs in here now!'

Nick bent to pull Webb to his feet, while keeping the gunman in focus. It was as if the gunman was now weighing things up. Finish off Webb or try to escape.

For a moment, Nick's gaze seemed to lock with that of the gunman even though he couldn't see his eyes.

Time stopped.

Webb clambered to his feet, getting his balance, grabbing at Nick and looking back at the gunman.

'Get me out of here!'

If it wasn't for the fact that Webb could testify against Blake, Nick frankly didn't care if he lived or died. But he was valuable.

And then the gunman raised his gloved hand. Nick could see he was holding a Russian-made Baikal 9mm handgun.

Crack! As if everything was at half speed, Nick saw the tendrils of smoke and the cartridge fly clear of the handgun.

A millisecond later, Webb lurched forward as the bullet came through the back of his neck and out from his throat with an explosion of blood and flesh.

Webb's body dropped to the floor and his head cracked on the tiles.

Nick blinked for a second, drops of Webb's blood in his right eye, trying to comprehend in those tiny fractions of time what had just happened.

By the time he glanced up from Webb's dead body, the gunman had gone.

'DI Hunter. Target has been shot. Require medical assistance. Location of assailant unknown, but he is armed and still in the building,' Ruth said.

WITHOUT THINKING, NICK TOOK OFF AFTER THE GUNMAN. If he had wanted to, he could have shot Nick right there and then. He was a professional and Webb was the target. No one else. At least that's what Nick was telling himself.

Nick heard the clatter of doors behind a giant freezer unit and saw the gunman push through the heavy plastic swing doors that led to the bakery and the back area of the supermarket.

As Nick crashed through, he saw terrified supermarket workers crouched down, shaking and hiding.

'Which way?' Nick shouted.

The woman pointed and Nick could see in the distance two large, metal shutter doors where the lorries would unload the deliveries.

The gunman was about fifty yards away. As Nick sprinted in pursuit, he could see the man's height and build. There was no doubt in his mind that the shooter was Terry Downes.

Workers that had been unloading crates scattered as the gunman ran through the loading area.

Nick clicked his radio. 'This is DS Evans. Gunman is heading for the delivery area to the rear of the building. Gunman is armed, repeat, gunman is armed.'

'Received. ARU en route,' came the response from Dispatch.

Nick was now thirty yards behind the gunman and gaining ground. Quite what he intended to do if he got close to the gunman, Nick wasn't quite sure. Tackle him?

The gunman sprinted through the delivery bay doors and out into the sunlight.

Nick could taste the lactic acid in his throat as he pumped his arms, pushing on despite the pain.

Suddenly, there was a screech of tyres.

Nick came out of the delivery bay doors to see the black Toyota screech to a halt. It was Mac.

The gunman got to the passenger door and turned back to look at Nick as he got in.

Nick stopped, pulling hard to get his breath. He felt sick. Were they going to get away? Where the bloody hell were the ARUs? It was a disaster. Webb was dead, and

346

Mac and Downes would probably disappear abroad, never to be heard of again.

There was a humming overhead as the police helicopter came in low and began to hover.

And then to the left, the deep growl of two BMW X5 armed-police vehicles that swung across the entrance and exit to the delivery area of the supermarket. Within seconds, several Armed Response officers had leapt from the vehicle with Heckler and Kosh MP5 carbine machine guns.

The Toyota slowed and stopped. There was no way out. They were trapped.

The Armed Response officers crouched, using the BMWs as cover, and took aim at the stationary Toyota.

The tension was mounting fast like a Mexican stand-off in a Western film.

Nick watched. How long before the doors opened, and Mac and Downes gave themselves up? There were no other options. They were going nowhere.

However, the Toyota's engine began to rev and Nick felt a sinking feeling. Were they suicidal enough to try to ram their way out of the car park through the BMWs?

Downes looked out of the passenger door and fired two shots at the armed officers, who ducked for cover. There was a metallic thud as a bullet hit the wing of one of the cars.

There was a squeal of tyres and the Toyota lurched forward, heading for the blocked entrance. They were going to smash their way out.

Crack! Crack! Crack!

THE AROS OPENED UP WITH THE MP5S HITTING THE tyres. The Toyota kept coming, faster and faster. The armed officers switched their aim to the windscreen, shattering it instantly.

Then like a child's toy with dying batteries, the Toyota slowed, veered to the left and then stopped.

For a moment, there was an eerie silence.

The armed officers approached slowly, guns trained on the Toyota. 'Armed police! Get out of the vehicle.' There was no movement from inside.

Nick began to approach cautiously, one step at a time.

One of the armed officers got to the passenger door and crouched as another officer covered the door with his MP5. He pulled the door handle, the door opened and Terry Downes' lifeless body fell out of the Toyota and onto the ground.

The armed officer quickly felt for a pulse and then looked up and shook his head. Downes was dead.

'Get a paramedic!' A voice shouted from the other side of the vehicle.

Nick got out his badge as he approached the jeep. He walked past Downes' body, showing his badge.

On the other side, Mac was lying on the ground, covered in blood. An armed officer was trying to resuscitate him.

'DS Evans,' Nick said as he came over. He crouched over Mac, who had a gunshot in his chest and whose shirt was drenched in blood.

Mac looked up as blood gurgled out of his mouth.

Nick reached for his mobile phone, then clicked on the record button and held it towards Mac.

'This is DS Evans. Record of interview with DC Macdonald.' Nick moved closer to Mac and said urgently, 'Come on, Mac. Do the right thing now.'

Mac looked at him for a moment and then looked

away. In that second, Nick wondered if it was a moment of shame or guilt.

'Who ordered the assassination of Callum Webb?' Nick asked.

Mac looked at him again. Was he going to clear his conscience now that he knew he was probably going to die?

'Did Curtis Blake order the assassination of Callum Webb?'

Mac took a moment, nodded and tried to speak. 'Yeah …' It was enough to have registered on the phone.

'And Owen Ankers?' Nick asked. 'Did Curtis Blake pay Terry Downes to murder Owen Ankers?'

Mac closed his eyes for a second, fighting for breath. More blood came from his mouth as his lungs had been severely damaged by the bullet.

'Mac, I need you to tell me if Curtis Blake ordered the murder of Owen Ankers.'

Mac moved his head as though he was nodding but he was struggling to stay conscious.

'Mac, I need you to confirm,' Nick said holding the phone to Mac's mouth. 'You just nodded to confirm that Curtis Blake ordered the murder of Owen Ankers. I just need you to say it.'

Mac closed his eyes as he slipped out of consciousness.

The paramedic came over with an oxygen mask, which he put over Mac's mouth.

'Sorry, sir, we need to get him to hospital now,' the paramedic said with urgency.

Nick moved away and turned off his phone. The moment had gone.

. . .

Ruth lit another cigarette. It was now three hours since the shooting and she was starting to get her head around all that had happened. The adrenaline was still racing through her body, making her feel jittery.

The sun under the clouds created a salmon hue, which signalled that the storm had passed. The wind slowed as if it had been racing for some time and it was now determined to rest. The atmosphere was no longer heavy and its lightness was a relief.

Half an hour earlier, Ruth had given her detailed statement of the events at the supermarket at a designated suite inside the station where the post-incident procedures were taking place. A post-incident manager, PIM, Inspector Shaw from St Asaph, had been drafted in. Police Federation representatives were buzzing around the station, as were the Force Professional Standards Department and lead investigators from the IOPC.

As the SIO, Ruth had given a brief overview of intelligence and operational planning before she and Nick had arrived to pick up Webb. She knew that she and Drake had assessed the high risk that Webb could be attacked. Armed Response teams were on standby and uniformed officers positioned to help secure the supermarket and deal with any shoppers caught up in the incident.

Nick was now in with his PFR and Drake, giving the exact details of how Mac and Downes had died. The AFOs would be doing the same in a different part of the building.

It seemed clear that Blake had ordered the death of Owen Ankers and Callum Webb. It had been Terry Downes who had murdered Owen, and Mac who had orchestrated the attack from the clifftops. It seemed no one had counted on Abi Mullen being with him at the time of the hit.

. . .

Ruth rang the doorbell for the second time and stood back a little. She had been waiting apprehensively outside Sian's front door holding a bottle of her favourite chilled white wine for about five minutes now. It was an unannounced visit.

Sian lived in a small cul-de-sac with lots of smart-looking new builds. It was a perfect summer's evening and small children rode their bikes around the close, laughing and shouting without a care in the world. Across the road, an elderly man was cutting his grass. He looked over and gave Ruth a friendly wave. She smiled and waved back.

What was taking Sian so long? Maybe she had gone out? Her car was on the drive. Ruth rang the doorbell again.

It had been a hell of a day, and Ruth just wanted to fall into Sian's arms, drink wine and make love. And she knew she had over-reacted when she had snapped at Sian the other day. The news of Kessler had thrown her.

Ruth went to the door. Maybe she should just give up and go home? As she was about to peer in for one final check, the door opened.

Sian looked at her. 'What do *you* want?'

Ruth gave her an uncertain smile and waved the bottle of wine gently at her. 'I'm … I'm not good at saying sorry, but … well, I'm sorry.'

'I did wonder how long you were willing to wait out here,' Sian said.

'You knew I was out here?' Ruth frowned.

'Yes. I was going to make you wait for at least another minute,' Sian replied starting to smile.

Then they looked at each other and all the tension and

petty anger of the last few days seemed to melt away in the evening heat.

'Well, are you going to stand there all evening or are we getting drunk?' Sian asked.

'Sounds like we're getting drunk.' Ruth's face lit up with a relieved smile.

They went in and Sian grabbed Ruth's hand as they headed for the kitchen.

'I said a few things ...' Ruth mumbled.

'Shut up and come here,' Sian said.

Sian pulled Ruth close to her and kissed her full on the mouth.

They paused and looked at each other. Ruth screwed the top off the wine and gulped two mouthfuls before handing over the bottle.

Sian grabbed Ruth's hand and led her to the lounge where the patio doors were open and the warm summer evening and the glow of the sunset cast a beautiful hue in the room. 'Come on.'

They kissed again. Ruth pushed her hips into Sian's and they began to undress.

'I forgot how fit you were,' Sian gasped as she stared at Ruth.

'Show me.' Ruth smiled.

'Bossy.' Sian grinned as she yanked Ruth's jeans down and pressed her onto the huge sofa, planting kisses over every inch of her.

An hour later, they had finished their second bottle of wine and were listening to soul music as they lay under a throw on the living-room carpet.

Chapter Twenty-Nine

It was pouring with rain as Ruth drove home from Llancastell. She had spent the day doing the paperwork in the lead-up to the enquiry into the supermarket shootings. Press speculation and stories had now stopped, and CID was getting back to some sense of normality.

As she turned off the high street, she noticed the people sitting at the bus stop, trying to shelter from the downpour.

She spotted a figure she recognised. Abi Mullen.

Pulling over at the kerb, Ruth wound down her window.

'Abi? Where are you going?' Ruth asked.

Abi blinked as she came over to the car. 'Oh, j-just to the halls. Don't worry.'

'Get in. I'll give you a lift.' Ruth gestured with her hand for her to get in.

'No, no, miss. You're all right.'

'Get in, Abi. It's filthy and you'll get soaked,' Ruth demanded.

Abi opened the car door tentatively and then climbed in.

'You up by the library still?' Ruth asked.

Abi nodded and looked awkward.

'How's it going?' Ruth asked. She wondered if Abi had seen any of the news about the Owen Ankers' case. The CPS and IOPC had made it clear in recent days that given the in-depth psychological report on Abi, they would not need her to give evidence about what she had seen that day at the inquest. It had been Downes on the beach that day that had attacked her and Owen. It had been Mac who had helped orchestrate and watched the whole event from the clifftops with binoculars and mobile phones.

Ruth had glanced briefly at Abi's psychological report. Through no fault of her own, Abi was a very damaged young lady who would struggle to live a normal life. It didn't seem fair that anyone should have to suffer like she and her sister had. The report had categorised her and Libby's physical, emotional and sexual abuse as 'chronic and severe'. Abi would spend her life prone to self-harm and suicide.

'Yeah, it's okay,' Abi mumbled.

Ruth's phone rang, and she answered it with her Bluetooth headset in. It was Sian offering a candlelit dinner on the patio.

'That sounds lovely. Very romantic. I'll get some wine,' Ruth said and then hung up.

Abi smiled over at her. 'Is that your boyfriend?'

Ruth smiled at her. 'Sort of.'

'Was he the man that came in when we were talking last time?'

Ruth knew that she meant Nick. She shook her head. 'No. He's not my boyfriend.'

Pulling over the car outside the halls of residence, Ruth smiled over at her and said, 'Here we go.'

Abi smiled back at her. 'I-I wanted to, to say thank you. You really looked out for me. No one's ever done that before.'

That was the most Ruth had ever heard Abi say at once. She was touched. 'That's fine. I know your life has been horrible up until now. I just hope it gets better from here on.'

'Yeah, so do I.' Abi gathered her bag of books up from beside her feet.

And then something struck Ruth.

A sudden thought that froze her and made her stomach tighten.

'You know you asked about my boyfriend? Did you mean the tall detective with black hair and a beard?' Ruth asked apprehensively.

'Yeah. Nice-looking,' Abi replied quietly.

This time a chill ran through Ruth.

'That's weird. Because when that detective came into the room, I was talking to Libby. Wasn't I?'

Abi shifted in the passenger seat and looked directly ahead. And then the atmosphere in the car changed. Ruth's mouth dried.

Abi looked over at Ruth and smiled. But it wasn't that innocent, awkward smile that she had grown accustomed to.

It was a smirk. A cocky, conceited, confident smirk.

And as Abi moved her shoulders and pushed her hair back, Ruth realised that she was looking at Libby.

'Surprise!' Libby did a little dance with her hands and body as she grinned at Ruth. The thick Scouse accent was back and the surly attitude. 'Libby or Abi? Abi or Libby?

You work it out eh, Ruthzie the Bizzy! I like dat, don't you?'

Ruth's stomach lurched. 'What's going on, Abi?'

LIBBY PULLED A MOCK BABY FACE AT RUTH WHO WAS NOW feeling scared. 'Poor lickle Abi.' She mockingly mimicked Abi's voice. '"Oh, j-just to the halls. Don't worry, miss." Here's Libby! I'm back now … Oh, you were so sweet, you know, Ruthzie. All dat bleedin' heart stuff. Gonna make me feckin' cry. I need to thank you for getting me off like. So Ruth, were you shagging that fit copper or what? Has he got a big cock? Did you suck him off in the police car when undercover? I would have.'

Ruth's head was lurching back and forth, as though she was watching a surreal film or was on some kind of bad acid trip. 'Are you telling me that there was no Libby?'

'Behave, girl. I am Libby, you daft bitch! There was no Abi. Don't you get it?'

Ruth felt physically sick now. 'So, where's Abi then?'

'Dead' – using her fingers as speech marks – '"committed suicide". Threw herself off a ferry to Ireland about three years ago. I watched her do it. To be honest, I gave her a bit of a helping hand.'

'You killed her?'

'No comment, Officer. Poor Abi couldn't cope.'

'So, I've never met Abi?' Ruth asked.

'Not unless you see dead people.'

'Jesus Christ!' Ruth couldn't help herself as she thought about the conversations with Abi. 'Why?'

'Why?' Ruth repeated, still horrified.

'Do you know how useful it is to have two passports, two identities? It's a blast!' Libby said triumphantly.

'And what about Owen Ankers?'

'I already told you dat. Went a bit over the top with the gore to make you think I was totally off me 'ead. But it was like I said. You know? That bastard agreed to meet up with me. Then he decided to reject me again. I wasn't gonna let him do dat and get away with it. I needed my revenge like I needed oxygen, you know?'

In nearly three decades of policing, Ruth had never experienced or heard anything like this before. She tried to remain calm to get as much information as she could.

'So, there was no attacker on that day?' Ruth asked.

Libby snorted. 'No. It was just little 'ole me. Put the blade in his thigh and twisted it. Saw it on some You Tube video. I watched the little bastard bleed out in a minute or two. Waited for a bit as the tide came in and then went home.'

'Abi's home? With David Sabatini?'

'Yeah, I'd been shagging him, pretending to be Abi. It was part of the fun.'

'And where is David Sabatini now?'

Libby shrugged with a smirk. 'No idea. I took 'im outta the hospital. Then he "disappeared" just like that.' She clicked her fingers on the final word.

'And now what?'

'Dunno. Probably be moving on somewhere. Got Daddy's ten grand to play with. You can arrest me if you like, but you know as well as I do, that no one is gonna put me on trial. Waste of money. And I have you to thank for dat. You made sure there was a thorough psychological report done. Ta, Ruthzie. You're a doll.'

'This isn't over,' Ruth warned her but knew that it probably was.

'Oh, I think we both know it is, Ruthzie Bizzy.' Libby opened the passenger door and slid out.

Ruth simply watched her go.

Chapter Thirty

There were about twenty people sat around in the small church hall. There were smiling faces and hugs. Like the survivors of some awful disaster, members of AA had a gratitude and joy in their continuing journey of sobriety. The sunlight of the fading day glinted off the large window like sparks and there was the smell of coffee and freshly cut grass.

Nick sat quietly in one corner next to his sponsor, Bill.

After the Webb shooting, Nick had been signed off work with anxiety and stress. Drake had been incredibly supportive. Curtis Blake had been arrested and charged with conspiracy to murder and supplying class-A drugs. It was a huge weight off Nick's shoulders. So this was Nick's chance to get his act cleaned up and get sober. This time he meant it. But then again, he had meant it every time before.

Nick's hands shook uncontrollably so the best thing was to sit on them. He was now four days sober, and it had been a rough time of sickness, shakes and sweats as his body detoxed from the alcohol. His nervous system was so used to being depressed from having alcohol in it, that it was now over-reacting. He had used small doses of Librium to take away some of the symptoms, but other than that, he just had to accept that he was going to feel terrible for a week or more.

The opening share was from Angela, who had over twenty years sobriety under her belt. She spent half an hour talking about her childhood, teens and her descent into alcoholism, before extolling the miracle of AA, which had saved her life and had given her a future that she never thought possible. It was a familiar tale of childhood anxiety, loneliness and fear. Her home had been a dysfunctional and frightening place to be. School was no better. Vulnerable kids got bullied. By fifteen, alcohol was Angela's solution to the pain of being alive. It continued like this for twenty more years, getting imperceptibly worse year by year. After two suicide attempts, Angela went into treatment, found AA and since then she had been blessed with a sober life.

Nick listened, wishing that he could find his way and stay sober. Various people began to share back, and it was then that Nick saw that his father had arrived a little late and was sitting at the back of the room. He was clean-shaven and wearing a smart shirt and slacks.

A young man had just finished speaking and Nick heard a familiar voice.

'Hi, my name's Rhys and I'm an alcoholic,' his father said.

'Hi, Rhys,' the room replied.

'Thank you for sharing with us, Angela. And thank you for everyone who makes this meeting possible. I particularly liked what you had to say about always thinking you were a victim, being full of self-pity. 'Cos that's how I felt for a long time. When I was a boy, I lived in a house that was full of violence and drink. And there was no love or care. And when I drank, I just felt bloody sorry for myself. My drinking and my behaviour was okay because poor Rhys had had such a terrible bloody life. And when my wife passed away, nearly thirty years now, that was another excuse to get on the drink. I took no responsibility for anything that I did. And I took no responsibility for my son who had been left without his mother. Because my feelings were the most important thing in the world. It was shameful.' Rhys' voice broke a little with the emotion of what he was saying.

Nick shifted in his seat to look round. He had never heard his father express himself like this before.

Rhys continued. 'I did a huge amount of damage to everyone around me. I destroyed my family. And eventually the drink took everything from me. And although I'm early in my sobriety, I never thought I could go a day without a drink, let alone a few weeks. And that's a bloody miracle.' Rhys nodded for a moment. 'And I'll leave it at that for now.'

'Thanks, Rhys,' the room replied.

When the meeting ended, Nick was feeling better and some of the anxiety had gone. Meetings were like that. They had a calming effect on everyone. He spoke to his sponsor, telling him he had a place in a Sunrise House, a police rehab treatment centre in Canaerfon for twenty-eights days. Bill agreed it was just what Nick needed.

As Nick walked out of the hall, he saw a small group of people including Rhys. His father looked over, nodded and then came over hesitantly.

'You all right, lad?' Rhys asked quietly.

Nick nodded uncertainly. 'Yeah … Getting there slowly.'

There was an awkward silence.

'Bill said you're going into rehab tonight?'

'Yeah. Twenty-eight days.'

'The force paying for it?'

'They've got their own rehabilitation centre out in Canaerfon,' Nick explained.

Rhys nodded and tapped the ash from his cigarette. 'Well, good luck, Nick. You know?' There was a moment between them. 'Look after yourself.'

'Thanks …' Nick was a little taken aback by his father's words. He looked at him. 'I liked what you shared today. It was good.'

'Ta … Maybe I'll see you when you get out?' Rhys said.

'Yeah. That would be good,' Nick replied, thinking how this conversation was one that he would never have imagined them having.

Rhys smiled to himself, turned and walked back to the group of people smoking under a tree.

Nick wandered towards the car park where Bill was waiting to take him to rehab.

RUTH, SIAN AND ELLA WERE IN THE GARDEN, SOAKING UP the evening sun and drinking. The stress of the Owen Ankers' murder case and the Llancastell supermarket shootings was dissipating. The media had been awash with the story for about a week and the station had been chaotic for some time afterwards.

North Wales Police were still trying to track down Abi Mullen but she had disappeared, leaving virtually no clues as to where she might have gone. Ruth knew that even if she was caught, there was little chance of the CPS threshold being met and her being charged with Owen Ankers' murder, despite her confession.

'More drinks?' Sian asked getting up.

'Of course!' Ruth said. It was a Friday night, Ella was staying over and sleeping on the sofa.

'Could I have some tonic with my gin this time please?' Ella joked.

'Why?' Sian asked with a grin.

Ruth knew they would spend the night drinking, chatting, laughing and listening to increasingly loud music. She couldn't think of a better way of spending an evening.

'Crisps!' Ruth shouted. 'I need crisps.'

Sian and Ruth wandered into the house arm in arm. They got to the kitchen where Ruth grabbed Sian and they kissed.

'Cheeky!' Sian said with a grin.

The doorbell rang and Ruth danced her way out of the room, into the hall and answered the door.

Standing there was Steven Flaherty from the Met. Her heart dropped to the pit of her stomach.

'Hi, Ruth. I've been up north, so I thought I'd pop in on the way home. I did text and ring earlier,' Steven explained quietly. There was something up. She could tell from the way he avoided eye contact as much as he could. Ruth hadn't checked her phone for a few hours. She had been having far too much fun.

'What is it?' Ruth asked, her mind racing with dark thoughts.

'Can I come in?' Steven asked.

'Of course … Come in.' Ruth gestured but she was feeling sick with anxiety. 'What's wrong?'

Steven came in and sat in the living room. Those few seconds were agonising. Ruth feared the day that someone arrived to tell her they had discovered Sarah's body.

'Have you found her?' Ruth asked.

ENJOY THIS BOOK?
Click here to the get the next one now
My Book
My Book

The Dee Valley Killings
A Ruth Hunter Crime Thriller
Book 3

Your FREE book is waiting for you now

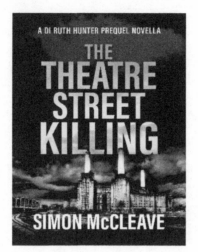

Get your FREE copy of the prequel to
the DI Ruth Hunter Series NOW
http://www.simonmccleave.com/vip-email-club
and join my VIP Email Club

AUTHOR'S NOTE

Although this book is very much a work of fiction, it is located in Snowdonia, a spectacular area of North Wales. It is steeped in history and folklore that spans over two thousand years. It is worth mentioning that Llancastell is a fictional town on the eastern edges of Snowdonia. I have made liberal use of artistic licence, names and places have been changed to enhance the pace and substance of the story.

Acknowledgments

I will always be indebted to the people who have made this novel possible.

My mum, Pam, and my stronger half, Nicola, whose initial reaction, ideas and notes on my work I trust implicitly. And Dad, for his overwhelming enthusiasm. Without their support and encouragement, these novels simply wouldn't exist.

Thanks also goes to my amazing Advanced Reading Team for their invaluable feedback on earlier drafts. Detective Sergeant Ben Wild of the North Wales Police Force for checking my work and explaining the complicated world of police procedure and investigation. My incredibly talented editor Rebecca Millar who has held my hand through the rewriting and editing process again and is a joy to work with. My excellent designer Stuart Bache for the incredible cover design and Bryan Cohen for the blurb and advertising copy.

Made in United States
North Haven, CT
16 February 2024

48804493R00232